assembling georgia

a novel by
Beth Carpel

ASSEMBLING GEORGIA. Copyright © 2009 by Beth Carpel. All rights reserved. No part of this book may be used or reproduced without written permission except in the case of brief quotations embodied in critical articles or reviews. For contact information go to www.bethcarpel.com.

Book design by the author
Cover design and photographs @ 2009 by Beth Carpel

ISBN 1-4392-2397-1
9781439223970

For all my parents

with love and gratitude

assembling georgia

1

WHEN GEORGIA GOT HOME from the factory, Albert was lying on the kitchen floor. He didn't move when she called his name, or stir at the tap of her footsteps as she crossed the linoleum and stood beside his still, limp form. He was clearly beyond hearing, so she gave him a poke with her toe.

"Albert," she said. "Wake up, you old booger. I'm home."

The basset hound twitched a nostril. His eyes traveled up her leg and passed over the nonessentials balanced in her arms, settling with contentment on the plastic sack dangling from one hand.

"He lives," Georgia pronounced, plunking the sack of chicken scraps onto the counter. With the back of her small, cold-reddened hand, she brushed away a renegade strand of hair that had escaped her braid. Then she sighed and shook her head. "Big lug. All you can do is lie there? You can't even say hello?"

Albert moved his tail a quarter of an inch but showed no inclination to actually rise.

Shoving papers and coffee cups to the side of the kitchen table, Georgia set down the box she'd picked up from the post office, along with a stack of ancient cassettes she'd finally brought in from the car. An old Moody Blues slid from the pile and fell, clipping Albert on the snout before skittering under the refrigerator. With the dignity of beleaguered royalty, the basset rolled onto his belly, sneezed twice, and heaved himself onto his stubby legs. "Sorry, old boy," Georgia said, reaching down to stroke his nose. "Didn't mean to clonk you." She scratched his head, garnering a pleased shiver of skin as she ran her short fingernails down his back.

After shedding her coat and scarf, letting Albert out into the backyard to pad through the snow and take care of the necessities, and finally serving him up a nice bowl of chicken scraps and kibble, Georgia stood leaning against the kitchen counter. The days, at long last, had begun to lengthen. The ungodly hour she had to start work in the mornings was finally paying off in the brief glimpse of daylight she got at the end. A last shaft of sunlight threaded between the small houses of her Minneapolis neighborhood and through her kitchen window, striking sparks from her brown hair, but she was unconscious of any hint of beauty, any last remnant of vitality. She was aware only of the weight of the braid down her back and of the sun's much-needed warmth after the chill of the factory. Hunger finally prodded her out of her stupor, but ten hours of stuffing internal organs up cold chicken butts had sucked the last particles of energy out of her. She couldn't face making dinner.

Her eyes drifted to the box she'd picked up from the post office, lying upside down on the table. Cookies from Mom, she guessed, and for once didn't mind how pathetic it was for a grown woman to be getting care packages from her mother. She didn't even care what shape the contents were in—the last batch had arrived so battered there were crumbs on the *outside* of the box—but hey, dinner was dinner. And afterwards all she wanted was a shower and bed. She pulled a steak knife from a drawer to slit the packing tape.

The phone interrupted her. Hesitating, her mouth already watering, she sighed as the second ring began, and laid down the knife.

"Don't put on your jammies," ordered her friend Corrine. "I'm coming by to pick you up."

"I don't think so, Cor," Georgia said.

"You haven't been out in ages, girl."

"So?"

"So, tonight's as good a time as any. Besides, this is my last chance to have a fling before Mama moves in," Corrine said. "My brothers are driving her up from Texas as we speak, with her grandmother's chifforobe tied to the top of the car and probably enough pots and pans to fill my entire house. So tonight you and me are goin' out. We'll pick up men and have wild sex in the balcony of the Bijou."

"Oh, sure. And then we can go over and pick up our prizes for best hallucinations of the month."

"You just get ready. Ten minutes," Corrine said, and hung up.

They ended up walking down to Manny's Pub, a few blocks away, taking Albert along. The owner knew Albert well from the basset's early solo forays (it had taken Georgia a while to find the hole in the backyard fence when they'd first moved in) and looked the other way. If the health department happened by, well, he guessed the mutt must have just snuck in, and of course it would never happen again. Albert sat happily under the table accepting his due of pets and adoring scratches behind the ear from the other customers, along with the occasional pretzel. For Georgia, a beer and a bar sandwich went a ways toward restoring her eroded spirits, but even more so the friendly banter and the warmth of the place.

Walking home, Georgia gave Corrine a hug around the shoulders. "You're a good friend, Cor. Thanks."

"Well, it was fun. And you deserve some fun. Ever since that sorry excuse of a—"

Georgia put up a hand. "Don't even mention Jimmy. If I can't even hang onto a jerk like him ..."

"What I was going to say," Corrine continued with manifest patience, "was that since ol' Jimbo came *into* your life, you haven't had a fair shake when it comes to good times. You never would see that you deserved better than him from the start. And maybe that's your problem—you *can't* see it...." She glanced over at Georgia's shadowed face. "Oh, hell, honey. I'm sorry. I didn't mean to give you shit. I know what kind of a year you've been having, and then that sorry-ass, no good *thing* walking out on you just when he could've been some use. You need more nights out. Now, if only pretty Davy in there with the shoulders wasn't ten years too young for us.... Mmm, mmm."

Georgia smiled. "Yeah, he was sweet. But *surely* he's only *five* years too young for us." She paused as Albert pulled toward the edge of the sidewalk. "Oh, Albert. Couldn't you at least wait till we got to a side street?" She rolled her eyes as he squatted under a streetlight. Corrine laughed.

Georgia dutifully pooper-scooped into a little gift bag she'd grabbed from her pantry as they were leaving the house. She dangled the bag a little ways out from her side as they walked on, keeping an eye out for a dumpster in the shadows of the alleys they passed.

In the next block of closed-up shops, Georgia glanced in at the window display at Minnesota Phats, a used CD and vinyl record shop. An album cover showed a woman in a swirling, gaudy-colored skirt. "Dance Samba!" the title commanded.

"Hey, look," Georgia said. "I should come back and get that for your mother. When's she getting in?"

"They said Saturday, but knowing Mama she'll want to drive straight through. Why don't you come for dinner Sunday. She'll want to see you. She says you've been neglecting her."

"I sent her a birthday card last month," Georgia objected.

"Don't tell *me*. Come over on Sunday and you can duke it out with Mama."

"Okay. What should I—"

Georgia felt something slam into her side. She staggered against Corrine, struggling to keep her balance. Her feet tangled in Albert's leash and she fell to one knee. "What—?"

"Jesus!" cried Corrine, grabbing for Georgia as she fell. "Are you all right? What does that *fucker* think he's *doing*!" She knelt down with her friend on the sidewalk and looked over her shoulder at the hooded figure of a man running off down the street. Then, to Georgia's astonishment, Corrine barked out a laugh.

"What?" Georgia followed her gaze. "Oh my God," she said. "He got Albert's shit." The mugger was turning into an alley on the far side of the street, the little gift bag clutched in his hand.

"Look at him go. Ha!" Corrine looked around. "Wait.... Where's your purse? Did he get—?"

"Didn't bring it. Just my wallet." Georgia patted her pocket.

Albert came over and licked her elbow. Georgia rocked back, sat down on the sidewalk with a small thump, and giggled. Then she began to laugh harder. "He got shit," she managed, and dropped her head to her hands.

Then somehow she wasn't laughing anymore, but leaking tears like an old rain gutter.

"Are you all right, hon? Did he hurt you?" asked Corrine.

"No.... No, I'm okay." Georgia shook her head and wiped an arm across her cheeks. "I'm fine." She pushed herself up. "Let's just go home."

Corrine helped Georgia up and untangled Albert's leash. Georgia unsnapped it from his collar as they turned down a side street toward her house.

"I just wish I could see that guy's face when he gets a good look at his loot," Corrine said.

"I hope he doesn't look. Maybe he'll just reach in." Georgia smiled a little.

"I hope all his buddies are watching," said Corrine. "And a girlfriend or two."

"Reap what you sow."

They laughed, but the warmth and light of the corner bar were far behind them.

Georgia stood in the shower. Her knee stung but there wasn't much she could do about that. Her hands, still aching from work—always aching from work—hung at her sides as the hot water flowed over her. At long last she began to relax. She breathed in the moist air and sighed it out. Loosening her braid, she reached for the shampoo.

There was a plastic rustling behind her. The blue shower curtain shifted, a gap appeared between the curtain and the wall, and the slightest of breezes touched her legs. Albert waddled into the stall and stood under the warm spray at her feet.

Two hours later Georgia woke up tangled in sheets. She was plagued by the thought of how powerless she'd been out there—blindsided and totally vulnerable. The guy had shoved her, that was all, but it could have been much worse and she wouldn't have been able to do a thing about it. She hated feeling this way. Hated the fear and hated the anger. And she needed to sleep if she was going to get through her overtime shift tomorrow, though at least she didn't have to be in until eight, thank God. Still, she didn't have time to be upset. It didn't do any good and besides, hadn't the shithead gotten what he deserved? Ha, ha.

No, she thought. He deserved more. He deserved ... Her imagination sputtered and failed. She turned over, kicked the sheets, and fretted. Her knee hurt. And she couldn't sleep. And tomorrow was going to be miserable if she didn't get some rest. She rolled on her back and listened to her stomach growl. She was still hungry, maybe that was her problem. And then she remembered—Mom's cookies.

The thought released her from her ineffectual struggle with the sheets. She shoved the bedding aside and headed for the kitchen.

The package and the knife were where she'd left them on the table. She sat down, turned the box over, and pulled it toward her.

Then she stopped and looked again. The box was not from her mother. Georgia's address was not scrawled in her mother's loopy script, but printed in a neat, firm hand. There was no flowery return address sticker from Wisconsin. There was no return address at all. Georgia couldn't think who would be sending her anything.

If she'd been an airline executive or a politician, and not just a tired chicken factory worker distracted by her ridiculous mugging, she might have paused. She might have appreciated how one small box could change the course of a life, and hesitated. But as apprehensive as she was of the world outside, the idea of hazard within her own walls didn't occur to her. She just gave a short grunt of disappointment as the idea of chocolate chip cookies slipped away. Then she opened the box.

In a padding of Styrofoam peanuts lay four objects wrapped with clean buff newsprint and clear tape. One was marked with a large dot. Georgia lifted it out and unwrapped it. It was a light, smooth metal cylinder, hollowed out from an irregular bottom, circled with grooved rings around the top. Small holes were bored through the sides. It gleamed with the barest sheen of oil.

There were two tags attached. The smaller one said, "Piston-1A." The other was a card, tied on with gold string like at Christmastime. "Dear Georgia," it read. "Please hold on to this. Regards."

2

"REGARDS"? Who on earth is sending me "regards"? Questions began combusting in Georgia's brain. Who has my address? Why would anyone send me pistons, of all things? Is someone trying to tell me my car's falling apart, like I don't already know? Is this some kind of mistaken identity? Why me?

The metal was cool and hard. It weighed in her hand with an unfamiliar solidity, a feeling of precision and the potential for ... what? Several things moved within Georgia at once. Bewilderment, suspicion, and something so rusty with disuse it almost didn't get started at all—interest.

She gave her head a small, convulsive shake. She didn't want *any* of those things. She hadn't asked for this and damned if she was going to let some anonymous prank get her rattled. Screw it, she thought. Screw him, and screw every bastard who thought he could mess with her life. She stared at the piston, and only then did her sense of physical vulnerability begin to catch up with her. A fear completely out of proportion to the object in her hand seized her, as if she'd bent to pick up a river stone and found herself holding a stick of dynamite. She sat paralyzed for a moment. Then she stood up, scraping her chair back. She spun to the trash can and flung the thing in. It didn't explode and shatter her life. It didn't blow a hole in her wall and leave her free and unsheltered. Alone, disconnected from its other parts, it landed with a dead thud.

Georgia dumped the box and the rest of its contents in after it, and washed her hands. Then, turning her back on all of it, she headed down the hall and climbed into bed. There she tried to lie quietly and get her breathing to organize itself. She finally gave it up as hopeless and twisted onto her side, giving the pillow an occasional punch or kicking the covers around.

An hour later, she was still inexorably awake. Finally she sat up, fumbled for the remote and switched on the TV. But in spite of infomercials and Chuck Norris reruns, her mind wouldn't switch itself off the way it was supposed to. Instead she found herself pondering those stupid, misguided questions that were such a waste of time, like why wasn't she happy, and why did she expect happiness in the first place. She had a job, a house with the payments almost caught up, good old Albert. She had her best friend Corrine living ten blocks away. She had loving if clueless parents in the next state. She was finally used to Jimmy being gone—not so big a loss when you came right down to it. After all, now she didn't have to make dinner every night, she could play whatever CDs she wanted, and she didn't have to listen to anyone whine about not having clean underwear while *his* idea of helping with the housework consisted of Windexing the TV screen. So what was her problem? Why was she lying here with a week's worth of empty pop cans piled on her nightstand and the remote tethered to her headboard with half a roll of dental floss so she wouldn't have to hunt for it if it slid to the floor during the night?

She threw off the covers. Shit. And now she didn't even have the consolation of Mom's cookies. She stalked into the kitchen, and opening the refrigerator, was faced with the meager remnants of her last trip to the grocery store, whenever that had been. She shut the door and stood there at a loss. Then she went to the trash can and gave it a small kick of frustration. She kicked it again, harder, and the piston—the unwanted, unasked-for piston—knocked against the side. She wrestled the trash bag out, unbolted the back door, and ran it out to the can waiting for pick-up by the alley. Back inside, she relocked door and scrubbed her hands clean.

She went back to the refrigerator, and after a moment began tossing out the few remaining vestiges of food—a black, limp banana, some probably-lettuce, a glass jar of orange juice whose lid strained under the pressure of fermenting sugars. Then she thought she might as well wash out the fridge as long as it was empty. Finally, spent at last, she staggered back to bed.

In what was left of the night, Georgia dreamed of spilled juices rising from a linoleum floor like Aladdin's genie, casting rings into the air, silver rings that landed in the weeds and couldn't be found. She stirred restlessly, feeling incomplete even in her dreams, and aware of being profoundly and determinedly asleep—unwilling to wake up for silver rings or dead chickens or anything at all.

In the morning she woke to her alarm, depleted but calm. There was a suspicious damp indentation next to her where Albert had snuck onto the bed once she'd finally fallen asleep, via the clothes bench at the foot of the bed that Georgia never seemed to get around to moving. A lapping noise emanated from the bathroom. "Ugh," Georgia groaned. "Albert."

Shuffling to the kitchen, she was momentarily startled, upon opening the refrigerator, to be faced with sparkling cleanliness. It was like a gift. She stood for a moment basking in its glow before resigning herself to the fact that there was still nothing there to eat. She turned to the counter for the last of the bread and plugged in the toaster.

As much as she tried holding on to the tranquility of a clean fridge, though, she couldn't help noticing a faint unpleasant odor hovering around the kitchen. She tried to shrug it off. It was like a wilted gardenia, or maybe—please God no—a hint of dead mouse. She changed her mind about breakfast. She put Albert out in the backyard and shuffled through her mail. There was another post office slip. She peered at it and scowled. There was nothing in the "sender" box, not even a zip code. Who the hell is sending me auto parts? she thought. Her alarm clock, forgotten on snooze, clamored from the bedroom. Albert simultaneously scratched at the back door to come in.

Fifteen minutes later Georgia sat out front in her Chevy Citation, listening to its tortured attempts to turn over. She pumped the gas a couple of times, automatically and unconsciously weighing the outside temperature in relation to how long the car had been sitting to figure how many times she could safely pump it without flooding the engine.

A rasping laugh made her look around, but she couldn't see anyone nearby. Odd. She let go of the key and listened. No, not laughing. A metallic "haw, haw, haw." And then a clank. The garbage truck, she realized, in the alley behind her house. There must be something wrong with it to make that noise. "Haw, haw, haw." Well, the joke's on me, Georgia thought. Somebody sends me few hunks of metal and I start hearing trucks laugh. Well, good riddance to anonymous pistons. She heard the truck move along the row of houses and stop behind the house next to hers. Only one more to go. Good.

The piston sat in Georgia's mind as clearly as it had weighed in her hand. It was an interesting thing in itself, no doubt about that. It seemed so perfect in its way, and surprisingly complicated. What were those odd holes and cutaways? She'd never actually seen a piston before. If she'd thought about it, she'd have assumed it would be a solid hunk of metal, but it wasn't. Like a heart, she thought. Like a chicken heart, just a little blob in your hand, but so complicated inside—this chamber and that chamber, and hooked up to all sorts of things. As long as the chicken was alive.... Disconnected, of course, it was dead.

Georgia wasn't conscious of opening the car door. She found herself moving toward the side of the house, the fingers of one hand touching lightly against the center of her chest. She walked between the houses. The garbage truck was stopped at her yard.

This is crazy. I can't be doing this, she thought, and broke into a run. "Wait! Hold on!"

But the man was tipping her can and didn't pause. Upended into the back of the truck, white plastic trash bags tumbled out.

Georgia stopped, dropping her arms to her sides. Well, that's it, she thought. Too late.

But for the second time in not enough hours, Georgia was swept by emotion. The fear and anger she'd felt last night turned itself inside out and was remade into a bewildering need, and alongside it, a sense of looming, irrevocable loss.

The crushing door began its descent.

"No, wait!" she croaked, and launched herself forward again. Rushing to the truck, she bashed her fist against the side. The man looked over at her in surprise and let go of the lever. The machinery stopped.

"There's something I need ... that I need to get," she stammered. "Please."

The bag wasn't far down in the hopper. She reached in, careless of getting dirty against the back rail. She grabbed a bottom corner of the sack, but in her haste the night before she'd neglected to tie the top. The trash went spilling out. "No," she cried, and her feet came off the ground as she lunged for the piston tumbling away from her. Her hand curled around it.

"It's okay," she called. "I got it." She held up the piston and waggled it back and forth. And again, faintly, "I got it." A puzzled look flitted across her face, and with a quick shake of her head she reached in to recover the box with the three unopened parts inside.

The garbage man just shook his head. He pulled the lever again as soon as she was clear, and the heavy door continued on its path, crushing the trash, pushing it into the belly of the truck. Georgia could hear its rasping guffaw behind her as she walked back toward her car. She wanted to laugh too, at herself, or at the oddness of the morning, but she couldn't quite manage it.

She looked down at the perfect metal thing in her hand and wondered if overtime shifts and sleep deprivation had finally sent her over the edge, or if she held in her palm some crazy kind of redemption, something that would hold an answer to her own disconnected heart.

By the time Georgia dragged herself home after work that evening, she was too tired to feel any emotion at all. The factory was good for that, she'd discovered long ago, for numbing the spirit along with the mind. She carried a new package from the post office. Only a box, after all, and whatever was in it would have to wait until she'd had a good night's sleep. She set it on the table beside the pistons, and nudged an inert Albert with her toe. "Wake up, old fart," she said." I'm home."

Then she looked around the disordered kitchen, and sniffed, and groaned. How could she have let things get so out of hand? What kind of a person was she? She put an arm, aching from cold chickens, over her face. She just couldn't cope with it with now. After Albert had gone out for his pee, Georgia showered and slunk miserably into bed with a jar of peanut butter, a box of Ritz, and a magazine. The TV droned.

Albert on his rug gave a deep sigh. He lay with a towel draped over him and gazed longingly at the bed. He'd been exiled to the floor ever since he'd acquired the habit of showering in the evenings.

. . .

Georgia's dreams were full of stinking things. A dead skunk, which was really a mouse, had come through a tunnel and was burrowing upward under her house. She awoke to damp dog. Albert had for once misjudged her sleep cycle. "Caught ya, booger," Georgia told him. "Down."

With a grunt, Albert resumed his place on the rug. But now, to her dismay, Georgia was wide awake again. Hunger and self-loathing wrestled with her aversion to decomposing rodents. The clock crawled toward midnight. Moonlight and shadow stirred faintly on the wall. Balanced on a fulcrum of inertia, her mind swung this way and that, looking for a reason to either get up or resign itself to a night of lying half awake. It finally latched onto the package in the kitchen, and with something like relief, Georgia sat up and switched on the lamp.

The box this time was oblong. It held a shank of metal. "Crankshaft connecting rod" was typed neatly on the tag, along with the number, "4B." There was no note.

Again a creaky response began to turn over within Georgia. Not suspicion and fear now, although those things still hovered at the back of her mind, but a growing curiosity. And more—a sense of possibilities beyond the tedium of work and home. A stirring of restlessness. Disgust at the dead-end she'd allowed her life to become.

Well, she was awake, and it wasn't going to do any good to go back to bed as long as her brain refused to punch out. She might as well deal with the kitchen. Short of vacating the little house entirely, she'd have to contend with it some time or other, and it wasn't going to get any better.

She began with the lower cupboards, filling the trash can with long-forgotten kitchen debris—newspaper once used as liners, old Brillo pads, congealed dish soap, but no mouse. She scrubbed the cupboards clean, then started on the drawers. By two in the morning she'd worked her way up to the sink. With a shudder of revulsion she plunged in and began stacking the chaos of dirty dishes onto the counter.

There was no mouse. There was only the humiliating realization of how low she'd sunk. What kind of a pitiful excuse for a human being would let her sink putrefy to evacuation proportions before she got around to washing the dishes?

The parts arrived in an ever-increasing stream, a new package every day or so, then one or two a day. Before long it was a flood—metal and rubber, pins and rings, sprockets and bearings, hoses and wires. At the end of the second week, when the exhaust pipes and two gleaming mufflers arrived, it dawned on Georgia that her mysterious packages contained not car but motorcycle parts. Her mind reeled. And eventually, with a wary but growing sense of excitement, it also occurred to her that it might actually be possible for somebody to put the parts together.

By the time spring, in its customary fits and starts, had made its way north, she'd settled into a ritual. Each time she brought another package home from the post office, she'd set it on the kitchen table until after her shower. Then she'd approach it like a new lover, with guarded hope and a sizzle in her stomach.

One day UPS left an engine block on her doorstep. Georgia wrestled the box into the dining room, now a parts repository, and stood looking at it, panting slightly. She thought something must be wrong with her heart, the way it was pounding. A faint roar seemed to be throbbing in her ears, transmitted through a firmament of doubt and fledgling hope, from a scarcely imaginable future.

Georgia told no one except Corrine about the parts. Corrine, she'd been sure, would inform her that she was out of her mind. That she should rip the parcel pick-up slips to shreds and set the cops on the lunatic, whoever he might be, that was bombarding her with metal. Georgia was half right. Her friend had indeed told her she was out of her mind to accept "peculiar gifts from God-knows-who." Then she proceeded to pump Georgia every day for news. "What came today? When are you going to start putting it together? Who *is* this secret admirer you've been hiding, girl? You've been holding out on me, all this time acting like nothing interesting ever happens to you. I knew there had to be more to your life than you let on."

Georgia began to examine the packages for clues, and asked UPS and the post office what they could tell her. All UPS could say was that the engine block had been sent from Cache, Illinois, which, they added, happened to be their biggest hub. The post office couldn't help her either. The postage varied, the postmarks were consistently blurred. She began to cut out postmarks and one night she spread them across her now-spotless kitchen table, determined to solve the puzzle. But after putting together all the letters she could make out and coming up with "Arfket Dolg, WN," she remained stumped.

She imagined her secret benefactor. He would have dark hair. She tended to waver between Marlon Brando in "The Wild One" and the elusive Jonathan Pryce in "Jumpin' Jack Flash," although occasionally Jamie Foxx came knocking. Her fantasies now, when she came home aching from work, were not of chicken parts hanging off her shoes, but the mud of dramatic landslides from which she would heroically rescue a half dozen children, carrying them on her back one at a time to safety until, verging on physical collapse, she would find her handsome lover arriving to gather her up in his arms. The children having been returned to weeping and grateful parents, he would carry her off to a mountain cabin, there to devotedly nurse her back to health, to adore and respect her for the rest of her days.

Other times, he was just an ordinary guy with sandy hair and blue jeans. But he was kind. Always kind. And he loved her. She didn't have to watch her step around him. He brought out her best qualities—her fine spirit, her joy in life. And when they argued, which was seldom, he'd never say, "You really thought I loved you? I just felt sorry for you, you loser." No, they would quarrel in bright, hot flashes that purified the air, and come together later in the night, filled with remorse and renewed love.

Georgia had always mistrusted hope. It was such a seducer. You couldn't talk it down; you couldn't kill it; you could only wait and watch it fade away in a long, lingering death. What was happening to her now was the sweetest of tortures. It was hope renewed every day, always with the promise of more, for who would send a tenth of a motorcycle? A third of a motorcycle? A half?

On the other hand, who would send her a motorcycle at all, and what nut would send it in pieces through the mail? She briefly thought of Jimmy, maybe some scheme he had, but Jimmy was not the calculating type. He had something and then he didn't. And he was so lacking in imagination that the idea of keeping water cold in the refrigerator had taken him by surprise. No, definitely not Jimmy.

Work was becoming intolerable. The factory was back to eight-hour shifts but even so, by the end of the day her hands hurt so much that even her feet and back seemed comfortable in comparison. The new girl next to her on the line actually spoke during her first few days but sank into morose silence by the end of the week. The country music station playing over the speaker system helped, but Georgia seemed to have lost the knack of numbing her mind as she worked.

When she'd first started this job, she'd survived on daydreams and the hopes of paying off her bills, of being able to own a house with Jimmy, maybe even starting a family. She could watch her pit of debts being filled in little by little, day by day. Then the physical effort of the work settled into a chronic grind and her dreams began to fade. Slowly her brain found a pattern of monotony to match the endless run of the chicken line.

Rita Solis had worked next to her then, a solid woman with a remarkable talent for talk, one of the few who didn't seem to be whittled down to silent efficiency. She'd talked with the rhythmic flow of a sea chantey. And she'd liked Georgia. Rita must have seen something in the younger woman that Georgia herself could not. Of all the women on the line she'd singled her out, treating her with affection, like a little sister or a niece. But then there came a midwinter day when the unfailing Rita didn't show up for work. It was as if some sweet, sure song that had been playing forever had suddenly gone silent.

Rita never came to work again. Three months later, the spring thaw brought a final and horrible resolution to her disappearance. Her body was found in a patch of woods near the river. Her note had said she was going to shoot herself, and that's what she'd done. How a woman who had endured nine years on the chicken line could suddenly be unable to stand another minute of life without going out and ending it with her own cold hand was more than Georgia could comprehend.

While Georgia struggled with her grief, and her guilt at not having seen Rita's desperation, not having taken the time to dig deeper into the big woman's life and somehow seen this tragedy lurking, Jimmy had taken the opportunity to walk out, saying little except that there were prospects for a guy like him in California.

All Georgia had left were debts and a line of chickens extending into infinity. She thought of quitting but didn't know what else to do. She couldn't seem to get her body to stop getting up and going to work. Her mind and heart ached as badly as her hands, but she involuntarily sought refuge in the familiar, hated routine. Anything that would require original thinking seemed beyond her capacity. And so, dazed and functioning on automatic, Georgia had gone on. Until the day of the motorcycle pistons.

Waking up is not always pleasant. Waking up and finding yourself looking at chickens' assholes all day is the rudest of shocks. Georgia's freshly revived nervous system found itself irritated beyond belief. Every moment became a test, and a marathon of such moments increased her misery beyond bearing.

The day she picked up what would prove to be the last of the packages from the post office, she set it as usual on the kitchen table. She showered as usual. Then she sat across from the flat, rectangular box and laid one hand on it. She didn't open it at once but made herself eat dinner and clean up. She wanted to linger over this one. There was no way she could have known it was the final package, but for the past week or so she'd sensed that the odd rain of wonders must soon end. Maybe she couldn't deal with many more disjointed parts. Maybe she was just ready—ready to move on, to face whatever all of this might mean.

Leaving the box where it was, she put on some music and sat down in the living room with a magazine, determined to read at least one article. Within the first paragraph, about a movie she'd most likely never go see anyway, her eyelids began to droop. A vision of chickens floated toward her, hanging from their cable in an eerie fluorescent factory light—a dry-cleaning rack from hell. Then, through the half-dream, a different light rose up to her ... the wavering glimmer of treasure ... a golden ignition key at the bottom of a deep pool. She came fully awake standing at the kitchen table with a steak knife in her hand, and reached for the box.

3

GEORGIA CUT THROUGH the packing tape and pulled the cardboard flaps back to reveal not metal or rubber, not wires or gauges, but a thick book. "ASSEMBLY AND MAINTENANCE" was printed across the front, and below that, in smaller letters, "G-1." Georgia could barely breathe. She paged through the book. In clear, professional-looking print and numbered diagrams were complete assembly instructions for the motorcycle. "Well," she said. "Well." She closed the book. "All right, then."

They were running a late shift at the plant. Georgia pulled on some jeans and searched her closet until she came up with a silk shirt her mother had given her one Christmas. She snipped the tag from its cuff and put it on. It fit perfectly on her small frame. Whatever else her mother did or didn't know, she had Georgia's size down cold.

"Come on, Albert," Georgia said.

The old basset seemed surprised but not displeased when she heaved him into the car and drove off, windows down in the balmy air of early summer, in the direction of the plant. Georgia pulled into the lot and rolled the windows halfway up so Albert wouldn't jump out, not that she thought he would. It had been a long time since he'd shown that much initiative, but on a night like tonight, who knew?

When she strode into the office she was surprised to see her usual day supervisor, Bill, a stringy, smirking man with a mortally inflated view of his own charm. He'd made all the women on his shift queasy for years. He looked her up and down with leering appreciation. "Hot date?"

"Not exactly," Georgia told him. "I'm quitting."

"Ha ha," he said.

"Do you want me to write it out for you?"

"No shit?"

She picked up a pen, and tore a sheet from the note pad on his desk.

Bill eased his bony butt onto the edge of the desk, a little too close to where she stood. "What, you don't love me any more? You know, honey, I always thought we could be real good friends. You just give me a chance and I bet I could change your mind—make you want to stay. What do you say?"

"Bill, you couldn't change the mind of a plucked chicken.... But you probably already know that." She headed for the door. "Have accounting send my paycheck."

"Hey, now, don't be that way. You know you're gonna miss me." He whistled an off-key rendition of "Sweet Georgia Brown" as she strode out.

She stalked down the hall and out to the parking lot, shuddering as the door closed behind her.

Then she looked around and took in the night. Beyond the streetlights, the sky was deep and starless. The air had a soft quality to it, like swimming in a lake, velvety and weightless. When they got out on the road, Albert hung his head out the window in ecstasy, long ears rippling, lips flapping in the wind.

Georgia drove north. She didn't have a destination in mind, she just wanted to get out and see what it felt like to *go*. But she soon realized exactly where she wanted to be. She pulled off for gas, considered the fact that she didn't have any overnight things, and decided it didn't matter. Uncle Emery probably wouldn't care if she wore the same clothes for a month. He most likely did himself, she thought. A self-sufficient old coot, shy with outsiders, he could wear whatever he wanted, living alone up there by the Boundary Waters. Georgia drove until she got tired, then turned off into a flax field and slept.

It was getting light when she pulled off a long track into a dirt yard and cut the engine. She sat there for a little while, listening to the ticking of the cooling metal, wondering whether it was too early to wake her uncle. When she finally went up to the cabin and knocked, Emery, evidently having heard her when she first pulled in and accepted her delay as simple country courtesy, met her at the door with two mugs of coffee. They sat on the narrow porch. Albert, with more joy in his step than Georgia had seen in a long time, went off to sniff around.

"How've you been?" Emery said as they sipped their coffee—freeze-dried, the height of modern convenience in his opinion. He was a slight man with gray hair and a hint of elf about him, as if, startled, he might vanish into the trees.

"Okay, I guess. How about you?"

"Not bad."

Georgia looked out past the low pines to the blue morning lake. It looked pure and welcoming, and she thought how nice it would be to take a swim.

"How much do you know about motorcycles, Uncle Emery?"

"Used to ride when I was younger."

"Could you put one together, do you think?"

"Depends on what shape it's in. Sometimes it's hard to get parts for the old ones, but yah, I could probably get one running."

Georgia smiled. "Oh," she said. "I've got parts."

. . .

Emery gave her a pair of old khaki pants to cut off, and a T-shirt, and Georgia went for a swim just as the sun was clearing the trees. It was like sliding through silk, the still microscopic algae sweeping her skin with the softest of caresses. Here and there a cold spring rose. She swam through the wayward pools of cold and warmth like a bird through clouds, toward the center of the lake.

Albert sauntered over to the shoreline and without so much as a pause, launched himself into the water. Georgia turned at the splash and laughed as he headed out to her.

"You'll never make it," she said. "You'll sink." She herded him back to the shore, found some rope, and tied him to a tree. Albert gazed sorrowfully after her as she swam out again.

Floating on the water, Georgia wondered what on earth she thought she was doing. Quitting the factory could mean losing her house. She should be out looking for another job right now. But, hell's bells, there must be more to life than mortgage payments. For the moment anyway, there was nothing better to do than let the water hold her. To gaze into the summer sky and watch the wispy clouds floating by. She gave herself up to the sensation of spinning, as slowly as the earth. She recalled floating like this as a child, turning under the sky.

It would be hot today but not as hot as in the city. Her shoulders eased as she arched back and floated her hair off her forehead. She swung her head a little from side to side, letting the fingers of the lake run through its long dark strands. After a while she swam back. She was met near the shore by Albert, romping in the shallows, trailing a chewed-through length of rope behind him.

She stayed all day at Emery's, weeding the garden and later cooking what she considered a pretty decent supper. In the evening she and her uncle sat outside until the mosquitoes drove them in.

Drove her in, really—they didn't seem to bother Emery a bit. Then they sat in the kitchen drinking Sanka. Emery's eyes kept straying to the stack of library books on the floor, but he was a good host. Rocking his chair onto its back legs, he listened as Georgia talked about Jimmy leaving, about quitting her job, about how their cousin Mary Anne was doing, about how crowded the Twin Cities had gotten. Finally she got around to the matter at hand.

Emery's eyes came back into focus when she said, "And then a couple of months ago something funny came in the mail. Pistons for an engine. I thought they were car parts."

He nodded, and she went on. "But they turned out to be for a motorcycle. Don't you think that's odd?"

"Yup."

"I almost threw them away. And then more parts came. They kept coming every day or so till there were so many I started piling them in the dining room."

"Who sent 'em?"

"I don't *know*! That's what I'm trying to say. Do you think it might be some whack job or something?"

"Dunno. Might be."

"But do you know what?" She paused and took a breath. "I don't think I care anymore. It's like, I'm not sure if they're really supposed to be mine but I don't know who else's they'd be, so I guess they're as good as mine. Anyway, there's an assembly manual and I want to put the bike together, but I think I'm going to need help. And I hate to ask you this, but do you think you might be able to come to the Cities for a while and give me a hand? I know you don't like it much there but it would really be great if you could come. Just for a while." She paused. "So, what do you think?"

"You gettin' another job right away?"

"What? Oh. Well I guess I'll have to. Pretty soon anyway."

"'Cause if you weren't, we could take my pickup down, haul

everything back up and do it here."

"You would do that?"

"Yah," he said, with a small nod. When Georgia hesitated, he added, "I'd stay out back in the trailer. You could have the cabin to yourself."

"Oh, no, you wouldn't have to do that. No, it's just that I hadn't really thought about it, leaving my house and everything. I'd have to figure some things out. How long do you think it would take to put together?"

"Don't know."

"Well, I could sleep on the couch here," Georgia said. "Or I'll take the trailer, if you wouldn't mind. I don't want to kick you out of your own house."

"All right."

"Okay, then."

Emery nodded.

Georgia looked at this small man, living alone out here in the middle of nowhere. What must he think of her unannounced invasion, all the disruption she was bringing to his quiet life. "Thank you, Uncle Emery," she said simply.

Emery shrugged and swirled the last drops of coffee around in the bottom of his mug.

"Uncle Emery?" Georgia said.

He raised his eyebrows.

"You can go read now if you want."

Emery drove with both hands carefully on the wheel. He kept the pickup on the straightest path down the center of his lane that Georgia had ever seen. They were barely on their way down to get the parts, and Georgia was suddenly overtaken by wild doubts.

What if it was all a mistake? What if the guy with the parts had thought she was someone else? Maybe he'd stolen the motorcycle and was sending it to somebody piece by piece. Someone else named Georgia Dunn—how likely was that? But who knew? Maybe she should see if she could get her job back. Again and again she went over the possibilities she'd already covered a thousand times during the past weeks, until she was so sick of her own thoughts she wanted to stuff her head into the glove compartment. Albert was sitting half on her lap, his big head out the window. Georgia leaned over and stuck her own head out.

Dogs like this? she thought. It made her eyes sting and loose strands of hair whip painfully against her cheeks. She pulled her head back in and turned on the radio, then glanced at Emery for consent, but he hadn't even seemed to notice.

While they were still close to his home ground, Emery drove slowly, glancing out the window at the countryside and commenting on changes. "Looks like Morrison's gonna be ready to harvest them Christmas trees this year." "That burn's growin' in pretty good." "Mary Dahl's got that south field fenced in. Wonder what she's gonna put out there." But as they got further afield he seemed more detached, and after an hour or so Georgia offered to drive. Emery sat stroking Albert's head and looking distractedly out the window.

Emery's eyes were on the land and towns rolling by, but his mind was elsewhere. Having a niece was a fine thing, he mused. He'd never dreamed, as a kid back in Baltimore, that he'd ever have any family at all outside of his mother. Aware only that he had grandparents somewhere in the Midwest, he'd never imagined any actual relationship with them. His unmarried mother had been adamant in her bitterness toward her family. She had vowed to accept nothing from them, short of an admission from her father that, her own transgressions notwithstanding, his had been the greater fault for throwing her out of his house—his own daughter. She'd accept nothing less, not even her mother's furtive gifts. One of Emery's few treasures was a thin gold chain with a small charm on it—a golden leaping horse—that his grandmother had once sent to his mother. A little boy with few things of his own, he'd fished it out of the trash and hidden it away, still wrapped in its pink tissue paper.

When Emery's mother died at thirty-one—drunk, unrepentant, and unforgiving—it was without having told her thirteen year-old son he had a half-sister, illegitimate like himself, living with her parents in Wisconsin.

It would be forty years before he knew. Then in one stroke, he learned he had a sister, a niece, and a fan of relatives that swept out to the far reaches of the Midwest and beyond. He was connected to the world through blood.

He was less stunned now, nine years after that first letter and the subsequent meetings with his sister, Iris, and her daughter, Georgia. But that wasn't to say he was exactly over it. Never mind—what with one thing and another he figured life had paid him back in full for the difficulties of his early years. And here, now, sat this young woman beside him, intently sweeping him up into her own unpredictable world. It might take some getting used to, he thought, but what a thing. If there was a God and he was giving out gifts, this was one he'd gladly accept.

He watched out the window as Georgia drove them into the city. It was even bigger than he remembered. The outskirts sprawled further, and Emery didn't recall there being quite so many buildings or so much traffic. But Georgia drove with confidence, heading straight to her small house. The place looked tidy enough but could probably stand a little maintenance. The windows could do with some recaulking, he thought, and he wouldn't want to make any serious bets on the roof.

"You guys make yourselves at home," Georgia said to Emery, and ostensibly Albert, as she let them in. "I'm going to pick up a few groceries. Uncle Emery, is there anything you want?"

"Whatever you get is fine."

When she was gone, Emery walked through the house, looking around. He noticed that Georgia didn't have many books, but she had stacks of CDs, a few new but most of them looking pretty well used. He looked at the CD player. He'd never had occasion to use one himself. There wasn't much to it, though. He slid the disc out. "Island," it said right on the silvery plastic, and in smaller letters, "U2-The Joshua Tree." Well, he didn't know what that was supposed to mean but he put it back in and pressed play.

In the dining room he looked in amazement at the chaos of motorcycle parts. It looked like enough for two or three bikes, but he knew that was deceiving. Maybe one and a half. He smiled to himself. Whatever this girl was thinking, she was in for quite a project. He hadn't even thought to ask if she knew how to ride. He went to look at the assembly manual on the dining room table. It seemed straightforward enough, but a couple things puzzled him. To begin with, other than a cryptic "G-1" on the front, there was no make or model number. Also, the book wasn't bound; it was put together with neat metal fasteners. He looked again at a few of the parts in growing amazement. They looked more than just okay—they looked *extremely* okay. Each piece was well made. There were no burred edges, no factory marks. Holy Goddamn, he thought. These were hand-made. With growing excitement he continued to inspect the parts.

When Georgia returned with groceries, Emery was sitting in the kitchen with the manual in his lap. He looked up at her with a grin.

Georgia looked at him. "What?" she said.

He shook his head. "Let's cook some dinner."

Emery sat at the table and chopped carrots, his eyes traveling continually to the manual he'd put safely off to the side, until finally Georgia couldn't stand it anymore.

"Uncle Emery," she said. "If you don't talk to me right now I'm going to toss these pork chops out the door. Albert gives me more answers than you do. Now, give."

"I want to ask you a couple questions first."

"Then ask. I can cook and talk at the same time."

"All right, then. First, do you have any idea at all about who's sending you this bike?"

"Not a clue. I told you."

"You're sure?"

"Yes!"

"Okay. Do you know anyone with a tool shop, or who has access to one?"

"Not that I know of. I mean, I might, but I can't think who. Why? Is something wrong with the parts? I could ask around if you need me to."

"No, there's nothing wrong with the parts. Not a single thing that I can see."

"So what, then?"

"Well, it's good and bad, as far as I can figure. Can you ride a motorcycle?"

"Uncle Emery!"

"All right. Look, what you've got here is not your average motorcycle. Did you happen to notice any make or model, any serial numbers on any of the parts?"

"No, I don't think so."

"I'll tell you why that is. Somebody made them himself."

Georgia furrowed her brow. "What do you mean 'made them himself'?"

"I mean by hand. Every piece."

Georgia sat down and picked up a round slice of carrot. She

tapped it on the table like a poker chip. "That would make it pretty expensive, wouldn't it?"

"This quality? You bet."

"But why ...?" She shook her head. "None of this makes any sense." She got up and went to the frying pan.

Emery watched her back, her slumped shoulders and bent head. He stood up and leaned on the counter by the sink. "Nope. It doesn't make much sense. I wouldn't get too down about it, though."

Georgia shrugged her shoulders. "I don't know. It just makes it worse, somehow. I could see fooling around with some ordinary bike. I mean it was sort of a joke, you know? A prank, and I could go along with it. But if this is really valuable, well, that makes it different. I've never even ridden a motorcycle before, to answer your question. I've been on the back of one but I've never driven one myself."

"It's not all that hard. I could teach you."

She looked over at him. "That's not the point. What if I messed it up? This belongs to someone, and it sure as shit isn't me." She went back to poking the pork chops. With a sizzle, they began to fill the kitchen with the mouth-watering smell of approaching dinner.

Emery felt an unaccustomed sense of recklessness. It didn't usually fall to him to convince anyone of anything. He always figured people would do what they wanted and he had no business trying to sway them one way or another. Now, though, he felt an urge to prod his niece along. He didn't like seeing her discouraged, for one thing. And to be honest, he was feeling drawn in to this adventure. He'd been about to tell her that if there were problems with any of the parts, he had no idea if she could get replacements. But she'd already managed to see the downside to the upside. So he said, "What the hell. Let's put the thing together at least. Then you can decide what to do with it."

She looked up. A tiny smile softened the corners of her mouth.

"Okay ... I guess we can do that."

After dinner, Georgia left her uncle absorbed in the manual and drove over to Corrine's house. The fading light had turned the sky a deep, luminous blue. The streetlights were bright blossoms against it, and the light from Corrine's front windows seemed to hold a golden warmth.

"Where've you been? I called and called." Corrine said when she opened the door, and grabbed Georgia into a hug.

"I quit the factory."

"You didn't!" Corrine held Georgia away from her with a wide-eyed look. "Why didn't you say something? You really quit?"

"I did."

"Unbelievable." Corrine led the way into the kitchen. "Although I really don't know how you stayed in that pit as long as you did."

Georgia sat down and savored a rich maritime aroma while her friend sautéed something in a black iron pan. "Jobs are tight."

"Not that tight."

"Well, I've done it. I'm officially unemployed."

Corrine looked over her shoulder while mincing parsley with swift little chops of a huge knife. "So what are you going to do? ... Why don't you apply at the bank?"

"Corrine, *please* watch your fingers. And no, thanks. I'm not going from one prison to another."

"Yeah, well, my prison doesn't have the rack, and it pays okay. And there are always promotions." Corrine turned back, scooped the parsley onto the side of her knife and flicked it into the pan. She swirled it around with a wooden spatula.

"I'm thinking of going up north for a while," Georgia said.

Corrine paused at that and looked at her friend. "North? Where? Has your secret admirer finally revealed himself? The mystery motorcycle man?"

"No. And I don't know if he is an admirer. He might be some psychopath screwing with my head."

"What, then?"

"My uncle's going to help me put the bike together."

Corrine nodded. She handed Georgia a tidbit from the pan on a paper towel. "Taste."

"What is it?"

"Just taste it."

"God, this is wonderful."

"How long are you going to be gone?" Corrine asked.

"I don't know."

"Do you need me to take care of anything at your place? I assume you're taking Albert."

"Yeah, he loves it up there." Georgia looked around the well-ordered kitchen she'd spent so much time in over the years. Deep red ceramic bowls of various sizes nested on the open shelves. The maple salad bowl she'd given Corrine a few birthdays ago sat at an angle, displaying the ringed grain. Shiny pans with blackened bottoms hung from a rack against the yellow walls, beside richly painted Brazilian carvings interspersed with down-home homilies on plastic plaques. She loved this kitchen.

"Could you just stop by and water the plants?" she asked. "Or let me bring them over here—that might be easier. I don't have a whole lot of them left."

"That's all right, I'll stop by and get them in a day or two."

"Okay. Thanks."

With mingled reluctance and anticipation Georgia stood up. "Well, I guess I'd better get going. My uncle's at home and I have to pack, and ... I don't know." She whooshed out a deep breath. "I've never just taken off like this before. I've never done *anything* like this before."

Corrine grinned. "Well, you go and have fun. Don't worry, be happy. Give me a call when you get back."

"Okay. Say hi to your mother for me. What *is* that, anyway?" Georgia asked, looking at the pan. "It's amazing."

"I'll tell you when you get back. I'll cook you dinner."

"It's not squid or anything, is it?"

Corrine smiled and walked her to the door.

4

FRANK MORROW WAS the kind of man who always seemed to be just out of the frame of the picture. One minute there he'd be, standing in the group at a wedding, or a picnic, or an aunt's retirement party, but by the time the shutter clicked he'd have invariably wandered off, leaving only a blurred arm behind, or the back of his head. In contrast to his brother Julius—a man always, unmistakably, in the picture—Frank had a tendency to appear diminished. Not that Frank was small. He was in fact moderately tall, with a lean build like a long distance runner. It was just that his brother was *so* big. He didn't so much loom over Frank as seem to have emerged into a different dimension. On the streets of Foxton, or in the bank, or in a store, a stranger passing by as the dark-haired brothers stood in conversation might pause a second, not sure what the problem was, and then smile as a solution sprang to mind. It was like seeing two images of the same person, one taken at a slightly greater distance, in a more subdued light.

It was perhaps inevitable that as a kid Frank would admire his brother, and almost as certain that he would resent him—his bigness, his sureness, his success. But Frank came early to an understanding that transcended either sentiment. It was Julius who was expected to carry the heavy loads, to be responsible, to keep up a good public image. Julius was the big one. Frank wasn't quite as useful. There was a time, in fact, when he believed he had no value at all.

Years ago a college girlfriend had asked Frank why he wasn't planning to work in the family wholesale foods business.

"Because I can't do anything right," he'd almost said. He changed it to, "Because I have other interests—I'm the artistic one."

"You're an artist?" she asked. "I thought you were a history major."

"No, not an artist. I just have the temperament, I guess."

Frank wasn't very surprised when the girl soon began hanging around with another boy, and only mildly disappointed. He'd found unexpected gratification in another aspect of college life—he'd somehow developed into an excellent student. In high school, switching from subject to subject throughout the day had left him still pondering algebraic axioms in history class, the point of the Stamp Act in science. In college he deliberately limited his courses to a narrow range (against his advisor's recommendation) and did well. He learned to focus in long blocks, and on weekends turned his attention to a succession of intricate projects.

Although his interests were sometimes initiated on a whim, once something caught his attention he pursued it intently. He experimented for hours with the tensile strength and elasticity of various fibers and devised a clock run by dripping water down a succession of threads into small vials suspended at their ends. He built model cars, quickly outgrowing even the most difficult store-bought versions and crafting elaborate variations of his own. He once happened upon a book on the anatomy of ballet and spent months researching the dynamics of the leap.

Frank's interest in women took on something of the same character. One day early in his sophomore year he saw a wide-shouldered girl leaving the gym, her hair wet from the pool or the shower. Hurrying toward her next class, she slung a backpack over one shoulder, at the same time flipping her hair back with a shake of her head. As she passed from the shadow of the building into a shaft of sunlight, droplets of water flew out from the tips of her hair and formed a fleeting cloak of rainbow around her shoulders.

In a single mesmerizing instant Frank saw that she, and all women, were beings more profound, more intense, than he'd ever imagined. They were suddenly revealed as a transcendental race imbued with wildly magical attributes. He would watch them pass by, trying to understand how one woman's movements differed from every other's, and just what it was about her scent on the air that made her unique. He was completely enthralled, not with one girl but with women in general.

Writing papers and studying for exams came as a reprieve to Frank during this time. It was when he left the realm of history and reemerged into the present that he was nearly overwhelmed with baffling sensations. It simultaneously bothered him and seemed perfectly reasonable that girls were too complex for him to even hope to comprehend, much less be of any use to. But as impossibly complicated as they were, he felt compelled to search for patterns, to try and see them clearly.

Frank first noticed Jill James on a chilly day in October as she clutched her zippered pink sweatshirt close against the cold and hurried into the library building. He changed course to follow her in. When she stopped at the coffee machine in the hall, he hung back and watched her put money into the slot. The way she bent her head to find change in her backpack—amazing. The lift of her arm and the way her body swayed forward as she inserted the quarters—a miracle. He suddenly wanted to know what she smelled like, and before he had time to think, he'd walked right up to her. She turned, and Frank immediately stepped back. The last thing he wanted was to frighten her. But the worried look on her face cleared and she gave him a small smile.

Every girlfriend he'd ever had disappeared in that instant. Frank felt as though he'd suddenly come upon a living work of art, a masterpiece. He didn't have a clue what to say to this wispy girl. It was not that she was classically beautiful, but that she was somehow, well ... perfectly original.

She cocked her head at him. "Getting coffee?"

"No ... uh ... maybe. I suppose coffee sounds good."

She laughed. "Well, 'good' might not be the most accurate word for it," she said. "But it's hot."

He reached into his pocket for change, and his eyes never left her face.

Jill had an air of pale fragility that Frank imagined in a young coal miner's wife, who could in reality be as tough and enduring as a roadside weed. He continued to be aware of the myriad of girls who passed before him every day, of their brightness or gloom, of the heavy compelling way one moved her mass through space, drawing him like a planetary body, or the airy, traipsing gait of another. But Jill was the one he wanted before him. He started learning the nuances of her character, and began to love her.

At Christmas she planned to go home to her parents' outside Pittsburgh. "You can come," Jill told Frank. "I just have to let them know."

"But do you want me to? Would it be uncomfortable? Is it too soon?"

"God, Frank," she said. "I thought you were the decisive one. I'm the wishy-washy one."

"No." He smiled at her. "I just always liked you more than you liked me."

Jill sidestepped that one. "It's fine if you come. It'll give me someone to complain to when my parents drive me nuts," she said. This wasn't quite the whole-hearted endorsement Frank would have liked, but then he caught a hint of a smile and he knew that behind her caution lay a subtle tease.

He couldn't bear to be separated from her. When he looked at her, his throat swelled with love. Each step she took reverberated up through the bones of his feet, through his legs, through his groin, and to his heart. So he went with her.

The plane ride to Pittsburgh was Frank's first. From the terminal he studied the propjet through the plate glass window, imagining the engines in motion, trying to get a look at the wing flaps. Glancing into the cockpit as they boarded, he was fascinated by the number of dials and instruments crowded into such a small compartment.

They took off in windy weather and Frank looked over at Jill with a grin that immediately faded. Her already pale skin had turned to skim milk. Frank felt helpless in the face of her distress. All he could think to do was pull the airsick bag from the seat pocket and hold it out to her. She looked at him as if he were the most pathetic creature she'd ever seen. He felt dumb as a tree. Then the plane pitched. She gripped his arm, a panicked wren clutching onto the only branch in sight.

Frank spent most of the flight worrying about Jill, and considering the structural forces of air molecules moving against the airframe. In fact, he spent a good bit of his spare time for the next year studying airplane dynamics.

Jill's mother was a surprise. Not an older version of Jill at all, she was large and dark-haired—Black Irish, she said. Jill's father was a small, morose man, polite enough but without much evidence of interest in life. A little girl was living with them, a blond pixie of about seven, introduced as Cousin Jessica.

Frank was accepted without much fuss.

There was a musty warmth to Christmas at the James's. Their house was small and filled with dark, worn furniture—a legacy of finer times from someone's distant past. There was a faint mildew smell that Frank noticed right away but soon got used to and accepted as an inherent part of the place, like the cramped, high-ceilinged rooms and the knock of the radiators.

He called his parents on Christmas Day. Although they'd expressed disappointment over his decision not to come home, he suspected they were at least partially relieved. And why not, he thought. What a pain he'd been to them growing up. Lacking judgment, forgetful, distracted. A terrible driver—he'd forgotten to read the driver's handbook and passed the written test on memories of his parents' driving and logic. How he'd managed to pass the road test was a mystery. And how he'd managed to survive *having* his license was an even greater mystery. He would start thinking about something—about his friend Georgia, maybe, although that was the last thing he wanted to think about—and he'd lose track of everything else. Where he was going, what the speed limit was, why it was important to stay on the pavement. And that had been typical of his whole childhood. His poor parents, he thought. He was a little surprised, though, at how the phone call made him feel. He wasn't sorry not to be there—still, there was a heaviness in his chest that felt like loss.

Being with Jill made everything all right, though. Their only complication was that the weather had turned bitingly cold. The long walks they'd planned were reduced to distracted fumblings in her father's car whenever they found an excuse to run an errand.

Jill's mother turned out to be an unexpected ally. "It looks like we're running out of milk, Jill. Would you go to the A&P for me? Wait ... here, I'll make a list."

"Sure, Mom."

"Maybe Frank would like to go with you, take a look at our little city?" She turned to him with a raised eyebrow.

"Okay, Mrs. James."

"But before you go, just put this turkey in the pantry sink to thaw for me, would you?"

Mr. James mostly sat in front of the TV with a newspaper in his lap. He tended to read during the programs and look up when the commercials came on. Frank wondered if his hearing wasn't quite up to par, and pondered the technicalities of a hearing aid.

One evening Jill asked Frank why he wasn't in engineering.

"Oh, I'm no good at it," he said.

"What do you mean? You're always fixing things and making things."

"That's just a hobby," he said. "I can't do the math."

"I bet you could if you tried."

Frank asked, "When geese fly, do you know why one side of the vee is longer than the other?"

"What?" she said. "Oh, I get it—you're changing the subject. All right, why?"

"Because there are more geese on that side."

She hit him in the arm.

"I hate the dentist," Jill told Frank. It was midway through spring semester and Jill was acting tired and thoroughly unreasonable. She sat on the bed in her dorm room, curled up against some pillows. Frank lay sprawled across her roommate's bed, propped up on an elbow. A stack of textbooks sat abandoned on the floor beside him.

"What's to hate? You go, you relax in the chair, and you let him look at your teeth. It's not the 1800's anymore. No pliers." He swung his feet to the floor and stepped over to settle down beside her. He took her head between his hands. "Here. Open up."

"No."

"Come on, just let me see."

"What are you going to do?"

"I'm not going to do anything. Just let me see. I can tell it's swollen even from the outside—I just want to see what it looks like."

She scowled, but opened her mouth.

"Turn more this way.... Jesus, Jill. You've got a broken molar. All right, conversation over. You have to get it taken care of." He sat back and regarded her frowning face. "Look, it's got to be killing you. What can be worse than feeling like you do now?"

"I don't know." She hunched up, wrapping her arms around her knees, then shifted to lay her aching jaw in a cupped hand.

"There's nothing to be afraid of. This guy's very good. I went to him last semester to get a filling replaced." He tapped his cheek.

"I haven't been to a dentist since I was a little girl," Jill said. "He gave me a shot with a needle that was a foot long and felt like a harpoon."

"And you haven't been since then?"

"No."

Frank looked at her and shook his head. "Well, you're going now," he said.

There were fish tanks in the waiting room and a palm tree in the corner. "Is this guy really a dentist?" Jill whispered as they came in. "I feel like we're in *The Little Mermaid*."

Frank went back with her when she was finally called. Jill climbed awkwardly onto the reclining dental chair and Frank sat in a folding chair by her feet. Jill eyed the machinery hanging on metal arms around her. A technician fastened a bib around her neck. The dentist chatted with her for a moment while he pulled on his latex gloves. Then he leaned over her mouth.

Frank watched, wishing he could do something about Jill's state of mind. She had the eyes of an unwilling roller coaster rider about to plunge into the abyss.

"Everything's going to be fine," Frank said helplessly. "Don't worry."

The dentist looked and probed, and then a technician jammed cardboard squares into her mouth for X-rays.

Jill wouldn't talk to Frank as they waited for the films to be developed.

"Well, the pictures look good," Dr. Garcia said, returning. "You'll need a crown, but it looks like there's no damage to the root." He began opening drawers in the cabinet next to him. "I'll put on a temporary now, and Anne will schedule you for the permanent one."

Jill swallowed and nodded. Frank leaned forward in his folding chair and gently squeezed Jill's ankle. He meant to reassure her, but it was like touching a dead branch. He didn't know if she even noticed.

Frank said, "So what would account for the swelling?"

"Swelling?" said Dr. Garcia.

"On the side of her jaw."

"Where?" The doctor leaned to look at Jill's face from the front, comparing the two sides. "Yes. I see what you mean." He touched his hand to the slight swelling as he asked Jill, "Has this been hurting?"

"No. Just the tooth."

He had her open and close her mouth. "Does it hurt here?" He put pressure on her jaw with the flats of his fingers.

"No."

He gently pressed the side of her jaw and her neck, and drew his brows together. "Jill, I can feel a lump here. Have you seen a doctor about this?"

She shook her head and whispered, "A lump?"

"That's what it feels like to me."

Frank, always so curious, always the first to examine any new and interesting phenomenon, sat paralyzed in his chair.

"You should have this looked at right away," Dr. Garcia said, looking her in the eye. "It might be nothing, but don't put it off."

Jill nodded.

"Do you have a regular doctor here in town?"

"No," she said.

"All right, I'm going to give you the number of a friend of mine, an internist. You call him and tell him I gave you his name. He's very good, Jill. He'll know whether this is anything to worry about, and he can refer you on if need be."

In the car on the way back to the dorm, Frank was concerned with Jill's pallor, with her lethargy, and most of all with the distant look in her eyes. "I've got a bad feeling," was the only thing she'd say.

Back in her room Frank took the slip of paper from her limp hand and dialed the doctor's number. Jill looked at the rug.

"I was afraid of the wrong thing," she said.

Four agonizingly long days later, but still too soon, too lousy a thing to accept all at once or ever, Jill's dread and Frank's worst fears were confirmed. Jill had lymphoma—stage 1 Hodgkin's disease. The doctor told her she had every reason to be optimistic. The success rate for treatment was very good.

Jill went home to Pennsylvania to begin chemotherapy and radiation. Frank tried to stay in Milwaukee and continue with his classes, but it was hopeless. He withdrew for the semester and followed her, renting a room and enrolling for a couple of evening classes at the University of Pittsburgh. He got a day job in a lumberyard.

Jill turned out to be as tenacious as Frank had once imagined her to be, a weed that refuses to succumb, beautiful and tough. The world seemed to run by them in a rush of motion as she struggled to come back again and again, even as the cancer, despite the doctor's earlier reassurances, continued to progress.

Frank hung on as hard as Jill did. Even when she tried to drive him away, while he acted docile enough, he was immovable. Why would he want to stay with her, she would demand, when she made his life so miserable with sickness and hospitals and the bleak future that loomed ahead of them? It was no future at all that she could see, beyond the depressing rounds of chemotherapy and partial remissions and always more cancer. "Leave me. Go away," she'd say. "It's not going to help anything for you to stick around."

But Frank wasn't about to leave. He'd failed people before.... He turned doggedly away from the memory that threatened to plunge him into an older, long-hidden torment. He couldn't afford to think about that now. He needed all his strength for the times ahead. He couldn't bear to fail Jill. He'd hold her to life with his love and his hope.

If there was a battle between them, it was one in which neither knew which side they were on from one day to the next. Neither wanted the other to suffer, but they didn't know how they were supposed to manage that. Jill talked to her parents about suicide, and they cried and made the doctor give her antidepressants. When she broached the subject with Frank, his mind spun through a spectrum of thoughts and emotions faster than the speed of light. "No, never," and "Anything that will make you not suffer," were the answers, and they blurred together in a gray miasma of sorrow.

But their days together had a richness about them, too. One Saturday morning in the first fall of Jill's illness, on a day when it seemed that even cancer had possibilities of brightness and love, they drove to a rocky outcropping and climbed. Frank reveled in the feel of his muscles working and his lungs pumping. He stopped to look around at the vistas below them, and thought of the forces at work over eons to form this complex rock and soil. Then he watched Jill up above him, lost in a world of stone, gazing in wonder at the colors and textures in the small universe right in front of her nose. Jill resting her cheek for a moment against the cool granite. Jill running her hands over a mossy area of dripping shadow.

Frank climbed up beside her.

"Don't say a single word about igneous, or manganese, or molecular mating," she warned.

"I wasn't going to." He laughed. "Molecular mating?"

They sat in a depression of rock and she leaned back against him, tracing the edges of moss with her fingers. They sat quietly for a long while. A chipmunk poked its head over a rock beside them. With a quick little movement it darted to the top and advanced a few feet. Jill lifted her hand instinctively, as if to reach out and pet it, and it retreated as quickly as it had come.

After a minute Jill said, "When I was a little girl I had a cat. My mother hated him because he peed on the furniture, so he had to stay outside. He had a life of his own, of course, but I always thought of him as purely mine." She turned her head a little, still gazing out over the valley, but Frank could see the side of her face, the soft curve of her cheekbone and the slight, heartbreaking hollow at her temple.

"Then one day I was sitting out on the back steps with my friend Amy. I was braiding her hair, trying to make it stick up on top of her head like one of our dolls'. It was hot and muggy and I remember thinking that nothing ever happened in the summer. School was out and everything seemed to slow down, more and more as summer went on. It was hard to imagine school ever opening again, or anything interesting ever happening. It was just plain slow and hot, and hardly worth the effort of slapping the flies away. Fuzz ... that was the cat ... was poking around in the weeds.

"Then all of a sudden this big dog dashed out from the trees behind the alley and went tearing after Fuzz. In one split second, instead of lazing around and catching crickets, Fuzz was racing for his life. It just happened so fast. It was scary and exciting." Jill shook her head. "Amy kept saying how sorry she was for the poor kitty, and that the brown dog was so mean, but all I could think of, once my cat was safe, was how the light suddenly seemed brighter than it had before, and how I'd never noticed the way the trees curled out of the shadows the way they did. I did feel sorry for Fuzz, but at the same time everything about him seemed more … I don't know … alive, I guess. Real." She glanced around at Frank. He gave a small nod of reluctant understanding.

"He wouldn't let me catch him," Jill went on, leaning back against him again. "He'd gone up onto the shed roof. Not even after my mom came out and chased the dog away with the hose. I think he came down at dinner. Mom let me keep him in my room that night."

Frank didn't say anything. He bent his head and rested his lips for a moment against her hair. He brushed a gnat off her cheek with his hand, leaving a muddy streak, which he wiped away with the sleeve of his T-shirt. He didn't know how a person's heart could feel both hollow and full to bursting at the same time.

"I think maybe we were both right, Amy and me. I always figured it was just a natural phenomenon, part of the nature of being alive. But now I think there are plenty of dogs that don't go after cats. Dogs that know the difference between a cat and a squirrel." She sighed. "Oh, well, I don't suppose you can be an outdoor cat without running some risk. He probably would have been miserable inside anyway, when I think about it." A breeze fanned them, bringing the scent of creek water and mint. They sat quietly.

A red-tailed hawk came into view, and then another, dipping and rising, each on their own path but clearly a pair, catching thermals, circling as they covered their hunting ground, then together passed from sight.

"Let's get married," Frank said.

She turned to look at him. "What? You're kidding, right?"

"No. I want to marry you."

"No."

He took her hand. "Please. Don't act like it's a crazy idea. I love you."

"It's a wonderful day, Frank. I love you too. But let's have today—this perfect day—just as it is. Besides, we're too young to get married. Ask me again after we graduate. Not before." She looked steadily at him for a moment and then turned back to the land spreading out below them. "God, it's beautiful here."

She must be rubbing off on me, Frank thought. He breathed in the air—the trees, the damp rock wall behind them, the faint whiff of mint, and Jill's own scent—and he felt, with unexpected peace, that it was enough.

But maybe, just maybe, there would be time ahead for a wedding.

Later they climbed, with many pauses, to the top of the rocks and got lost coming down the other side. It was dusk before they made their way back to the road, and then they had to hitchhike down to the car.

"I told you we should've gone back down the way we came," Jill said, crabby with fatigue.

"You're right. I thought I knew the way."

She grunted with exasperation. "Would you please stop being so reasonable," she said.

"Okay," said Frank. "Fuck you, then."

"Yeah, you wish."

"Oh, baby."

On a fine evening in September, not quite a year later, Jill lay breathing shallowly in a Pittsburgh hospital bed. Frank was there beside her, and her mother and father as well, but Jill was no longer aware of them. They'd been called back to her bedside from their brief forays walking the hallways or gazing blankly at cafeteria food, by a floor nurse who judged the time was near. Jill's pain was behind her, her despair and fear over. Her ragged breaths diminished and grew further and further apart until at last there were none. There was no particular moment when they knew she was gone, only a gradual, ultimately undeniable quiet.

Later, as Frank walked out of the hospital alone, he hesitated at the doors for a moment, compelled to turn back. But there was nothing left for him to do. He forced himself on, stepping through the doors and crossing the parking lot into a world that was forever broken and bleak. He breathed air that would never contain the exhalations of her breath, would never be stirred by the movement of her body. He walked to his car on weak limbs, not understanding how emptiness could cut like shattered glass.

5

GEORGIA AND EMERY RETURNED to the cabin late and tired, and hauled all the motorcycle parts in from the truck. Despite falling gratefully into bed in the little trailer she'd be using as her bedroom, Georgia did not find her first night back in the country a restful experience. The next time someone from the sticks complained about city noise she was going to counter with bullfrogs and crickets. How did anyone ever get any sleep?

The next morning she rose early, eager to get started. When she came into the house, Emery was clearing a space against a wall—pushing a chair off to one side, moving away a trunk and some odds and ends he'd been working on. Together they spread a canvas tarp on the wooden floor, and brought in bookcases from Emery's bedroom. After breakfast they began to sort parts, laying out the smaller pieces in neat rows on the shelves. Each part had come tagged with its name, reference number, and the section of the bike it belonged to. There were even directions and hardware to make a stand for the bike. The parts marked for later assembly they stored in boxes in the corner.

That afternoon, Georgia tried to make up for her lack of sleep with a nap on the couch while Emery was out cutting wood, stocking up for winter. She woke disoriented and groggy to the sound of Albert pushing his nose against the screen door, making it slap lightly against its frame. After stumbling over to let him in, thinking she should make some supper, she reached for the phone instead of the cupboard door, after which she opened the cupboard only to stare blankly at the canned peas for endless seconds before realizing she'd meant to look for potatoes. When she progressed to nearly cutting off the tip of her finger while slicing an onion, she decided she'd better sit down for a while. Emery found her asleep with her head flopped against the back of the couch, her finger wrapped in a swath of toilet paper. He checked to make sure she wasn't still bleeding, washed off the vegetable knife and finished cooking. They ate as the lengthening evening faded to night.

Georgia had never before spent much time with her uncle. She was surprised not just by his kindness, but also by his intelligence. If she'd been asked to guess, she might have classified him as rustic with a certain amount of horse sense. But his clear grasp of the world put her own city-girl oblivion to shame.

For all that, he was easy to be with. After the first day or two, as her cut finger healed, and the factory ache in her hands subsided, and afterimages of chickens faded into leaf and lapping water, her nervous chatter dwindled off. They fell into a pattern, working in the garden in the cool of the morning, coming in for breakfast, and then working on the motorcycle until lunch. Georgia drowsed in the early afternoons or found small projects to do while Emery took care of his own business—tool sharpening for the Forest Service, or small repair jobs that people brought to him. As time went on and Georgia gained confidence, she found she could work on the bike on her own. The manual was clear and the illustrations flawless. When she was tired or unsure, she'd stop and make dinner. Sometimes Emery would come in and find her still at work, and then he'd put a meal on. Neither of them made anything elaborate, although for a while Georgia felt obliged to try. After her first stab at coq-au-vin, however, and Emery's valiant but transparent attempts to express appreciation, Georgia gave up and fell back on stews and spaghetti.

In her idle moments, Georgia discovered a talent. She realized she was able to sit and stare into space for considerable amounts of time and not get bored or count the time wasted. It was a revelation to her that every minute didn't have to be filled with talk, or TV, or work. This was worlds away from the chicken factory—the mindless hours on the line had been heavy with worries, or blank with indifference. Here she could contemplate the quality of the air, or let her mind drift into dreamlike dances—old stories, images conjured by the scent of damp earth, thoughts of Corrine's irrepressible mama and her teasing banter—all configuring together in brand new ways to the sound of the lake slapping the shore as the breeze played across it and then floated off through the pines.

One night after dinner, Georgia and Emery pushed back their chairs and sat enjoying the quiet of the evening. Emery had been sharpening saws all afternoon. Instead of reaching for a book as he usually did, he locked his fingers behind his neck and closed his eyes.

After a while Georgia broke the silence. "My mother used to talk about you," she said.

Emery looked over at her, surprised. "She did?"

"Well, not about you exactly, but about having a brother she'd never met."

He gave a little nod.

"She always wanted to meet you."

Georgia wondered how Emery's life would have been different if he'd had the opportunity to grow up with a family, with her outgoing mother as his sister. From what her mother had gleaned and told to her, his had been a poor, dim existence—not without love, perhaps, but narrow. All the half-dreamed possibilities of life would have existed outside of family, beyond his alcoholic mother and unkempt house.

"Did Iris even know my name?" Emery asked.

"I don't think so, not until grandpa died. Well, great-grandpa, but I just called him grandpa."

"Was he mean?"

"Grandpa? No, not at all."

Emery turned his head toward the window. "I always thought of him as mean."

"Because he kicked your mother out. I know…. It was hard for me to understand that," Georgia said. She followed his gaze and saw that night was closing in, although at this time of year true darkness wouldn't come until quite a bit later. The light seemed to pool over the lake. Georgia very much doubted that Emery was seeing what lay outside the window at the moment, though. "I suppose times were different then," she said.

"Hmm."

Georgia got up and started clearing the dishes. "Anyway, he wasn't mean."

Emery looked back around. "Well," he said," I wouldn't worry about it."

"I'm not." She ran water into the dishpan. Then she turned and leaned back against the edge of the sink. "Well, maybe I'm worrying about it a little."

Emery looked over at her and sighed.

"I mean *we* always had it all right," Georgia said. "We had family around and never gave it a second thought. But you and your mother—"

"Georgia," Emery interrupted gently. "It's okay."

Later, as Georgia and Albert headed out to the trailer for the night, Georgia paused in the doorway, looking back at her uncle in his easy chair, which was inched over toward the center of the room to accommodate the encroaching motorcycle parts.

"Uncle Emery?"

He glanced up from his book, raising his eyebrows.

"Thanks for having me here."

He ducked his head and shrugged.

On impulse Georgia took a couple of quick strides across the room and gave him a peck on the cheek, startling him so much he almost knocked over the lamp.

The next day was Sunday, and Georgia decided to take the day off. She and Albert went for a swim in the lake. She'd completely given up on trying to tie him—the old guy was remarkably resourceful when it came to chewing through rope or slipping his collar. But basset hounds simply aren't built for swimming, and she was afraid he'd never resist trying to follow her. So she made him a pair of water wings. Emery helped her. They'd found an old life vest and modified it into a dog harness, adding a little extra flotation at the front, and making numerous adjustments and trial runs with a very willing Albert until they had it right.

Slender, silken ropes of algae were beginning to form in the water. She swam out, Albert trailing behind, until she reached a cold spring that spilled upward, a lake within the lake, and there she lay on her back and floated until Albert tried to use her as a raft.

Later that afternoon she drove into town. Although it had originally sprung up as a logging town and still had some of its woodsy working flavor, much of the town now catered to fishermen and canoeists visiting the Boundary Waters Canoe Area. The locals had a friendly air just barely tinged with the disdain that so often takes root in resort areas. Georgia wasn't quite sure of her own place. Did she belong or not? As the relative of a local, even an outlying, hermetic one, she felt she was entitled to slightly more respect than an outright tourist, but not nearly as much as someone who toughed out the bitter winters and marginal economy full time.

Her first stop was the drugstore, where she stood in front of the hand cream contemplating which one would soothe her cracked skin, which one smelled best, which was the best value, and in what size. Not that there were many choices. She dropped into a dreamy daze and stood staring right through the plastic bottles into a land of drifting waters and speckles of sunlight endlessly shifting on ground so thick with duff it sprang back up with every footstep.

A thin boy came over, stiff-shouldered and blushing. "Uh, do you need any help, ma'am?" he asked.

Her mind came back to the shelves in front of her. "Oh," she said. "No, thanks. I'm just trying to make up my mind."

His blush deepened. "Let me know if you need help finding anything." Georgia would have bet money this was his first job.

"I will. Thanks," she said, and watched him escape to the front of the store where he wielded a clicking gun, sticking prices on cans of bug repellent.

She grabbed a bottle of lotion and found the calamine, and gave the boy a friendly smile as she passed him on her way to the register. Georgia tried to imagine Uncle Emery at his age but somehow couldn't. Awkward as this teenager was, she could envision him as a man grown confident with age and easy with his peers, selling them fishing line and joking over a beer at the end of the day.

Georgia walked out onto the bright sidewalk and crossed the street to the grocery store, squinting against the glare. She shopped for pizza ingredients. She figured she could manage that much cooking. Homemade pizza was one of her mother's specialties, and as a girl Georgia must surely have learned *something* from helping her. She rolled her cart to the produce aisle for garlic and mushrooms and exchanged pleasantries with a young woman wearing a butterfly clip in her hair and bangs that looked like they'd been rolled around a steel pipe. Then she found a rack of sunglasses and tried on one after another until she found a pair that had just the right color lenses, and sat on her nose just so, and didn't rest on her cheeks where they would leave creases.

Being in town, idling away the time, was just what she needed, she thought, to soften the culture shock of the last week. But two aisles over, just past the paper towels, she found herself face to face with the motor oil and a little rack of household tools. She suddenly wanted to be back at Uncle Emery's, listening to the birds and crickets, and fitting motorcycle parts together. She finished her errands and headed home.

She wondered what she'd really do once the motorcycle was finished. She wasn't sure she could see herself riding off into the sunset. She supposed she could get a job somewhere and ride to work every day, but wasn't this bike meant for better things? Didn't it demand a life that lived up to its potential, its quality? When she handled the beautifully crafted metal parts, the plastic and rubber pieces molded so carefully and hand-trimmed, with no edges left rough or ragged, she began to see how a life could go beyond the ordinary.

For all these years, she'd been living her life however it happened to present itself. She'd lived with a man who just happened to be there when she thought she needed a man. She'd worked the dullest jobs—whatever turned up, or whatever a friend turned her onto. She thought now what a shabby and careless way that was to pass away the days.

But was she capable of more? She didn't know the answer to that one.

On an early evening after a hot, muggy day, Georgia looked up for the tenth time from helping her uncle stack wood. She felt as unsettled as the trees, which stirred and swayed in restless eddies. A thunderstorm was blowing in and Albert was nowhere to be seen. As Georgia and Emery got the last of the day's wood put up and the chainsaw under cover, Georgia looked around and whistled again for the dog.

"Go find him," Emery finally said. "I'll finish up."

The wind was picking up as Georgia headed for the deep stand of pines behind the cabin. Calling as she went, she walked from the clearing into the woods. It was like stepping into another world. A hushed peace enfolded her. Sounds became muffled, the needles so thick beneath her feet she seemed to be traversing a dense but bottomless mattress. The wind that blew so raucously over the lake was buffered by the mass of trees, groaning distantly above her as the storm rose. Within a few steps the gloom made it hard to see, a dark world that was gauged by time rather than distance. "Albert!" she called, and her voice was absorbed into the foliage and the thick carpet of needles.

Was he hurt, or lost? Had he gotten so domesticated and lazy he'd forgotten all his innate dog sense? A distant voice reached her. Uncle Emery was shouting a caution, "Georgia, don't go too far. You'll get lost.... Can you hear me?"

"I'm right here," she yelled, realizing with a shock how reckless she'd been. These woods didn't end in suburbs and strip malls, but in hundreds of miles of labyrinth waterways, swamps, and more forest. She turned back, until through the branches she could see the faded blue travel trailer, and beyond it the cabin and glimpses of the lake. She kept the water to her left as she skirted the edge of the pines, yelling into the wooded depths like a reverse image of a bereft child at the seashore calling to a loved one swimming far out beyond the crashing waves. She turned and tried the other direction, and finally returned to Emery in the clearing.

"Maybe he followed something and couldn't find his way back," Georgia said. She caught up the loose end of a flapping tarp Emery was drawing over a snowmobile he'd been working on for a neighbor, and held it abstractly while her eyes scanned the shore.

"Maybe he caught something and he's sitting there gnawing on it," Emery suggested.

She snorted, "Albert? Can you imagine him actually catching anything?"

Emery smiled and cinched down the last edge of the tarp. Georgia followed him as he headed over to secure the canoe. Together they carried the aluminum boat up to the side of the cabin and tied it down to cleats. The first drops of rain were falling. "Let's get inside," Emery said. "Albert's probably found someplace to hole up by now." As they headed for the door the rain began to come down in sheets. Georgia reluctantly went inside, Emery behind her.

"Do bears eat dogs?" she asked.

"I wouldn't worry about bears."

"He might be hurt. Maybe a snake or something."

"Nothing poisonous this far north. Why don't we start dinner. Do you have any dry clothes in here?"

"No. All my stuff's in the trailer."

He took a flannel shirt from a hook and handed it to her.

"I'm okay," she said, but put it on anyway over her damp top.

Then she stood chewing on a cuticle as she looked through the window above the sink, out into the deepening gloom.

Emery didn't really know how to help his niece but he figured keeping her busy might be good, so he went out to the freezer on the back porch and got a package of ground venison wrapped in white butcher paper. He thumped it onto the counter in front of her and moved the heavy cast iron pan onto the stove.

Emery had always liked storms. He felt an elemental joy in the resonating thunder, the smell of wild air and all the lazy scents they stirred up and sent flying around him. His wiry body awoke to the vibrations rolling through him, the muscles of his belly relaxing to the deep music of it all. He would take great, full inhalations, feeling like they were the first real breaths he'd drawn in a long time.

Now he paced the living room. Having someone, especially a worried someone, in his house made it difficult to surrender to the storm in the way he was accustomed. Suddenly, without any conscious decision, Emery picked up a flashlight from a shelf and a jacket from the hooks by the door, and went out into the downpour.

"Uncle Emery!" Georgia protested, but the door closed behind him.

He walked along the side of the lake where he remembered seeing Albert sniffing around earlier in the day. In this weather there was no hope of finding tracks, and the noise made it unlikely the old dog would hear his calls. There was a racket of rain and gusting wind, and under it came the low booming thunder that rolled from across the flat woodlands, across the ever-mutable water, across the enduring granite of earth's childhood, all churning to the crazy, noisy beating of the storm. Emery was drenched and buffeted by the shifting forces of the wind. It was oddly comforting to feel the weight of air, usually so passive it seemed without substance, but now making itself known, working passionately across the land. Lightning flashed erratically through the wild dusk. The rain that soaked him was threaded with spindrifts, bringing the smell of the lake to him, saturating his clothes and his thin tangled hair.

Hollering for Albert without much hope, Emery nevertheless found peace in action, in trying. In being out here, while inside the cabin his niece chewed her fingernails. In making a stand against loss and fear. He continued down along the east side of the lake. Although night was falling, the summer sky behind its mass of clouds still held a final glow of evening light. A momentary parting of thunderheads to the west gave Emery a diffused view down the shore. Perhaps among the rocks and dark clumps of brush the basset lay sad eyed, waiting for rescue. The rain swept down in heavy gusts.

Then Emery paused. He heard something, but couldn't make out what it was or where it was coming from. A faint, eerie sound emerged—not from along the shore but from deep in an area of mixed pine and old hardwood. There it was again—a low, aching siren. Emery entered the trees, following the almost constant wail of sound. By the light of his flashlight, well back in the thick woods, he found the old dog.

Albert was in his glory at last, baying rapturously by the foot of a red oak tree. Emery laughed out loud with relief. Good old Albert—his stubby legs planted wide, his ridiculous figure proud and true, his long ears swept back—raised his head upward and sang out the fulfillment of his destiny. He had found prey, and treed it.

Emery peered upward but couldn't see what hid among the branches until he climbed partway up a neighboring spruce and shined his light over. He glimpsed the dark rump and the long tail of a fisher, a large mink-like thing. It twisted its head around at this new disturbance with a disgruntled look. Emery climbed back down. Using his belt as a leash, he looped it through Albert's collar and dragged the unwilling hound from his quarry.

Disturbed earth, and a smell of blood that even a man could detect, caught Emery's attention not far from the tree. A dead porcupine lay belly-up between some roots. Emery reconstructed the scene in his mind—the fisher hunting the porcupine, then, engrossed in his meal, suddenly becoming prey himself as the dog picked up his scent and movement.

At the edge of the woods, Albert slipped his collar and made a beeline back through the trees. Emery had to fight his way through the branches again. Finally, notching the collar tighter, he succeeded in dragging the conquering hero home through the pounding rain.

. . .

Georgia had alleviated her anxiety by cooking. She had a sort of venison chili going when Albert and Emery walked through the door smelling of ozone and wet leaves. Her uncle seemed very pleased with himself. Albert looked blissful.

"You bad thing," she cried, dropping to her knees and hugging the dog. Looking up at Emery, she added, "You too. You had me so worried." She rose and gave her uncle a quick hug. "You better go get dry," she said, and turned away to reach for a towel before Emery had a chance to get flustered.

Emery told her over dinner about Albert's adventure.

"Oh, I wish I'd seen it," Georgia said.

Emery nodded. "He was pretty proud of himself. It was a good-sized fisher."

"Fisher?"

"Like a big weasel."

She reached down to where Albert was lying at her feet and scratched his damp head. "And you chased it up a tree all by yourself."

Albert gave the floor a single thump with his tail and sighed.

A new battalion of thunderheads was riding over the cabin and the night cracked and blazed with lightning. Georgia thought how secure she felt in this little cabin, warm and dry, protected from the storm. Rain slammed against the windows in uneven bursts, and ran down, defeated.

Done with their meal and their talking, Emery and Georgia cleared the table and Georgia turned on the tap to wash up. All she got was a sucking sound.

"Pump motor's out. Happens sometimes." Emery told her. "We can use the hand pump, but it's probably better to wait till morning anyway. Lightning can come right through the pipes."

Georgia stepped back from the sink and Emery laughed. "Don't worry. It can happen just the same in town, you know."

Georgia grinned a little. "I know. The phone lines too, but I don't usually give it much thought. It seems like nothing's really safe."

Emery shrugged.

Georgia walked over to the big window looking out over the lake just as a flash of lightning revealed the expanse of dark water. "It's pretty, though."

Emery nodded behind her and sat down in his easy chair, picking up a book from the side table. He didn't open it, though, just sat looking out the window. He reached over and turned off the lamp beside him. Georgia stepped across and switched off the kitchen light.

The sound of the storm seemed instantly louder. Rain hit the cabin with gusty force, carrying with it woody debris from the forest, pine needles and twigs, ancient nests, assorted bits of unprotected life. A chorus of trees sang from behind the sturdy notched logs of Uncle Emery's snug and sheltering home. The wind shifted, and from somewhere came a soft, high keening, almost beyond the range of hearing. Georgia shivered and glanced through the darkened room to where the woodstove sat cold and empty. But she had no desire now for its comforting crackle, or for any light other than the periodic flash of lightning. She savored the sense of the real world—the rough, vital world she'd been hiding away from for so long.

She thought of the fisher in its tree and wondered where it took shelter during its life, what it ate, how it survived thunder bursts and bitter winters. She wondered what it would be like to join its musky-smelling family in some den or hollow, to feel their warmth, to live as they did, touching the world directly, dependent on it, at its mercy.

She stepped over to gather up a blanket from where it lay draped across the couch. Wrapping it around her shoulders, she went back to the window. A shuffling in the dark behind her told her Emery had risen from his chair and was heading to his bedroom. "You can sleep on the couch tonight if you want," he said in a quiet voice.

"Okay, I might."

"Well, good night, then."

"Good night, Uncle Emery."

Left alone, Georgia stood thinking about her uncle setting out into the storm the way he had, and of Albert, fearless and purposeful, treeing the fisher. A whole universe of creatures lived in the world, with danger and hardships, with the exultation of a successful hunt or a narrow escape, the satisfactions of a dry den, a full belly, another day before them. What courage would it take to reap the rewards of such an existence—the heightened senses, the intimacy with the elements? But it was one thing to risk the world's odds when you weren't yet aware of the consequences, the pain that could come out of nowhere and steal your life, your body, your innocence. She didn't know what it would take to walk out there with open eyes, with the fear that comes from knowledge.

Georgia left the window and walked over to the front door. She turned the knob and opened it, holding tightly against the demands of the wind. The wet air swirled into the cabin, pressing against her face and her chest with its fierce power. She straightened against it, breathing in the complicated scents, letting the moist coolness play against her. The lake and sky brightened with a flash of lightning whose source she couldn't see, and a moment later the thunder reached her. She shut the door, relief and longing in her lungs, her eyes, her ears, and the feel of the wind still on her skin.

6

FRANK THOUGHT he was doing all right after Jill's death. He immersed himself in philosophy courses, discerning complex meaning in a thought, universes of shifting perception in a well-developed idea. He saw every philosopher who built upon the ideas of the last as a magician revamping the entire world.

Frank's friends were the first to worry. Not the simplest thing—a hamburger at Wendy's, or a car door—was exempt from his contemplative scrutiny. It's just tedious, said a few. He needs professional help, said others. He'll get over it—he needs time. He's a genius—they take things hard. He's a jerk—he needs to get over himself. Yeah, he's a bore. No, he's cool.

His family might have been concerned, but his letters and phone calls home were determinedly reassuring. He kept his grades up even though he'd lost more than a semester and had changed his major.

Frank told his parents he wouldn't be home for Christmas. He said he wanted to stay at school and make up some work. He flew instead to Jill's parents' house near Pittsburgh, where he showed up unannounced on their doorstep.

"Well. It's certainly a surprise to see you here, Frank," Mrs. James said when she opened the door. The faint shock in her eyes was quickly covered.

"Sorry I didn't call," he said. "I ... I just thought I'd stop by and wish you a Merry Christmas." With one hand he thrust a large candy box tied with ribbon in her direction. In his other hand he held a duffle bag. A pang of uneasiness prompted him to set it down outside the door. Of course he should have called ahead. He'd just hoped ... well, he didn't know what.

"Just stopping by?" Mrs. James said. "From Milwaukee?"

"Well ..."

"Yes, well. Anyway, come in, dear. How are you?"

"I'm all right." Now that he was inside, he felt more lost than ever. He didn't belong here. The house seemed at once familiar and strange—and with the Christmas tree dominating the living room, smaller than he remembered. The light appeared weak and dim, and Mrs. James's efforts at holiday spirit anemic. Still, he didn't know where else he wanted to be. He was instinctively avoiding his own parents—shielding himself from their eyes, not willing to face whatever it was he imagined they might see in him.

"Who's there?" said a light voice from the hallway, and Frank had a weird moment of disassociation, the intonation and timbre evoking Jill's own vanished voice. But in the next instant Jill's little cousin, Jessica, now nine, ran into the living room. She pulled up short as she turned to look at him. "Oh," she said. "It's you."

"Hi, Jessica."

"Hi. What are you doing here?" Seeing her troubled face, Frank suddenly thought how it must be for the girl, having him show up in the midst of her Christmas, now that Jill was gone. Even in the long, last days of Jill's illness, when he'd haunted the hospital and the house, and at the funeral afterward, it was as if he'd carried Jill's presence with him. Now it was just him alone.

"I came to say Merry Christmas." The gift he'd brought for her, a tiny wooden puzzle of a bird perched in a tree, sat forgotten in his pocket. All Frank's illusions of life, of the world of philosophy that had seemed so real to him through the past months, were seeping away at an alarming rate. The house pressed down on him—he couldn't seem to suck in enough oxygen to keep himself reliably upright. He sat down on the edge of a chair. He couldn't imagine why he'd thought coming here would be a good idea.

Mrs. James offered him a cup of coffee and he almost whimpered with relief. He would drink it and leave. He barely noticed Jessica slip out of the living room and head back to her room to play.

Mrs. James went to the kitchen and returned with coffee and cream. "Phil's out getting some last minute things for me," she said, sitting down. "He should be back soon."

She handed him his cup and they faced each other across the coffee table, Frank and the woman who most surely would have been his mother-in-law. If things had been different. If Jill had lived. If he'd had the guts to overcome Jill's objections and make her marry him, no matter what.

Finally, after an awkward delay, Mrs. James asked, "Will you be staying for supper, Frank?" And then, as if she couldn't help herself, though knowing she'd regret it, "And for Christmas tomorrow?"

He'd have to sleep on the couch, Frank thought. There wouldn't be a motel room left in town, and he knew neither of them could face having him sleep in Jill's empty room. A part of him wanted desperately to accept her offer. He was narrowly spared from collapsing into her hospitality by some fragile membrane of decency, a relic from a sane past. "Thank you," he said, "but I have to go. Thanks, though." He rose suddenly, bumping his knee against the coffee table. "It's ... it's been good to see you, Mrs. James."

"You're leaving already?" she asked in surprise, getting up from the couch. "You haven't even finished your coffee. You should at least stay and say hello to Phil."

"No, I'd better not. I have a flight," Frank lied. "I'm going to my parents'. I wanted to wish you a Merry Christmas, that's all." He felt almost frantic to be away. But looking into Mrs. James's lined face, he suddenly caught a confused and fleeting image of Jill, and of a mother's love for her child, and of all the things this meeting could have been. His cup was still in his hand. He set it down clumsily. Fighting tears, he stepped over and hugged the older woman. "I wanted to say I loved her," he whispered, and fled out the door.

He walked downtown and found the bus station, where he sat drinking black coffee and trying to decide what to do. He felt simultaneously too young and unformed to make a reasonable plan, and too ancient to weather the consequences of any decision he could possibly make. When he couldn't tolerate sitting still any longer, he went walking through the cold, grimy town. By dusk he was shivering with caffeine and cold, breathing shallow, ragged breaths. He'd have to do something soon, he realized, or run the risk of having to be rescued from hypothermia and stupidity, lying in some snowbank, not that it wouldn't serve him right. But he couldn't bear the thought of ending up as somebody's Christmas good deed.

The final bus of the night was heading west and he bought a ticket home. He felt like one of his model cars with its props removed before the glue had set, falling apart piece by piece. He sat numbly in the bus station and couldn't think of a single coherent precept or axiom. He couldn't remember what Thomas Aquinas wrote or imagine why he should care. Kierkegaard and Nietzsche were just dark and distant names. There was nothing left to keep his memories from engulfing him.

A face kept rising before him, not the beloved face of Jill, fresh and smiling, but a nightmarish imitation, a sunken mask, gray, dominated by haunted, protruding eyes. If he'd had enough energy left in him, he would have been tempted to find a blunt object and beat himself unconscious with it just to relieve himself of that vision.

But he wasn't capable of anything of the sort. His body seemed to have quit on him. The shivering had subsided, leaving only minor tremors and a maddening twitch on his upper lip. Melted snow dripped from his hair, but when he tried to brush it away his arm was wildly uncoordinated, unhinged.

Other images began swirling through his mind. He no longer had the strength to hold his nightmares at bay. A young girl he had failed ... no, more than one ... that he had failed to protect, because he had been a coward—a miserable, stupid coward. Confusion, shame, and grief roiled through him. Tangled images. Frizzy red hair ... no, long dark hair flowing free, silky with youth; a girl twirling around and around; a girl curled up on a basement floor weeping; a pale haunted face in a corridor.

Had he thought his love for Jill could save him? But how could it possibly, when he couldn't save *her*? He couldn't save her any more than he could save the others, though he loved her with every fathom of his flawed being. Maybe she'd been doomed from the moment she'd met him.

Once Frank started crying, he couldn't stop. The tears flowed intermittently but relentlessly—as he boarded the bus, as he rode through the desolate countryside. It distressed him that crying could be so utterly involuntary. When he stepped off the Greyhound briefly at a rest stop somewhere in Indiana, fellow travelers regarded him with curiosity, and perhaps pity, but he was impervious to their glances.

When the bus crossed the state line into Wisconsin, Frank began to look toward home. For once he didn't worry about how he'd appear to his family, about his mother being upset or his father disapproving. There was a bed there, and a room with a door he could close. That was his goal and the only thought that kept him upright in his seat throughout the long hours.

He arrived home like any traveler, he thought, still feeling the road in his bones. Depleted, a little disoriented, just like any traveler. But not for the first time he misjudged himself. His brother came to the front door when Frank, keyless, knocked numbly upon it. Frank saw the look on Julius's face turn from surprise to grim concern. A massive arm went around him as, with a glance toward the family room where the TV churned out sounds of a Christmas special, Julius gently hustled him into the kitchen. Frank sat hunched at the table while his brother brought him a drink and a wet washcloth. Apparently judging Frank unfit even to wash his own ravaged face, Julius wielded the cloth himself.

After checking to make sure that their parents were still occupied, he got Frank upstairs and into bed. "I'm going to get you something to eat," he said, and left. He reappeared sometime later, whispering, "Are you still awake? I brought you some soup." But Frank was lying just as Julius had left him, staring blank-eyed at the wall, tears still seeping sideways onto the white pillowcase. Julius insisted he eat, and Frank sat up and obediently swallowed, his famished body seeming to absorb the hot liquid as soon as it ran down his gullet.

"I'm going to tell Mom and Dad you're sleeping," Julius said.

"That would be good."

"I'll be back up in a while."

"No, I'm okay, J. Thanks."

"You're definitely not okay, but I'll leave you alone for awhile. I'll be in to check on you, though. Try to sleep."

He's such a good brother, thought Frank. He never once asked me a question I couldn't answer.

Frank missed Christmas completely, sleeping fitfully, waking like someone in a fever, dry-mouthed and sweaty. He felt bad for his mother. He knew she must be worried, as she always was, over this son of hers who could never manage to be just okay, just normal. Julius, typically, took charge, even setting up an appointment at a mental health clinic a few days after Christmas. When Frank insisted on returning to school, he arranged for him to see someone in Milwaukee.

Frank reasoned that he should be able to finish his coursework and graduate on time, despite his dropped semester. What he most wanted was to get back into the limbo he'd achieved during the fall. But it wasn't possible. Back at school he had a rocky semester, working steadily for a few weeks and then losing his concentration.

He felt like a man who's lost his last, best chance. Jill was the only person in whose eyes Frank had been able to see himself as a competent man, a good man who'd have the courage and ability to stand up and do the right thing, if need be. To risk himself for justice, or to save someone he loved. And now she was gone. He hadn't been able to save her. He didn't think he'd ever have the audacity to imagine himself in that light again.

His days had an uncertain quality to them. Each movement was like walking through heavy fog. His ability to take things for granted deserted him and every step seemed fraught with ambiguity and potential danger.

A thin strand of wire would become his lifeline.

Frank sat in the library, his eyes turned to his textbook, which, in fact, he was not at the moment reading. Instead he was watching a scene, completely imagined, of himself and a girl walking through a desert. When she began to fail in the heat, he wrapped his arm around her and led her to a rocky overhang, shaded from the terrible glare, and there he soothed her and gave her water. He made repeated forays to find hidden watercourses where he would dig until the life-giving liquid was revealed, and each time more and more of the poisons within him were sucked away by the scorching air and the intensity of his efforts. It was a satisfying daydream, simple and finely crafted, feeding a craving he'd found no other way to appease. He'd been traversing this same desert for eight or nine weeks. The time he spent there was at first carved out of his spare moments, but had lately been finding its way into any unattended second and lodging there, expanding like ice, cracking off chunks of his study time, even his class time.

When he felt a tap on his shoulder, Frank had to travel a long way in order to arrive in the present and hear the voice of the professor at his side.

"Could I speak to you for a minute, Mr. Morrow?"

Frank reacted with instinctive politeness, though a muscle in his neck tightened in rebellion at being wrenched from his dream. He nodded, carefully gathered his books, and followed the professor outside into the cloudy day.

As a freshman, Frank had taken a class in comparative religions from Professor Chase. He didn't know much about the heavyset, middle-aged man apart from the energetic way he conducted his seminars. Word was he liked to do some kind of metal work, soldering or something, in his spare time, and considered himself something of an artist. They'd never spoken outside of class.

Chase's current project, as he explained it to Frank, was an intricate three-dimensional time-line using wire and engraved platforms to illustrate the history of world religions. His main problems at the moment were time and engineering. It had come to his attention that Frank, although not an engineering student, had a gift for models. The professor paused, a hint of discomfort flickering over his features, and Frank wondered what else had come to his attention. That Frank was perhaps a little obsessive, perhaps not a hundred percent stable? But Chase went on—would Frank be interested in working with him in exchange for credit or a small stipend, whatever he could work out with the department?

Frank didn't immediately take to the idea. The project seemed pointless, an art project disguised as a history lesson. He agreed reluctantly to take a look. In a side room off the welding shop, where Chase had managed to claim a niche for himself, he showed Frank what he'd created so far. He stood with a mixture of pride and the anxiety of a fledgling artist awaiting a critic's judgment of his work.

An airy nest of wires rose two feet from its base and there sagged precariously. It was clear that without help it was going no further. There was a sort of beauty to it, but it was in danger of being lost in the randomness of the tangle.

"This can't be how religion started," said Frank.

"Actually," said Professor Chase, "although it's impossible to determine all the early forms, from the archaeological evidence—"

Frank sighed. "What I mean is, you have all these wires springing up out of a flat field."

Chase looked at him for a moment, and then his eyes widened. "Yes. That's it," he said excitedly. His hands rose into the air as if levitated by an updraft of creative enthusiasm. "They'd have come from an extant culture, which would already have a form of its own...." And he was off.

In spite of himself, Frank was amused. Ultimately, though with some reservation, he decided to accept Chase's proposal. Frank began to spend his free time reviewing the subject of world religions, making sketches of wiry, three-dimensional family trees of doctrine and lore, and researching metals. He declared a second major in engineering, and so began to define the course of his life.

It took them two and a half years to present a finished project. They finally wrapped it up under pressure from the University, despite the fact that Chase still regarded it as incomplete. It stood, depending upon the observer, as an eyesore or a work of magnificence; a futile effort at tracking religion to its most ridiculous reaches or an outstanding piece of scholarship.

When the project terminated, so did Frank's college career. An engineering degree within sight, he'd had enough of campuses. The wire that had saved him had not ultimately led him into the world, but had wrapped itself around an abstract idea. There was a part of him that craved the grounding of the outside world. He accepted a job in Chicago as a technical writer for a company that published trade magazines.

It took him weeks to pack up and leave his apartment. Transitions had never been easy for him, and here he was abandoning a place he'd known and worked in for nearly a quarter of his life. Was liberation supposed to make your heart pound and your bowels churn? The hope and exhilaration he'd felt when first leaving his parents' house to enter college had faded to an almost incomprehensible memory.

Though he enjoyed his work in Chicago, Frank was lured back to Milwaukee after a couple of years to take a job as a technical services writer for Harley-Davidson Motorcycles after a friend urged him to submit samples of his drafting work. It was a good time to move closer to home. Frank's mother hadn't been well—plagued by painful circulation problems in her legs, she couldn't get around easily on her own. Frank found it both satisfying and irritating to finally be of use to his family. He drove up to Foxton on weekends to help out.

One Saturday when he arrived with the week's shopping, he found his mother at the kitchen table. He put the groceries away while she sat drinking tea.

"Is Dad around? I got him some of the tobacco he likes from that shop in Milwaukee."

"No, he's down at the bar." She tipped her head in the general direction of downtown. She'd recently gone through a phase of dying her hair. It was now at that stage where the stark line between youthful chestnut and tarnished silver was beginning to give way in mingled streaks.

"Already? Gambling?"

"Of course. You know he doesn't go there to drink." She gave Frank a mildly reproving glance.

"I've always wondered how they get away with gambling at that place."

"They've got a back room. They call it private, so all the old men can go lose their money."

"Dad doesn't lose a lot, though, does he?"

"No, not too much. Just the price of entertainment, he says."

Frank rearranged a few things in the freezer. "He never seems to be around much anymore," he commented.

"Your father can do what he likes. He's earned his retirement."

"I know, Mom." Frank moved around to put the canned string beans and soups into the slant-shelved cupboard he'd built in high school, designed so the cans would roll to the front and nothing be left forgotten in back.

Frank's father, twenty years older than his wife, had long ago carved out a pleasant life for himself apart from his family. It wasn't that he didn't love them, Frank knew. He'd worked hard to build Morrow Foods into a successful business, and had taken good care of his wife and children. It was just that it had been a while since he'd really been needed, and he'd apparently settled into the idea. Not having him around now, though, must be hard on his mother, and also on Julius, who took on most of the added work.

Frank went to the sink and began washing apples.

"It's nice of you to do this, dear," his mother said.

"It's no problem."

"Well, it's a lot for you."

Frank shot her a look over his shoulder. "Julius has been helping out for years, Mom."

"But you were never as outgoing as Julius," she said.

"Outgoing? I'm not sure what that has to do with putting away groceries."

"Well, nothing really. Not 'outgoing' exactly. It's just that you were always a little temperamental."

"Was I?"

"Not tantrums or anything. Just the opposite. You kept to yourself. I never knew what you were thinking. That's hard on a mother, you know."

"I guess I never thought of it that way."

"You did turn out to be quite a bit smarter than we expected, though."

Frank laughed, opening the refrigerator to put away the rest of the fruit and vegetables.

"Not that we ever thought of you as retarded, exactly—"

Frank emitted a dry hoot into the crisper and shook his head.

"—but you just didn't show the promise of other children your age. My word," she said, her eyes turning heavenward, recalling old vexations. "I remember when you were in grade school. I'd start you on your math homework and twenty minutes later you'd still be looking out the kitchen door at your bicycle, and if I didn't keep my eye on you, there you'd be, out there fooling with the wheels or something. It was a trial—it really was. And when you finally did start on your homework, it just seemed to take you forever. And then getting you to bed! ..." She blew out softly through pursed lips.

"Well, you're grown now. I just wish I could've done more for you, dear. Maybe I wasn't the best mother for a child like you. It's sweet of you to come back home, though, and try to help me out now, with my bad legs and all."

Frank didn't quite know what to say to all this. He closed the refrigerator and as he slipped past his mother to put the vinegar away, he leaned down and kissed her cheek.

. . .

Frank's mother died at home, alone, on a Friday night, while her husband was away on a weekend fishing trip. She'd sometimes accused him of not fishing at all, but of going off on some Las Vegas junket or other. He was, in fact, at a friend's fishing cabin in the woods, listening to old records and playing cards.

Bea Morrow was in bed, watching a rerun of "Who's the Boss?" She just loved that Tony Danza. She'd always said so, and she especially liked it that he was so crazy about a woman who wasn't movie-star beautiful. In fact, that lady boss of his was a little homely, if you came right down to it, but she had a nice brightness to her—and that was her name too, wasn't it, Light? Well, good for Tony.

A blood clot broke loose in her left leg. It traveled through her bloodstream and lodged in her pulmonary artery. She cried out in sudden pain and couldn't catch her breath. She tried to turn onto her side to reach for the phone. The pain seized her again. She clenched her arm to her chest, and lost consciousness.

When Frank came to the house the next morning and his mother wasn't up yet, he put away the groceries, fixed himself scrambled eggs and coffee, and went out onto the porch to eat. He noticed that the mowing service hadn't been by to do the lawn. After loading the dishwasher he peeked into his mother's room and saw that she still wasn't up. She'd left the TV on as usual, and he didn't turn it off. She seemed to like the noise and the sudden silence might startle her.

He went to the back shed and, knowing his mother would disapprove—what did they hire the service for anyway?—he fired up the old mower. By the time he was done it was almost eleven, and between the late hour and the noise he'd made as he finished up in the side yard, he was sure his mother would be awake. He went to see if she needed help.

She was lying on her side, exactly as she'd been when he'd looked in on her two hours before. He shut off the TV and called softly to her, but in the silence he knew. He went around the bed and sat down beside her. He reached for her wrist but it was an empty gesture. He checked for her pulse only because he knew that Julius, always competent, would have.

Frank felt like a little boy for a moment, sitting there on the edge of his mother's bed. But looking at her, so still and helpless, he suddenly felt as if *she* were the child. She'd made a good life, he supposed. But had she been happy? Fulfilled? He realized with sadness that he'd never know.

He couldn't look at her face for long. She was pale and bluish, her lips almost purple. He was glad her eyes were closed. He sat beside her for a while more, then reached over, not looking at her directly, and stroked her hair—just once, and another light pat.

Julius, of course, would want to make all the funeral arrangements, knowing it would be too much for their father. But it suddenly seemed to Frank that this was meant to be his own task. Julius had a wife and children to take care of and certainly didn't need more to do. But whether or not Julius wanted this responsibility, the big man was used to running things and it might seem unreasonable for him to stop. If Frank really was going to take over—a daunting thing—he'd have to be resolute. Little Frank, the squirt who hadn't even known how to change the TV channels until Julius taught him. Frank, who could never be trusted to stand up under pressure. If necessary, Frank decided, he'd fight for the right to do this dreaded duty.

The smell of grass came in through the window—mown grass. He'd have to call the lawn people and tell them not to come this week. But first, of course, he'd have to figure out how to contact his father, and then there were the other calls. He went to the kitchen to begin.

While he gathered his courage to start, he made a list. He tried desperately not to wonder—if he had tried to awaken her when he'd first come in instead of having a leisurely breakfast and taking it upon himself to mow the lawn, could he have gotten to his mother in time, called an ambulance, saved her life? But in between looking up his aunts' phone numbers and trying to think which funeral home they'd used when his grandfather died, Frank remembered the feel of his mother's cold skin under his fingers. No, he realized, she'd been gone for a lot longer than an hour or two. There was nothing he could have done. With a sharp inhalation, he pushed back the grief that was beginning to overtake the numbness of first shock, and picked up the phone.

The ceremony was meticulously arranged. Frank's thin nervousness was not in evidence, except occasionally when he sat, jiggling his knee up and down before catching himself at it and desisting. Julius's elegant wife, Laura, came up to Frank afterwards and gave him a small hug.

"A beautiful ceremony," she said. "So sweet and loving, but not sentimental at all. Thanks for taking care of everything, Frank."

"How's Julius been doing?"

"Okay, I think."

When Frank had told his brother he would take care of the funeral arrangements, it seemed at first that he might object. In retrospect, it might have been better for Julius if he had. All at once he had no props under him. There was nothing he was required to do. The realization that he was not indispensable threw him off balance. The big man's life had grown into a shape dictated by the pressures around him—they propelled him, and bounded him, and it now appeared, held him together and kept him upright. When

Frank stepped in and began to organize everything, Julius stumbled in the vacuum.

At the house after the funeral, Julius wandered around or sat looking dazed, until even his children thought he was acting weird. Only three-year-old Gina persisted in trailing after him, tugging at his jacket or trying to crawl up into his lap. He stroked her hair with such a distant touch that she shivered and huddled even closer.

One evening a couple months after their mother's funeral, Frank stopped by to drop off a few things from their parents' house, their father having finally decided to move to an apartment. Laura, so perfectly self-contained as a rule, answered the door and reached for Frank's arm before he headed back to Julius's study.

"Can I ask your advice about something?" Her voice sounded strained.

The idea of his sister-in-law asking him for advice was a little startling. She had, he was sure, always seen him as someone who couldn't even manage to hold himself together half the time.

"I'm worried about Julius," she said.

"I can see why. He's a mess."

She gave a short bark of laughter. "He is. He keeps forgetting things—calls he's supposed to return, bills to pay. I'm really worried. He left Kelli and Jason waiting after their piano lessons last Thursday. I just don't know what to do. He doesn't seem to be pulling himself together."

"Well, I'd say give him something to do."

"But that's what I'm saying—he keeps forgetting to do even the little things."

"Then don't give him little things."

"What? What do you mean?"

"I mean don't give him little things."

"So, what should he be doing?"

"I don't know. Is there anything he's been wanting to accomplish?

Restructuring the business? Setting up a charitable foundation? Hell, I don't know, but it has to be something big, that needs to get done."

Frank was uncomfortably aware of his own part in Julius's present emotional state. And he was more than a little dismayed by all he'd ended up taking on himself. In some ways he would have been happy to hand everything back over to Julius—the final paperwork of their mother's affairs, the house, their father's move, in fact all of Dad. Checking medicines, appointments, car registration renewal. He didn't know how long their father had been relying on others to keep his daily life running. Maybe Julius had been taking care of all of these things, or maybe Mom, but his father now seemed to take it for granted that Frank, newly willing and able, would be the one to relieve him of all these irksome details.

But as much as he would have liked to go to Julius and dump the whole thing into his lap, Frank's pride wouldn't allow it. He imagined he'd blow it, anyway—he could just hear himself blurting, "Well, you need something to do, big brother, so I'll let you take care of Dad. Just out of charity, you know, not because I'm not capable."

He wasn't proud of taking over the way he had. In overcoming his fear of screwing up, he felt like a driver who's seen a chance to make his move and blasted ahead, not caring about the wrecks he might leave in his wake. But he was caught now. He couldn't give up the lead, even though he felt like a fraud—in danger of veering out of control and taking the rest of the field with him.

So, as he left her, he said to his sister-in-law, "If there's anything I can do to help, just call me."

7

HALF ASSEMBLED ON the cabin floor, the motorcycle looked like a dismembered mechanical chicken. The completed engine lay there—a shiny, useless carcass; the frame and fork—glistening bones. Georgia stood looking down at it glumly, her hands on her hips.

The project was at a standstill. Uncle Emery was out looking for his friend, Mel, who owned a local garage, to see if he could help them out, but meanwhile Georgia was in a funk.

Everything had been going so well. Working from the Mystery Motorcycle Man's exquisite drawings was a joy. Every item was identified and precisely ordered, fitting together easily, truly, every joining snug, every gap perfectly planned. Georgia had only herself to blame for their current predicament, although she wasn't willing to let Albert completely off the hook.

The morning was already hot when Georgia had awakened sweaty in the early hours. She went for a swim, knowing from experience the route through the water to the coolest springs. Albert, or course, went with her, paddling happily away, buoyed up by his water wings. He refused to stay near the shore anymore, no matter how far she swam. If the stubborn old noodlehead thought he was a Labrador and ended up having a heart attack from the exertion, well, so be it; at least he'd die happy and wet.

Afterwards, while Georgia rinsed herself under the pump and went to the trailer to change, Albert had apparently decided to check out the cabin. Bumping his head against the unlatched screen door until it bounced slightly ajar, he stuck his nose in and wedged it open. He strolled in, found the only thing that could be ruined in the entire place, and lay down on it. Georgia fervently wished it had occurred to her the night before to close the manual and remove it from the couch, where she'd stayed up late reading it. Uncle Emery would have, she was sure. He'd have put it up on the shelf, or at least on the table. But not her. She'd just headed off to the trailer to bed.

It may not have been quite such a disaster had Albert simply lain down on the manual, then gotten up and departed. But, sopping and smelly, he'd settled on it just long enough to saturate the exposed pages and then, deciding it made an uncomfortable bed after all, had not risen but slithered to the floor dragging waterlogged pages with him as he went. Two pages, front and back, were hopeless. A couple more were barely salvageable. At Georgia's cry, Emery ran inside and the two of them looked from the damaged manual to the unperturbed hound, shreds of paper sticking to his belly and trailing from one back claw.

"Albert," moaned Georgia. "How could you?"

Both she and her uncle, it was clear, had grown not only dependent on the manual in a practical way, but emotionally attached as well, and the loss momentarily stunned them. They were not willing to wing it without at least moral support from an expert. So Emery went in search of his friend, or the library, or a bookstore, or all three. Georgia thought she could probably skip ahead and assemble another portion of the bike, but she didn't want to. She gazed at the completed sections on the floor and on the little workbench they'd set up, and at the rows of parts organized along the wall.

She fell into the dreamlike state she'd become adept at, her eyes reflecting the gleaming parts but not focused on them, her mind drifting. She had somehow circled back to point A—she had no clue what she was doing here. And even if she did have even the slightest notion, it would probably shift by tomorrow. How insane was this—to quit her job to build a motorcycle in the wilds of the north woods? On the face of it, it was a way to get out of her rut, to get out of the chicken factory and over Jimmy. But getting out of a rut was supposed to mean you were headed someplace.

Some people thought God was behind everything, with a plan firmly in mind, but what kind of God sent motorcycle parts raining down on a person? Nuts and bolts and carburetors, falling like manna from heaven? Well, she couldn't wait for a detailed manual from God. If there was a plan, she'd have to figure it out herself from the pieces she had, wherever they came from.

Perhaps there was some mission she was meant to go on, something she should achieve. Or something she was supposed to find out. The thought of hiring a detective had occurred to her more than once. Or of doing some detecting on her own—maybe she was more competent than she'd once assumed. She was building a motorcycle, wasn't she? Maybe she could track down this mystery man. On the other hand, maybe it was better that she didn't know every last thing. There were too many parts, too many things to keep in her mind at once.

It had been so nice up until now, just having one thing after another to do. All that was required of her was to follow directions, fit one part into another, tighten this, assemble that, check the tolerances. But it wouldn't be so straightforward once the bike was done. Then she'd have to start figuring out on her own what to do next. Now, *there* was a frightening thought.

She envisioned her fear as an enormous chasm. One misstep and she would fall into an abyss of never-ending terror. But then another idea drifted into her mind. The chasm might not be unconquerable. If she could nurture her underlying excitement, her fledgling sense of hope, she realized that the chasm could fill with joy like a quarry with water. It was crossable. And the other side was not only reachable, but the swim across might be as exhilarating as whatever awaited her on the other side.

Georgia wasn't usually inclined to self-analysis, it just wasn't her nature. But self-knowledge is not always the result of deep thought. She was discovering capabilities and feelings she'd never before imagined. She felt her life expanding.

She took a deep breath, put her thoughts away, and reached for her gardening gloves.

Georgia was weeding the squash bed when a vintage red Ford pickup bumped into the yard. A tall, skinny man wearing coveralls stepped out. The wrinkles on his mahogany face seemed to put him at about Emery's age.

"Mel Johnson, at your service," he said, tapping the bill of his baseball cap with a forefinger. "I hear you've had some muddy-dog problems."

"Oh, we sure have. Meet the culprit. Albert, say hello to our rescuer." Albert, showing not the slightest trace of remorse, trotted over to greet the newcomer.

"Emery should be along soon," Mel said, leaning over to stroke the top of Albert's generous muzzle. "He got snagged by my wife and had to sit down for coffee and hjortebakkels—that's Norwegian for death-by-cholesterol-but-what-a-way-to-go. But I managed to escape. Snuck out the back."

Georgia grinned. "And why don't I exactly believe that?"

"Uh-oh. You got me. She sent me to the store for milk and I absconded with the grocery money."

Georgia laughed. "Well, we better get some work done before she sends the posse after you."

Mel and Georgia were fast friends and the motorcycle was back in production by the time Emery returned, walking with the deliberate gait of a man full of baked goods and coffee.

That evening Georgia picked up a book from the top of her uncle's stacks and tried to read it. She had to go over the first sentence three times before she understood it. She put the book back and went to find something useful to do.

After dinner the next night Emery slid a paperback across to her. "Thought you might like something to read," he said. "This here's a pretty good one."

It was. And maybe she wasn't so dumb, either. The book was about the Everglades and was full of river grasses and sloping beaches, and all sorts of semi-tropical wonders. It reached across eons in a way Georgia had never experienced before. It was like traveling in time and space without ever leaving the house. It was geography and science and history, subjects she'd ordinarily have avoided, but here so interwoven with characters and events that before long she was completely engrossed. From that time on, she and Emery often spent quiet evenings together, each immersed in their own reading. Emery seemed more comfortable after that, as if a social weight had been lifted from him. He'd fulfilled some unspoken, uneasy responsibility he felt toward her, to make sure that she was entertained, content.

Emery didn't own most of the books he read. He had an arrangement with the town library to borrow their volumes for as long as he liked without fines, in return for occasional minor repairs on the little building.

Georgia was touched by Emery's air of proprietary pride the first time he took her in with him.

"Hello, Delores," he said to the plump woman at work behind the desk. "This is my niece." The librarian looked up, startled at hearing her usually silent patron speak.

"Georgia Dunn," said Georgia, extending her hand. "Nice to meet you."

"Likewise," said the woman. "Your uncle's a great reader. Here all the time—or whenever he gets to town, I guess. Isn't that right?"

Emery nodded with a shy, pleased smile. Georgia loved that he was showing off, introducing her—his family—to this librarian who treated him with fond respect.

There was little need to show Georgia around. It was just a small place, really, but Emery clearly knew it intimately, its books and its housing. Like a good host he pointed out the sections that might interest her, but he soon went off on his own, as relaxed and easy as if he were in his own cabin.

Georgia wandered up and down the aisles while Emery filled out an interlibrary loan request and then went browsing. When he returned to her with a few books he thought she might like, she'd found the how-to section. They left with an eclectic selection ranging from *Hornblower and the Hotspur* to *Organic Composting*.

"How'd you get so interested in reading, Uncle Emery?" Georgia asked, as Emery drove them home. "Did you read much as a kid?"

"No, not when I was young. At my foster home I did."

"You had a foster family?"

"Yah. After my mother died."

"What were they like?"

Emery smiled. "Big," he said.

Georgia raised her eyebrows.

"Not big people," Emery explained. "Just a lot of them."

"Was that in Baltimore?"

"No, they picked me up on an Illinois highway and brought me home with them to Minnesota."

"Uncle Emery! Really? Who were they? What were you doing out on the highway? How old were you?"

In shy bits and pieces, Georgia got the story out of him. It took her a good part of the week, but she managed to extract enough information to piece together a tale. Emery clearly wanted to concentrate on the happier times, but Georgia also caught some sense of the harshness of his life in the years before he left home, a newly orphaned thirteen year-old with a vision in his mind of the Rocky Mountains glowing in the western sky like Shangri-la.

Hard as it was for Emery to believe that Georgia really wanted to hear about his life, he eventually told her most of the parts he thought worth telling. But he remembered it all. He remembered, but did not relate, his mother's cycles of over-protectiveness and neglect, her drinking, her bitterness toward the outside world. And he remembered his own contact with that world.

One of the only poor kids at a public school in a middle-class section of Baltimore, Emery hadn't been so much outcast—he'd never been *in*—as studiously avoided. He didn't smell good. His clothes weren't new, weren't even washed sometimes. He farted a lot from his haphazard diet and even when he didn't, his shoes, which he rarely had socks for, reeked with a pungency easily mistaken for bad sanitation. The Tomara boys were the only ones who'd consistently speak to him, and that was only to tell him to wipe his ass before he came to school. He lived in a stupor of humiliation and dropped out of junior high the day his mother died. After the funeral, he packed up what few things they actually owned and stowed them in a park storage shed he'd been using as a hideaway since he was seven, there to be found or to rot—he didn't care which, as long as he never had to see them again and the landlord so despised by his mother didn't get his hands on them.

With a few necessities rolled up in a towel tied across his back, Emery hitchhiked west. He was scrawny and small even for his thirteen years and he worried that the cops would catch him and throw him into juvenile hall. It wasn't the first time he'd stuck out his thumb for a ride, but it was the first time he'd done it without a mother and a house to come home to, such as they were. His arm felt like it was weighted with lead. He kept looking behind him. Every passing car might be a cop, or some good citizen eager to turn him in.

When a battered pickup finally pulled over, Emery climbed in with relief. The driver, a scruffy fellow smelling of axle grease and cigarettes, looked him over, gave a slight shrug, and drove him out to the highway. He spoke to Emery as if he were an equal. "Where you headed, man?" and "Look at that Bel Air. What a piece of shit." He pulled out his cigarettes and shook one up from the pack, extending it to Emery. Emery shook his head and the driver, without offense, stuck the cigarette between his own lips. Emery's confidence began to grow.

His next ride came without much delay. A shiny blue sedan pulled over. The passenger door swung open from the inside even before Emery reached the car, and the driver, in slacks and a white button-down shirt, was clearing a stack of papers off the passenger seat. He seemed happy to have company and especially pleased to offer "words to the wise" to his "young friend." Emery was surprised to discover that, though nice enough, the man wasn't particularly bright. It confused him that he, a misfit dropout, could know more, or at least think more intelligently, than an adult who had his own car—and a new one at that.

Though he had a few long waits, Emery had no real misadventures. Most of his rides were locals heading to town, or "up the road a-ways." Many of them went out of their way to take him a few extra miles, to the next town or crossroads.

Then in Illinois, a station wagon stopped for him. A big green Oldsmobile pulled up immediately behind it. The two cars were packed full with one big family headed home from a wedding in

Aurora. The mother was at the wheel of the station wagon, but Emery ended up crammed into the Olds with the father and five of the kids. Mr. Vogel had plenty of questions for Emery, and he seemed less than satisfied with the answers. Young Emery fell asleep with questions still pelting him.

He woke at a gas station by the side of the highway. The family surged from the cars. While the children jostled to line up at the bathrooms, the parents went into a huddle in the shade of an oak out front. Emery watched them for a second, and then thought he might as well save them the trouble of giving him the boot. He grabbed his things and headed west down the highway, facing straight ahead, his thumb out to his side.

He heard running footsteps behind him and turned.

"Mom wants you to come back," said one of the middle boys, a redhead with a sunburned nose.

Emery frowned doubtfully.

"She wants to talk to you." He paused, looking back toward the station, then confided, "I think she wants to take you home."

"Why would she want to do that?"

"Dunno. But she said to get you."

Emery returned to the service station where the boy delivered him triumphantly to his parents.

"Here he is," the child announced with a flourish.

"We see that. Thank you, Henry," his father said.

Henry stood smiling.

"*Thank* you, Henry," his father repeated.

Henry reluctantly went to join the line at the bathroom.

"So," said Mrs. Vogel. "Your name is Emery. Emery what?"

Emery looked down.

"Are you in trouble, son?"

Startled at the "son," Emery glanced at her, but he saw that her expression was concerned, not condemning. "No," he said.

"John tells me your mother died?"

"That's right." Emery's grief was private. He could feel it under his skin and in his chest, but wouldn't allow it to enter his eyes or his voice.

"And you don't have any family to go to?"

"No. Not really.... No one I know of."

"There might be someone, then?" The parallel creases between Mrs. Vogel's eyebrows eased momentarily at this thought.

"I don't even know what their names are."

"What if we could find out for you?"

"No." He looked down the highway, restless for the next ride.

"You're sure?" She frowned again, in deep reflection, as she appraised Emery.

"Yes." He looked at her. She was a short woman and their eyes were nearly level. "Thanks anyway," he added.

Mrs. Vogel exchanged a look with her husband, who stepped forward. "How would you feel about coming home with us?" he asked. "Staying for a while, until you know what you want to do with yourself?"

Emery fidgeted with the strap on his makeshift pack. The thought of all those kids made him nervous. He might just as well be thrown back into school to be despised and pitied all over again. The ones in the car had seemed okay, but the father had been sitting right there, so they were probably on their best behavior. What about when their folks weren't around and they all got together in a pack?

"I kinda wanted to see the mountains," Emery hedged, looking back down the road again.

"Well, you have to do whatever you see fit. We'd like you to come, though," said Mr. Vogel. "I tell you what. We don't turn north till Des Moines. We're dropping Eddie and Marla off to stay at their grandma's—"

"That's my mother," interjected Mrs. Vogel

"—for the week. So you'd have a while to think about it. Ride with Gem—"

"That's me," said Mrs. Vogel.

"—and if you decide to come home with us, that'll be fine. You can always change your mind later," he added.

They both watched Emery as he struggled with the idea. He almost blurted out, "You won't call the police?" but of course they wouldn't say so. He figured he'd just have to trust them or not.

"I guess I'll ride along to Des Moines, then," he said. Mr. Vogel looked like he was going to clap him on the back, but restrained himself. Emery was surprised Mr. Vogel had come on board at all. He wouldn't have thought this man, who'd acted so suspicious in the car, would have liked the idea of taking Emery home with him. But if there was anything Emery was learning about people, it was that there were a whole lot of different kinds in the world and it was just about useless to try and figure them out.

Emery ended up going home with the bountiful Vogel clan and staying with them for the next four years. It wasn't always easy. He almost picked himself up and left three or four times before Mrs. Vogel's younger brother moved to New York and left his travel trailer behind. It was a small rounded camper with a little stove and sink, and a narrow bunk. The Vogels decided to give it to Emery, then fourteen. They set it up in a strip of trees separating two sections of family farmland, and Emery hauled water and propane from the house.

He repaid the Vogels by working hard on the farm, becoming adept at fixing machinery and jury-rigging the innumerable parts and pieces that kept a farm running. He absolutely refused to go to school, so Mrs. Vogel started him on a homemade course of schoolwork using an assortment of her children's books. He'd sit at her kitchen table with his head in a textbook while she went about her housework. She'd look over his shoulder at intervals to correct this or that, or start him on a new task.

And that's how Emery finished growing up. He came to like quite a few of the Vogel kids and kept in touch with some of them after he left, at age seventeen, to mine taconite, a low-grade iron ore, on the Mesabi Range up north, and later to work for logging outfits until he'd saved up enough money for some land of his own up by the Canadian border. He loved Mrs. Vogel without reservation and in time he came to think Mr. Vogel was pretty swell, too.

So the boy without a family had found a bigger family than he knew what to do with. Good people, too, Emery told Georgia. The best foster family a person could hope for.

And now on top of everything, he thought, he had a half-sister and a niece. Whatever life had deprived him of in his early years, it had made up for with abundance.

Georgia and Emery fell into a habit of passing along interesting information they gleaned from their reading. It reminded Emery of his time with the Vogels, and the prized, patchwork schooling he'd gotten there.

Emery was sitting in his usual easy chair one evening after dinner, Georgia stretched out on the couch with Albert on her feet. "All right, imagine a particle," Emery was saying.

"A particle. Uh, huh.... A particle of what?"

"Come on, now."

Georgia smiled, "Oh, okay, a particle. Got it."

"Now this particle is heading out in one direction, passing through a tiny slit and hitting a piece of film on the opposite wall. It might hit anything in an area of a circle."

"Mm hmm."

"Now, imagine a bunch of particles and two slits."

"Two slits."

"Georgia?"

"Uh, huh?"

"Are you sure you want to hear this?"

"I do, I really do." She squirmed a little to get her legs in a more comfortable position, and Albert grunted. "I'm just having a hard time concentrating right now. I keep thinking, what if we have to lower the seat because of my height—what else would we have to change? Is there enough room to do that without messing with the rear suspension?"

"Well, we'll look into that. I doubt if it'll be a problem at all, you know. Whoever this mystery fellow of yours is, he seems to have thought of everything. He probably knows your height to the hair."

"Yeah. Okay." She wasn't quite sure how she felt about that, but was willing to put the thought aside for the time being. "So, you were saying … 'particles.'"

"Maybe that's enough for tonight." Emery shut the book he'd been leafing through to refresh his memory, and set it on the lamp table.

Georgia went back to the idea she'd been pursuing, off and on, all day. "Do you think I could find an old beater bike to learn on? I mean, what if I fall and screw this one up?"

"You've decided about riding it then?"

"Oh … well, no. I was just thinking."

"I'll ask Mel if he can find something for you. He said he'd come by this weekend and help us true the flywheel."

"Okay, that's great." She pulled one foot free from under Albert's head and used it to rub his belly. "I've been meaning to drop by when I'm in town and thank him for helping us on the missing pages. Maybe I should bake him something."

Emery discretely raised his book in front of his face to hide his grin.

"I saw that," Georgia said. "Okay, so maybe not baking. I'll think of something."

On Saturday Georgia went into town to run some errands. Stepping out of the A&P, she found herself cut off from her car by a good portion of the town's population. It occurred to her that there might be more people *in* a small town parade than left over to watch it.

Scattered groups of spectators waved and called to the participants by name. The feathered and beaded children on the Anishinaabe dancer's float were pelting people with a rain of candy. On the sidewalk, squalls of kids swirled around, darting into the street to gather up the treats. Mothers, if they were quick enough, snatched the youngest ones back by their nimble little arms. A float sponsored by the local bank rolled by. "Throw money! Throw money!" hooted teenagers along the route. A small, resplendent marching band strutted past, followed by a procession of classic cars, including an ancient Studebaker that had either run out of gas or just plain bit the dust. Four men in shiny shoes pushed it down the street while their soft-cheeked granny sat hunched over the steering wheel sporting a sheepish grin, intermittently overcoming her stage fright to wave at the spectators, blushing and laughing till her eyes watered.

Behind the cars, a controlled chaos of motorcycles filled the street. Georgia had only recently begun to notice how many motorcycles there were in the world, awakened as she was by her own budding relationship with one. This was a varied collection of vintage, make, and model, a few with spectacularly inventive customized paint jobs. They wove around the road, looping back and forth. She didn't know whether she wanted to clap as they came roaring along, or clap her hands over her ears, but in any case she was hindered by the grocery bags in her arms. She stepped over to the store's brick wall and set the bags down, straightening back up in surprise when she heard her name called out. Mel Johnson, upright and begoggled atop his restored 1949 Vincent-HRD Black Shadow, waved to her. Two or three of his buddies waved too. A heavy-set old guy in a fringed jacket called out, "Hey, beautiful! Want to go for a ride?"

And she suddenly did. She wanted to run out into the street and throw her leg over the saddle of this stranger's bike and ride. She laughed and waved back.

More floats and then the horseback-riders followed—rodeo kids, ladies in turn-of-the-century calicos, trappers in beaver caps, and a wagon drawn by two enormous draft horses. The whole cavalcade was rounded off by the two town police cars, lights flashing, their uniformed occupants waving out the windows to their friends (and possibly a foe or two) along the way.

Georgia went home happy.

Emery was frying up some fish when she walked in. Albert lay sprawled next to him.

"There was a parade in town," she told her uncle.

"That'd be Founder's Day," he said.

"It was fun." She began to unpack the groceries and put them away. "I saw Mel. He was riding his Vincent."

"Great bike. He got it in trade, it must have been twenty years ago now, from some Canadian orthodontist. Guy couldn't lay off the booze and blamed the bike for not staying on the road. Mel shines it up every year for the parade. Well, this is about done," Emery said, and turned with the frying pan in his hand to fill the plates sitting on the edge of the counter.

But Albert chose that moment to rise and belatedly greet Georgia. Instead of stepping neatly over the dog as he'd been doing all day,

Emery's foot was interrupted in its course by Albert's surprisingly solid mass, and he lurched forward. The frying pan went flying, spraying hot oil and bouncing back off the corner cabinet with a crash and a clatter. Emery reached out for something to stop his fall, but he missed the counter and landed heavily, his right hand meeting the hot pan on the floor.

Georgia could hear the sickening sizzle through the clanging and grunting. She dropped a jar of mayonnaise from her hand and ran to help. Emery rolled onto his side and lay there, half stunned, holding his hand in the air. Georgia kicked the frying pan to the side and knelt beside him. "Is your neck hurt?"

"No, I don't think so," Emery responded through the pain of his hand.

"Your back?"

"Uh, it's okay."

Georgia reached both arms around him and heaved him upright, hauled him over to the sink, and turned on the cold water, running it into the basin and plunging Emery's reddening hand into it.

"I think my wrist's broke, too," Emery said after a minute.

Georgia sat him down in a chair and filled a deep bowl with more cold water, instructing him to keep his hand in it. Albert, inching toward the hot fish on the floor, seemed unharmed. Georgia put him outside, where he contented himself by licking the splattered oil off his coat and paws.

Georgia gripped the steering wheel like death, her head thrust forward. Trees flashed by in an endless rush and the distance to town seemed to have quadrupled.

"Might be a good idea to stop at that stop sign up ahead," Emery said mildly. "State highway, you know."

Georgia let up on the gas and took a shaky breath. She reached one hand over and gave her uncle a tentative pat on the shoulder.

By the time they got to the little hospital in town, Georgia's adrenaline was wearing off. She was drained and shaky but Emery seemed perfectly calm. The on-call doctor commended Georgia on her actions, saying the cold water had saved her uncle from more severe burns and had probably even helped the wrist, which was indeed fractured.

Georgia felt awful. Here she'd lurched into this nice man's life—moving in with her dog and her truckload of metal, disrupting his routine, talking her head off. Disturbing the peace. And as if that weren't enough, now she'd gone and landed him in the hospital.

"Shut up, Georgia."

"What?" She looked up, shocked. Uncle Emery sat in a chair by the side of the X-ray table while they waited for the films to be developed. She stood by the door keeping him company, not that he'd want her.

"I said, shut up what you're thinking."

She didn't know what to say. She stood there with her mouth open, and then she started to bawl.

"Aw, Jesus," said Emery.

"I'm sorry."

He looked pained.

"I'm really sorry."

"I know you are," he said. "It's okay, though. Not your fault."

Just when things are going well, thought Georgia, that's when it all comes crashing down. Nothing was safe—she'd known that since she was barely twelve. Now it would be Emery's turn to pull back. Georgia knew how hard it had been for him to open up to her in the first place, and now he'd surely want to go hide away and recuperate, take cover from all the pain and disorder she'd brought on him.

Emery watched her curiously as she sniffled and pulled tissue from her purse. "You did good, you know," he told her. "You ought to do just fine on that motorcycle. You've got a cool head."

"The motorcycle?"

"Yup. I was thinking I might get myself one too, just to ride around on, keep you company while you're learning."

"Really? You'd really want to do that?"

"If you wouldn't mind."

Georgia shook her head, trying to absorb this. "I don't know how you can even think about motorcycles at a time like this," she said.

He gave her a grin. "Oh, you bet. Motorcycles and drugs, like in that movie ... what was it, *Easy Riding*? The doctor *did* say he was getting me some painkillers, didn't he?"

She laughed uncertainly. "I'll check."

"No, it's all right. They'll get around to it."

Georgia started to cry again. "You're so nice," she blubbered.

Emery gave her a crooked smile.

"You are," she insisted.

"And you're not so bad yourself," he said.

A nurse poked her head in the door. "Everything okay here?" she asked.

"Oh, yes, ma'am," Georgia told her, dabbing at her nose. "We're the greatest. Could you find out about my uncle's drugs, though?" The nurse withdrew.

Georgia looked back at Emery. "Do you think maybe I should go back down to the Cities for a while?"

"No. Why?"

"I don't know. Just for you to take a break."

"Well, I'm not going to be much good helping with the bike for a while, but that's no reason to leave. You don't really need my help with it anymore, anyway."

"Yes, I do."

"You'll be more help to me than I'll be to you."

"Oh, of course. I wasn't thinking. Of course I'll stay and help you out. I got you into this in the first place."

Emery shook his head. "You didn't get me into anything."

"Your hand. Your wrist."

"My hand and my wrist hurt like hell. What does that have to do with you staying or going?"

She looked at him doubtfully.

In a quiet voice he said to her, "I wouldn't have missed all this for anything. I count myself lucky."

"Lucky?"

He nodded.

Georgia wiped her eyes and gave a deep sigh. She pulled a chair over from the corner of the room, and together they sat waiting for the X-rays.

8

IT TOOK FRANK another hemisphere and twelve more years of forging ahead before he was finally compelled to stop and look back.

After his mother's funeral, he'd gradually gained confidence in his ability to manage his life. His view of the world shifted in large ways and small. He began to notice the color green, for example. He saw patterns of green in shadows and waving leaves, and wasn't daunted by the complexity of them. He relied less on a complete understanding of things and more on his ability to survive disorder and loose ends.

But when it came to work, his old attention to detail stood him in good stead. Harley moved him from tech services to product development, where he immersed himself in design and the essentials of production.

Then Julius appealed to him to come work at his new subsidiary. Frank had never quite shaken the lingering guilt over his role in his brother's troubles after their mother died, nor could he forget his brother's kindness to him after Jill's death. So when Julius asked for his help, he went. It was a difficult move. He didn't really like the new job and didn't much care for working for his big brother. He couldn't help feeling subtly inferior, operating so completely within Julius's sphere.

With every day Frank stayed in Foxton, a desire grew in him to move far away. So he did his best for Julius, banked his money, and looked for other work. After a year and a half, when he felt the business was running smoothly and could do just as well without him, he landed a job with a mining company in Western Australia and said goodbye to family and friends.

It didn't take long for the mining outfit to decide Frank was underutilized. Pressed for mechanical engineers, they urged him to finish his engineering degree, which he did gladly, and for the next decade he moved wherever the company sent him—Peru, Indonesia, back to Perth again, whenever and wherever they needed him. It was an interesting and demanding life, and he was successful in his work.

But as the years progressed, Frank was able to do his job proficiently while engaging less and less of his mind, and old demons began finding their way though the gaps. Frank's life, it seemed to him, had been lived in sections. Childhood. Jill. The years after Jill. The mining years. It was the way he'd always managed. It was the way he'd studied in college, the way he'd done everything, immersing himself completely in one project until it was done, then moving on to the next. But there was one part of his life that was not done. He'd tried to put it away from him, and had more or less succeeded for a long time, but it would never really let him be. It was from a time even before Jill. From his teenage years ... from one year, one hour, one eternal span of time within that hour. And from a moment two years afterwards when he realized that what had happened was not over, nor could it ever be.

He couldn't let it go and he couldn't face it, so he worked, tried to forget, and carried on as well as he could. Antidepressants helped. He even thought for a while he might try and settle down with someone, a girl in his office. It was his final defense against memory, but before another Australian summer was over he knew the strategy was failing.

...

"I can't open it. I tried."

The peaches in Penny McGuire's canning jar pressed against the inside of the glass, imprisoned forever. Well, maybe not forever ... just till the damned thing would come unscrewed.

Frank was annoyed, not because Penny couldn't open it, but because as soon as he walked in the door she turned helpless. Did she think men liked that? He could do very well without the act. She was perfectly competent. On the other hand, maybe he had fallen for it at the beginning. He'd dated Penny from the first week she came to work at the Perth office. She was a pretty Australian girl, fair-haired, and very feminine. Eight months later, he found himself entrenched and unhappy.

His dreams lately had been of suffocating in froths of sharp blue water, bubbles and roiling waves tumbling him onto an ocean bottom littered with jagged shells he couldn't see. The panicky feel of water up his nose and down his throat. But he wouldn't wake. He'd hang on to the point of drowning until something finally would turn the dream around. Sometimes he'd find salvation in a looped rope or the sudden ability to propel himself upward, beyond the reach of the sea. Sometimes the dream would change to something else entirely—to horse racing, or to green rivers under willow trees.

But the image of obscuring froth remained with him. He increasingly felt there was something he couldn't quite make out, something he was missing. Always in his mind, dreaming or waking, was a subtle undercurrent of lines—mechanical drawings of machinery, isometric maps, stark horizons beyond bleached-out landscapes. He vaguely imagined the lines to be the unifying aspect of his consciousness, holding the potential to tie together all the separate fragments of his life, if only he could grasp their significance.

He was finding it hard to concentrate. The over-decorated house didn't feel like his own anymore. Where he saw openness and room to breathe, to think uncluttered thoughts, Penny saw empty spaces that needed filling. She was a bakery cake heaped with sugar icing. She was just what he'd craved, but now he was so full he was ready to spew. For the first time in his life Frank was faced with the dilemma of how to break up with someone. What he truly wanted to do was flee. Just run, take off for the outback, go and see the red earth of Uluru.

"It's too tight," Penny said with a petulant tilt of her head.

Frank knew he needed to figure out something soon when he found himself visualizing her face pressed up against the inside of the jar, looking out at him like a fish-faced peach. He imagined putting the jar back up on the shelf and shutting the cupboard door, and laughing like a maniac. With an effort, with arms that seemed heavy and nerveless, he took the jar from Penny's pink hands and did not throw it through the window. He tapped it on the counter and focused on grasping the metal lid and twisting it from the glass jar, releasing the yellow peaches and their thick syrup. He handed it back, the jar in one hand and the lid in the other.

"We need to split up," he said.

And this woman he'd lived with for nearly a year, who bored him almost to tears, who never seemed to have an original thought, at last surprised him.

"I knew it!" she shrieked without a moment's hesitation. "I just knew it!" She slammed the peaches down, and the syrup slopped in a surprised wave over the lip. "You were just waiting until I was well caught in this relationship to throw me onto the street. Do you know how many better men I've passed up, being with you? I could've had my pick, but no, I stayed. Look at me, trying like bloody hell to be the perfect woman for you, busting my sweet behind to make a nice house after working all day. You think I don't work just as hard as you?" She pointed her finger at him. "You're a spoiled little bastard. You're a self-indulgent, lying, cunt-fucking shit, just like every other man out there. You think you're entitled. Well, you're not entitled to me! Go fuck yourself! *Twice!*" She picked up the heavy drainer full of dishes with her two little hands, and dropped it loudly and dramatically to the floor. Stalking to the living room, she grabbed her purse from the end table and turned to look at Frank with a face like a mottled fruitcake as she pulled out the car keys. Then she marched out the door.

Frank stood rooted to the floor, his mouth open, and watched her go. When the door slammed shut he shook his head like a boxer who's just been clocked a good one, and exhaled in a whoosh. "Well," he said, after a moment. "That was easy."

He was less sure about that when Penny came by the next day with an unshaven bloke in leather who loaded up her stuff, not stopping to differentiate between Penny's knickknacks and Frank's furniture. He also found the office environment less than congenial after she'd finished sweetly trashing his reputation and casting doubt on his mental, not to mention his sexual, competence.

A week later Frank awoke to knocking on the front door at five in the morning. He rose and pulled on some jeans. There stood Penny, dressed for work, her leather purse hanging from her shoulder. "I'm sorry it's so early, Frank," she said. "Can I come in?"

He was strongly tempted to say no, but he let her into the bare living room. Penny viewed the neat but stark house with dismay.

"You can't live like this, Frank."

"I actually prefer it."

"No, you're just saying that. Look, maybe I made a mistake, breaking up with you the way I did. It's not like me, really. I don't know what got into me. My Aunt Zelly had just called that morning, and you know how she goes on. She just kept on and on about my hair, my job, my clothes.... Maybe I was just in a bad mood. I had a headache." She put her chin down and looked up at him. "Do you think maybe we ...?"

"Penny," said Frank. A thousand things went through his mind. If she wanted to think she'd broken up with *him*, that was fine. His first instinct was not to hurt her feelings. But if hurting her feelings would help him avoid whatever situation she had in mind to suck him back into, it would be worth it. He could be the bad guy. He *was* the bad guy. So he steeled himself and glanced around to see if there was anything left that she could break. Then he looked at her.

"Penny," he said. "No way in hell." Then he added, "Nice of you to stop by, though."

"You're not being reasonable, Frank. Just think about it."

He walked her to the door.

"Who else are you going to find who'll put up with all your shit? You can't speak two words without acting superior or—"

He closed the door behind her. He knew people who'd had some ugly breakups, but supposed there would have to be passion in the first place for there to be pain at the end. He felt only relief.

It was then that Frank began designing the first motorcycle. He'd played around with some ideas while he was still at Harley, and now at last he had the time to develop them. He had no deep motive when he started, just the need for something to keep him busy. It was amazing how much time and energy being with Penny had consumed. He suddenly found himself with an enormous store of ideas and the freedom to focus on them. He spent many of his spare hours on the beaches outside of Perth, looking across the water and going over details in his mind. At night he drew them up at a drafting table he'd set up in the living room.

But then it became something more. In his first rush of liberation and enthusiasm over the project, he'd let his prescription for antidepressants run out. Side by side with his absorption in the motorcycle, old troubling memories grew increasingly insistent, drawing him down to the more difficult places of his mind.

He finally went to a doctor he'd seen in the past and asked her to write him a new prescription. They talked about his recent break-up, and then for awhile about Jill, but Dr. Sokolov wasn't satisfied. "It's clear there's something more, Frank," she said. "I don't know whether you're just not willing to talk about it, or whether you're sincerely repressing it. But if you're going to make any progress we have to examine it."

"I don't believe in all that."

"In repressed memories or in talk therapy?"

"Both. Repressed memories. It seems to me they're just an excuse for a person's problems. Invented memories would be a better description."

"That's sometimes a risk," she told him. "There are certainly cases of false memories. But Frank, we need to explore the possibility that there's something else going on with you. Something relating to the past. You've been circling around it for quite a while now."

"If there are things I'd rather not discuss—"

"You came to me for a reason. Do you want to go on feeling the way you do? Or do you want to make some changes? That's the real question."

"Of course I want to feel better. I'm not a complete fool. But I'm here because I need you to prescribe my medication. Whatever did or did not happen in my childhood has no bearing on it. It's brain chemistry, pure and simple. I do appreciate that your education compels you to probe my psyche, but I'd be grateful if you'd keep it in the present."

"You're convinced the past has nothing to do with your state of mind?"

"I'm convinced the past is none of your business."

"All right, we'll table it for the moment. But please keep an open mind. It's quite possible that whatever it is you're not willing to face is having an ongoing impact on that brain chemistry of yours. You're a smart man, Frank, and I'd hate to see you rationalize your way out of productive therapy."

"And you're a smart woman, Sarah. I'd hate to see you waste your time on a bunch of repressed memory theories that have no bearing on anything. Not to mention that it's my dime."

"Noted."

Frank sat back and sighed. He looked out the window and they didn't speak. "I'll think about it," he said after a while.

The doctor looked at him, eyebrows raised in expectation.

"But don't push it, Doc."

She smiled, "No, of course not. I wouldn't dream of it."

But Frank's memories were not repressed. That was the problem. He couldn't keep them down. They were a relentless part of his life, confronting him daily, ready or not.

As a boy, Frank had been uncommonly neat. He didn't scatter his toys randomly around his room to be played with helter-skelter. He was scrupulous and single-minded. It annoyed him when his friends chose toys without regard to their size and relative proportions. How could a five-inch car possibly be part of a street with three-inch houses? This aspect of his personality eventually fed his strengths—his fine eye for design and detail, but also his weaknesses—his tendency to get lost in those same details, to lose the larger perspective. All in all, though, he'd been happy growing up, with friends and interests, not terribly troubled about being considered odd by his family.

Frank's mother might have thought him a fragile child, deficient in some undefined way, but the truth was he'd had no real problems until something had happened. And it hadn't even happened to him.

. . .

Georgia Dunn had been an exuberant child. People smiled when they saw her, unless of course she happened to be driving them up a wall at the time. Frank remembered her well from those early days.

He remembered standing alone by the little backyard fishpond at her sixth birthday party. He was nine years old, and felt very silly in his blazer, with a party hat tilted so far back it must have looked like it was growing out of the back of his head. He'd only come because his mother and Georgia's mother were friends. He had a perfectly good derailment going on at home and was anxious to figure out why car #5 had stayed on the tracks. He stared morosely into the pond.

But Georgia, glimpsing him across the lawn, wasn't one to let anyone get away with moping around at her party. In her own inimitable way she took matters in hand. *She* had all her friends here, her reasoning must have run, and her mommy had a friend, but poor Frank didn't have a friend, so to make him feel better she picked up a rock from the garden, a nice, heavy one, bigger than her hand, and snuck around through the trees to the pond. When Frank looked over his shoulder at the shrieking children playing blind man's bluff, Georgia stepped quickly out, threw the rock into the pond, and ducked back into the trees. Frank turned just in time to get a face full of pond water. With an "Aargh!" he jumped back, hands flying in the air. He caught his foot on a tuft of grass, stumbled backward, and landed flat on his butt. Georgia, beside herself with glee, ran out from the trees, knocked him backwards, and sat on his belly. "You're so funny," she cried, bouncing up and down. Then she dashed away.

Frank scrambled to his feet. "You little brat!" he yelled, yanking off his hat and chasing her furiously across the grass. She screeched with delighted terror, fleeing through the trees and back out to the safety of her little friends, who dodged and clung to each other as she darted among them, with Frank flying after her into their midst. He retreated in embarrassment, though, when faced with twenty giggling first-graders.

"Babies," he muttered from the vantage of his superior years.

His blue jacket was splattered with pond water and he took it off as he stalked away. He hated the thing anyway and couldn't believe his mother had made him wear it, or that she'd forced him to come to this stupid party in the first place. He went around the corner of the house and up to the screen porch, where he sat sulking on the faded cushions of a wicker couch. After a while he moved onto an old rocking chair, turning it so he could see Georgia and her friends playing. They were in the middle of some game involving bits of paper and everybody acting like animals. Georgia crouched on the ground and slunk toward a boy who was running around clucking like a chicken. Frank thought he could do a better chicken than that. He strutted around the porch a few times flapping his wings and then sat back down in the rocker. After a minute he let loose with a rooster crow, and then subsided again.

Now Georgia was standing on tiptoes like a ballerina. She spun herself around and her hair flew out in a swirling arc, the sun shining through it, transforming the brown into a fan of light.

Now she was unwrapping presents, flinging birthday paper with abandon and laughing at all the wonders that awaited her inside cardboard boxes and cellophane. From somewhere, a hot-pink feather boa came to be slung around her neck, shedding occasional feathers that floated on the slightest breeze, lifting when it seemed they should fall, imbuing the air with depth and whimsy.

Over the years they saw each other often, Frank and Georgia. They came to know each other well, better than Frank knew most of his own cousins. Frank displayed the required disdainful condescension when they met but could never keep it up for long. Georgia was a fun, uncomplicated girl, and she really wasn't at all obnoxious to play with.

But those memories were not the ones that now swirled mercilessly through Frank's brain. It was something else that haunted him, working its way into his waking mind as well as threatening his sleep. He was back on antidepressants but they were no match for the memories that had taken hold and were growing increasingly insistent. He couldn't understand why this was happening to him now, after so many years. He continued designing the motorcycle in all his spare time, often during sleepless nights, sitting up at his drafting table until dawn.

One morning as sunlight crept into the living room, Frank sat up from his work and realized with shock that the calculations he'd just made for cooling the cylinders were dangerously flawed. The engine would overheat. Frank knew he was seriously sleep deprived. He was not eating well. And now he was having mental lapses concerning critical engineering details. The engine would overheat, seize, tear up the transmission, crack. Frank realized he had to get help.

"I need something stronger," Frank told Dr. Sokolov in her office a few days later.

"Why do you say that?"

"Well, I've been having a hard time concentrating."

"Have you been getting any sleep, Frank?"

"Sleep? Well, not a lot."

"Something's been keeping you up?"

"I just can't sleep much. I get up and do stuff."

"And what sort of things do you do?"

"Oh, just projects. Mechanical things, designs."

"I see. And it's obvious you're not eating enough. So, when you can't sleep, what thoughts are going through your mind?"

Frank hesitated, his eyes darting away from her.

"Frank, stop looking at the door. It's true you can walk out of here and go find some other doctor to write your prescriptions, but do you think that's going to change things for you?"

"Okay. I've just been thinking about some things that happened back when I was a kid. A teenager."

"Something happened to you?"

"No, not to me." Frank's knee had begun to jiggle up and down.

"Not to you…. Something you did, then?"

"Yes … no … something that happened to someone else. But it was my fault."

"How old were you?"

"Thirteen. Fifteen. No, thirteen"

Sitting in a swivel chair with a pad in her lap, she made a note and nodded her head for him to go on.

But although it was why he'd come, Frank didn't know how to begin. He hedged and dodged the doctor's leading questions again and again until finally she raised her eyebrows and leaned back in her chair. "You have some choices here, you know. You can either jump in, or you can walk out, or you can sit here and waste the hour," she said. "It is, as you once so aptly put it, your dime."

Well, it was, but that was beside the point. It was his life. He'd come here determined to resolve something, to get some help—but now he wasn't sure he could do it. The alternative, though, was looking increasingly bleak. "All right. It was something …," he said, "well, something at church. After church."

"Yes, go on."

"All right." Frank took a breath. He forced his hands to go lax on his knees, and his knees to be still. "All right. There was a kid," he began. "His name was Donny—Donny Gerber. I didn't have much to do with him. He was a couple years older than me. He was tall. Blond. He had his own friends, I guess...." Frank trailed off.

"Church," he began again. "... I guess I should mention, first of all, how bored I was there. I must have had a fairly rich sideshow going on in my head most of the time, because in church I could feel it all grinding to a halt. I wouldn't be able think of a single interesting thing. It was painful. I'd count how long each breath lasted, or how long it took for someone to turn a page. Everything seemed to take forever, but it would hardly make a dent in the time still left to go. I'd get a sick feeling. I suppose it was depression, but of course I didn't think in those terms then.

"The feeling would stay with me after the service, too. I'd have to be polite, say the right things to my parents' friends. But even when they'd finally let us go play, while they had their meetings and things, I'd still be left feeling like the world on Sundays would always be slow and gray. Like a lead cloud on my chest."

Dr. Sokolov underlined something on her pad.

"But that's not what I meant to be talking about. It's just that because I was bored ... I, uh ... well, that's why I happened to be where I was." Frank rubbed his forehead with the heel of his hand.

"Anyway, I saw ... heard ... something." Frank shook his head. "I don't know why I'm so disorganized about this. I know I can get it all sorted out if I try."

"Don't worry about sorting it out. Just tell it as it comes to you and we'll worry about the sorting later."

"All right. Okay ... so after services we were allowed to go play, and the younger kids went to Sunday school. In winter we'd go downstairs to the rec room, and little ones would go to the classrooms off the side of it, but in summer, if the weather was good, the older kids would go to the side lawn, or the basketball hoop in the parking lot, while Mrs. Pearl held Sunday school on the grass out front. Donny was usually around, I guess, but I'd never paid much attention to him." Frank looked down at his knees, and again stilled them. He tried to take a calming breath but it ended up a jerky gulp. He plunged ahead anyway, feeling suddenly that there wasn't enough air, that he could die right here in this chair, drowned in a riptide of bad memories. He closed his eyes. "About what happened ... I'm not sure how it started. I don't know if it was something that had happened before, or if what I saw was, well...." Frank opened his eyes, shook his head, and took a quick breath. "I was hiding when I saw them. I was in a storeroom next to the classroom, because I was so ... bored ... and, well, that's why I was telling you about that. But forget that, it's not the point. The important thing is that I saw them—Donny and a girl."

Frank could see her so clearly, a little girl with frizzy red hair, whose name he'd never learned. "I didn't know her. She was only a kid, maybe ten or eleven. She wasn't one of the regular church kids, she was a relative or something from out of town. Her hair was red and she had those knobby knees that kids sometimes have. I don't know why I remember those knees but I do. They made her seem so young, I guess. She *was* young. I couldn't understand why Donny was interested in a kid like that—why he'd even bother to talk to her—because he was always so cool, you know, so self-assured.

"I was where I could see them but they couldn't see me. The other kids were all outside. The two of them were alone in the classroom. And, uh ... he kept talking to her," he faltered. "Flattering her." Frank's knees were beyond his control, his hands clenching convulsively to some syncopated interior rhythm. His eyes darted around the room.

"Then ... well, I guess she started to look scared...." Frank looked back at the doctor and swallowed. "That's when I noticed he was between her and the door to the hall. And the same thought must have occurred to her." He stopped. His eyes lost focus and drifted over the doctor's shoulder in the direction of the window.

When he didn't go on, Dr. Sokolov asked quietly, "Why was she scared, Frank?"

But he still didn't answer.

"And how old were you?"

He looked back at her. "Me? I was thirteen then, and Donny must have been fifteen or sixteen. I wasn't really into school, you know, and I wasn't into sports or anything. I was a runner, though. I'd thought about joining the track team, but it seemed like it would just be one more thing to drag me away from my own stuff. Sometimes I ran on my own, when I needed to think things over, or when I just felt restless. I wasn't a weakling, in other words, but it wouldn't have occurred to me that I could take Donny. But that wasn't it, really." His eyes went away again. His body had grown still. "It wasn't so much that I was a physical coward. I was a moral one."

The doctor was asking him something, but Frank suddenly couldn't seem to get his mind in order. It was as if he were caught between two worlds. He could relive that time as it had been, or he could take control of it, make it the way it should have been. But that wasn't right either. He couldn't change the past. He really should know that by now. He opened his mouth to speak and he didn't know which world he'd end up in. Maybe neither. The inside of his head felt as if it were churning, alternately buffeted between a sucking vacuum and an unbearable pressure. He thought his skull might burst apart from the force of it. For an instant the idea flashed through his mind that maybe he *was* drowning, in the ocean, and was only imagining himself, in a dying delusion, to be sitting here in this room with his psychiatrist. He blinked and took a breath.

He knew exactly where he was. He looked over at her—so apart from him, so calm, waiting. It was a mistake to come here, he realized. Nothing he could say would matter. It was all a mistake.

He closed his mouth.

"Frank?"

"What?"

"Why do you say you were a coward? What happened?"

He looked steadily at her. "Nothing. I don't know why I'm even telling you about this."

"You've made a good start, Frank. That's important. But don't give up there. Now, take a second if you need to, have a drink of water—"

"No. That's all. It was nothing.... I didn't like what was going on." He stopped, but just as the doctor began to speak again, he overrode her in a rush. "I could see Donny inching his chair toward the girl, cornering her. She tried to get around him, but he stuck his arm out and caught her ... so I ran out of the side room I was in, into the hall, and around to the classroom door. I knocked on it and yelled something about the Pastor coming downstairs. I can't remember what excuse I made up. But after a few seconds the door opened and Donny stood there. He must've seen something in my face that he didn't like, because the look he gave me was pretty cold.

"Maybe if he'd threatened me outright, things would've been different. But he just looked me up and down, like he was trying to figure out what to do with me that wouldn't get his shoes dirty."

"And then?"

"Nothing, that was it."

"That was it?"

"Yeah, except ..."

"Except what? ... Frank?"

"Nothing. Forget it" He brought his hands down on his knees. "You know what, doc? I think I can figure this out on my own. Thanks for listening, but talking about it isn't going to help me." He rose with a jerky motion and turned to the door.

"Frank, how different?"

"What?"

"You said if he'd threatened you, things might have been different. What things?"

"Nothing," he said. And then again, his voice turning dull with defeat. "Nothing. Just bill me for the hour."

Frank made one more appointment with Dr. Sokolov but he broke it. He never went back. He found another doctor to write his prescription without asking unanswerable questions. A couple of years later he left his job in Perth and returned to the U.S., to Foxton, a liar now as well as a coward.

9

"CHICAGO?" Emery asked.

"Yeah, a friend of mine from college invited us to come. You included," said Georgia.

It was the end of July. The cast was still on Emery's arm, but barely, as he'd irritably whittled it down to a vestige of its original form. His wrist was coming along fine and the palm of his hand, toughened as it was from years of work, had healed well from the burn.

Georgia was sitting on the porch, looking up from her just-completed, belated card to Corrine, thanking her for arranging to have her second cousin Brenda rent Georgia's house for July and August. Emery had come up from the workshop a few minutes ago, an alternator in one hand and a toolbox in the other. After setting them down, he'd ducked inside for a minute and come back out with two peaches, handing one to Georgia. He now sat in the shade of the porch, wiping peach juice from his hands with a handkerchief and looking at his niece quizzically.

"Well, the bike is almost done," he said. "I suppose this is as good a time as any for you to take a break." Georgia had admitted to being afraid of riding even the old Honda 450 Nighthawk Mel found for her to learn on, much less balancing atop her gleaming mystery motorcycle. Emery could see where a person might need time to make up her mind to do a thing that scared her, even if it was as clear as day she'd wind up doing it in the end. But as far as him going with her to Chicago.... Well, Emery didn't know about that.

"I thought you said you didn't go to college," he stalled.

"Well, I did for a while but then I dropped out. So what do you say? Will you go with me?"

He hemmed and hawed for a few more minutes and finally told Georgia he'd think about it. "I better get out there and sharpen a saw or two before dinnertime, though," he said. He abandoned the porch, the alternator, and the immediate question, and strolled casually but quickly down the steps.

He sat in the shade beside the shed, grinding down rakers on a chainsaw and fretting. What would an old hick like him do in a city like Chicago? He'd look like a fool for one thing—he may as well have wood chips in his hair and a blade of straw hanging out of his mouth. He got up, nervously hitching up his sagging work khakis, and shifted his jig and wheel over a few feet to stay in the shade as the sun edged around toward him. It was one thing to run to town for his groceries and library books, and maybe to stop in for a beer. But he knew from the TV in JJ's bar how fast everything moved in cities like Chicago. He was pretty sure he'd get himself lost if he was left on his own for more than a minute and a half. No, it would probably be better just to stay put. He had an awful lot to get done around here anyhow. The summer seemed to be just flying by.

It had been a nice idea, though. He sighed. It might have been interesting to see some new sights. Too bad he was so busy.

Georgia wouldn't let him get away with it, though. At dinner she said, "You know you want to come, Uncle Emery. When was the last time you went anywhere? You're going to shrivel up like an old squash if you don't get out and do something new every now and then. And of course," she added, "it would be a big help to have you share the driving."

He fidgeted, and he scratched his cheek, and he finally said, "Well, I guess I could finish putting up the wood when we get back if I use the old timber from that beaver cut over on the south end. And I suppose folks could get Art Demsen to do repairs for them if they need to."

Georgia smiled with contentment.

The next day Emery went to town and bought a brand new suitcase. Throughout the week he alternately packed it to the gills, throwing in everything he thought he could possibly need and more, then unpacked and started over. His usual self-reliant confidence deserted him in the face of old fears about not fitting in, and he kept asking Georgia nervous questions about his wardrobe.

"What if we go to a nice restaurant?"

"Do you have a jacket and tie?"

"I got a suit I bought once for a funeral." He rummaged through his closet. "Here." He held up a stolid wool suit on its hanger.

"No, you don't want to take that. You'll have to buy a sports jacket. But why don't you wait till we get to Chicago? We can go shopping there. It'll be fun."

Emery had his doubts about that but went sorting through his shirts, asking her opinion on this one or that. Finally Georgia rolled her eyes and said, "Chicago can't be all that different from here. It's not Outer Mongolia or anything. Just wear some jeans and throw in another pair of pants and a few shirts, and you're done."

"Well, then, I guess that'll be okay." But a few shirts turned into half a dozen, and Emery snuck off to town and bought himself some nice trousers, a new tie, a pair of shoes. "I don't want to look like some rube," he told Georgia when she caught him coming back laden with shopping bags.

They budgeted a careful allotment of funds for motels and meals. In Chicago they would stay with Georgia's friend for three days and then head back. Georgia had planned to drive straight there and back but Emery objected that if he was going to travel, then he wanted to see a little bit of country along the way.

They decided to stop in and say hello to his foster sister, Janet. In his younger days, after Emery had built his cabin, one or another of the Vogels used to come up to see him now and then, usually Janet. A sweet natured, homey person always interested in the doings of her clan, she was as good a foster sister as anyone could hope for, but she was also the one who made Emery most seriously doubt his fitness for family life. His head would begin to spin after half an hour. After an hour it was all he could do to keep from running for the pines. He'd usually make his escape by going out in the canoe to catch some supper. In the early days, Janet would stay around the cabin being a mother hen, tidying until he returned, and then cook dinner for him.

After she married, she'd sometimes bring her son, Mark, who had Down's syndrome and was as good-natured and outgoing as his mother. Emery couldn't help admiring the boy, a man now. He seemed so fearless. He took the bus every day to his job at Goodwill, met new people, and even had a volunteer job as an assistant swim instructor.

Janet and Emery had stayed in touch but rarely visited anymore. Emery had never been to the house where she now lived. When he'd called to ask if he and Georgia could drop by, Janet's voice came pealing through the phone lines with such thrilled enthusiasm that Emery was sure it could be heard into the next county. He almost got cold feet and backed out of the whole thing, but he told her they'd come for lunch, and got detailed directions to her house.

Emery, who had once set out to travel across the country with a rolled-up towel and a few meager necessities, with no map, no money to speak of, and no idea where he'd end up, now wanted to know exactly where they would sleep, what route they would follow, and what they would see. The Windy City loomed like the Emerald City at the end of an uncertain road.

Most of their preparations went smoothly until one day Emery suggested that they might stop in Foxton.

"No," Georgia said at once. "My parents aren't there, they're in Florida."

"We could just drive through. It's not far out of the way."

"No. No one's there." She said it with such curt finality that, other than looking at her curiously, Emery didn't press it. He'd never seen the town where his mother had grown up. Where, pregnant for the second time without a husband, she'd been banished from her father's house. Where, under other circumstances, Emery might have grown up with a sister, with cousins, aunts, and uncles. But Georgia was uncharacteristically grim and he let it be.

There were plenty of other things to think about, and soon the day had come to leave and it was time to load up the car. They'd done a temporary trade with Jeanette Tourilla, the owner of one of the lake resorts out on the highway. Emery sometimes did repair work for her, and over the years they'd built up a quiet friendship. It was agreed that Emery would lend her his pickup to haul her new boat, while he and Georgia took her old Lincoln, complete with air conditioning and bounding shocks. Emery had to throw in a little engine work but he thought it was a fair deal considering the miles they were going to put on it.

Albert obviously knew something was up. Instead of sniffing once around the cabin and then plopping down on the grass for the remainder of the morning, he made sure he was constantly underfoot. But when all the packing was done and the cabin checked—windows shut, taps closed, generator turned off—Georgia couldn't find him anywhere. She whistled and yelled in vain until she and Emery finally decided to sit down for another cup of coffee, hoping he'd show up on his own.

"We'll have to check around the lake," said Georgia when they'd rinsed out their thermos cups under the hand pump and he still hadn't turned up. Georgia headed east and Emery trucked off down the shore to the west. He was just starting to wonder if Albert had returned to the scene of his past glory, the great treeing of the fisher, when he heard Georgia calling, "Uncle Emery! I've got the old booger here. Come on back." When Emery returned, it was to the strains of Georgia's scolding. "You are the most exasperating dog. I swear, if you didn't have that goofy face I'd boot you right into the lake. Look at you, what did you think you were doing, making us hunt all over creation for you?"

"Where was he?" asked Emery.

"Here."

"Where?"

"Here! In the car. The whole time. I came back to get my sunglasses and here he was." She headed for the driver's side shaking her head. "I swear!"

As they rolled onto the highway, Emery felt an excitement course through him that made him think of the time he'd been talked into sampling Jeanette Tourilla's homemade blueberry brandy. He glanced at Georgia. Her mouth was still in a pout over Albert's stunt, but her eyes were smiling, and soon there was a little twist at the corner of her lips. She looked over at him and they both looked back down the road, grinning silently as they headed south.

They got to Janet's in time for a late lunch. Her son, Mark, had gotten the afternoon off to be there. Before Emery even had a chance to ring the bell, the door swung open and he found himself swept through a hallway into a smaller version of the farmhouse kitchen where he'd spent so many hours as a youth. Janet gave him a kiss on the cheek and then held him at arm's length with her strong, gnarled hands, to take a good look at him. Emery glanced over his shoulder to see Georgia receiving an even more extravagant welcome than he was getting. Mark was giving her a bone crunching hug and saying,

"Hello, Georgia, Uncle Emery's niece. I'm Mark and Mom says we're sort of related now, because you're his niece and my mother is his foster sister, which is like a sister, so ..."

After more handshakes and hugs, they were soon sitting at the kitchen table eating a colossal lunch. To Emery's relief, most of the attention stayed focused on Georgia. But every now and then, between asking Georgia about the trip and checking to make sure everyone had enough lemonade, Janet would look over at Emery, shake her head, and smile to herself. It seemed that just having him sitting at her table and eating her cooking was enough for her today. Emery felt exactly the same. He looked around the table at this family of his, and sighed with a kind of contentment he'd rarely felt in his life. He took another bite of egg salad and sat back to enjoy watching as Georgia was plied with food and questions. She was obviously having a wonderful time.

Mark couldn't get over the idea of someone sending Georgia a motorcycle. "But who *is* he? Is it hard to put a motorcycle together? I can put a bicycle together, that's my job, putting bicycles together. But who *sent* it?"

"I don't know," said Georgia. She threw her arms out in a wide shrug, the look of incredulity on her face a match for Mark's.

"Does it work?"

"I don't know. We haven't finished it yet."

"Well, if it works, that's the important thing."

"You're right," Georgia agreed.

"But who *sent* it?"

Emery finally talked Georgia into going through Foxton by a combination of temptation and petulance. "Did you know the main Harley-Davidson factory's in Milwaukee?" he asked her when they stopped for gas in Eau Claire.

"It is?" she said. "Do you think we could go there? Could we go inside? Take a tour or something?"

"Well, I don't know. Never been there. You could call them and find out." He pulled out the map and laid it flat on the expansive hood of the Lincoln. "Let's see. We could take Highway 10 to 41, and then down."

"But the interstate goes right to Milwaukee," she objected. "Look."

"I sure am tired of this highway. You can't see anything. What's the point of traveling if you can't see anything?"

"We'll see plenty when we get to Milwaukee."

"Well, I don't know if I really want to see another city. I'm not much of a city person, you know, and Chicago'll be sufficient for me."

"Uncle Emery, if you want to see Foxton, just say so."

"Well ..."

"All right, all right. We'll go."

"Georgia?"

"What."

He looked at her, his eyes worried. "We don't have to, you know. I just kind of wanted to, now that I know my family came from there. But I can live without it. If it brings back bad memories or anything." He looked away, out over the weedy field that bordered the gas station.

"No," she said after a moment. "It's okay—let's go."

"We don't have to stay long, just drive on through."

"All right."

"And then on to Milwaukee."

"Then on to Milwaukee. Harley-Davidson, here we come."

They drove through a few towns that wouldn't have brought

back memories to anyone much over the age of ten. Downtowns had been renovated and new construction had made several developers and a realtor or two very comfortable, at least for a while. Foxton retained much of its old flavor, but even here changes had occurred in the years Georgia had been gone. New houses had sprung up and there was a walled development of tidy manufactured houses. Georgia drove past them to an old neighborhood that had somehow survived almost completely intact. She took Emery down the shady streets and pulled over at the corner of a quiet intersection.

"There," she said, pointing across the street to a yellow two-story house with shiny black shutters on the windows. "That was grandpa's house. It used to be white."

Emery just nodded.

"The trees are bigger," she said, looking up at them. "It's like a forest now."

"Where did you live?"

Georgia waved her hand. "Over that way about a half mile," she said.

Emery thought Georgia might simply drive out of town then, and that would be that, but she sat looking out the car window for a while longer, then drove downtown and stopped in front of a coffee shop.

"This didn't used to be here. Let's get something."

They had pie and coffee while Georgia looked out the window onto the street. Emery's concern for her vied with his curiosity about the area. He stirred restlessly in his seat. "I'm going to take Albert for a walk," he said at last.

"Okay," said Georgia without looking around.

"Nice town," he said to Albert, who was taking a dump in some trash and leaves down by the river. "Good boy." Emery absently kicked a hole in the dirt with his heel, nudged in Albert's mess, buffered with leaves, and then kicked dirt back over it. "Nice place to grow up in, I guess. Didn't seem to make Georgia happy, though."

Albert, on his typically delayed timetable, scraped back a kick or two of dirt, then turned to sniff. He looked around in alarm.

"Gone, buddy," Emery told him. "Dead and buried."

Moving on, Emery dragged Albert away, and they ambled along the riverbank. They followed the water for a while, but Albert seemed a little preoccupied, so before long they headed back to the coffee shop. As they walked up the hill, Emery could see Georgia outside waiting for them. She was leaning back against the side of the Lincoln, her feet on the curb, her head turned away from them, gazing up the street.

Emery noticed a man standing on the other side of the street. He was dark haired and ordinary enough to look at, except for the intensity of his eyes and the stricken look on his face. He was staring directly at Georgia's back. He took a few hesitant steps in her direction.

A woman came out of the real estate office behind him, closing her purse and straightening her skirt. She touched the man's arm and spoke to him. He looked at her with a start, then with a last glance in Georgia's direction he turned back to her, nodded, and they walked off down the street.

Emery and Albert continued up the hill to meet Georgia.

Frank had begun stopping by the real estate office most days at noon. The owner was a nice woman, a couple years older than himself, and a cheerful sort, not disheartened by two divorces. They'd been dating off and on for about six months. Frank enjoyed her company, but was concerned from the first that he'd be wasting her time. She was obviously the marrying type, and he certainly was not. She was an optimist, though, and as long as she was willing to go out, even after Frank told her outright he was not looking for a permanent relationship, then he wasn't going to argue.

The weather had eased in the last couple of days from sweltering to just plain hot, so instead of going inside the office, Frank tapped on the window. When Susan looked up, he motioned that he'd wait outside. In the slim shade of the building, he leaned against the wall and folded his arms.

When he saw Georgia walk out of Alma's Coffee Shop across the street, his breath caught in his chest. He dropped his arms and began to step forward. He stopped, torn between a compelling force drawing him onward, and a strong impulse to flee. He watched her walk to an old, pale blue Lincoln parked at the curb. She glanced down the street, then turned around and leaned back against the side of the hood. Frank looked around for a motorcycle but there was no sign of one.

All at once he felt not just dazed at seeing her, but extraordinarily stupid. An idea that had seemed so perfectly reasonable from a world away in Perth, even somehow from here in Foxton, as long as Georgia had been safely in another state, now looked at best like a ridiculous flight of fancy. At worst it appeared a stalker's ploy. All he'd wanted was to give her something—something within his ability—to help get her life going, and perhaps ease his guilt a little. He had imagined her, all this time, as mired and helpless, but she was obviously doing all right for herself. She looked good—healthy and fit. Only her expression, the brief glimpse he'd seen of it before she'd turned around, was tense, as if she were waiting for some terrible thing to jump out at her and not knowing where it might be coming from. Well, it already had, Frank thought. No thanks to him. And nothing he could dream up was going to take away the wrong that had been done to her.

Idiot, he thought. I'm an idiot. With his brain berating him and his heart feeling like a stone he'd swallowed, he was drawn so powerfully toward Georgia that it felt as if his eyes would be torn from his head. He wanted to turn and run, but his renegade legs had ideas of their own, and he took another step in her direction.

Like a switch clicking him out of one world and into another, he heard the snap of Susan's purse behind him. Ripping through a weft of consciousness, he turned toward her and made himself hear her words. "So how about the Chinese place down on Third?"

He nodded.

Susan acted as if she didn't notice Frank's pallor or the haunted look he cast, compelled against his will, across the street, but as they began to walk, Frank was aware of her surreptitious glance back. All she would see, though, would be the lunch crowd beginning to trickle into Alma's, and leaning against an old car, the back of a woman in a short sleeved work shirt, her dark hair pulled into a low braid. Nothing to be alarmed about.

Susan touched Frank's arm and began talking about their plans for the weekend. "I hear there's a new dinner theater opening. I thought we could drive over …"

Frank had never been a drinker and he'd never had any inclination toward drugs, but he suddenly felt a terrible craving. He wanted to run home and down a couple of … he didn't know what. Scotch, antidepressants, Sominex, he didn't care.

"Are you okay?" Susan finally asked him.

Speaking from a great distance, he managed a distracted, "Yes." Then he looked at her as if coming awake. "I'm sorry Susan," he said. "I have to go do something." He turned around and walked away, leaving her gaping after him.

The car was pulling away from the curb when Frank came abreast of it. An older man was at the wheel and suddenly Frank mistrusted himself. Maybe he'd only imagined all of this. Through the side window of the back seat a mournful dog looked out at him, its wet nose pressed against the already well-smudged glass. The dog turned his head to watch him as the car moved away.

But then Frank forgot both man and dog as he glimpsed the back of a dark head beside the driver. The car turned onto Binder Street, heading toward Main. Frank began to walk more rapidly up the hill. He broke into a run. When he reached the end of the block, he turned the corner and sprinted to the end of the street. Looking desperately up and down Main, he thought he'd missed her, but then he saw the big car pulling away at the light, heading out toward the highway. Then it passed Malvern, where the road curved right, and was gone. Frank stood panting, sweat streaking down his face, feeling stunned, foolish, forlorn. He imagined the car in his mind, block after block, until it reached the highway and turned onto it. He shook his head to clear it, and only then wondered what in hell he was doing. The street in front of his eyes started to waver. He leaned over, putting his hands on his knees, and dropped his head.

What was supposed to have been simple—something to propel Georgia out into the world, to free her from the wreck her life had become and give her back some of the spirit of her young childhood—now seemed weird and confused. He'd been shamelessly underhanded, sending the bike anonymously, employing her unsuspecting cousin Mary Ann to feed back reports on her welfare, but since he'd sent off the last of the parts and the manual, he'd deliberately stayed away from the restaurant where Mary Ann worked. He'd wanted to release Georgia, not only from her old life, but also from his watchful eye. To let her find her own way. That was to be his gift to her—mobility and freedom. He *should* free her —he had, after all, been responsible for her imprisonment. But how had he thought her life could be fixed with a motorcycle? What kind of insanity was that?

And what had he been thinking just now, running after her the way he had? He felt as if he'd been sucked into the center of a tornado. He took a few deep breaths, straightened, and when the world steadied enough, walked back the way he'd come.

He thought of poor Susan, left standing there while he'd torn off up the street. He'd have to apologize. Susan was a perfectly fine person and pleasant to spend time with. He certainly didn't want to hurt her feelings. But placid contentment of that sort was not real, not like living in the true world. It was more like living on top of a sheet of acetate that kept everything above it nice and clean and level, but never let anything down into the deeper parts. Down where the monsters lived, but also the mysteries.

Steadiness—that's what he'd wanted once upon a time. He'd thought that if he could only keep his head level and above water, he'd be satisfied, and never want anything more. How we fool ourselves, he thought. We deal for our lives, then the future comes along and we want to renegotiate. Well, he hadn't asked for a deal. He hadn't. He'd only thought that if he could stop his mind from its spiraling hopelessly downward, he'd be content.

He knew, of course, that he wasn't good for people. Not for anyone he really cared about. He told himself to can the melodrama, but he couldn't dismiss the notion, not altogether. Sure, he was perfectly functional now, but it was a mild world he'd made for himself. He was no good under pressure. He'd always do the wrong thing, make the wrong choice, hurt someone.

And seeing Georgia out of the blue like that.... He never had any intention of pursuing her, especially not literally, through the midday streets of Foxton. And any romantic notions, of course, would be obscene under the circumstances. His headlong rush was simply to see her, to make sure she was okay. And if by some chance she was, then maybe there was also hope for that other girl, the little red-haired girl in the church basement.

10

LIBBY FALKMAN LOOKED up from her counter as Frank's white shirt flew by the window. She put the invoices aside and strolled to the door. What a goofball. He always tried to act so composed, but his real charm was that underlying ... well, something, she didn't exactly know what. She just had the sense that there was some raw, real person under there. She'd seen Frank Morrow around for a while now, ever since he'd come back from wherever it was he used to work, someplace overseas. Carol Oskaush at the Title Company next door said he worked at her brother-in-law's engineering firm now.

He always seemed to have a lady friend. Libby must not be the only woman to pick up on that subtly lost look he had, and that intense interest he took in whatever was before him, like a dog whose whole existence at any particular moment hung on a single scent. He appeared to be the perfect gentleman, though, serious and polite. Libby bet that even his break-ups were civil. No tantrums in the middle of Main Street, no rumors of abortions or torched automobiles. So what was he doing running down the sidewalk at high noon under a blazing sun?

It touched on that hidden something beneath his smooth exterior. She sensed it somehow, and it made her feel ... well. She shook her hands as if to cast off built-up static.

Libby was a boyish, slim-hipped woman, full of contradictions. She had big hands and a sweet, light voice, reddish blond hair and dark eyes. She was clever but klutzy when nervous. She had no mechanical aptitude, but she worked at a medical supply company surrounded by equipment and was good at her job. She relied on advice for the trivial aspects of her life, but when, four years earlier, it had come time to nurse her dying husband, she'd stepped up with absolute conviction—once the doctors had done what they could and failed—and had brought him home with her until the sad and bitter end. She'd raised her twins, a girl and a boy, with no hope at all of being a particularly good mother, and they loved her and had gone off to college with the same mixed feelings of liberation and covert homesickness as countless other well-adjusted children. Libby had grown up poor, married rich, lost most of her money—due to terminally flawed insurance—in an avalanche of medical bills, spent the rest of it on her kids' college tuition, and come out dead even—meaning dead broke. Despite this, she didn't care much one way or the other about money as long as she could take care of her family.

They'd almost met a year ago, Libby and Frank. They might have ... if it weren't for the green bicycle on the sidewalk.

Libby had been a widow for three years then, and her twins were leaving for college. Hating the idea of putting herself "on the market," she hoped nevertheless that she might somehow stumble upon a nice guy. So she kept her eyes open, even though she was sure most of the good men would already be taken. The few who might still be out there would certainly be swooped up by more proactive women. When she'd noticed Frank with his dark hair and distracted manner, he'd caught her interest. She remembered seeing him around the neighborhood years ago, before Joey got sick. She assumed he'd have settled down by now, but apparently he was an established bachelor. He must work nearby, she thought. She occasionally saw him walking down Binder Street at lunchtime.

He intrigued her. Each time she saw him he seemed somehow different from the time before. One day he might look lean and intense, like he'd just spotted some fascinating insect specimen on the sun-baked pavement outside Alma's Coffee Shop. On another he might have the appearance of a businessman complacently returning from lunch with the mayor. In the winter he seemed to savor the cold, not hunching up like most people against the sleety wind, but opening himself to it, facing it down, his face reddened and his eyes sinking back into their sockets, but never turning away. It was hard to get a fix on the man. There seemed to be more than one of him.

And then one day she'd had a real turn. At the grocery store, she saw a man who almost made her drop her oranges. She felt like Alice in Wonderland, only it wasn't she who was getting bigger, but the man. For just an instant she was sure it was Frank from Binder Street, and that he'd suddenly grown into yet another aspect of himself—a giant version. Then he turned and she could see his whole face. He looked very much like Frank; they could be—must be—brothers, but this person was an entirely different sort. Not better or worse, she thought, just different. He had different worries, and eyes that focused on things not intensely near or philosophically far, but at an ordinary distance. Libby shook herself and laughed at her notions. She'd *better* get out there and start meeting people before she *did* fall down a rabbit hole.

So the day she'd walked out of Knutsen's Medical Supply and had seen Frank coming down the sidewalk toward her, she straightened her posture with as much grace as she could, given her armload of invoice books and the carton of oxygen canister replacement tubing balanced on top. She made up her mind to smile at him as they passed. A good smile, she decided, not one of those wimpy ones she sometimes gave when taken by surprise, smiling a little and then looking down at her big feet. A good one, like the women on TV did, in bars, that made a man feel like he was welcome. She should have practiced this at home, she thought. She took a breath and began to walk toward him, hoping she wasn't turning crimson. She looked right at him and got ready to flash him a nice, open, friendly smile—but not too friendly, of course, or he'd think she was slutty or maybe just plain crazy. He was looking up. He must have seen her for a split second, and if it weren't for the green bicycle, she might have succeeded in making eye contact with him.

But young Kenny Martinez, who'd gone into the newspaper office to tell his mother that Mr. Lance said he was going to pull his ads unless they stopped parking the news van in front of his store, had left his bike leaning at its usual precarious angle against the brick, and when Frank looked up he must have brushed lightly against it. Not much, but enough to overbalance the iridescent metal. The front wheel turned inward and the bike started a slow rolling plunge to the pavement, whacking Frank on the shin and causing him to spill his carry-out coffee.

Shit, thought Libby, as she passed him and continued on down the street. Such magic I possess, that I can make a man fall all over himself even *before* he looks at me. She shook her head and decided that one of these days she really would like to meet that man.

So when, a year later, Frank flew by like Ichabod Crane, Libby went to the window and watched him. He sprinted to the corner and stopped, panting, looking down Main. Then he bent over with his hands on his knees.

He looked dazed and a little pathetic as he turned and came back along the sidewalk. Libby took a step out the door. She had no idea what she was going to say, but she placed herself in his path and turned to him.

"It's a pretty hot day," she said. Brilliant, she thought. Now what? "Do you want to come in for a glass of water?" She flapped her hands and added, "I saw you running, and I was thinking … well … you might need some water." Now I'm a duck, she thought, corralling her hands. She felt like sinking into the ground, but she was committed now. About two seconds before she would have fallen over dead of embarrassment, Frank seemed to come out of his daze. He nodded, and followed her into the cool office. She was the only one working the front until Nicole returned from her obstetrician at two. Rob and Darren could be counted on to stay holed up in their offices until they were done for the day. So Libby sat Frank down on a chair and brought him a cup of water from the cooler. She pulled up one of the display wheelchairs and sat across from him, tucking a flyaway wisp of hair behind one ear.

"Thanks," he said. "Much better."

She realized then that he truly was in need of attention. His face was pale, except for a red streak along each cheek that made her imagine him as a kid, skating out on the river until his cheeks were aflame and ice formed on his eyebrows.

He pulled a handkerchief out of his pants pocket and sopped up cold water from his cup, wiping his forehead and neck with it, letting dribbles of water run down under his shirt collar. "I don't know why I did that," he said.

She looked at him questioningly. "Why you …?"

"Ran like that. I saw someone I used to know." He shook his head. "Sorry," he said, extending his hand. "I'm Frank. Frank Morrow."

"Nice to meet you, Frank. I'm Libby Falkman…. You must work around here."

"A couple of blocks," he inclined his head to indicate the direction.

"I've seen you once or twice, walking by at lunchtime."

She hoped he'd say something to let her know he'd noticed her too, but he didn't. Instead he said, "Have you ever felt like you don't know what year it is? I mean, for a split second you're back in the past, your age is ... well ... irrelevant. You're fifteen, or you're nine. You've never left those ages behind you—they're still part of you—and there you are? ... Just for a second? I'm sorry," he said again. "I'm rambling."

"Yes."

"I'm rambling?"

"No, I know what you mean. Sometimes when I wake up in the middle of the night I feel like that. I sit on the toilet in the dark and wonder for a second why the window's on that wall instead of the other one, and then I remember I'm not in my mother's house anymore." God, she thought. I'm talking to a complete stranger about sitting on the toilet.

"That's it," he said, and smiled a little. She had the distinct impression that he knew what she was thinking about the toilet, and that it was okay. "That's the feeling. Well, I just had it in a big way. Thank you for rescuing me."

"My pleasure." Now ask me out to dinner, she thought.

He stood up and held out his hand. "I'm all better now, Libby, and I should let you get back to work. Thank you again."

"Would you like to have dinner sometime, Frank?" Her head felt like it was going to spin off into outer space. If this was what dating was like, she didn't know if she could stand it.

"Yes. I would." Although it seemed to be an effort, he was focusing intently on her. He pulled out a card from his wallet and handed it to her, and then to her relief he pulled out another and asked for her number. She wrote it on the back and handed it to him.

Libby felt both exhilarated and exhausted after he left. She made two errors in her inventory update, but by the time they would come back to haunt her she'd have more important things on her mind.

Foxton, Milwaukee, Chicago. To many it would have seemed as ordinary as eggs, but for Georgia and Emery it was a whirlwind of a trip, and they came home feeling as if they'd just returned from a carnival, tired and sated and wondering where the time had gone.

Getting home was both a comfort and a little bit of a letdown. And disconcerting. They'd been jolted out of their usual grooves, and instead of slipping back into the familiar routine and easy pace, they both felt like they were jumping from one thing to another in a less than organized way.

"I've got to change gears," Emery told Georgia one morning while they were working on the bike. "I feel like the place is standing still, and I'm scooting around all over it and can't get any traction."

She smiled. "I know exactly what you mean."

"I'm glad I went on the trip with you, though," he said.

"Yeah, me too."

"Too bad your mother wasn't home. I would have liked to see her."

"How long has it been?" She could see his reflection in the chrome of the headlamp housing she was attaching. He was sitting on a stool behind her with the manual on his lap, sorting through a small box of fasteners, one foot propped up on the toolbox.

"Quite a while. Going on three years now, I guess."

"It must have been strange when you two first met."

Emery looked up for a moment, considering. "Nine years ago." He remembered sitting, slightly dazed, on an overstuffed couch in a house in Minneapolis, where Iris was visiting a friend who'd tactfully gone out for the afternoon so brother and sister could have time together. "Your mother is quite, uh …"

Georgia laughed. "Yeah, she is. And she's mellowed from when I was a kid. Back then she was always pumped up over some political cause or other. Then she'd give a good fart and be on to something else."

Emery tried to frown. "She's a good person, though."

"Of course she is. She's still pretty political, but now it's closer to home. City council meetings and letters to the editor—that kind of thing. She can still get good and worked up, though."

Emery thought of how Iris had chattered away about the Foxton utility company tearing up the streets *twice*, because some idiot had decided to install inferior water lines the first time around to save a few bucks, and where did that money go, anyway? She strode around her friend's house, pulling out photograph albums from her suitcases and piling them in front of Emery on the coffee table, taking cookies from a tin and dealing them onto a dinner plate, stepping out onto the back patio to retrieve a large plastic jug of pale sun-tea, which she proceeded to doctor with lemon and sugar. "Ice?" she said, and immediately answered herself, "Of course you want ice, what am I thinking?" She'd brought to mind Emery's foster sister Janet, although next to Iris, Janet's domestic energy seemed positively calming.

He'd sunk back into the couch like a chipmunk backing into a knothole, to observe the bustle from a safe refuge. He spoke only when he couldn't avoid it. The more Iris tried to make him feel welcome, the stronger his impulse was to retreat.

It finally occurred to Emery that Iris might be just as nervous as he was. "My long-lost brother," she kept calling him. So he began to tell her a little about his part of the country, the cabin he'd built, his modest sharpening and repair business—elevated for the moment to a "business" rather than the neighborly barter operation it mostly was. He reeled her in with his quiet talk, until finally she sat across from him, listening with interest. Then she told him all about her daughter, Georgia, and how proud she was of her. She was a good girl, only she wasn't fulfilling her potential. She could have gotten a college degree but instead she was wasting herself on a bum.

They'd talked about the lost years between them. "I knew you existed," Iris told him. "I used to have this make-believe brother who helped me all the way through elementary school. He told me not to worry when I forgot my homework four days in a row, and he stood up for me when Dotty Dinskoe deliberately tripped me with the jump rope every time it was my turn."

"I must be kind of a disappointment, then," Emery said ruefully. "Not exactly your knight in shining armor."

"No, you're just fine," she said. "I had you a little taller, though."

"And not so scrawny, I bet," he grinned.

"And maybe a little more hair," she allowed.

He laughed and ran his fingers through his thin gray locks. "I never thought about having a sister," he said. "But I bet it would have been nice."

"Oh, I would've been a big pain in the derrière, I'm sure."

They felt better then. Iris leaned back and began to tell him about the rest of their family. Before long she was up again—this time not from nerves, but to hunt for a pencil and paper. "I'd better draw it," she told him. "Your own family tree."

It made him feel a little sad, that his whole life had gone by without ever knowing this fundamental history. Family tree projects at school had taken him about two seconds—him and his mother. She had hated those projects. "Why can't they keep their goddamned noses out of our business," she'd say, and clam up.

Iris drew with the swift sure movements of a person who'd been drawing family trees all her life. She had to think a moment, to place some of the more distant cousins and the by-marriages and the twice-removeds, but never mind. She had the important part. "Here *you* are," she said, pointing with the tip of the No.2, leaving a series of little dots next to his name as she jabbed at it with satisfaction. "About time, too. I could have killed grandpa when I found out the truth about you and your mother.... *our* mother. Except he was already dead." She shook her head in a small gesture of combined sadness and frustration. "That's when we found out, of course. He'd told us she'd run away, but that was a damned lie. I wouldn't have expected it from him in a million years. Aunt Rose brought me up like one of hers, of course...."

"Uncle Emery?"

Emery looked at Georgia and blinked. She was holding out her hand. "Hmm?" he said.

"The twelve-millimeter?"

"Oh, sorry," he said, recollecting himself. "Out wool-gathering." He reached down to the toolbox and handed her the wrench.

"I know. I've been like that for days. Can't seem to settle down."

Emery nodded and set aside the box he was sorting. "I tell you what," he said, closing the manual. "Why don't we go out and you can take a practice ride on the Honda."

"Oh, yeah," she said dryly. "That'll settle me right down."

"It might."

"Well ... maybe you're right. Anyway I'd better learn to ride soon, if I'm not going to chicken out."

"I don't think there's much chance of that now."

"You wouldn't let me even if I wanted to," she teased. "Alright, let me just finish this up."

"I don't want to go to my grave without seeing you sail off down the road." Emery said, getting up and walking around to the other side of the bike. He knelt down to look at the wiring she was securing to the frame. His smile turned wistful. "I always wanted to see the Rockies, myself, you know." He glanced up at Georgia. "I think you should do that."

"You do it yourself."

"Well, I might—but if I don't, you do it for me.... Here, hold this," he said, twisting a clamp into place, "and I'll see if I can tighten it from this side." They worked for a while in silence and then Emery said, "Have you ever been out West?"

"Nope ... well, actually, yes," Georgia amended. When I was about eight or so, we went on a family trip to Yellowstone. I haven't thought about that in years."

"Was it nice?" Emery asked.

"Yeah. I think so. I don't remember a lot. I do remember a hot stream—so hot you could boil an egg in it. I walked over to it, and a Park Ranger came out of nowhere and started yelling at my mother to make me get back. I guess I was walking on some sort of a thin crust, and if I'd gone through, that would have been the end of me."

"Was she mad at you, your mother?"

"Some, but mostly at herself I think."

"And your father?"

"I can't remember—probably not. Oh, and I remember that we met a man with white hair who was hitchhiking all over the country. He had a mirror hanging up in a tree—a side mirror from an old car—that he looked into to shave, and he screwed his face up into all kinds of funny shapes." She looked across the bike at her Uncle and shrugged. "I was eight."

"How about the mountains? Were they as big as they look in pictures?"

"I honestly don't know. My ears popped a lot, though, when we were driving up and down the passes. And the air was cold, and it smelled good."

Emery sighed. "I guess I'll just have to go one day." But he made it sound like an impossibly distant dream.

Emery woke up one morning with the unaccountable sense that the cabin had shifted. He knew it couldn't be so. He'd built the place himself, had sunk the foundation well past the frost line and plumbed it true. Throughout the day he found himself putting things down, and a minute later picking them up—he'd swear—an inch to the left. Even Albert, that evening, started off flopped next to the couch and later rose from a spot almost in the kitchen to follow Georgia out to the trailer.

"I've slipped a gear," thought Emery that night in bed. After lying awake for almost fifteen minutes—his version of insomnia—he actually went and got out his four-foot level and laid it across the living room floorboards. The bubble floated dead center, no matter which way he turned it.

He sat in his chair thinking about frost heave and shifting ground, continental plates and cardinal directions. What had happened to his dream of the West, of the Rockies, he wondered? Maybe it had just been an excuse, a destination after his mother died, when there didn't seem to be much else to point him one way or another. It was a dream that had lingered ... but if he was going to start losing his mind now, well, he might never make it. He picked up a book and switched on the reading lamp.

The motorcycle was almost done. Maybe that was it, he thought, looking up again. Maybe that's what was shifting. Georgia would finish the motorcycle, and he'd teach her to ride, and then she'd be gone. And what then? Back to normal, he thought firmly. He'd miss her, maybe, and the hound. But wouldn't it be nice to cook for one, to not worry when she didn't come back from running errands when she said she would, to walk from one end of the cabin to the other without having to step around anything that didn't belong to him? He held resolutely to that thought.

And then one day the motorcycle was done. Georgia and Emery stood wiping the last smudges off the cowling, reluctant to step back. Neither of them knew what to say.

"Start it," said Emery at last.

"Start it?"

"Why not? I've got gas in the shed."

"Oh, God, I don't think I can."

"Humph," Emery grunted.

"Well, I mean I can. What if it doesn't work?"

Emery didn't bother to answer that. "Unclamp the front wheel from the stand and we'll back it off—make sure it's out of gear." Together they rolled it over the doorsill and down into the yard. Georgia couldn't take her eyes off it. It was cream colored and gleaming with chrome, a little retro in its low curving lines, a roadbike that wouldn't mind a little dirt now and then. When Emery returned from the shed with a red gas can and a funnel, she was standing with her hand on the right handgrip, gently putting pressure on the accelerator, not enough to twist it much, just to feel its resistance.

"We should have a bottle of champagne," she said. "Or a voodoo blessing or something."

Setting the gas can and funnel on the step, Emery changed course and went into the cabin. He returned a few minutes later with something wrapped in a small piece of faded pink tissue paper. "Here," he said. "For you."

It was a small charm on a thin gold chain. She took it from the tissue and held it up—a little horse, poised as if jumping over a great fence.

"Uncle Emery. Where did you get this?"

"It's kind of old. But I can't tell you where it came from."

"Why not?"

"I just can't. But it's for you, now. It's not much, but maybe it'll bring you luck," he said. "… Don't cry."

Albert padded over and sniffed the bike. "Don't you dare lift your leg," Georgia told him, wiping her nose. "Jeez, I'm going to have to get you a sidecar."

"He can stay with me when you go," said Emery.

"Hold on. You're getting ahead of me here," Georgia said. "Number one, I don't know if I'm going to ride this thing at all."

Emery nodded and didn't even crack a smile.

"And two, maybe you'll be coming with me. I don't know if I want to take off without some company. And three," she looked at Albert, "... he's my buddy. I'm not sure I can stand to leave him behind. Just look at him." Albert had flopped down facing the lake, looking perfectly content.

"Well, you should probably start thinking about it. And you might want to think about going soon, unless you want to wait out the winter."

Georgia looked uncertainly up at the sky, as if expecting it to suddenly start spitting snow. Then she looked out around the lake, and noticed for the first time that some of the trees were changing from their deep summer green to a lighter hue, vaguely golden in places, rusty in others. When did that happen?

"Let's just start her up and see how she sounds," Emery said.

Georgia got some oil from the back of Emery's truck and filled the bike's reservoir. Emery handed her the funnel and together they ran gas into the tank, ceremoniously tucking a rag under the funnel when Georgia lifted it out, so no stray drop would sully the pristine machinery.

"Prime her a little," said Emery.

There was no more hesitation. Her moves went smoothly from one step to the next as she opened the gas valve and pulled the choke, rolled back a little to make sure she wasn't in gear, turned the key, and pressed the starter.

11

IF GEORGIA WAS EXPECTING disappointment, she was way off the mark. When the motorcycle came alive, when she felt it and heard it, it was completely new, completely surprising, and absolutely, unconditionally right.

For the next few days she and Emery made minor adjustments on it, and Georgia spent a lot of practice time on the Honda. And then finally it was time to try the new baby out. They chose a morning after a light drizzle, when the dirt road was dampened down. Mel came out from town to help with the test drive. His wife Barbara came along with him. She wouldn't let them start until she'd taken pictures of Georgia on the bike, and Georgia with a grinning Emery on the bike, and one, which she later framed, of Georgia straddling the bike with Albert draped placidly across the touring seat behind her, one leg hanging down and his head propped up for the camera by Emery's disembodied hand.

Emery and Barbara stood back and watched as Mel, with Georgia behind him clutching his skinny waist, took off on the first trial run. After the sound of the motorcycle receded, the other sounds of the day settled back into place. Emery pulled folding chairs out of the shed and they sat down in the yard to wait. The humid air still had a morning coolness. The leaves were turning brittle and the lank breeze set them rustling against each other. Throughout the summer they'd filtered the sunlight in shifting deep green shadows. There was a mellower cast to the air now. The insects and birds no longer sang out with youthful abandon. All the bustle of bird families—

the nest building, the frantic feeding, all the comings and goings as parents brought friends and relatives around to admire their broods, the dippy antics of the fledglings—all of that had changed to the packing-up of fall. Blackbirds made conspicuous trial runs, flocks collecting and circling, extending farther and farther as the season progressed, gathering up the neighborhood for migration.

Presently the sound of the returning motorcycle could be heard down the road. Mel and Georgia pulled up. "Beautiful," Mel said. "Beautiful."

Georgia didn't seem to be able to speak.

They left the bike running while Mel had Georgia listen to the various thrummings and revvings. "All right," he said at last. "Are you ready for a solo?"

She wasn't as scared as the day she'd first taken off on the old Honda a month ago, but her heart surged with an excitement and a fullness she'd forgotten existed. She felt her pulse throb against the helmet's strap when at first she pulled it too tight. Her feet were steady on the ground, though, as she righted the bike. The motorcycle felt solid and balanced under her, the padded seat smooth and familiar. She kicked the stand back and toed the gear lever into first. The clutch had a different feel from the Honda and she lurched a little as she eased out, but then she was off and riding.

If home was the air, or the road, then she'd found it. Home was movement. How could she have forgotten this? She used to run as a child, she suddenly remembered. Run everywhere—through the neighborhood, to the store, down to the creek to play on the rocks. She remembered ... But first she had to concentrate on the bike, on the road. Focus or crash. The motorcycle was steady and sound. She would paint a red zigzag down the cream white, like an eggshell ready to hatch. She'd sell her house.... The road curved and she leaned into it, just like she'd practiced, but now as she focused her mind and settled into it, she felt herself and the bike moving together as a single body. It suddenly didn't feel like simply a lean. It felt like a thought—an intention made real.

Once, a long time ago, she'd ridden a stallion—a gray four year-old, too big for her and way beyond her ability—that belonged to a friend's father. The horse was well trained, though, and perfectly secure in his movements. Her body and her mind together had felt his motion, his immense controlled power, as they rode at a walk, then a trot, over the green weedy hills. They descended into a gully to cross an old creek bed. Her friend's brother, riding with them, had warned her that the stallion liked to take off up the slope on the far side. The warm leather of the reins hung lightly from Georgia's small hands, along the dappled neck, to the bit in the horse's mouth. At the exact split-second she felt his haunches tensing behind her, she twitched her fingers back a fraction. The big horse responded immediately. Holding back from his intended leap out of the gully, he walked politely up the slope.

"Guess he didn't feel like doing it today," said the brother. Georgia realized the boy hadn't even noticed the communication between her and the horse—it had been so instantaneous, so perfect.

Her body remembered the feeling of that long-ago day as the bike responded to her movements with contained power. She briefly touched the fingers of her left hand to the notch of her throat, where the little horse on its chain hung hidden against her skin. Then she just rode.

When at last she returned, rounding the final curve, Georgia could see Uncle Emery standing by the edge of the road. As soon as he caught sight of her, he sauntered back over to his chair and sat down in a pretty fair imitation of nonchalance.

"Do you know what you're going to do now?" Emery asked later, after Mel and Barbara had gone. Georgia followed him around to the side of the cabin. He carried a bucket and scrub brush and began cleaning off the bottom of the upended canoe.

Georgia sat on the ground with Albert's head in her lap. "I guess I'll be going back home."

"You can stay here as long as you like, you know. Once you get the bike registered, you might want to spend some time getting used to it before you take off."

"Thanks, Uncle Emery. I'd really like to, but I think I'm going to have to get a little money together first. And, oh—I didn't tell you!"

"What?"

"I'd forgotten all about it. It came with the manual and I taped it inside the back cover so I wouldn't lose it, and then completely forgot. A gift certificate—for a paint job. Can you believe it?"

"I have a hard time believing any of this, frankly."

"I know. I was supposed to have used it before putting the bike together, in case I wanted to change the color. I like the color, though.... I think I might get a blaze put across it." She felt unaccountably shy about mentioning the hatching-egg idea. "The place is in the Cities, though. So I figured I'd go down and get the bike registered down there."

"You'll be needing a ride down for it, then."

"If it's not too much trouble. I hate to make you go down there again, but ..."

"No trouble," said Emery. He continued to scrub the canoe, keeping his unexpectedly damp eyes safely trained on a patch of dried algae.

Georgia stretched out on the ground next to Albert and absently stroked his head. For a long time there was no sound except the small lapping at the shore and the sweep of a scrub brush against aluminum. "You've been so wonderful to me," Georgia finally said to Emery. "I'm going to miss you." She looked at him but he only nodded, his head turned away as he reached across the canoe and worked at a particularly resistant spot.

After a moment he cleared his throat and said, "When do you want to go?"

"Tomorrow, I guess."

They drove down in the morning, Georgia in her old Chevy, Emery behind in his pickup with the motorcycle tied down in the bed.

The following day Emery returned home alone. He sat down in his easy chair. Georgia, the dog, and the motorcycle were gone. He had the whole place to himself. He regarded the empty shelves that had held rows and rows of o-rings, shims, washers, bolts. Well, now he'd be able to reshelve the books that had sat stacked in the corner of his bedroom all this time. He could pull out that old generator he'd been restoring and get back to work on it. He could move the old trunk back out here, along the wall where he was used to having it.

He looked around at the strange emptiness. His shoulders sagged and his eyes filled with sorrow. "Good luck, niece," he whispered. "Don't be a stranger."

That evening in Minneapolis, Georgia sat in Corrine's kitchen as dusk fell, taking a breath after telling her friend all about Emery, the bike, Mel and Barbara, Albert's antics—everything and everyone.

"Your uncle sounds like a sweetheart," said Corrine, pulling a sack of flour from a cabinet.

"He is. I can't believe the way he just took us in like that. And all the work he did, acting like it was nothing. I wish I could knit or make him a quilt or something. I don't know how to begin to thank him."

"I tell you what. You give me a ride on that bike of yours and I'll bake him whatever you want. You can start with that."

"It's a deal."

"So," said Corrine, continuing to assemble ingredients for her current recipe. "The bike's ready to go."

"Yeah, just about," said Georgia.

"And you got a gift certificate from the Mystery Motorcycle Man."

"Yeah."

"My, oh my," drawled Corrine. "You do know how to pick your fairy angels. So when are you thinking about leaving on your travels?"

"I'm not sure. I went down to Manpower today and got a temp job packing nuts. By the time I've got a little more cash in the bank, I just hope the weather's still good. I want to get out on the road with enough time to see a few things before I have to turn around and beat winter back. I wish I didn't have to wait. Wouldn't it be great to just take off, not worry about time or money? ... I've thought of selling my house."

"You're kidding."

"No. It's just a drain, now that I've had to buy Jimmy out, and without his income. It was never my dream house anyway.... I don't know what I'll decide. I'm just thinking about it."

They heard Corrine's mother come out of her room and stop at the hall mirror. Corrine glanced out the window at the light drizzle just visible in the streetlights. "Could you get the umbrella down from the closet?" she asked Georgia. "Mama won't take it unless I put it in her hand, and then she complains about her hair going all tight."

Mrs. Perriera sashayed into the kitchen, swirling the flowered skirt of her size 22 for their approval.

"You look very nice, Mrs. P."

"Lookin' good, Mama," Corrine seconded.

"Gotta get me some new shoes to go with this, though. These old things are the best dancing shoes I ever had but they ain't gonna last, the way Carl's got me going every night."

A car door sounded out front. "Here he is now," Corrine said. Her mother gave a last flounce and went to the hall.

Georgia trailed her out of the kitchen and found the umbrella in the hall closet. Mrs. Perriera opened the front door to a tall, grizzle-haired man snazzily outfitted in a silver-gray zoot suit, and gave him a good looking-over. "My, yes," she said. "You're looking sharp tonight, Carl."

"And you look mighty fine yourself," Carl replied, "Pretty as can be." He took her arm to help her down the front steps. Georgia darted out at the last second and pushed the umbrella into Mrs. Perriera's free hand. "Thank you, honey," the older woman said, opening it. "I better not show up looking like a drowned rat tonight, of all nights."

Georgia rejoined Corrine in the kitchen. "They're taking pictures for the community newsletter," explained Corrine.

"Oh. Well, your mother sure knows how to make the most of life, doesn't she?"

"She wasn't always like that. After daddy died she just kind of went through the motions. Then when she and my brother Aaron got in that accident, when Mama hurt her head so bad, and her eye and all, Aaron got real depressed, feeling guilty, you know. So once she started walking good again, she made him take her dancing. She called it her balance therapy, but I think it was more for my brother. He even ended up meeting his wife there at the dance club. Anyway, he and Mama got pretty good. You should see them together. And Mama's been a dancing fool ever since."

"Well, she's my hero."

"Yeah, me too. Some days."

Georgia laughed. "So. What are you making?"

Corrine was mixing ingredients, as always, without the inconvenience of measuring devices. Cornmeal and flour were poured directly from their bags into a large bowl, followed by pinches of this and handfuls of that, in addition to which Corrine was able to talk and to keep track of the soccer game turned down low on the little TV in the corner.

"Hush puppies."

"Hush Puppies? This late?"

"Just the batter. Mama's gonna want some tomorrow."

Georgia knew for a fact Corrine's mother hadn't said a word about hush puppies. She also knew that when tomorrow came around, Corrine would be proved exactly right. Her sense of food was one of the great mysteries of the modern world.

Corrine looked up while she stirred. "I'm serious about getting a ride on that motorcycle of yours, you know."

"Okay, sure, if you trust me enough. I'm pretty new at this. I've got to get it registered first." Georgia paused, then said. "You should come with me."

Corrine cracked an egg one-handed into the dry mixture.

"On my trip," Georgia clarified, but Corrine knew what she meant.

"Oh, yeah," she said. "I can just see my fat butt riding a motorcycle across America."

"Mine's gonna be."

"Honey, I got you all beat to hell in the hip department. Well," Corrine shrugged, "Who knows? Maybe I will." They both knew she wouldn't come in the end, but they liked the idea anyway.

"We could go see your grandpa in Texas."

Corrine smiled. "Oh, I can see us wheeling up to old grandpa's tidy little house, in his tidy little neighborhood, with all his prissy neighbors watching through their curtains. We'll have to go get ourselves some tattoos first."

"Motorcycle Babes."

"Harlots on Hogs."

"I heart Mom."

Corrine put her hand over her heart. "A big one right here and a neckline down to here." She went back to her stirring. "So, tell me. Are you going to give the bike a name? You've always named your cars."

"I don't know. I want to get the feel of her first."

"Like an Indian kid."

"Yeah." Making swirls in the dusting of flour on the countertop with her fingertips, Georgia was silent for a while. "It *is* kind of a spiritual thing, you know."

"I know, honey. You don't go quitting your job, and selling your house, and taking off on a motorcycle that fell like manna from heaven into your front yard, without having some thoughts about your soul. Mama thinks you're crazy and she loves it. She's in a real go-get-'em phase right now."

"Good for her."

"Well, this is ready to go." Corrine covered the bowl with Saran Wrap and slid it into the refrigerator. "You want to go spy on her?"

Georgia laughed, "Who, your mother?"

"Why not? They're just down at the Community Center."

"What are we going to do, drink beer and sneak around through the bushes to peer in the windows?"

"That, or walk through the front door."

"Will they make us dance?"

"What do you care? You're a wild woman, remember?"

"Oh, yeah, I keep forgetting."

Georgia broke down the motorcycle just enough to remove the

gas tank and take it over to be painted with a bright red zigzag down each side. Taking it apart and putting it back together made her miss Emery, but also gave her a surge of pleasure in her ability to use the manual on her own. It was suddenly making so much sense—it was no longer just a pile of parts to be put together by rote, but had assumed a comprehensible form based on logic and function.

Once it was back together again, she had to borrow a pickup to get it to Motor Vehicles. She couldn't believe that the first person who came into her mind to ask was Jimmy. Of course she rejected him even before the thought was fully formed, even before she remembered that he probably wasn't even in Minnesota anymore. Instead she asked Corrine's cousin Brenda and her boyfriend if they wouldn't mind.

A matched set, Georgia thought when she first saw them. They'd probably live together forever, ending up as charming, shrunken little bookends. Either that or they'd get so sick of each other by the end of winter they'd never want to see each other again. For now, though, they worked together in apparent bliss, helping to roll the bike up a makeshift ramp into the back of Keith's truck and tying it down like a professional team.

The State of Minnesota had a surprise in store for Georgia. Two, in fact. The vehicle inspector was a bored young man who looked increasingly less bored and more worried as he checked over Georgia's motorcycle. "Is this factory or reconstructed? ... Where are the numbers? ... This can't be right, there aren't enough digits.... I think you've got a problem here, lady. You need proof of ownership or you'll have to get it bonded."

Georgia waited dejectedly in the registration line to see what she should do, while Keith and Brenda went out for a Slurpee.

But a better surprise awaited Georgia at the counter. The clerk listened to her story, looked at the inspector's form, and typed the information into the computer. She changed screens and continued typing for a remarkably long time, then handed Georgia a printout. "Sign here," she said.

Georgia signed. The woman reached down to a shelf and put a small license plate onto the counter.

When Georgia continued standing there the woman said, "That's it, you're done."

"That's it? Why did the guy tell me I needed all that other stuff?"

"Oh, you did. It was already entered."

"What?"

"Already in the computer. Unusual. And paid for."

"Paid for? Who paid it?"

"It doesn't say. Look, ma'am, there are a lot of other people waiting."

Nobody Georgia talked to, that day or later, had ever heard of a registration on a home-built motorcycle going that smoothly.

Her next step was to get her permanent motorcycle license, to replace the learner's she'd gotten when she started practicing on the Honda. She passed the test with flying colors. Things were moving along so fast that it was all over before she had time to get nervous.

"Are you going to ride it home?" Brenda asked.

But Georgia chickened out at that. "I think I better have you drive it there. There's an awful lot of traffic and I don't think I—"

"No problem," said Keith.

By five in the morning the day after registering the bike, Georgia was so keyed up she gave up trying to sleep. She couldn't eat either, or sit still, so she finally got dressed to ride and went outside. The motorcycle stood before her, low and sleek and gleaming, still its original eggshell color but now with its newly painted zigzagged stripes. It had dark brown leather seats, the front one sitting low, the touring seat behind it stepped up a little higher, plus saddlebags and a fair-sized trunk mounted on the back. Triple-plated chrome reflected the first sunlight.

Through the side streets of the early hour, with no Mel for guidance and no Uncle Emery for moral support, she rode. She felt pretty shaky at first. It wasn't like on the dirt road at Emery's—these streets were hard and indifferent. And soon there was traffic. She rode with fear and self-conscious pride. She was so exhausted by the end of an hour she could hardly trust herself to get back home.

Her next ride was better, and the next one better yet. Her spirits began to rise and then to soar. She wasn't sure she trusted feeling this euphoric so she tempered her happiness with a more familiar emotion—worry. The whole idea of setting out cross-country was unsettling. She'd miss her dog. And what if she fell off and broke her neck, or got so smashed up she'd suffer the rest of her life in pain. No, she wouldn't think about that. But there was also the nagging worry that she'd take off on her trip only to find that life all over was the same old grind. Maybe there was nothing new to discover in the world—now wouldn't that be depressing?

She thought maybe she ought to just park the bike in her shed, get a job, and wait to see if whoever had sent it would come to claim it. And if that happened she should charge a big damn bundle for all the labor of putting it together, not to mention the loss of her job and the psychological trauma of thinking her life was changing forever, opening up, just to find it slamming shut again. But no, if she put it in the shed, *she'd* be the one closing the door. And anyway, hadn't the experience of building a motorcycle put her way ahead of the game already?

She knew she had to make a decision soon. If she waited too long, winter would be here and she'd be forced to hunker down with a regular job. But making decisions was like riding the bike itself, a matter of confidence and balance. Hesitation was perilous, but so were hasty moves, and she didn't trust herself to always know the difference. She decided to put away a little more money and then to take off if the forecast looked good.

The nut packing ended, and she took another temp job doing inventory at a plumbing supply company in south Minneapolis. She'd ride the motorcycle to work. It would be good practice, she thought.

She was waiting at an intersection when a semi tried to make a left turn onto her street. It hadn't gone wide enough and the driver motioned for her to back up, but she was blocked in. By the time she maneuvered out of the way, the light had changed. The truck cleared the turn and a car behind her honked for her to go.

She was still a little flustered as she reached the stretch of road that opened up to 50mph. Traffic jockeyed for position in the rush to work. An airport van cut in front of her.

She never saw what happened in front of the van to make it stop so abruptly. All she knew was that the back of the van suddenly seemed to be way too big, she was too close ... and then time lost its meaning. If she swerved to the right, she might just barely have room to squeeze between the van and the SUV in the turn lane, but although everything seemed to be going in slow motion, there wasn't even an instant to act. It was already too late. She slammed on her brakes.

The front wheel locked and the bike folded up under her.

Georgia lay on the road. For a moment it seemed like everything might be all right. Then she breathed. The pain in her leg overtook her with the same speed as the rush toward the van. Her arm was bent under her, but when she tried to move it, she gasped as her shoulder muscles caught on something that should not have been there. This was all wrong. She could see the motorcycle lying on its side a little ways from her. Its cracked-egg motif looked prophetic now, a bloody omen—not of birth, but of shattered dreams. Humpty Dumpty. The bike's front wheel spun slowly, a defunct hope in a useless breeze. Bent metal glinted under the sun of a fresh and promising fall morning.

The sky was clear, the sunlight warm on the skin while the crisp, cool air swept the city with the scent of northern plains. But what Georgia was left with was the smell of leaking gas, of pavement under her nose, of her own blood and snot, and the feel of the world closing in as people came to help or to look. They formed a wall around her, blocking out the little bit of horizon that had been visible at the end of the long converging lines of the road ahead.

Her parents came from Wisconsin. They tried persuading her to go back with them when she was released from the hospital, but she wouldn't consider it. It was just too much of a strain to be around them. She tried to act cheerful so they'd go away and leave her alone, and finally convinced them she was fine, she had plenty of friends who could give her a hand if she needed it, and besides, she'd get better faster at her own house since she'd have to do more for herself. It would build up her strength. Her mother reluctantly bought the argument, but only because she could tell Bernie was anxious to get back to Foxton, and he bought it only because he could tell his daughter wanted them to leave.

"I'm glad you came, though," Georgia told them, and she was. Even though she couldn't wait for them to be gone, it was reassuring to know they loved her.

Once Georgia was home, Corrine came over often with offerings of hot food and DVDs. She sat by the bed trying to get her friend to say she was feeling bad or that something hurt, so she could at least try to do something about it, but Georgia told her the painkillers were working fine and a broken leg wasn't the end of the world. Finally Corrine's patience wore thin.

"That's right, it's not the end of the world. So why are you acting like it is?"

"I'm not," said Georgia.

"You haven't even asked about the motorcycle."

"You told me they took it away."

"Well, if you want to know, your Uncle Emery is coming down tomorrow, and he's taking it back up to his place to see if he and his friend can fix it up. He said he'll be here around one."

"That's nice."

"Jesus, girl! It was an accident. I'm getting tired of you sitting here feeling sorry for your poor self. I'm leaving now. I'll be back tomorrow, probably late—I got Mama's doctor's appointment after work."

"You don't have to come. It's probably too much trouble."

"Well, it's *my* trouble. I'll come if I want to. Shit," she said, and left.

Everyone got pretty much the same response from Georgia. She was polite and closed off. She thanked Emery for taking the bike, but told him not to fix it until she could make some money to pay for it. Corrine accused her of trying to drive everyone away so she could pity herself better alone.

Her right leg was broken, her pelvic bone chipped, her collarbone broken, she was generally banged up and had lost some skin, but her doctor told her that with physical therapy and commitment there was nothing that wouldn't eventually heal, especially with a good diet and a course of exercise at home.

Right, thought Georgia. Her main problem now, as she saw it, was money. When she quit her job at the chicken factory, she'd lost her insurance and hadn't thought twice about it. She hadn't signed up for the temp agency insurance deal either, wanting to save every penny and thinking she'd probably be there for only a few weeks anyway. She had her house listed, but it hadn't sold yet and another payment was coming due. For once Georgia accepted help from her parents, just so she wouldn't lose the house. She got a job making phone sales from home and found it wasn't as hard as she thought it would be. The people who were going to hang up on her or yell at her were going to, no matter what she said—she didn't take it personally, and in fact saved up a few choice comments for possible future use of her own—and the people who were going to buy something probably would have anyway, for the convenience. But it was a lousy way to earn a living. Maybe if she had four children running around and a wild sex life, she would have welcomed a spell of boredom during the day. As it was, she felt isolated and depressed. But at least it wasn't the constant cold and endless repetition of the chicken line.

She healed slowly. She hated her physical therapist, who apparently had one default mood—joviality—and she didn't have the money for him anyway, so after a couple of weeks she quit. It took a winter of aching and irritation before she felt like doing anything other than the bare necessities, except in unpredictable bursts of furious efficiency. If it wasn't for Albert she might not have gotten anything resembling exercise at all. She tried to give him a little walk each day, although when the sidewalks were icy she was afraid of falling and resorted to letting him wade through the snow in the backyard while she made a show of throwing snowballs for him. He would invariably regard her with blank pity and return to the door to go inside.

One evening in early spring, Corrine came in with a covered bowl and set it down on the kitchen table, where Georgia sat stirring through a clutter of magazines and junk mail. "Mama made you balas de batada doce—Brazilian sweet potato balls," she said.

"Thanks. I'll give her a call tomorrow." The soundtrack of an old movie could be heard faintly from the TV in the bedroom.

Corrine put her hands on her hips. "Okay, Georgia. That's enough."

"What?" She hunched her shoulders slightly, and poked at a coffee-stained pizza coupon.

"You've got to snap out of it."

Georgia looked up at her with a haunted look. "I know."

Corrine sat down, and for once didn't jump in and start talking, but just watched her friend and waited.

"I'm scared," Georgia said. "I want to snap out of it, and I keep wanting to be brave and fun again, but every time I start thinking of all the things I could do if I really tried, I start to freak out. It's like there's this all-or-nothing button inside me now. The All keeps wanting to bust out, but then the Nothing jumps in and wrestles it to the ground."

Corrine nodded, smiling a little at the image, but with a line of worry between her eyes. "I never thought about you being afraid of anything."

"I'm afraid of everything," said Georgia, looking down. "Always have been."

"Afraid of what?"

"I don't know. Maybe that if things start going good, something bad will happen. Case in point...." She spread her arms, exhibit one.

"Honey, that's not how the world works. Bad things happen, sure, but not just to beat you down. You've got to take your chances with the good stuff where you find it."

"Well, maybe I'm not sure I know what's good."

While Corrine tapped her fingernails on the table, taking this in, Georgia took the cover off the bowl of potato balls and looked in at the little cakes. She pinched a little piece off one and put it in her mouth, tasting the luscious sweet potato, the hint of coconut. She imagined Mrs. P. in Corrine's kitchen baking these wonderful treats. Balas de batada doce, a recipe she'd probably learned as a young child in the slums of São Paulo, if they ever had money for ingredients, that is, in the years before her father had had the unimaginable good fortune of landing a job with an American company, and eventually moving his family to Houston. Then she thought of Mrs. P. grown, a young widow, a mother dancing with her son after the accident that took her eye—the son she never once blamed even after the police cited him as at fault—and somehow finding the strength to dance both of them back to health.

Corrine reached over for one of the potato balls and said, "Mama's friend Carl wants to know how you're doing, by the way. I said I'd give you his best."

Georgia gave a small smile. "No, tell him he better save that for your mama. She'll get jealous if he gives it to me."

It was lame but better than nothing. Encouraged, Corrine said, "I tell you what. Let's go out this weekend. How 'bout it?"

"Sure."

"Really? That's great. Where do you want to go?"

"I don't know. The wheelchair races? Shit, sorry." Habit, thought Georgia. I need to stop doing that.

"Don't be mean, now. You walk just fine, and anyway we could do worse than watch people having fun." She tapped her foot a few times. "How about a movie?"

"Okay," Georgia agreed. "And maybe some shopping?"

"Now you're talking."

"I need some clothes. I've thought of maybe of trying to get an office job. You know, filing or something."

"Good. Good girl. See you Saturday, then?"

"If the creeks don't rise."

It was a beginning, but a slow one. By summer Georgia was

working at a store selling telephones and electronic toys. Her house finally sold in August and she moved into a small duplex, settling into a routine that mimicked her old life—going to work, walking Albert, eating, flopping into bed. If she'd been asked, she would have said she was satisfied with her life, but it felt more like resignation, illuminated only by small flickers of happiness or hope, quickly dampened.

The money from the sale of the house, after the bank got its cut and Jimmy got his, went to pay off the doctors and the hospital. She watched her checkbook and her bills. She took Albert to the vet when he got a burr deep in his ear. She had dinner at Corrine's every couple of weeks. She even dated a couple of times—a man her boss introduced her to. She didn't like him much, but at least she got to go to some new places and think some new thoughts. He took her to the planetarium once, and once to a concert. She wasn't sorry when he didn't call a third time. They didn't have much to talk about, and besides, he had hair transplants and a Hummer.

She dreamed late in the night and woke troubled in the morning, but couldn't remember why.

12

SUMMER PASSED. Another winter settled in, closing down the light and dulling Georgia's guilt about sleeping so much. Then for two weeks in January the temperature plunged, hovering well below zero. An odd thing happens when it gets that cold. Chance passersby greet each other with friendly smiles, neighbors become downright cheerful. People help each other out with a camaraderie that's brief and treasured. Faith in humanity is restored.

It was during this spell that Georgia came home from work one evening, and as usual, opened the letter box beside the door to her duplex. There, peeking out from amidst the envelopes, peachy and delicious like an enticing edge of lingerie left deliberately exposed, was a parcel pick-up slip. Georgia grabbed the mail in her mittened hand, leaving the slip caught between white envelopes, waiting to get safely inside before taking a look. She felt her blood pounding through her as she fumbled for her key.

"Hey Albert!" she hollered, shutting the door behind her. He slid off the couch with a thump, his only greeting a charitable wave of his tail as he lumbered majestically past her, stopping only when his nose touched the door.

"Okay, wait," she said.

Standing in line at the post office, she looked at the slip again, smoothing out the wrinkles her clutched hand had made. There was nothing written in the space for sender, no name or zip code. She couldn't understand the thumping of her heart. She'd already made a mess of the motorcycle and didn't expect, nor would she accept, any more handouts. Uncle Emery and Mel had finally stopped working on the bike when she told them she'd take a sledgehammer to it if they didn't. "If anyone's going to fix it," she said, "it'll be me."

But she couldn't do anything about the fluttering in her stomach as she waited for her package. When she got up to the counter and took it in her hands, she was surprised to see a return address label in the corner. In an instant, all her expectations flew out the window like the absurd birds they were. Her mother's flowered sticker, and the solid looped cursive of Georgia's name and address, beamed up at her. Now, why couldn't her mother print like you were supposed to? Georgia had repeatedly told her you were supposed to print addresses, but she never would.

"My handwriting is perfectly legible," her mother maintained.

"One of these days they won't deliver your letters."

"And on that day I'll begin to print."

Georgia opened the box in the car. Salt water taffy from Atlantic City and a letter from her mother with "Georgia" written largely across the envelope, the flap stuck down at the tip with a lick of her mother's tongue. Georgia had forgotten her parents were going on vacation. She'd have to call them next week. But right now she had the stupidest urge to cry. What on earth had she been thinking?

That night she couldn't get to sleep for anything. She ate half the box of taffy but it only made her feel bloated. She finally looked at Albert on the floor, sighed, and hauled him onto the bed. She stroked one long ear while she thought of all the things she needed to do the next day. Bills first, then shopping. She was out of cereal. She had to call about her auto insurance rate before the next premium was due. Toothpaste. All these things skipped through her head and she knew she'd forget them by morning unless she got up and made a list, especially since it looked like she'd be getting less than five—no, four—hours of sleep.

When she finally began to drift off she had a vision of the motorcycle, but it was green, and.... She jerked awake, grunted in irritation at finding herself conscious again, and began an interminable course of counting backward. Toward dawn she slept for an hour or so, and woke to a roar surging up from her dreams—a locomotive ... no, a four-stroke engine, and a view of dappled pavement flowing toward her beneath a tunnel of trees.

She had a miserable day at work. There were almost no customers until noon and then they flooded in with dirty, dripping snow boots, with demands and returns and questions, which Georgia on any other day would have accepted as a normal part of the electronically-uninitiated learning curve, but which today seemed just plain ignorant. The afternoon slowed again to an excruciating near-standstill. She could hardly keep her eyes open. She tried to keep busy with whatever small tasks she could find, and then she tried to at least look busy.

Her boss had an earache but had come in anyway, sitting grumpily and unproductively in the back office. After the third time she told Georgia to straighten merchandise that didn't need straightening, Georgia almost walked out. She played one-way conversations in her head—"If you feel so lousy, why don't you go home?... I'm doing my job just fine. If you don't like it, then fire me and see if you can find somebody half as good.... I have better things to do than stand around here all day."

But she didn't have anything better to do. Her daily life had spiraled down to a monotony approaching the deadly tedium of the chicken factory. Her bones were mended, her debts were almost paid, she had no pressing worries, and she was bored to tears. She sensed that even Corrine was getting seriously tired of her lack of ambition. Anyway, Corrine was busy now with her daughter, Joelle, who was home for a visit.

When Georgia walked in the door that evening and smelled a dead mouse in her sink, she stood poised for a moment between two courses of action, two worlds. Her whole life seemed to hang in the balance, until it seemed impossible *not* to do something, whatever that something might be.... Either to take that final comforting plunge into despair, or to dive the other way into the icy quarry waters of the living. She wobbled for an agonizing moment, and then instead of dissolving into tears and crawling into bed with taffy and the remote, she picked up the phone and called her uncle.

"Can I come up this weekend?" she asked him in a voice that sounded more pitiful than she liked. "Just for a visit?"

"Yup."

"Oh ... okay then. I'll see you on Friday probably, if I can get off early. It might be late. Is that all right?"

"Yup."

"Okay. Good. Well ... I'll see you then."

The wind was shifting around to the south and more snow seemed likely when Georgia got off work at noon on Friday. She waited impatiently while Albert did his business in the back yard, then loaded him and her suitcase into the car, which was already gassed up and ready to go. This was different from a year and a half ago, when she'd driven to Emery's filled with excitement—mystified but ready to embark on something brand new. Now she had already tried and failed to face her fears, and she honestly didn't know why she was running back to him. She told herself it was just to get away for a while, to alleviate the blues that were growing on her with the scanty daylight and imprisoning cold. She couldn't expect to be patted on the back or to find an indulgent ear to listen to her whining. Emery was a good old fellow but he couldn't be expected to understand how paralyzing her life felt. Second thoughts almost made her pull off the highway at Hinkley and turn around, but the idea of looking at her apartment walls for two more days was enough to keep her headed north.

She underestimated Emery. It's true he wouldn't have known how to coddle her with sympathy and muffins and tell her everything was going to be okay. But that turned out not to matter. Her car crunched into the frozen yard, and Albert gave a short yowl of recognition. Emery came out of the cabin with a battery lantern in one hand and an extension cord looped over his shoulder.

"Jesus, Uncle Emery, put some shoes on. It's 20 below."

"You got more than one suitcase?"

"No, but...!"

He was bending down looking at the front of her car. "Go on in. I'm just going to plug you in." He unplugged the engine heater of his truck, reconnected it to a splitter, and ran the second cord to the plug hanging from her front grill. He hopped back into the cabin and stripped his socks off. "Cold," he said.

Georgia laughed. "Told ya." She was suddenly very glad to be there. The big braided rug and the shabby sofa felt as familiar as her childhood pajamas. With a smile at her elfin uncle dancing around, pulling out blankets, telling her she'd sleep on the sofa if that was okay 'cause there was no heat in the trailer, she went to the kitchen and put the kettle on. Emery seemed very happy to see her. Albert stood in the middle of the floor and sniffed the air, then, content, flopped on the rug like he'd never been gone.

The only difference was that the chair and the old trunk Emery used for storage were back in their pre-motorcycle place against the wall. Georgia couldn't help glancing over at them as she sat on the sofa to drink her Sanka. Her uncle, in his easy chair, caught her look. "The bike's in the shed. We can take a look at it in the morning if you want."

Georgia thought for about half a second before she knew she'd already made up her mind. "Yeah," she said.

The bike wasn't as bad as she'd imagined, but it was bad enough. The handlebars had taken a hit, the back wheel was bent, and one saddlebag was a dead loss. Emery said they'd have to true everything up again and Mel wanted to x-ray the frame to make sure it was sound. The clutch lever had snapped off but somehow the cable—in fact all the cables and wiring—were intact. The rest was cosmetic. The trunk had a pretty good-sized dent in it.

"I'm going to have her painted green this time," she told her uncle. "Like that." She pointed to a faded scrap of corduroy shirt that was folded up on the rag pile. It was a soft, smoky olive green.

"Let's roll her inside before the snow flies," Emery said.

The temperature had risen the night before, and they'd awakened to a late dawn, snow clouds raking in from the west. The air at ground level was absolutely still. A quiet expectancy hung over the frozen lake. Together they pushed the bike to the cabin and ramped it up the steps. Emery had built a deck during the summer. He looked a little embarrassed over Georgia's compliments. "Well, it's not much. I just kind of liked those ones down at the resorts. Used a lot of my own wood."

"You did?"

"Yah, there were some dead cedars over by the creek," he pointed, with what Georgia correctly assumed was perfect accuracy, through the woods to the northeast. "I've been sitting on them for a couple of years, waiting for them to cure, and just figured I'd better use them. Nice straight grain."

The snow started falling about midday, sparse little flakes at first, thickening through the afternoon. Georgia and Emery stripped down the motorcycle, taking stock of what needed replacing and what could be fixed. Georgia took pleasure in handling the metal, the tools fitting into her hands like old friends. She and Emery worked amiably, having to turn on lights by early afternoon as the snow came down more heavily. They kept at it through the weekend, building up the fire in the woodstove at intervals, eating when they felt like it. They ran into a few problems that couldn't be solved without going into town and getting parts, but there was plenty to do in the meantime, so on Sunday afternoon Georgia was glad to look outside at the accumulated snow and realize that driving back to the Cities would be impossible. "Snowbound," she declared with satisfaction. And then she had second thoughts. Stuck here without the parts they needed, without a lake to swim in, would she get on Uncle Emery's nerves? No, not at all, he told her, stay as long as you like.

The phone line was out on Monday, and Georgia's cell phone never worked at Emery's, but her uncle had a solution for that. He had her bundle up, and they snowmobiled across the lake to a neighbor's place on the county road. The phones were working there and Georgia called her boss to explain, without regret, why she wouldn't be in. Then she called the parts place in town to make sure they had what she needed in stock, or could order it.

"You know, what you get from them won't be quite like the original parts," Emery said. "They ought to do, though."

Georgia nodded. Nothing was like the original. Not ever. But life was a messy business and whatever would get her going would be all right.

They stayed for lunch with the neighbors, a fifty-something couple who'd taken early retirement and moved permanently to their summer house on the lake. They were happy to have company, and broke out a couple decks of cards. They insisted on teaching Georgia the rudiments of bridge, over her objections that she didn't even know how to play "Go Fish." She didn't make too much of a fool of herself and was warmed by the thin, hot coffee and good nature of her hosts. Christina told her to come back any time.

Then she and Emery were on the snowmobile, flying back across the lake. The open expanse seemed to embrace the winter light and at the same to time set it free. The world was a limitless place, where both friendship and survival were possible.

Frank Morrow's news of Georgia was delayed and distant and third-hand.

There was a fish restaurant by the river, a place called Bulwarks, where Georgia's cousin Mary Anne worked. Frank had been avoiding it for a while now, but when Libby suggested going there one night, he couldn't think of a reason to say no. He and Libby had been dating throughout the fall and winter, and what Frank had initially sensed as a comfortable connection had fast deepened to something more. He picked her up at her house and greeted her with a quiet kiss, brushing a wisp of soft coppery hair off her forehead and putting an arm around her to help her over some snowy patches as they walked to the car.

When they entered Bulwarks, Mary Anne greeted them, and taking two oversized menus from the stand, she led the way toward their table. As they crossed the room to a booth by the window she mentioned that she'd heard Georgia was up and about again, and doing okay.

"Again?" Frank was confused.

"Well, you knew about her motorcycle accident didn't you?"

Somehow Frank kept moving, although he could no longer feel his legs under him. He felt as if Georgia's bones were breaking right in front of him, her skin tearing, her blood welling up and flowing over his own hands. Mary Anne in her black skirt and white hostess blouse, holding the menus to her chest, looked back at him and paused in her explanations as she caught sight of his face. "She's fine now, though," she said. "Uncle Bernie told my mother she's working again, at some electronics gizmo store."

Frank slid into the booth and Libby sat across from him.

"Well, you two have a nice meal," Mary Anne said as she handed them their menus. "Say hi to Julius for me," she added over her shoulder to Frank, as she turned and headed toward a new group of customers waiting at the hostess stand.

Libby leaned across the table and put a hand on Frank's arm. "Are you all right?" she asked.

The muscles of his forearm moved under his jacket as he clenched and unclenched his hand. He looked at Libby with haunted eyes, and when she didn't turn away he stilled his hand.

"Let's talk later," he managed. "If that's all right with you."

She nodded.

They looked at their menus and listened to their server recite the specials. With the initial shock wearing off, Frank entered a bizarre state that somehow fused paralyzing lethargy with a restless explosion of nerve endings. He took deep deliberate breaths when he remembered to, his eyes darting to Libby's face and then away.

As the meal progressed, Frank regained some of his composure, and sensed Libby's relief. They began to talk a little about this and that, but mostly ate in silence.

Afterwards, they went to a quiet bar and sat in a back corner with coffee. Frank took Libby's hand for a minute, then he gave it a little squeeze before letting go. Maybe it was the shock still upon him, or maybe it was the sense of clarity and strength he felt in Libby's presence, but he was sure now of what he intended to do. He didn't know how, after so many years, he was going to open himself up, especially to this woman he'd known for so short a time but had already grown to care so deeply about—the single person he now most feared losing. He only knew that whenever he looked away from her he saw desolation, he saw the people he'd hurt, he saw Georgia's blood and her life in ruins. And whenever he looked back at Libby's face he saw a person who was here and now, whose heart reached out to his. He saw hope and the glimmer of a future. But he knew that if he was going to love her, he'd better first give her the chance to flee.

"I had a childhood friend," he began. An icy fear in his gut told him to stop before he went any further, but he had a greater fear now. He looked into Libby's eyes and his panic ebbed. He knew he wouldn't stop now until the end. "She was a few years younger than me, but she was a neat little kid…."

He told her everything. For the first time, he told the whole story, the truth. What happened. What he did and didn't do. Why he was to blame for Georgia's life being a shambles. And his belated and misguided attempt at atonement—the gift of the motorcycle. Libby heard him out quietly, listening not only to the details of events but also to the depth of his guilt.

"But I've only made a worse mess of things," Frank concluded. "Whatever I do, or whatever I don't do, I just seem to screw up her life. I'm not good for people, Libby. I can see that." He looked up. "I think you might not want to see me anymore. It's probably—"

"Frank," Libby interrupted. "I know you're upset up about this, but—"

"No, listen, Libby. I like you—more than you know—but whatever I decide is bound to be the wrong thing. So I'm going to leave it up to you. But my honest opinion is that you should probably break it off." He looked at her earnestly for a moment and then dropped his eyes. "I know this isn't fair. I don't want you to feel like you're bailing out or anything. But I don't think I could stand to see someone I care about hurt again. You have to make the decision for us. I'm trusting you on it."

Libby shook her head. "Well, I'll think about it, Frank. That's all

I can tell you now."

"Good, —"

"But I think you're taking too much on yourself. You made a mistake, Frank, a bad one, but you're not the bad guy. You were just a kid anyway, a scrawny little adolescent kid."

Frank didn't answer. Libby tapped her fingers against the table. Frank sensed she wasn't finished but she didn't say anything, just sat there looking more and more troubled ... and gathering steam.

He was just about to tell her it was all right, he'd take her home, when she finally leaned forward and blurted, "But who do you think you are anyway—God? To know how things are going to turn out?" With quiet passion she went on. "And the girl, Georgia—what happened back then was another matter, but she's a grown woman now. She didn't have to take the motorcycle. Things happen, Frank, and people have to make up their own minds. Maybe you should give yourself a break." She slumped back and let out a breath. Her eyes were still on him.

"I think we should go now," she said. "I have to think."

It occurred to Frank, sitting in his house later that night, to wonder why he'd stayed so fixed on a single point of view for a quarter of a century. What had happened back then was something he'd never forgive himself for. But it had taken Libby to make him think it was at least possible to have some compassion for the scared kid he'd been. But to do harm by not doing something, and then do harm again by trying to do something—well, how could he see himself as anything but bad news?

It had taken a lot out of him to reveal himself to Libby. His mind was clamoring with dissonant thoughts, and the very noise of it made him want to lay his head down. He went to the bedroom, took his shoes off, and without even bothering to undress, dropped onto the bed and slept.

. . .

Libby, on the other hand, paced, tried to watch TV, played a game of computer solitaire, vacuumed every room of her house, watered the plants, and finally, at two in the morning, resigned herself to sitting in an easy chair and staring into space while her thoughts tumbled unproductively around, like clothes in a broken dryer spinning around and around and never getting dry.

Frank was a good man.... Frank might be a little unbalanced.... Frank was loving and caring.... Frank was nothing but trouble.... Frank needed someone.... *she* needed someone.... Frank wasn't worth it.... Frank was worth everything.

She could visualize him in a workshop somewhere, intently carving out motorcycle parts in some plan to redeem the world. And she remembered how he'd looked in that restaurant booth. He could never lie or be unfaithful, she decided. His pale skin and his dark, expressive eyes would be foolproof lie detectors.

She'd surprised herself with the anger she'd felt listening to him blame himself so bitterly. Certainly Frank had made a bad mistake, and was compounding it by clinging so tightly to his guilt, but who was she mad at? Frank, for not being the uncomplicated companion she sought? Or herself, for being the kind of person whose instinct was to jump ship at the first sign of trouble?

She must have slept, because the next thing she was aware of was waking stiffly in the living room chair with morning light in her eyes. A shaft of sun penetrated the room through a gap in the blinds, and for a while she watched the dust motes drift in the air. Then she got up to go to the bathroom. The same morning light that had awakened her passed through the depths of an old blue glass bottle on her bathroom sill, lighting it to a wondrous, glowing cobalt and casting blue angels on the opposite wall. Inside Libby's morning brain a sequence of childhood memories flashed, almost too fast to fathom. Her first delight at the color of a Bromo-Seltzer bottle on her grandmother's bathroom shelf—her best friend at a sleep-over, the two of them peeking into the medicine cabinet to giggle over grandma's hemorrhoid medicine, coming upon the beautiful blue glass, holding it up to the light. Midnight discussions of favorites, with that childish affinity for defining yourself by whatever your "favorite" was—favorite animal, favorite ice cream, favorite color. Blue, pink, yellow, green—

Libby's thoughts tripped and stumbled to a halt. She suddenly found herself sitting on the edge of her bathtub wondering about the social metaphors she'd also learned in childhood. Was she green with jealousy over Frank's childhood friend? Georgia certainly claimed more of Frank's emotional life than Libby did, maybe more than she ever would.

Libby wondered if this was a world she wanted to enter—jealousy, worry, hard decisions. But what if it was the only world where love existed?

She decided half a dozen times, throughout that day and the next, to break things off with Frank. What had seemed a promising relationship was, she could now see, doomed from the start. It would clearly be better to find someone less complicated, less haunted by the past, and try again. She'd succeeded in overcoming her reluctance to start dating, so she could surely get out there and find a decent guy somewhere. She'd had one good marriage—Joey had been a wonderful husband and father, and she'd loved him. Maybe she could find another good man somewhere. Or maybe she should take the promotion her company had offered, move to their headquarters in Lansing, and start over there.

But then Frank's face, his dark eyes and knitted brow, would float up before her and she'd think, but there *is* something special here. He might well be the one for me. For better or for worse, maybe, but I can't turn away from him, not without at least giving it an honest try.

Until an hour later when she'd change her mind again.

By Wednesday, Libby was so tired of her own thoughts she asked Rob and Darren from the office if she could join them in their traditional mid-week beer. They were obviously surprised, and acted so self-consciously jovial as they sat down at the bar after work that she momentarily regretted inviting herself. After a couple of glasses, though, they settled down, or maybe she just didn't care anymore. The evening achieved its purpose in one way—Libby did get a break from brooding about her dilemma. But the noise in the bar gave her a headache, and she never got drunk enough to fully appreciate the wit of her fellows.

When she got home, she went on a maudlin tour of her old photo albums. She slept, and dreamed of Joey.

All through work the next day something nagged at her. That evening she pulled out the photo albums again. She'd all but forgotten the time she and Joey had driven to California on vacation and had fought so much she'd threatened to fly home alone. She hadn't, but they'd driven without speaking for two days, and forever after she'd thought of the beautiful Yosemite Valley with aversion. And how many times had they disagreed over significant things? They could barely look at each other at election times. There was a picture of them together at her sister's wedding in '92. Joey was drunk and leaning away from her, his arm wrapped around the slim waist of some girl—a Republican probably—while Libby stood with an elbow jutting out like a poisoned arrow aimed at her husband's ribs. It wasn't always like that—of course it wasn't. They had a good marriage, better than most. But as much as they loved each other, it wasn't all paradise. There were times when she'd have just as soon been on her own. It certainly would have been easier.

So, she decided, I'm not saying I'm going to marry Frank, but I won't let the first snag that comes along make my decision for me either. We'll date.

She called him from work on Friday morning and asked if he wanted to have dinner. The sound of his voice made her glad she called. He didn't sound like a person who was about to go off the deep end any time soon. More than simple relief, Libby felt a great comfort. She was amazed at how much the tone of his voice communicated, without the awkwardness of extraneous words. It acknowledged the effort she must have made in coming to a decision, but it also reassured her that she wasn't committing to anything besides dinner. That was enough for now.

They were on the same wavelength, she realized, and that was no small thing. And aren't we all a little neurotic when you come right down to it?

13

THERE WAS A THAW in February that tricked the lilacs outside Georgia's duplex into budding. Georgia stroked one of the fattening buds with a finger. "Not yet," she said. "You'll freeze and die. Winter's not over." But she couldn't help cheering them on, despite the odds.

Indeed, winter did close in again. It seemed, in that trying season so typical of northern climates, as if spring would never come. When at long last the days began to warm, people found themselves stripping to shirtsleeves as soon as the temperature soared to a rousing 32º. Georgia felt like a liberated prisoner when she stepped from her apartment one day without having to don the burdensome layers of clothing—sweaters, parka, boots, mittens, earmuffs, not to mention long johns and extra socks. Patches of pavement emerged from under the packed snow that surfaced the side streets, and the bare branches of the trees swelled and shimmered with anticipation of spring.

Throughout the winter, Georgia had gone up to Emery's every chance she got, working on the bike, fixing it, even making a few improvements. She found some handlebars that suited her, putting her hands at a slightly better angle, taking a little strain off her wrists, which, even after all this time away from the chicken factory, still sometimes gave her trouble. Once everything was done, she'd broken the bike down and brought the parts she wanted to have painted down to the city, to the paint and powder-coat place where she still had credit on her original coupon. That done, she and

Emery had assembled them once more.

She quit her job and let her apartment go in May, and she and Albert headed north. Georgia's car overheated near Sandstone, had a flat outside Cloquet—she broke a rusted lug nut fixing it—and barely made it up the muddy bog of a road to Emery's cabin. It just generally made her glad she wouldn't have to look at the old beater again for a while.

She'd fine-tuned the bike—ad nauseum, Emery finally grumbled—on her last visit, and was ready to ride as soon as she arrived. Because of the condition of the road, they loaded the bike into the pickup and Emery drove her to the state highway. She was full of shaky courage as she made her first start.

By day three she was looking ahead with more confidence. In the morning she and Emery ramped the bike up into the truck bed and tied it down. When Georgia went to get into the cab, though, Albert was waiting, his snout lifted up to rest on the door.

"Okay, bud, you can come, if Uncle Emery doesn't mind."

"Not at all," said Emery, so Georgia hoisted Albert in.

But the old dog wasn't done. When they got to the highway, where they unloaded the bike and packed it with provisions for a more extended day's trial, Albert stood by the bike and gave a pitiful howl.

"I think he wants to come," said Georgia.

"He could probably do it. If any dog can sit still, it's Albert."

"You really think it's possible?"

"Up to you."

They ended up unpacking the bike's trunk and removing the lid. It was a tight fit, but Albert let himself be lifted up and stuffed into a position that was at least stable. "Heavy dog," Emery observed. "Thick bones," said Georgia.

"All right, I'm going to try it," she said.

Albert didn't flinch at the sound of the now-familiar engine starting up, but Emery told her afterwards that he'd looked surprised when they took off. "For Albert, anyway."

"What did he do?"

"Well, nothing really. Just his eyebrows went up, like this."

Georgia laughed. "I think you've been spending way too much time together. Well, anyway, I'm glad to know something can still surprise him."

Georgia ended up using the saddlebags for all her things and modifying the trunk into a dog bed. Emery got the Honda Nighthawk back out, and together they went on a few day trips. One time Mel joined them and they rode all the way to Winnipeg for a couple of days. "I'm getting too old for this," Emery complained at the motel restaurant that night.

"Me too," said Mel. They both looked at Georgia, younger by twenty-some years.

"I'm not saying a word."

They laughed. "And you're doing just fine, I take it," Mel teased.

Actually her hip was sore and her back ached, but she wasn't about to admit it. Instead she reached into her purse and pulled out a bottle of Tylenol. "Hors d'oeuvres anyone?" she asked.

Georgia, with Albert sailing along behind her in the converted trunk, rode down to the city to pick up her last paycheck and finish up some business. She couldn't help wanting to show off a little, too.

Corrine was suitably impressed. "Look at you," she said, shaking her head in wonder. "I like the new color. It makes me think of olive groves on a Grecian hillside."

"You're a poet," Georgia said lightly, but it made her happy.

The next day she left Albert at Corrine's and ran up to the chicken factory at lunchtime to say hello to some old friends, and maybe to rub her old supervisor's nose in it a little. Bill followed the small group out to the parking lot, but hung back at the door, leaning against the doorframe and lighting up a cigarette. He never said a word as Georgia basked in admiring comments and choruses of envy. He stubbed out his cigarette before they were halfway done and went back inside.

Georgia found herself missing Rita Solis. It didn't seem complete without her there, interested and talkative. Georgia wished something good could have happened for Rita before despair had claimed her.

She left the plant feeling a little sad. She finished her errands, resenting the city fumes and the traffic, but taking pride in navigating the busy streets with competence, not letting her fear get the upper hand. When she got back, Corrine was already home from work. Georgia washed up and joined her in the kitchen.

"Albert seems a little tired," Corrine said.

Georgia looked under the table at her dog. "He always acts that way."

"I know, but even for him."

It was hard to tell about Albert, but she scratched his back and decided to keep an eye on him. When she took her shower that night he didn't follow her in. She even called to him.

"Maybe he's not used to your shower," she said to Corrine.

Corrine nodded but didn't answer.

Georgia took Albert to the vet the next day. "Nothing wrong with him that I can see," he said. "But he's getting up there. He's ... let's see here, twelve?"

"That's right."

"Bassets sometimes get back problems, a little arthritis. If he seems stiff you can give him one aspirin a day with his meal. Make sure it's buffered, though, and if he shows any signs of gastric problems stop right away." Georgia felt old worries swirling back around her.

Corrine was forthright. "You can't take him," she said as they ate dinner that evening.

"But he likes it," said Georgia, although she knew her friend was right.

Corrine cocked her head and looked at Georgia.

"I know, I know," said Georgia. "I'm acting like a spoiled brat. 'I want my doggie.'"

"No, not spoiled. Just like someone who's going to miss her dog like crazy. But if you're going to do this thing, Georgia, you know it won't be all easy."

Georgia stuck her fork in a cube of browned potato and slid it around her plate. "I know. You're right. I just get waves of being scared, not wanting to go through with it."

"But you're going to."

She put the fork down. "Yeah."

"Take off with no plans."

"Yeah."

"Do you even know what direction you're going?"

"Nope. Not yet."

"Do you know *when* you'll know?"

"Nope." She laughed. "I'll write when I get work."

"You better do more than that," Corrine said "You better call me."

"I'll probably be calling you every day," Georgia said, reaching for the iced tea pitcher and refilling their glasses.

"That'll be fine to start with. I know you won't, though, once you get going…. Mama wants picture postcards, by the way. She wants one of Mount Rushmore, don't ask me why."

Georgia and Corrine sat up until late, talking and eating ice cream. In the morning, when Georgia loaded Albert into his seat for the ride north to Emery's, the two women hugged and said their farewells.

"Look at you, girl. It's good to see you cry," Corrine said.

"Yeah, great. How am I supposed to see the road?" She settled the helmet over her head and started the engine. She couldn't talk anymore or she'd get weepy again, so she blew Corrine a kiss, lowered the visor, and took off with a wave.

In the end she decided to leave Albert with Emery. She knew he'd be happy there and her uncle seemed pleased. "Us two old fellows," he said.

She and Emery put the trunk back together and loaded it up with tools and supplies. Georgia had a rolled-up air mattress and a new down sleeping bag in a waterproof stuff bag battened down to the sissy bar behind the seats. Maps of North America were folded neatly into the pocket of a saddlebag.

Mel and Barbara came by the day before Georgia left. After lunch on the deck, while Barbara helped Emery clear, Mel took Georgia off to the side.

"Here," he said, handing her what looked like a large pocketknife. "Just in case you need it. You hold it like this and push here."

"Jesus Christ, Mel. It's a switchblade."

"I had a troubled youth," he said. "Don't tell Barbara I gave it to you. She knows, but she's pretending not to. She hates it, and you should too, so practice with it but don't count on it for defense unless it's absolutely necessary. Oh, and by the way it's illegal most places, so ..."

"Got it. Thanks, Mel." She put it away, not knowing if she felt better or worse for having it.

. . .

The roads were barely dried out. Georgia prepared to leave on a morning of light drizzle, deciding to go before more rain turned everything back into soup, and also, she thought, before she lost her nerve. Emery stood around while she got ready, standing on one leg and then another, looking everywhere but at Georgia. Finally he mumbled something about having to run into town. "You have a good trip," he said. "Let me know if you need anything…. A good, safe trip." He looked at her for a brief moment, gave her an awkward kiss on the cheek, got into his pickup, and took off. No good with goodbyes, Georgia concluded. Well, that was all right, neither was she.

Leaving Albert was the hardest thing, but at last she had to go. She left him lying in the front yard, his head on his paws, watching birds fly over the lake. She didn't see him turn and watch her as she rode off down the road.

"The idea for the bike?" Frank said. "I don't really know."

Frank and Libby were sitting in his living room one Sunday afternoon, and Libby had finally gotten up the courage to ask about the motorcycle.

Frank frowned for a minute and Libby thought the subject might be too touchy, but then he said, "When I was at Harley I was always thinking about things that could be improved, or things I thought other companies did better. Harley's a great bike, I'm not saying it isn't, but I guess my mind just works that way. So while I was in Australia I started working on some ideas. My boss at the mine was into motorcycles. Once I had my designs on paper, he invited me out to his house and ended up letting me use his tools—

his presses and lathe and everything, until I could get a workshop of my own together at my place. He had a friend with a regular metalworking shop, too." Frank took his feet off the coffee table and reached across for a pistachio nut. He didn't eat it, just cracked the shell and sat shifting the nut back and forth between the two halves.

"That's all I spent my money on for the next couple of years. I took some anatomy classes too, to get an idea of the ergonomics of the thing. That was especially interesting. The whole thing reminded me a little of college, when I always had some project or other going."

Libby noted the shadow that came over his face, but just nodded and waited for him to go on.

"On my last vacation back in the States, I'd run into Mary Anne, and she told me Georgia was working some kind of dead-end factory job, and living with some low-life asshole—her words, not mine—so I guess I had that running around in my head, too, while I was working on the first bike. I designed it from top to bottom, putting all my ideas together. I made my own frame but I didn't have access to the best bending equipment at the time and it wasn't as good as it should have been."

Libby would have bet that "not as good as it should have been" would have been totally perfect for almost any other human on the face of the earth, but refrained from saying so.

"When I started working on Georgia's, though, I found a shop in Kalgoorlie that let me use their benders and showed me some of their techniques. It made a real difference."

"So you made two bikes?" Libby asked. "What happened to the other one? Do you still ride it?"

"No, I never did. I ended up selling it to the shop owner's brother. I liked designing and building them, but couldn't see myself riding. Or I *could* see myself riding … for about two seconds, and then careening off the road and over a cliff or something. But then I woke up one morning with this idea—I could see Georgia riding.

"I can't explain it. I never wanted to put her at risk—that was the *last* thing I wanted—but I could see her escaping from the life she was in, that I'd helped put her in. I see now how presumptuous it was." He looked down at the pistachio.

"Anyway," he went on, looking back over at Libby, sitting on the couch with her arms wrapped around her bent knees. "I finished the prototype and made a few design changes—mechanical improvements, adjustments for her size, that kind of thing. Also, I wanted her to be able to repair and replace parts without spending a fortune, and that meant staying within some standard parameters.

"Then, when I moved back to the States, I had the bike shipped to myself in pieces—engine, trannie, frame, front end—and when it got to me, I broke it down even more and went over everything to make sure nothing had been damaged in shipping.

"I think that's when the idea of sending it to her in parts came to me. I thought just getting a motorcycle out of the blue would be too much, you know? I mean how could a person get on a bike and ride it without knowing anything about it? Not knowing where it came from would be bad enough, but not knowing anything about how it worked? No, it seemed it would be better if she built up her knowledge and her confidence first. I'm sure I wasn't that logical about it. I may have rationalized some of this afterwards." He sat back and looked out the window. A couple of little kids across the street were whacking away at a plastic pop bottle, using it as a puck. They disappeared around the corner of a house, the youngest one, a girl with an awkward limp, unhesitatingly leading the way. Then the street grew quiet again.

"Sometimes it seems like the whole idea came up from out of some deep, dreaming sleep," he said. "I never would have thought of doing it that way if I'd sat down and logically planned it out. I might have never thought of doing it at all. It seemed right, though, and it appealed to a sense of ... I don't know ... mystery, I guess. Deeper things. Getting down to a place where I could help lift Georgia out of the pit she was in."

Libby watched his eyes, which seemed to have gone to whatever subterranean part of himself he'd been remembering. He glanced up at her with a troubled look.

"I did consider that she might think I was stalking her or something. I mean, what would a person think? I worried she might be freaked out by the whole thing. I suppose it was wrong for me to risk that, or any of it, really, but the way the idea came to me, and then afterwards.... It seemed the right thing to do and the right time, that's all, and I couldn't wait any longer just hoping she'd find a way to break free by herself." He shook his head and put the pistachio down.

"Here I go again. Who am I to decide something like that?" He stood and went over to the window. "Looking back," he said, his voice subdued as he stared at the street, "I can see how arrogant I was—to think I could know what anyone needs." He turned around and leaned back against the ledge.

"She could have rejected the whole thing, I suppose—in fact I thought she might. A few weeks into sending the parts, I went over to Bulwark's and tried to find out from Mary Anne if she'd heard anything. I didn't really intend to spy on Georgia, I just wanted to know, but Mary Anne never mentioned anything about it.

"And then—I'm reluctant to admit this—I did something else I'm not very proud of. I went to Minneapolis and I really did spy on her. I went to her post office when I figured she'd be getting off work, and waited for her to pick up one of the parts ... I think it might have been the shift cam assembly, it was right around that time anyway. I didn't know if she'd come. For all I knew she might've thrown out the delivery slips, and I wouldn't have blamed her. But I suppose I didn't truly think she would.

"She didn't come the first day, and as embarrassed as I was about what I was doing, I came back the next. I couldn't just leave. I don't know what I'd have done if she never came—just stood there day after day, I guess, until I was hauled off by Homeland Security or something. But she came on the second day. She stood in line—she looked tired, with her purse dragging over her shoulder—and then she pulled out a little MP3 player. I guess she'd gotten tired of standing in line day after day with nothing to do. I hadn't thought of that and felt bad, but she looked okay. Her eyes were closed for part of the time and every now and then she moved her head a little to the music. After five or ten minutes, she was up at the counter and smiling and talking to the clerk. They were getting to be old friends, and I got a good feeling in my chest, which got even better when she took the boxes and turned to leave. She looked happy. That was all I needed to know and I came home."

Libby felt closer to Frank after that day. He'd trusted her with his private thoughts, for one thing, but she also felt she could see a little more into his heart. Not just the guilt, but the generosity of his nature.

She still wasn't over the idea that he was going to be trouble, though. In fact she thought he might be a lot of trouble. She decided she should keep her options open. A sales rep asked her out and she accepted. The man seemed nice enough, and he was good-looking. The problem was that he thought so, too. Libby wanted to give him the benefit of the doubt, thinking maybe he just had first-date nerves, but by the end of dinner she was just goddamn sick of how wonderful he was. He apparently thought the date had been a great success and asked her out again. This was the part she hated. She was no good at making polite excuses. So she said something about not feeling ready to date seriously. "No problem," he said. "We can just do stuff together when I'm in town. Do you like to work out?"

"No, I'm sorry."

"That's okay, no pressure. How about a movie?"

"No, Dave. I mean I guess I'm just not ready to date at all." It made her feel ridiculous to lie. Why couldn't she just say she was already seeing someone? That at least was mostly true.

"Sure, I understand. I'll be making some sales calls next month, though. I'll see you at the store. You might change your mind by then." He wiggled his eyebrows.

Sure, she thought. When I start liking escargot in slime sauce.

Libby still wasn't ready to give up altogether. She worried that she'd get serious with Frank, and then the very next day, or the next week, she'd meet the perfect man, a man with no baggage and every attribute, the man of her dreams. Just around the corner, she thought. Then she thought, now that's a lousy way to live—thinking that the perfect *anything* is right around the corner. She was taking a yoga class at the community college with Nicole from the store, who was trying to stay fit through her pregnancy, and Libby tried to learn to breathe with deep, slow, yogic breaths and keep her mind in the present, but she wasn't very good at it yet. Her mind kept veering off whenever the idea of marriage or commitment strayed into it. What was that mantra? "Be here now?" How could she be here now and still make rational decisions about the future?

She went to a classical music concert in the park with Frank one Saturday. He brought two collapsible cloth chairs and a beach umbrella. They sat in the muggy air and let the sounds wash over them. By the end of the first piece, Libby, without any conscious effort at all, found herself breathing steadily, her diaphragm relaxed, her shoulders loose. Her mind stopped skipping around and settled into an easy peace. This is Frank, she thought. This is how he makes me feel.

Even with all her concerns about what life would be like with him, even doubting and skeptical and indecisive, just being with him was good. She reached for his hand and he took hers. She snuggled her chair up to his and rested her head on his shoulder.

They got engaged a couple months later, and soon after that had a small wedding, just family. Julius was thrilled for his brother. He loved Libby immediately, without reservation—with her soft strawberry blond hair and her big hands, and the way she walked with the awkward grace of a camel. Libby was a little overwhelmed with this huge bear of a man, but thought he'd make a fine brother-in-law.

Her children came and were perfect human beings, supportive and happy for her. They liked Frank, and if he fell short of their expectations in any way, they didn't let on. Libby knew he wasn't their father, but she also knew that for her Frank Morrow was the man, not perhaps of her dreams, but of her heart.

14

GEORGIA WANTED to see Niagara Falls but didn't want to go through Wisconsin because it felt too much like backtracking. She wanted to see Hudson Bay but wasn't sure she was ready for the wilds of Canada, and it was still too early in the year to ride north anyway. She'd always wanted to go to New Orleans and seriously considered heading south, working her way through the heartland. But she mostly wanted something totally new, some road she'd never traveled before, and south would mean passing all the way down through Minneapolis before hitting fresh territory. So she thought of Corrine's mama and headed west, destination Mount Rushmore. Her westward-dreaming uncle would approve, she thought.

She rode through farm country on secondary highways, and every place she stopped, for food or just for a break, people asked about the bike, or told stories of their own motorcycles at home or the machines of their youth. When she happened upon other motorcyclists along her way, there was no end to their courtesy and interest. She hadn't had any idea, when she'd straddled her new leather seat and set off, that she'd be entering into a community.

But what she liked best was the sense of being in the world. Every inch of air she rode through was on a direct line to her senses. She smelled the damp woods and the newly turned soil of the fields. Not secondhand, seeping through a car window a half-mile after she'd passed through, but with every breath. She felt every change in air temperature—the cool hollows, the wet chill of a creek breeze, mysterious warm spots. The air was a sea of currents and textures she'd been denied her whole life. Why had she always thought of it as *just* air? If she'd thought of its qualities at all, they'd been limited to wind and temperature—static things defined by degrees or by whether she wanted to go outside for lunch or stay in. Things went through it. She'd never really considered the air itself.

Georgia imagined something like the sea charts she'd seen on a fifth grade field trip to the nautical museum. But that would be impossible—air was too alive, too changeable, from morning to noon to night, day to day, season to season. She wondered how the birds navigated this world of theirs. Could they actually see air? Did they use some other sense to make their way? The immediacy of everything as she flew through the countryside made her feel, for the first time, a part of the natural world. A noisy part, she knew, but still ... it was glorious.

The first night, she stopped at a small campground. She hadn't camped since she was a little girl. It was good, pulling into her campsite, tired and sore, and feeling as if she were coming home. She spent some quality time with the bike—cleaning it up, checking nuts and bolts, brake and clutch cable adjustment, oil level. Then she went into the woods and collected dead twigs and small branches to make a fire. She pulled out the hotdogs and coleslaw she'd picked up at the Piggly Wiggly in the last town she'd been through, and set them optimistically on the picnic table while she tried her hand at fire building. In the stone-encircled fire pit she built a log cabin of twigs, dropped the grocery receipt in the center, and lit it. With enormous satisfaction she watched her creation take light with the first match, and almost wished someone else had been around to see it. She admired it until it nearly burned itself out before she remembered, with a start, to add more wood. Soon she had a proper little fire going, and as the sky deepened to indigo and the light faded from the world around her, she stuck two hotdogs on a stick and held them over the flames.

The next time she'd have to remember to find a stick that wasn't bone dry, she thought, after the third time she had to pull it back to put out the little eruptions of flame that licked along it. She finally ate the hotdogs half charred on one side, nicely done on the other, and a tad cool in the center, with a garnish of burnt wood bits. She thought she'd never tasted anything so wonderful in her life. The coleslaw went down fine, too, shoveled in with the camping utensils Emery had bought her at Bogg's Hardware.

She blew up her air mattress with a little hand pump from the same establishment and unrolled her sleeping bag. She stood undecided for a moment, thinking of snakes and insects, and finally set up her bed on the picnic table. In sweatpants and a loose T-shirt she lay down and looked up at the sky. Framed by a black lace border of branches and rustling leaves, the sky was brimming with stars—no moon in sight.

Georgia smelled of wood smoke, her hands were dirty and sticky with sap that wouldn't wash off, she was tired, and full, and she knew she should be sleeping like a bear. But her head was full of the day's images. It was like a crazy movie, the world slipping by in a geometry of fields, a blur of roads, pure sky blue, the new green of trees. So much green. Winter had finally thawed from her mind, melted away in the eager atmosphere of spring.

She turned to ease her sore hip. A distant sound of someone's camper door closing came through the trees, and then the night was quiet again. Georgia was suddenly aware of how exposed she was, without any walls or doors to guard her. After a minute she reached down into her pack on the bench beside her. Feeling around with her hand, she found the pocket of her jeans and retrieved Mel's switchblade. Slipping it under the rolled-up sweatshirt she was using for a pillow, she made sure she could reach it with a quick grab. When the night cooled enough for her to pull her sleeping bag around her in a comforting embrace, and with the knowledge that she'd done all she could to protect herself from the world she was determined to enter, she drifted off to sleep.

In the morning she awakened to the heavy throbbing of a V-twin motorcycle engine. She opened her eyes upon a huge, hairy fellow idling a Harley on the dirt in front of her campsite. The bike seemed as massive as the man—plenty big enough for him, plus what looked like enough gear to get him to Argentina and back. Georgia sat up in her sleeping bag on the picnic table. The man nodded to her.

"Morning," he said.

"Morning." She felt stiff and groggy but alert enough to see that his eyes were drawn to her motorcycle, not her.

He shut off his engine. "That's really something," he said.

"Thanks."

"What is it?"

"Kind of a mix," she said.

"Interesting." He took off his helmet, a minimalist thing that probably just barely got him past the helmet laws.

She nodded. "The frame's modeled on a Harley…. an FXR Lowrider." She got that from Mel.

"What's the engine?"

She climbed out of her sleeping bag. Her neck was sweaty and her mouth dry. "Coffee?" she offered, taking a fledgling leap into this newfound world of motorcycle camaraderie.

They sat at her table with coffee, some Entenmann's crumb cake the man produced from somewhere, and the last of the hotdogs. She'd shown off her fire-making skill with assumed nonchalance. "Good breakfast," he approved through a mouthful that encompassed half a dog at a time, though she doubted it was more than an appetizer to this hulk of a man. He wore a sleeveless denim motorcycle jacket framing heavy arms covered with tattoos. His black jeans were so tight over his thick legs she wondered how he could straddle a bike all day. In short, he was her archetypal image of a biker.

They talked motorcycles. In a surprisingly brief time Georgia's tension eased and then faded away. Not only that, but she began to feel as if she'd done this forever—welcomed strange, large men with hairy arms to her breakfast table beside a crackling campfire. He told her about the motorcycle club he usually rode with and talked about some of his favorite destinations. She had to see the Crazy Horse monument, he said, and of course the badlands. "There's nothing like the badlands," he said. "You got to see 'em. They're not everyone's idea of great scenery, I guess, but you decide for yourself."

Eventually he lumbered to his feet. "Well, I gotta roll, my old lady's expecting me home by tomorrow. Good to meet ya." He shook her hand and then reached for his wallet. "If you ever need anything, you just call me." He handed her a card with "Rowe and Frankel" and the name of his biking club embossed across it. In the corner in small letters it said "attorneys-at-law" with a phone number. "I'm Rowe," he said. "Tina's idea to keep the Frankel. She's a big feminist."

"Well," Georgia said to herself, watching him go. She dowsed the fire, and began to pack up. "That was an eye opener."

The day lay before her and she was ready. She'd take care, but she'd also take hold of it—all of it, whoever and whatever happened her way.

She loved the badlands. They were like nothing she'd ever seen before. I'm on another planet, she thought, made of elephant skin.

That night she called Corrine from a restaurant.

"Well, it's about time," Corrine said. "I told you you'd forget all about me."

"Blame my phone—I can never get a signal when I want it." Georgia told her. "But Corrine, this area is amazing. You should be here. It's like a desert. It *is* a desert. It's so cool. I don't know how the Sioux could have survived here, but it's beautiful."

"Hang on a sec," Corrine said. Georgia heard her yelling to someone in the background, "Okay, okay, I will." And then back into the phone, "Mama says do you have a video camera?"

"No, but I thought I might get one of those little plastic snapshot deals."

"No, she doesn't," Corrine yelled. "What, do you think she's traveling in a Winnebago, for God's sake? No, Mama, I'm not swearing." Back on the phone again, she confided, "Mama's boyfriend is having trouble with his knee, so she's cranky. Anyway, is it like you thought? Are you having a good time?"

"Yeah," Georgia said. "I am. I thought I'd be lonely, you know, but I'm not." She paused for a second. "It's an odd thing, though. It keeps occurring to me that I've never really felt like an adult, ever in my life," she said. "No, I mean it—I've felt a hundred years old sometimes, but never really grown up. I think I always had this idea of adults as being confident, in charge, and I never got it straight in my head what it really did mean. But all of a sudden here I am doing this completely juvenile thing, taking off like a kid with no responsibilities, and for some reason *now* I feel like an adult. Is that crazy?"

"Well, I don't know. Maybe it is and maybe it's not. You are in charge, though, you know."

"You're right, I am. Not of much, but of my own little part of the world, I guess. Of what I do, anyway. How bizarre is that—that I've gone all this time without ever taking charge of my life."

"Oh, Georgia," sighed Corrine. "I just want to reach through this phone and give you a hug."

"Me too, Cor. I wish you were here to see some of this stuff.

And to meet the people." Her mind was a whirl of images, of all the encounters she'd had in just a couple days of travel—at gas station cafés, campgrounds, scenic overlooks. "It seems like every person I meet has some sort of story. Everyone's got a passion—motorcycles, or astronomy, one guy has a collection of caterpillars on trays that take up the whole back of his car. Maybe it's just that everyone's on the road. It makes them lose their inhibitions. Or maybe I'm just attracting all the nuts. A nut magnet."

"Nobody's giving you any trouble, are they?"

"Oh, no. Everyone's been great. Well, there was a waitress who seemed to think I was invisible, or stank or something. I happen to think wood smoke smells good.... Oh, I've been camping out. I can build campfires and everything. I think I'm a natural."

Corrine laughed. "Well, you make sure to take care of yourself. Don't let any bears get at you. Or wolves either, hear?"

"I won't. Well, I've got to go. My burger's ready."

"Burger? You better remember to eat right. No, mama! No ... okay, I'll tell her. She says you should carry a gun."

"Jesus, Corrine. Is your mother *on* something these days or what?" She decided not to mention the switchblade.

"I don't know." Corrine lowered her voice, "But I tell you it can be a real trial having a character for a parent. Don't tell her I said that."

"You tell her I said she should find a man with good knees. Well, you take care and I will too, I promise. I love you both."

"Love you too. Bye, hon."

When Corrine got off the phone, she confided in her mother, "I'm worried about her out there."

"I know, baby. Me too."

"You are?"

"Sure I am. Nobody ever said this world's a safe place. But would you be happier watching her shrivel away in that little apartment of hers? Never get on with her life?"

"No."

"And I noticed you didn't try to stop her from going, either. Why's that?"

"I know what you're trying to tell me, Mama. But can't you just let me worry for a while?"

"Why sure, baby. You go right ahead. Meanwhile, me and Irene's goin' to the mall. You want to come with us? You can do your worrying there."

"No, thanks. How are you getting there?"

"Irene's driving."

"Irene's *driving*? She can hardly see, even with her glasses on! Where's her son?"

"He's in Iowa at some meeting or other. She's still got her license."

"Okay, I'll go—but I'm driving."

"Well, now. If you want to drive that'll be just fine." She went to her bedroom to get her comfortable walking shoes.

Corrine narrowed her eyes and wondered how she'd managed, in such short order, to get herself sucked into taking Mama to the mall.

Mrs. Perriera got her picture postcard from Mount Rushmore. Georgia sent a nice scenic one for her, and another joke one for Corrine showing Cary Grant from "North by Northwest" clinging onto a nose hair hanging from Teddy Roosevelt's stony beak, with the president looking just about set to sneeze. When Georgia called, Corrine told her that her mama had been a little peeved because Corrine got the better postcard.

"Tell her I'll send her one from Yellowstone. Maybe grizzlies doing a Busby Berkley number around the geyser. Or how about Ginger Rogers taking a spin with a moose?"

"I was out that way once during a wet spell," said Corrine, "and I thought for sure I saw mosquitoes doing the mazurka. Maybe they've got a postcard of that."

Getting to Yellowstone, though, turned out to be serious business. Georgia hit terrible weather going across Wyoming, rain and wind. She could see it coming, too, from miles away. She rode into it like a knight into first battle, her anxiety growing mile by mile as they approached each other with terrible speed. The wind hit her first, smelling of sage and ozone. Then came the rain in horizontal bursts. The road glistened malevolently, and she slowed down even though she desperately wanted to get through to the next town as soon as she could. After a terrifying gust almost blew her off the road, she took refuge in a ditch, trying to shield herself under some sagebrush. Huddled there in the gray light, the storm surging around her, she wished she had Albert for company, although she could imagine his sad, wet mug, and was glad he was safe in Minnesota.

He would have loved all the smells of traveling, though. She was learning to know the various scents of trees, of creek water, of town swimming pools and farm silos. She couldn't even imagine all the smells his superior nose would detect.

When she got back on the road after the worst of the turbulence, she was wet to the skin despite her rubberized rain gear. The wind buffeted her, straight on and all around, pumping air in and out of her jacket and pants like a bellows. When she finally found a motel, she used some of her meager savings to hole up for the night and recover from near-hypothermia and a bad case of nerves.

The next day started better, but by mid-morning turned stormy again. By the time she hit Cody, Wyoming, she was exhausted from driving with her heart in her mouth, expecting at any moment that a gust of wind would send her skidding across the slick road and into oblivion.

She walked, stiff and rummy with fatigue, into a sandwich shop and sank down at a table as far from the door's draft as she could manage. The man behind the counter had white hair that wisped outward on one side like a cloud caught in a high altitude gust. He had bright blue eyes that smiled even though his mouth didn't. It was as if the years had worn out his face unevenly—the top, still in working order, had taken over the expressive functions, leaving his mouth free for less demanding tasks like sucking toothpicks. A yellow one now waved like a miniature baton from one corner. Without a word, he came and poured Georgia a cup of coffee. Regular, hot, black coffee. He set it in front of her with a menu and walked away.

It wasn't till her first sip that she really started to shake. It began as a shudder and progressed to a lesser but persistent shivering. She went into the bathroom with the dry clothes she'd brought in, and stripped off her rain gear and the damp clothes underneath. She couldn't stop shaking. She wished with all her heart for a sauna to appear in the wall before her. Her very bones felt chilled. The funny thing was that she hadn't been aware while she was riding of just how much warmth was being leeched out of her. Dangerous, she thought. Gotta watch that. She stumbled back out to the table and sat down. Feeling too tired to even pick up the menu, she leaned over on her forearms to read it. The only thing keeping her awake was her continuing intermittent shivering.

The white-haired man came and stood with a green order pad and a pencil at the ready. A girl in a pink T-shirt had taken his place behind the counter and was serving customers who, even at four in the afternoon, trickled steadily in and out, sucking up buffalo burgers and BLTs.

Georgia's brain seemed to be stuck in neutral. She was no closer to deciding what to order than she'd been when she first sat down. She shook her head and began, "I'm not sure ..." and the man walked away without a word. When he returned a minute later he was carrying a huge bowl of chili, with shredded yellow cheese melting on top, and saltines in little cellophane packets. He spoke two succinct words in a high, cracked voice, "Buffalo Chili." After refilling her coffee cup, he again departed without ceremony.

She was more grateful than she could express, as much for the fact that she didn't have to think as for the hot comfort before her. She ate, and drank her coffee, and gradually her shoulders sank to their proper position and her jaw unclenched. Her butt was sore but at least her legs were in a new position. The muscles inside her thighs were cramped and aching. All she could think about was taking a hot shower and lying down in a warm bed.

There was a motel across the street that looked cheap and was close, her two main concerns, and to her relief it had a vacancy sign. She used more of her precious savings and never doubted that it would have been worth spending the whole bundle if she had to.

15

THE NEXT MORNING, in the bright sun of the rain-washed town, she crossed the street back to the restaurant and asked for a job. She told the old man right off she'd only stay for a couple of weeks. To her amazement he hired her. His dishwasher had just quit after one of the waitresses had spotted needle tracks in his arm. So Georgia started off washing dishes, but a high-school kid was hired for that the next day and Georgia was put on waitress duty. There were two other waitresses, but the younger of them, Maria—the pink one Georgia had seen the first day—had vacation time coming, so Georgia took her place. The older waitress, Mary, was a ranch woman who was as matter-of-fact as she was foul-mouthed. She had three teenaged boys at home.

The old man was Harry Luvinsky. Georgia was amazed to find that once he got going, he could talk a blue streak. Working the breakfast rush, when it was all she could do to keep her orders straight, he'd be dealing out food and chattering away about seafood restaurants of the world, or donkey races in Peru. He liked to travel every November. He'd gone with his wife until she died a few years before, and more recently with his special lady friend who, he complained, stubbornly refused to get married. A free spirit was fine, Harry told Georgia, but marriage was finer, and he missed it.

He considered for a second. "She's messy, though, so maybe it's just as well."

"Messy?"

"She leaves gobs of toothpaste in the sink."

"Oh, well then," said Georgia.

Harry was a student of people. Not that he would have called himself that, but Georgia watched him sometimes, going quiet as he observed some new specimen. As much as he breathed out information, he breathed in his examination of the world. His likes and dislikes were a matter of some interest to his employees. Mary and Georgia made small bets on whether or not he'd take to a certain customer—the heavy-set woman with the thick glasses and even thicker Yankee accent, the boy with the spiked hair and dirty ears. There was really no telling who'd strike his fancy and who'd reap his disdain. They couldn't always tell by watching him, either. Bets weren't settled until later when he verbally dissected his finds like tenth-grade frogs. Georgia wondered what he'd said about her when she'd first turned up, but thought it must have been all right, judging by the blessings of coffee and chili he'd bestowed upon her, and the fact that he'd hired her.

Mary took Georgia home with her after the third day. She wanted her boys to see that a woman was good for something besides tits and high school proms.

"A motorcycle," she said with satisfaction. "That'll get their attention." She stuffed her purse into one of Georgia's saddlebags, produced a helmet she'd borrowed from her brother-in-law, and climbed onto the back of the bike, leaving her car in the lot. They rode out into the country about thirty miles before she pointed to a dirt road and they turned into the ranch. The three boys were home and had apparently finished their chores. A head appeared at the living room window and disappeared. It popped back up like a jack-in-the-box to see its mother come riding up on the back of a motorcycle. The other two boys arrived at the kitchen door in time to see their mother and Georgia pulling off their helmets. "Cool," said one. "Shit, yeah," said the other.

Georgia gave up her motel room and moved to the ranch for

the remainder of her two weeks. She helped out with groceries but Mary wouldn't accept rent.

"You don't have to do anything at all," Mary told her when Georgia worried she wasn't helping enough. "Just having a female out here that doesn't have hooves is plenty for me. Smell that?" She took a deep sniff. "Men. Cow shit. Teenaged boys who haven't brushed their teeth in a week and think I don't notice, not to mention that they've been dipping into their Daddy's chew. I swear I don't know which end smells worse."

Not having to shell out for a room helped considerably, and after her two weeks in Cody, Georgia had enough money to set out again with a little bit of a cushion against foul weather and mishaps. She entered Yellowstone a happy tourist, and Mrs. P. got her postcard. Two angels sitting on a cloud, looking down at the tourists oohing and aahing over Old Faithful. One shaking his head and saying to the other, "*Look at all these people. You'd think they'd never seen a bidet before.*"

Corrine told Georgia she was now off the hook—mama had laughed herself silly. "She won't let me say 'damn' but she thinks bathroom humor is the greatest thing since the ark."

A week later, Georgia called Corrine from Whitefish, Montana. "I just talked myself out of a ticket," she told her. "The grumpiest highway patrolman stopped me, but he was really sweet in the end."

"I wish you'd be more careful out there, girl. You know better than to speed."

"Oh, no, not for speeding. For going too slow. I couldn't stop looking at all the scenery. I got a little digital camera and I kept stopping to take pictures. He said I was a danger to traffic."

And a couple days later, "I picked up my first hitchhiker."

"You can't do that!"

"He was the nicest kid, a Nez Perce Indian whose car broke down. He and his grandmother live down in this little hollow next to a creek, and after I took him into town, and he got a friend to tow his car in, I gave him a ride home and they made me stay the night. And then the next morning this chipped-toothed sixteen year old kid with a broken-down car tells me I should be careful out there and tries to hand me five dollars for gas money."

By the end of June she was on the Olympic Peninsula.
"Hi Corride."
"What's wrong?"
"I've got a cold. I'b miserable. I wish I was hobe."
"Where are you?"
"Wait…." Corrine listened to the sound of Georgia blowing her nose. In a voice only marginally less stopped up, Georgia moaned, "In a campground in the middle of the dampest hell on earth, and the showers aren't even hot. And there are two people camped next to me who are the filthiest human beings I've ever seen. They asked me if I wanted some hot cocoa last night and I said yes. I hadn't seen them in daylight or I never would have gone over. I thought the mug they gave me was some kind of heavy hand-made ceramic, and I was halfway done before I realized it was just a regular cup that was caked with I don't know how many months worth of crud. I almost puked."
"Oh my God, that's disgusting."
"And do you know what they do for a living? They're moss gatherers! I'm not lying. They climb trees and gather moss."
Corrine started to laugh.
"I know!" said Georgia. "And of course that kind of moss grows only in the rainiest places on earth. Imagine wanting to live in the rain all the time. *Ah-choo!*" Georgia exploded. "Ow," she groaned.

"My nose is so sore. And I think I've got a fever."

"You should find a motel and rest up awhile."

"I know, but I don't want to stay around here. It's so beautiful, but I hate it. I just want to get someplace sunny."

"Oh, baby, I wish I was there with you."

"Me too," Georgia said and sneezed again. "Or I was hobe in bed. Not that I even have a hobe anymore." She couldn't stand the sniveling self-pity in her voice, and knew she was about to cry. "Well, I'b no treat to be around right now eddyway. I just wanted to complain to subbody and you're it. Sorry."

She'd wanted to see British Columbia and Alaska, but now she couldn't face any more of the dark looming trees and depressing drizzle, so she headed south. She thought she'd try and get at least as far as Oregon, but by the time she passed Olympia she didn't care where she was and checked into a motel in Tumwater, in a shitty room overlooking the freeway. She holed up there for three days, nursing a fever and watching TV. When she finally hit the road again, the weather had cleared and she decided to head for the coast.

She felt reborn. Hugging the Pacific, she gloried in the curving coastline and the pure salt air. The motorcycle ran like a dream, responding to her every desire, as if this assemblage of parts was a God-given connection between her and the road.

In a cluster of shops in an Oregon town by the ocean, she passed a sign saying "Olivia's Market." She didn't stop, but the name kept sounding in her head like a song as the miles passed. Olivia, the engine purred. Olivia. By the time she stopped for the night, the motorcycle, at long last, had found itself a name.

There were a lot of motorcycles along the coast. Everywhere, people asked about her bike. She stopped in Santa Rosa and worked for a couple of weeks, then got back on the road again. San Francisco was a dream of food, street music, and people-watching. Every time the fog rolled in, though, and then suddenly floated off, she felt as if she were being swallowed by a whale and then spit back out again into the sunny light of day. There was so much to do and see, she was worn out after four days.

She ricocheted around California for a while—she drove through the cool Sierra to Tahoe, she bounced down to Mojave, she rode with some folks who were going to Santa Barbara and stayed in their guest-house for a few days like a movie star. She skipped Los Angeles altogether—too intimidating, and besides, she was low on money again. She almost got heat stroke getting to Barstow, the hot winds sucking her dry.

After recovering for a day, she drove through the dark desert night to the Grand Canyon, arriving just as the sun rose. Looking across that vastness, her mind couldn't take in what it was seeing. Her eyes and her brain hadn't adjusted to the scope of the landscape. She stood there for the longest time with a dumb look on her face, seeing only textures and colors, like a blind woman with a sudden onset of sight, but without the capacity to make any sense of it.

"There's so much out there," she told Corrine that evening, her voice subdued with awe. "In the world, you know. All of it. It's a little overwhelming."

"It sounds amazing." Corrine breathed out a sigh. "What a time you're having."

"I am. It can be exhausting at times, but there's nothing like being here. I mean actually being out here, standing here breathing the air and ... oh, I don't know how to say it. Just *being* here. And the landscape itself.... Uncle Emery would be over the moon."

"I bet he would. How's the bike doing?"

"My Olivia? She's wonderful. A little idle adjustment here and there, but that's normal. Oh, and I ran out of gas one day last week, but I literally had not even come to a stop when a couple on a totally decked-out Yamaha Royal Star pulled over to help. Other than that she's been as sweet as can be."

"It all sounds so great. I really miss you though, hon. Have you thought any about when you're coming home?"

"Soon, I think."

"Any plans for after you're back? I just want to make sure you know you can stay here while you look for a place. Joelle's leaving to go back to school at the end of the month, and once I muck out her room it'll be yours for as long as you need it. She says hi, by the way, and thanks for the silk bandana. She's calling it a neckerchief, and on her, God bless her, it's the height of fashion."

"Tell her she's welcome. I'm sorry I'll miss her."

Georgia had been thinking there was nothing to go back to Minneapolis for, only another cold winter and bleak job prospects. There was Corrine, though, and Uncle Emery up north. And of all the places Georgia had been, fabulous as they might be, she couldn't think of anywhere else she'd want to stop and live. It took more than nice scenery to make a life. San Francisco, maybe, but she didn't think she could take the schizophrenia of the weather. At least you knew what you were getting from one hour to the next in Minnesota. "Thanks for the offer, Cor. I'll let you know," she said. "You're really the best."

Georgia spent long stretches of road thinking about the Mystery Motorcycle Man. She realized she was being a chauvinist—why couldn't it be a woman?—but she couldn't get that picture into her mind for some reason, which annoyed her. It was like getting a map one way in your head and never afterwards being able to turn it around. It was hard enough just to imagine anyone at all doing this thing, sending such a gift, piece by piece from who knew where, to her, one lone woman out of all the billions in the world. She systematically reviewed all the people she could think of in her life, and rejected one after another.

Her thoughts turned once or twice to Frank Morrow. He'd always been kind of an odd duck, hadn't he? And wasn't he some sort of an engineer now? Mary Anne said he'd asked about her recently. She couldn't put it together, though. The main problem was motive. They hardly knew each other, not since they were kids. She couldn't think of a single reason for him to do anything like this.

Or it could be someone she didn't know at all. Maybe it was some crazy private lottery someone had thought up, and she was the winner. Or Candid Camera on a grand scale. The most troubling idea was that it might be some demented stalker playing with her head. Someone trying to insinuate himself into her life using this irresistible lure. Someone with a sordid ulterior motive. Maybe she should have had the parts fingerprinted when she first got them.

A rabbit shot across the road and Georgia swerved sharply, barely missing it, her mind jerked back to the present. Jeez, she thought. A close one. Another few inches or another second and there would have been nothing she could've done.

She pulled onto the next side road and got off the bike. She shook her hands to relieve the tired numbness. That felt so good she progressed to shaking her arms, then bent over and shook out her whole front end—hands, arms, shoulders, and she swung her head gently back and forth to ease her neck muscles. Then, pulling a candy bar from a saddlebag, she stepped out into a bracing walk up the dirt road. It felt good to move. She didn't like the state of mind she'd slipped into. Not productive. If there was one thing she was learning—that she was intent on learning—it was to stay focused on things that were good, things that could promote her survival.

And that meant staying in the moment and not getting sucked into despairing thoughts of some terrible future. That was as bad as or worse than dwelling on a painful past.

Frank Morrow came back into her mind. Well, one of these days she'd have to look him up. Maybe she'd take Uncle Emery for a ride out to Foxton, really visit this time, not just breeze through. He deserved it, and she wasn't afraid of riding with a passenger anymore if he was up for it.

The tense antipathy she'd once felt for her hometown didn't seem to be a barrier anymore, either. She felt around for it, probed her feelings in search of it, but it wasn't there. Something in her had let go of it while she had her mind on other things.

She remembered how she used to make her mother read to her when she was a little girl—what was it? Hansel and Gretel—again and again, until one day she realized with a sad jolt that she'd outgrown it. It no longer moved her, or scared her. In a perverse way she felt a similar sense of loss now. She'd held on to her aversion to Foxton for a long time ... but that was an old story and she'd just as soon get over it.

She rode on with alert confidence, an equilibrium that was slowly but surely becoming second nature. Through the breathtaking sunsets of New Mexico, through the mountains and sudden plains of Colorado. Through Kansas, where a waitress, when Georgia asked her to fill her thermos with hot water, walked it over to the sink and ran it full of hot tap water. Well, thought Georgia. I could have done that myself. She wondered if the rolling endlessness of the land had done something to this woman's brain. Whatever it was, she hoped it was not irreversible.

Then on through hot days and muggy, sweltering Missouri nights, through Iowa, and finally Minnesota, the fields thickly gold, heavy with crops, the woods fertile and rife with mosquitoes. All of it, every rapture and dissatisfaction, every adventure or numbing stretch of road, and the people—the fat man driving a donkey buggy, the bikers, the waitresses and grocery store clerks, the bratty children making their mothers' lives a misery at the Laundromat—all of it merged together into a new geography in her mind. And to think, even with all the places she'd been and things she'd seen, it was just a bare fraction of the world, one little section of North America. There was an infinite world out there. If, with all that, she couldn't find a way to have an interesting life, then shame on her.

Still, she was a little worried about coming home. The city seemed like a big, impersonal Venus Fly Trap ready to imprison her, to lure her in and close around her. Just thinking about it seemed to suck energy out of her. But she did want to see Corrine. She wanted to talk to her for hours, and then go dancing with Mrs. P. at the community center. Now, while she still felt alive, her mind buzzing with interesting tales and visions of an expansive life.

She pulled up in front of Corrine's house and cut the engine. When knocking at the front door produced no results, she followed the path around the side of the house. She found Mrs. Perriera in paisley pants, hacking away with a spade at the weeds in the zinnia bed.

"Well, hey there!" Mrs. P. shouted out when she spied Georgia. "Grab a shovel!"

And so she did.

Georgia stayed a couple of days and then headed up to Emery's. She'd called him every now and then while she was on the road, and therefore knew about Albert having chased a porcupine, and the inevitable results. Emery had removed most of the quills with pliers, but a couple under Albert's chin had worked their way in too deep and the vet in town had had to get them out.

Georgia pulled into the yard in the late afternoon. Albert padded over to greet her. "Hello, my sweet boy," Georgia crooned, kneeling down to hug him. "Let's see your battle scars. Oh, my."

Emery walked out onto the deck. "Welcome home," he said.

"Hi!" Georgia wanted to run to him and give him a hug, too, and a buss on the cheek, but she could tell by the way he was standing with his thumbs in his belt loops and his shoulders hunched forward that he was out of the habit of such things. Well, she'd just have to work on him.

They picked corn and beans from the garden and talked about Georgia's plans. He thought she could find a job in town if she wanted to.

"The summer folks are heading home so a lot of jobs are done for the season, but there's still some work through the winter if you want it. Especially with so many young people moving to the cities. Pete at the dry cleaners is looking for someone."

"No thanks to that," said Georgia. "I can't stand the smell of those chemicals."

"How about the Kentucky Fried?"

She looked at him suspiciously. "No, I don't think so."

"Oh, well," he said. "I suppose you could ask Mel if he might have an opening at the garage. Seems to me he was looking for a manager, now that he's cutting back on his work schedule."

"Uncle Emery! Do you think he'd hire me? I don't know much about cars or managing a business."

"I think he might. He's got a lot of faith in you. You learn fast."

She thought about it. "I think I'd do okay there," she said. "I'd have to find my own place in town."

"You could stay here awhile, though. Till you get settled, you know. If we get early snow you could always keep your car down at the Dahls' and use the snowmobile to get to it. Just till you get settled." He shrugged.

Georgia talked it over with Mel the next day and they came to an agreement. She'd do whatever motorcycle work or small engine repairs she thought she could handle and let Mike Takkunen, the full-time mechanic, do the rest. She'd do all the paperwork, cashier, and take on-call shifts with the wrecker.

"Will Mike be okay with this?" she asked Mel. "He's been here a long time. Having someone—a woman—coming in...."

"He hates the office. All he wants to do is work on cars and mind his own business. Don't worry about him."

Mel would show her how the business was run for a week or so, but after her training she wanted to take a couple weeks off before starting in permanently. "I want to take Emery on a motorcycle trip," she explained.

Mel laughed. "Good for him. The old fart could use an airing out."

"I haven't asked him yet. Oh, also, do you think you and Barbara could take care of Albert while we're gone?"

"I don't see why not. Let me give her a call."

"I don't have to know right away."

"She'll want to know you're back. She wants to have you over for dinner."

Emery chewed it over a little but finally agreed to take the trip out to Wisconsin.

"I owe it to you," Georgia said.

"No." He said, looking down at his feet. "You don't."

The way he said it, reverting to his old shyness, left Georgia unsure how to respond, so she didn't say anything at all. Emery nodded and went back to the lawn mower he was working on.

Albert was not thrilled about being left behind. Georgia could tell by the way he lay on Mel and Barbara's kitchen floor. He flopped on his side with a look of selfless martyrdom. She thought briefly of taking him along, but the idea of him getting worn out and maybe sick on the trip decided her against it. She never considered where she'd have put all their gear if the trunk was full of basset hound.

They set off on a clear, fresh morning. It gave Georgia a tiny qualm—it was uncomfortably like the bright morning when she'd set off down a Minneapolis street and ended up in a bloody heap on the pavement. But the dirt road leading out from her uncle's held no surprises other than the shifting shadows of late summer. Emery was an easy passenger. If Georgia ducked her head down and to the side a little, she could catch sight of his grinning face in the side mirror. Though he kept his body still, his head waggled back and forth, back and forth, looking around like he'd never seen the woods before, or the boggy meadows, or the creeks connecting the cool lakes in musty-smelling currents.

Southward, Georgia and Emery rode, then east, through the countryside that opened before them, revealing itself around curves and across fields, in pastoral watercourses and no-nonsense towns. Georgia kept waiting for her doubts to seep in, but finally forgot to do even that. It was pretty country, she decided, and even with all the glorious landscapes she'd seen on her travels, and despite all the old worries about going home, this place fit her like a favorite pair of jeans.

Foxton sat on the river, the newer sections replacing the old in a creeping renewal that had been both the bane and the redemption of the town. The trees made a shimmering canopy as they drove up to Georgia's parents' house.

"Oh, my goodness. Look at you," her mother exclaimed, coming out of the house. "And Emery!"

"Hello, Iris." Emery shocked both Iris and Georgia, and possibly himself, by pulling his helmet off and coming forward to kiss his sister on the cheek. Iris took his hand and began to lead him to the house, talking a mile a minute and smiling back at Georgia every so often. Emery let himself be led, managing to look both embarrassed and proud at the same time. Georgia laughed out loud, and reached her arms out from her sides in a bone cracking stretch that embraced the day, and her family, and even this awful old town.

16

THE ANNUAL FOXTON Boys' Club Benefit Barbeque was held at the park by the river. Libby and Frank went down with Julius and his two oldest kids. Julius immediately went off to supervise something or other, the kids disappeared with friends, and Frank was recruited to take a shift at one of the grills, so Libby sauntered down to the dock and sat at the end with an oversized cup of ice, dangling her feet over the water. It was a hot, muggy afternoon. Two little girls were squatting a little ways back from the edge, dropping fishing lines through the cracks between the boards, trying to lure whatever fish might be hiding in the cool shadows.

"They like these," the smaller girl explained to Libby, holding up what looked like a tiny pink marshmallow. "But if it rains, they like these better." She dug around in her little bait jar and came up with a round, red pellet that she squished between her fingers. "That's because fish are schools." Though not quite following her logic, Libby nodded attentively. She liked the commitment of the child to making sure her big, possibly slow student understood this important information.

"Have you caught anything?" she asked.

The child dismissed this as a typically dull question. "Oh, sure, but I threw them back. You can't keep anything smaller than this." She held her hands about three inches apart.

The older girl looked up and rolled her eyes, but didn't say anything.

The hollow sound of footsteps reverberated along the dock, and they all looked around at a small, wiry man with thinning gray hair walking down the wooden planks, his thumbs in his belt loops. He stepped more quietly once he saw that the girls had fishing lines, and paused before he got to them, until Libby smiled and told him not to mind them. Then he came and lowered himself on the far side of the girls, dangling his legs over the edge, his old boots well above the waterline. Libby had taken off her sneakers, and every now and then reached out a toe to the river's cool surface. The man leaned over to look into the water, then looked up at the sky.

"Pretty hot day," Libby said.

"Yup," answered the man.

The younger girl, as if she'd only been waiting to see if he could speak, took this as her cue. "They *like* it when it's hot, 'cause they can hide in the shade and don't have to go to work," she told him.

Libby said, "Is that right?" The girl looked around at her for a split second and then turned back to the man.

"And they can kiss each other all they want without getting overheated."

"The fish," Libby said, to clarify.

"The fish," agreed the man.

The little one chattered on about kissing until the older girl jabbed her in the ribs with a sharp elbow.

"Ow! I'm gonna tell mommy," the little one said and shoved her back. Her big sister took this as a matter of course, leaning over with the shove and springing right back up again.

"Don't look at me," Libby laughed, answering the man's unspoken question. "I'm just an innocent bystander."

The older girl pulled in her line, wrapping it neatly around a yellow plastic cylinder that looked like a kite string holder. She stood, and without looking back, walked off the dock. Her little sister wadded her own line into a mutinous tangle and scrambled after her. "You didn't have to *hit* me," she complained, her voice receding as they stepped onto the sandy grass. Drifting back on the heavy air came the phlegmatic reply, "Dipshit." And then the children were absorbed into the throng.

"Kids," Libby said, shaking her head.

"A handful," the man agreed.

"Aren't they, though?" sighed Libby. "I've got two in college. Not that they squabbled awfully much when they were growing up, but when they did, man, they had some doozies."

"I can imagine," he said, drawing a baseball cap out of his back pocket and pulling on to shade his eyes from the glare of white sky over the water.

"How about you? Have any kids ... or grandkids maybe?"

"Nope, never married. I've got a niece, though."

The two of them sat for a while, listening to the river around them and the picnic behind.

Then Libby said, "I just got married…. Well, my first husband died a few years ago, so I guess I should say 'remarried.'"

"Remarried. Now, that's nice." He looked over at her and smiled. His boyish face looked sincerely happy for her.

"I don't know why I'm telling you this."

"It's a nice thing."

"My husband's up there right now slaving over a grill full of hotdogs, and here I am just lazing around. I suppose I should feel guilty, or go help out."

"Oh, no," came the immediate reply.

Libby laughed. "You're my kind of guy." She shook her cup of ice and sipped some of the melted water. They continued to sit quietly, watching the river.

After a while the man said, "My niece and I are visiting her mother ... that's my sister. If anyone should feel guilty, I suppose it's me. I haven't seen her in awhile—in fact I only just met her for the first time a few years back—and here I am hiding out. I'm not used to socializing much."

"You only just met? That must have been something. I can understand about the socializing part, though."

He looked over his shoulder at the people milling around the park, carrying paper plates piled with food, juggling pop cans and diaper bags, or sitting at the picnic tables swatting insects. "It seems I've got a bunch of cousins and second cousins too. They appear to be nice folks."

"Where are you from?"

"Northern Minnesota. We rode down on her motorcycle, Georgia and me." He grinned. "Hard on the butt, but more fun than I've had in quite a while."

"Georgia Dunn?" Libby said. Her heart gave a little lurch. She turned to face him.

"That's her. You know her?" He looked at her curiously.

She was afraid he'd read in her expression, or hear in her voice, the sudden apprehension that came over her at the thought of Frank face to face with Georgia, and she tempered her response. "Oh," she said. "No, I don't know her myself but I know someone who does."

Libby wasn't sure what she should do. She thought she should tell Frank right away, but she was worried about what his reaction might be. Would he want to see this woman? And more importantly, would she threaten the peace of mind he'd so laboriously achieved? Libby had always had the uneasy feeling that Georgia was going to mean trouble, and now suddenly here she was in Foxton.

Libby realized she'd have to tread carefully with this nice little uncle, in any case. The relationship between Frank and Georgia was complicated, and not hers to reveal.

"Are you going to be around for a while?" she asked.

"Uh, at the barbeque? Or in town?"

"Both I guess."

"Well, let's see. Iris'll probably want to stay at the park awhile.

She gets to talking, you know—she's got a lot of stamina. But I might ask Georgia to run me back to the house after awhile. Here in town, well, another four, five days, I suppose. Georgia's got to get back to work on the first."

"Are you staying with the Dunns?"

"That's right."

"Well, I may know someone who'd like to say hello." Or who might not, she thought, or who would feel compelled to, despite all his wife's reservations.

The rumble of a motorcycle is not uncommon in summer. If the sound of Georgia pulling into the parking area reached Frank at his grill, it didn't penetrate his conscious mind.

The cooking area was set up behind a row of folding tables covered with plaid plastic tablecloths. A line of people flowed past, piling their plates full. Hotdogs, hamburgers, and a stupefying quantity of baked beans and potato salads that Kiwanis Club members had spent days preparing, were served up at a gratifying rate. People drank gallons of lemonade and soda pop in the humid heat. Adults shook their heads at the energy expended by kids as they chased each other around in frantic rushes or wrestled in the grass, whether in fun or in earnest it was sometimes hard to tell. Occasionally a child or two would be corralled long enough to eat. The heavy air and the lush old trees muted the sounds into a traditional, happy picnic babble.

Frank turned hotdogs with his tongs, taking it all in through the wavering, smoky heat and the rich aroma of grilling meat. He reached for another package of hotdogs from the plastic cooler behind him and took a moment to hang his face over the cool air of the melting ice. As he closed the lid, his eyes traveled past the row of shade trees to the line of vehicles along the street. His attention was caught by one motorcycle, soft green and gleaming ... and oddly familiar. He looked again at the unique lines with dawning recognition.

"Are you all right?" Marcie Gordon, a Kiwanian with lacquered curls, was beside him. Her round face floated above a flowered apron. "Here, you need to sit down." She turned Frank around and sat him on the cooler, waving Julius over.

"What's the matter, Frank? The heat get you? Put your head down," Julius took the package of hotdogs from his brother's hand.

Marcie produced a paper cup of lemonade. "Here, honey, drink this."

"I'm okay," Frank said, his hands propped beside him. He was leaning partway over, looking at the grass between his feet with great intensity. It was trampled flat. Individual clover stems lay limp and bent among the green blades. Julius took the cup from Marcie and squatted down, thrusting it forward. "Drink." Frank took it and drank. The drink was sweet and cloying but at least it was cold.

"I'm okay, stop hovering," Frank told his brother.

"All right. You're done for the day. I'll get Oscar to finish up."

"Don't tell Libby."

"What? Why not?"

"Oh, she'll just worry."

"All right, got ya."

Frank sat on the cooler for a few more minutes. When he felt he could stand up without making a spectacle of himself, he tipped the rest of the lemonade onto the grass and went to refill his cup with ice water. Stepping out from behind the serving tables, he scanned the crowd. People sat at the rows of picnic tables set up for the event. More milled around, or sat at scattered tables that were a permanent part of the park, or on blankets under the trees. Some kids had taken over the little side street that divided the park from a playground area and bathrooms, and were rollerblading in some societal ritual order incomprehensible to adults. Frank wandered around, not knowing if he hoped to see Georgia or not. He caught a glimpse of Libby coming up from the dock but didn't go to her. Instead he turned around and sat down at a table.

And there she was, twenty feet away, a braid down her back, sitting cross-legged on a blanket. She was talking to an older couple on folding lawn chairs. Frank recognized them as her parents, in the brief instant before his attention locked on Georgia.

Georgia looked good. She looked like an ordinary, happy woman at a picnic in the park. With a feeling of unreality that suspended surprise, he noticed that her hair had a strand or two of premature gray glinting in it. There were fine sun lines at the corners of her eyes. She was only a few years younger than himself, but he'd somehow clung to an image of her as a little girl, or as a very young woman struggling with her fears. Even the time he'd seen her in the Minneapolis post office had receded from his mind, pushed away by older, stronger images. It was all coming back now like a tidal surge. He might have been able to convince himself for a while that what he'd done had just been a youthful mistake, but that "mistake" had had devastating consequences that were borne by others, and the reality of it, in the sudden presence of Georgia, washed over him in a cold rush.

She was talking now, gesturing with her arms, her back straight and supple, leaning into her words. He couldn't hear her voice, but then she laughed, and the sound came to him clear and low. This is how he remembered her as a child, he thought. She'd possessed such clarity and joy, it had made him happy simply to be around her.

"There you are," said Libby, coming up behind him and sitting down on the bench by his side. She looked over at him and her concern solidified. "What's wrong?"

He shook his head and tried to answer casually, "Nothing. Good turn-out, huh?"

"Frank. You're as pale as a ghost. Something's wrong. Tell me."

"Georgia's here."

"I know," she said, nodding. "I just met her uncle—I was coming to tell you."

He raised his hands in a gesture of uncertainty. "I don't know what to do."

"Well, I can't tell you. She's your friend." Her tone straddled an ambivalent middle ground between compassion and a sharp asperity triggered by worry.

Frank's eyes went back to Georgia. With difficulty he managed to say, "I should go say hello." But he didn't stir.

"Are you asking my permission?"

Frank caught her tone but only looked more distressed and not diverted at all from his dilemma. "She might not even remember me."

Libby sighed and relented. "Just go say hi," she said quietly.

They sat for a moment, Libby with her misgivings, Frank reluctant to break through the wall he'd constructed in his mind. For such a long time his relationship with Georgia had been one of cause and effect, and always from a distance. That had been bad enough. What else would shatter if he actually spoke to her? Sitting by his side, Libby hugged her arms, though the day was as hot as ever.

Dreamlike, Frank began to move his limbs, pulling himself free of the picnic table. Georgia, leaning back on her elbows as she listened to her mother, loomed slowly larger as he made his way toward her. She turned her head and looked up as he reached the edge of her blanket.

Their eyes met and immediate recognition registered in Georgia's face. Frank wondered what she saw. Not the Frank Morrow of her youth, but a thinner, paler man with a sheen of sweat covering his face, and fear and guilt in his eyes.

"Hello, Georgia."

"Frank," she said, smiling and sitting up. "How are you?"

Georgia's mother looked around. "Why, Frank!" she exclaimed. "How nice! I heard you've been back in town, but I guess we just haven't run into each other. You must be keeping busy." She turned to her husband. "Bernie, you remember Frank Morrow."

"Of course," Georgia's father said. He got his stocky legs under him and struggled to his feet.

"Don't get up," Frank said.

"Oh, I need to move around every now and then and see if the old legs still work. Good to see you again," he said, shaking Frank's hand. He turned to his wife, "Want some more Pepsi?"

"Okay. But wait, I see Jean and Lou over there. I'll come with you ... we'll let the young folks talk. Nice to see you, Frank." She stood and followed her husband, stopping to chat here and there as they made their way over to the table selling cans of pop fished from galvanized ice tubs.

"How've you been?" said Georgia. "I heard you got married."

"Yes."

"That's great. Congratulations."

"Thanks." Frank stood with his arms at his sides, not having any idea what to say. Surely there were polite conversational phrases ordinary people said to each other, but for the moment he couldn't think of a single one.

"Come on and sit down."

He sank into one of the vacated lawn chairs. "Uh ... how are you?"

"I'm good," said Georgia.

"You look good." He wanted desperately to ask her about the

bike but didn't know how. "What've you been doing lately?" he finally came up with.

"God, lots of things. I'm living up in northern Minnesota now, up by the Boundary Waters, and I've just started a new job managing a garage. And I've been doing some traveling. On a motorcycle." She smiled.

"Is that right?"

Frank felt the blood rising up his neck, into his cheeks, the blush that had betrayed him from his earliest years. Georgia looked at him with a frown. Then one eyebrow flickered the barest fraction.

"Frank, are you okay?" she asked.

"Oh, sure."

"Then can you tell me why you're turning into a beet right in front of my eyes?"

"Am I? ... I don't know. It must be the heat."

"Really," she said.

"Uh, look, I should probably be getting back." He leaned forward in his chair, but Georgia reached out and put a hand lightly on his knee to stop him.

"When you were a kid you used to sit over in a corner talking to your friends about rockets, or how to make an electrified goat fence or something. I'd come and tease you about it sometimes, do you remember? And you'd act all mad and tell me to mind my own business."

"I remember." He sat back a little, helpless, and Georgia took her hand away.

"You'd get all embarrassed and act like you had twenty girlfriends waiting for you at home and you couldn't be bothered with a little baby like me."

"I did? I'm sorry. I guess I was pretty shy in those days, but that doesn't mean I had to act like a jerk."

"No, it was okay. I thought it was pretty funny. I think I just wanted to torture you."

"Oh."

"Yeah, I was a brat."

"I don't know—I thought you were pretty cool for a kid."

"But Frank, the point I'm getting at is that the only times I ever saw you actually blush were when you were lying about something or trying to hide something."

"Oh." There wasn't enough air. He wanted to leave but his legs had turned to wood. He wanted to turn away but couldn't stop looking at her.

"So?" she said.

"I'm sorry, Georgia," he said huskily. He gave his head a quick shake and put his hands on the armrests of the lawn chair. "I have to go."

But she went on, testing him, he thought, testing her theory. "I've been riding a motorcycle, Frank. It's quite an interesting story. Don't you want to hear about it?"

He couldn't answer, but he stayed where he was, his fingers gripping the chair arms.

"It was very odd," she said, watching him closely. "Someone—I don't know who—sent me a motorcycle. Piece by piece—pistons, wiring, shocks.... I didn't even know what half the stuff was at first."

He didn't speak. The color was now drained from his face. He breathed through his mouth in deep, unsteady respirations.

"I ended up quitting my job and taking the whole kit and caboodle up north to my uncle's to put together," she said. "I learned quite a bit about motorcycle mechanics. It turns out I'm not too bad at it.... And then I wrecked the bike. But you knew that, didn't you?"

If it was possible, Frank went even paler.

"Mary Anne told you, right?"

"Oh. Yes ... right."

"And of course I didn't have a job, or insurance, and I had to sell my house."

"I'm sorry," Frank whispered.

"And it took me a while, but I got back on my feet again—got a brand new start, with a little help, and fixed the bike. And then I took an amazing road trip on it, all over the West. And here I am. Back home where I started." She paused. "Frank?"

"Yes."

"Do *you* happen to know who sent me that bike?"

He couldn't lie to her, but he was incapable of saying the words. He wanted to, he tried ... but it was impossible. He wasn't ready. He couldn't ...

With an abrupt, graceless motion, Frank stood up, and without speaking, walked away.

"But why, Frank?" Georgia called after him, "All I want to know is *why*?"

But he didn't turn around.

Georgia sat on the blanket and watched him go, as mystified as she'd ever been. There was no doubt in her mind that Frank was the one. Her childhood friend had spoken as clearly without a word as most people did in an hour of talking. But it seemed that solving the identity of the Mystery Motorcycle Man was going to be a mixed blessing. In one way it was a relief—to know at last. Her mind could finally stop circling around the question in its fruitless, dizzying dance. So that craziness was gone. But gone also was the knight in shining armor the child inside her had half hoped for. In its place was the more complicated mystery of Frank Morrow. A nice married man who blushed like a boy and couldn't even admit out loud that he'd given her this amazing gift. Reality was just too complicated, like a thousand motorcycle parts and no manual.

At least her fears of a stalker were gone. She couldn't picture Frank in that role. On the other hand, he wasn't the most stable of people. Could he have a hidden side, a sinister side? She wanted to laugh at the thought of Frank being able to hide anything deep and dark, but her smile faded in bafflement as she thought about how successfully he'd hidden his identity as the Motorcycle Man for so long. And whatever his motive was, it remained as obscure as ever. For a man who couldn't lie, he was pretty damned good at keeping things to himself.

In the next few days, aware she might be treading on sensitive ground, Georgia spoke discreetly to some people about Frank but didn't get any further in understanding what would have possessed him to do such a thing as building and sending her a motorcycle. She knew he'd had some problems in the past when his college girlfriend had died from cancer, but mostly people seemed to think well of him. Mary Anne said she thought he was on some sort of medication. "That's just what someone at work told me," Mary Anne said. "I don't really know. He seems like a nice guy—just a little intense sometimes."

Well, that was true enough, but it didn't bring her any closer to an answer.

Libby's fears were growing. She watched as Frank submerged himself in work—staying late at the office, bringing plans and papers home. He slept fitfully if at all. In the early hours of morning he began slipping out of the house and across the lawn to his workshop in the detached garage out back. When Libby secretly followed him, she found the door locked. She could hear the electric sizzle of the welding torch, though, and see an erratic blue light coming from the gap under the door.

In just a few days, Frank grew gaunt and hollow eyed. He forgot things—his wallet, the door left open behind him, the breakfast he'd just made and left uneaten on the table. He avoided Libby's eyes.

"Sit down and eat. You have to eat," she told him one morning when he came downstairs and headed for the door to leave for work. He looked at the eggs she'd made for him, and sat down at the table but didn't pick up his fork. "Frank, you have to tell her," Libby said, setting coffee beside him. "You know you'll feel better if you do. It's keeping it inside that's tearing you up."

Frank just shook his head. "It's not how *I* feel that matters."

"Well, it matters to me." Libby said. She paused to change tactics. "And you said yourself she deserves to know, right?"

"Yes."

"Well, then?"

"I can't."

Libby turned to the sink muttering, "Then I hope she goes back to Minnesota soon, so you can get back to your life." But she said it low enough for Frank not to hear, not that he was listening.

That afternoon when Libby came home from work, she was surprised to see Frank's car already in the carport. She found him in the workshop, the door for once unlocked. She went in and took the dark-lensed goggles from their peg by the door, holding them to her eyes while she waited for him to finish a weld. Then she came up beside him.

"Frank? You're home early. Did you finally finish the Walther project?"

He didn't answer. He lifted the TIG torch to start on another section of whatever it was he was building, but she laid her hand on his arm before he could begin, and spoke again.

"Frank?"

He didn't turn the torch on, but he didn't respond to her either. Libby reached over and lifted the front of Frank's helmet, pivoting it up over his head. He remained focused on the metal piece before him and Libby became truly alarmed. "Frank?"

He finally turned to her. "You're home," he said.

She had him take off his welding clothes and walked him to the kitchen. She put orange juice and toast in front of him, and looked up the number for his psychiatrist in Milwaukee.

As she dialed, she said, "You'll have to take a day off from work." The owners of his small engineering firm were a couple who, while serious about their deadlines, were quite flexible, within reason.

But Frank said, "That's all right…. I'm off."

She looked at him. "What do you mean? Why?"

"They said to take some time off."

This wasn't good. "How come?"

"They said I should take my sick days, or my vacation time. They talked it over."

Work had always been Frank's salvation. If he was having problems at work, Libby thought, it was *really* not good.

The doctor's receptionist answered then and Libby explained the situation.

"Is he on his medication?"

"Yes."

"Does he need hospitalization?"

"What? I don't think so—he's just kind of out of it."

"Well, we can put you in for Friday afternoon at 4:30."

"No." Libby said firmly. "The doctor can either talk to him on the phone right now or you can get us an appointment for tomorrow morning. Or both."

"Well, he was just about to leave the office—"

"Good, then he can speak to him now."

"All right," the receptionist conceded. "I'll see what I can do. Hold on."

Libby spoke to the psychiatrist and then handed the phone

to Frank. She listened to Frank's rote answers, and although she couldn't make out the doctor's words, she could hear the resonance of his deep voice from the other end of the line and was aware of the slight delays before her husband replied, like pauses for translation in a bilingual interview.

Frank extended the phone back to Libby.

"Can you bring him down early tomorrow?" the doctor asked. "I can see him at, let's see, 8:30. He might need an adjustment in his medication."

"I don't think his medication is the problem. Or at least not all of it."

"Well, bring him in and we'll take it from there."

Libby was worried, and tired, and as frustrated by the doctor's casual manner as she was by Frank's passivity. She felt like she was the only one to see that Frank was in serious trouble.

She suddenly found herself furious at Georgia, and didn't care if it was completely irrational. Georgia and her uncle were leaving town tomorrow, something Libby had been looking forward to, but now all at once it seemed as if Georgia were running out on Frank. If Frank was going to resolve this, Libby thought, it would have to be face to face, and it looked like it would have to be now.

She looked up the Dunns' number, and sitting right there in front of Frank, called and asked to speak to Georgia. When Georgia got on the line, Libby explained that Frank had something he needed to talk to her about, and asked if Georgia could come over. Libby watched Frank carefully to see what his reaction would be, and was gratified to see that at least he had one. He looked confused, and then he swallowed and looked scared.

When Libby hung up, she was overcome with second thoughts. What the hell was she doing? She didn't know what she might be risking. What if Frank fell completely apart? She should call the psychiatrist back. She should call Georgia and tell her not to come.

She forced herself to calm down, although her stomach felt like she'd swallowed barbed wire. Maybe she was making a terrible mistake and *she*'d end up being the one to spend the rest of her life not being able to forgive herself. But she cleared away the empty orange juice glass and the uneaten toast, and then sat down at the table with Frank. They waited in silence.

She reached for his hand and held onto it until they heard the sound of a motorcycle turning into the driveway, and the empty sound of its engine stopping.

Georgia saw the side door open up as she got off the bike. Libby ushered her directly into the kitchen, where Frank was at the table facing away from them. He didn't turn around.

Georgia was immediately aware of the tension, the undertone of anxiety. The evening light seemed suddenly to define every detail of the room. The scrape of the glass carafe sliding out of the coffeemaker and the little ting of Libby's bracelet tapping against the glass as she tipped it to pour were small, sharp edges in the air.

Other than the coffee, there were none of the usual amenities, no "how have you been" or "glad you could come." Georgia sat down across from Frank. Libby took the chair beside him. Nobody drank their coffee, although Georgia stirred hers nervously.

Libby began. "I called you because Frank needs to tell you something, but he's having some problems and I'm not sure if he can manage it. Frank? Do you want to start? Or do you want me to?"

There was a long pause. Finally Georgia couldn't take the silence anymore and asked, "Is it about the motorcycle?"

At last Frank raised his head and looked at her. "The motorcycle," he said. "Could I see it?"

"Yeah, sure. It's right outside." Georgia stood up, grateful to at least be moving.

The sun had dropped low behind the trees but there was still some light in the sky. They filed out into the driveway. Georgia and Frank went to the motorcycle. Frank ran his hand over the gas tank. He squatted down to look at the drive belt, peered at the parts and connections that he knew so intimately, then stood and walked around the bike. He looked at the modifications Georgia had made, the new saddlebags and the padded sissy bar, over which hung a small knapsack she could slip off and carry on her back. The handlebars were different, too, the handgrips at less of an angle. Frank nodded.

Impulsively Georgia asked him, "Do you want to go for a ride?" and wished at once she could take it back.

But together Libby and Frank said, "No."

Then, to Georgia's horror, Frank started to cry. Silent tears ran down his cheeks that he didn't try to hide or wipe away. She didn't know what to do, or what all this could possibly mean. She looked over at Libby.

Libby kept her eyes on Frank, her hands gripped tightly in front of her, as if she had to physically hold herself back from going and wrapping him in her arms.

"What's going on?" Georgia said. "Frank?"

Frank closed his eyes. In a bleak voice that seemed to have been dredged up from some fathomless depth he said, "I did something bad."

"What? What did you do?" She didn't know if she wanted to hear this. The day had abruptly changed and she wasn't sure she could face the wreck that threatened. But it was too late. Maybe it had been too late from the very first day, when she'd opened that first mysterious box and unwrapped that first piston.

When Frank still didn't answer and another intolerable silence threatened, she went over to him and put her hands up to his shoulders—whether to force words out of him, or in sympathy for whatever struggle he was going through, she herself didn't know. "What?"

"I didn't tell."

"Didn't tell what?"

"When he hurt you, I didn't tell."

Libby said, "No, not her."

Georgia stepped back. "What? What are you talking about?"

Frank had begun to gulp air.

"Lean over," Libby said.

"Sit down," said Georgia.

The women together pushed Frank into a sitting position on the driveway. He was backed up so close to the motorcycle that when he finally straightened, breathing deeply but with at least some semblance of control, his shoulder brushed against the front shock. Georgia sat down cross-legged in front of him. Libby squatted beside them.

"Why don't you start from the beginning," Libby said.

Frank looked at her. "The beginning?" His eyes came back to Georgia. "I didn't even know her name," he said. Then he shook his head. "It was a girl...."

17

FRANK'S EYES CLOSED briefly. Once out of cowardice and humiliation, once out of a misguided attempt to make reparations, and now—well, he didn't know why now except that the time was finally upon him—he was inflicting inexcusable pain on Georgia. He felt as if the weight of it might crush him, but then he pulled himself together and looked at her, and he spoke with a sort of last gasp strength that came from a lifetime of shame capped off by a year of loving Libby. He found, almost beyond hope, that a small part of his mind seemed to have detached itself, like psychic flesh torn free of the body, and was looking on from at least a small distance. He clung to this as the only thing that could both take him back into the past, and maybe, if he held to it tightly enough, keep him from becoming utterly lost in the telling.

So he began. He knew that as careful as he tried to be, there was no way to do this right. He couldn't tell all the details, of course—it would be too hard on Georgia and pointless, but about himself, about his part in it, he'd keep nothing back. He began, clinging with his last strength to truth and intelligibility and a final despairing effort to do no more further damage than necessary.

"You were only ten then, and I was thirteen," he said. "It was at my church." He took a breath. "It was a Sunday ... just a regular Sunday—dreary and boring, but ordinary. After the service the other kids ... most of the other kids ... went outside, but I didn't. I snuck down to the basement. There was a room there, a storage room...."

He saw it clearly, as familiar in his memory as any room he'd known before or since. Once a cloakroom, it had Dutch doors leading off to classrooms on either side. The top half of each door was made of a cane weave, like the patterned webbing on a kitchen chair. The room had been used for storage for years, filled with boxes, broken desks, stacked chairs.

Afflicted with a standard case of adolescence complicated by painstaking intelligence, young Frank knew his way into this storage closet. With so many boys and girls together in the repressed atmosphere of church, it was inevitable that a certain amount of sexual tension would arise. While there was some risk involved in masturbating in a storage room, and in a church of all places, it was less so than might be imagined. In the cocoon of cardboard boxes and discarded drapes, sounds were muffled. In addition, the room had been locked and out of bounds since an Easter afternoon two years before when little Charlie Dietz, while playing hide and seek, had been knocked unconscious by a toppling box of psalm books. The key that Frank carried in his pocket was not stolen, but was the product of experimental probing into the plastic properties of various materials used for impressions and metal casting. And just having turned thirteen, Frank was desperate for a private place to go when boredom, in combination with the charged air of adolescence, overcame him.

On this sunny afternoon, while the other kids were outside and their parents in committee meetings and study groups, Frank sauntered down the stairs to the cool basement, slipped unnoticed into one of the side classrooms, and from there into the storage room, making sure to lock the door behind him. He made his way to the center of the closely piled boxes and furniture, and sat down at a cramped, slightly listing desk.

"The room was my secret place," he told Georgia. "I was stupid and thirteen and church made me crazy, so I went down there sometimes.... To masturbate. That's why I was there that day. That's why I was there and saw what I did."

Georgia nodded. She looked puzzled, but then all at once her face took on an apprehensive cast.

She knows, thought Frank. Or suspects. She knows it's going to be bad, anyway. He plunged ahead, before the sight of her face growing pale in the fading light could immobilize him once more, the way he'd been immobilized all his life.

"That's what I was doing when I heard a sound, and I froze. It was from one of the classrooms—a door closing. And then I heard their voices. They were muffled, but I could tell it was a boy and a girl. I was scared of being caught but I shifted a couple of boxes anyway, as carefully as I could, so I could see between them through the panel on the door into the room. I knew they couldn't see in but I could see out. I could hear them better then, too. I don't know why I did it. I could've just gone out the other door, snuck out without anyone knowing I'd been there, but I didn't.

"He was sitting on one of the desks. It was Donny Gerber. He was ... Georgia? Are you—"

"No ... go on."

Frank paused for a moment. Georgia looked like she was going to be sick, but he saw her swallow a few times and take a deep breath. She set her face and said again, "Go on."

"There was a girl with him. She must have been about your age then. Ten or eleven. I didn't know her, and I never saw her again after that day. I don't know what happened to her."

He couldn't bear to focus on Georgia's growing dismay so he concentrated only on the scene in his mind.

Tall, fair-haired Donny Gerber was perched on one of the little laminated desks that served the Sunday school. Frank knew him only slightly. He wasn't one of the kids that hung out with Julius's crowd, and he wouldn't have considered being friendly with the younger boys like Frank. Frank didn't know the girl, except for having seen her at the service for the last couple of weeks. She was a relative of one of the newer church members, he thought, visiting from Omaha or Oregon or somewhere. He was surprised that Donny would be bothering with a kid like her.

"He seduced her," Frank told Georgia. "He manipulated her. Flattered her and made her feel grateful to be there with him."

The girl had giggled and blushed as Donny reached out a hand and gently pulled on a swatch of her frizzy red hair with his thumb and forefinger. "You seem so much more mature than your age," he said. "I mean it—you could pass for fourteen at least."

Blushing even more, the girl put her shoulders back, and tipped her head a little to the side.

"Oh, for sure," Donny told her. "At least." He tugged again at her hair, and she stepped a fraction closer. "I bet you've kissed plenty of boys," he said.

The girl's eyes widened a little. "Not really."

Donny raised his eyebrows.

"Well, some, I guess," she amended. "Sure, I have."

So, step by step, with a sly combination of flattery and subtle threats of rejection, Donny led her into the opening moves of sexual intimacy. Young Frank watched, fascinated, as Donny ran his fingers lightly over the front of her little blouse, and then gently opened a button, then two. The girl pulled away and Donny sat back frowning, folding his arms across his chest. "I thought you liked me," he said. "But maybe you're too much of a baby after all."

"I'm not a baby. I do like you—it's just that ... well ..."

"You can't just tease a boy and then back out."

A flicker of resentment flashed in her eyes that Donny read with consummate accuracy. With the guile not to arouse her suspicion or temper prematurely, he changed tack. He said with a hurt look, "It makes me think you don't trust me."

She hesitated, then took a small step closer to him.

"You like me, don't you?" he asked. "You trust me, right?"

She lifted her chin and nodded. She bit a fingernail and said something so softly that Frank could just barely make it out. "Only touching?"

"Of course," said Donny, and finished unbuttoning her blouse, pulling it back off her arms to reveal a blue slip over scanty swells. Donny left the blouse hanging by its tail from the back of her skirt, and put his hands on her shoulders....

From the poisonous detail of these memories Frank was desperately extracting only what was necessary to tell Georgia—who sat listening in tense silence—though there was nothing he didn't remember. "Donny got her to let him open her blouse," he told her, "and she was still okay. But then things changed. All of a sudden he pulled down her slip, quick and hard. She wasn't expecting him to be so ... so abrupt. I think that's when it occurred to her that he could overpower her. That he might. She was nervous before that but she still trusted him, I think. He told her it would be only touching and she believed him. But everything changed then. She was afraid."

Georgia's face was immobile, inward. But the appalling knowledge of what was to come lay deep in her eyes. Frank forced himself to go on. He had to ignore the feeling of tearing inside him. He couldn't stop now or he wouldn't survive, and maybe neither would she. She had to know the whole truth, though. It was too late to stop ... she had to know the other thing.

But even so he hesitated. Even among the lacerating thrusts of shame that were Frank's internal life, this one went deep, that his first sight of a real girl's breasts, and his thirteen year-old body's reflexive reaction to it, came in such a terrible and twisted context. In the synapse-fast debate that determined how to continue, he did not take into account his incomprehension, at the time, of what was unfolding. Only that it would sound like what it was—the most worthless of excuses. Only that relating it was bound to sicken her further. But, finally, it had to be told—an inextricable link in the chain of events. So he stumbled on.

"When he pulled her slip down," he said, "something else happened. With me.... It's the thing that made ... the reason, one of the reasons ... I turned out to be such a coward. It's .... When he pulled down her slip and I saw her so unexpectedly like that, I ... well ... I came. I didn't mean to; didn't want to. But it doesn't matter. I did.

"And so I didn't know what to do. Things were happening so fast. Donny was getting more insistent. He was still talking to her, but he wasn't letting her say no—he kept on and on.... I knew I should do something. I knew it. She was too young, too little, just a little kid with skinny legs, and things were going way too fast. I knew it, but I didn't know what to do. I was afraid. Afraid to go running out there like I was, with come all over my pants, afraid of the humiliation and the ridicule. And I was afraid to confront them, too. Afraid of Donny, and afraid of the girl, too—for her to know I'd seen her half naked like that. So I stayed hidden. I stayed where I was and I didn't do anything. I didn't ... didn't stop what was happening."

When Frank had looked back through the caned panel into the room, Donny had moved off the desk and into one of the small chairs. Sitting sideways to Frank's view, his partially distended penis released from his pants, he held onto the girl.

Everything was different now. The girl was truly frightened, but Donny's arm held tight around her hips. He ran his other hand over her small chest. One of her thin legs was unwillingly pressed against his exposed flesh. "It's okay," Donny told her. "You're really good. You're doing great."

In the dark storeroom, Frank had sat paralyzed with shame and fear. When he finally moved, it was not to stop what was happening but to bury his head in his arms. And there he stayed, frozen and horrified, hiding in the musty darkness. The girl didn't cry out at once, but he could clearly hear her words of childish reluctance, "I don't think I want to do this.... No, please, I don't think this is right...." in escalating tones of distress. Although at every new stage Frank writhed in increasingly agonized indecision, his self-hatred growing, he became more and more deeply entrenched in his inability to act. It'll be over any second, he kept thinking. He'll stop, or it'll be done. Now ... now.... Any second.

"It's okay," he heard Donny breathe. "All girls have to go through this, it's fine.... Shhh." Toward the end he must have put his hand over her mouth. But Frank could still hear her, the panic of her muffled cries and thwarted struggles.

When Donny had finished, it was quiet for a minute. Frank lifted his head and warily looked through the cane weave into the room again. The girl lay on the linoleum floor with Donny crouched over her, leaning down, his mouth close to her ear. He whispered something to her, something that seemed to take a long time. Then Donny stood, zipped up his pants, unlocked the classroom door, and walked out.

The girl rolled onto her side and grabbed her panties—blue flowered print to match her slip—wiping herself frantically with them. Frank looked away, but glanced back again when he heard a rustling sound, to see her wrapping them up in colored Sunday school art paper and throwing them into the trash can. Her back was to him as she pulled her blouse back on, tucking it in with shaking hands. She carefully opened the classroom door and looked out, then ran to the bathroom in the hall.

Frank sat crying silently in the storage room. He stayed there for a long time.

"He raped her," Frank said.

Georgia nodded, her face almost lost in the darkness. Almost lost, but not quite. The last of the light revealed the bleakness in her face, in her eyes. She shivered once, a small shuddering movement in the night air, and then was still again.

"And I didn't do anything. I hid my head and I let it happen."

He was almost done now. There was just the one last thing.

Because then Frank had committed his final offense—the one he continued to commit each moment of every day. His other unforgivable act. He told it to Georgia now, although of course she already knew.

"I didn't tell," he said, misery and shame roughening his voice. "I never told anyone."

Two years later Frank had learned—from a friend who'd overheard it from his father, a courthouse clerk—that Donny Gerber had raped again. The Foxton D.A. had filed charges against him for the assault and rape of twelve-year-old Georgia Dunn.

Georgia sat in the middle of Frank's driveway listening with a sense of numb disbelief.

"I could have stopped him," Frank said. She saw his hands opening, lifting through the darkness. It seemed for a moment as if they were rising to cover his face, but they didn't continue upward. It may have been simply a gesture of futility, of hopeless apology. In any case, his hands halted, fluttered erratically, and fell again to his knees. "I could have stopped him."

The light was almost gone. Georgia and Frank were the only two people left in the world. Georgia looked into Frank's sunken eyes, until he dropped his head.

You could have, she thought, feeling battered and sick and numb. You could have stopped him and saved the girl. You could have stopped him then, and I would have had my life. But she didn't say it. She was filled with such a confusion of anger and pity and pain that she seemed to have lost the ability to feel anything at all.

They didn't move for what seemed like a very long time. Georgia could hear their breathing, hers and Frank's. She leaned forward, and hardly knowing what she did, reached out a hand. She touched Frank's bowed head briefly with the tips of her fingers. Then she got up and walked away down the street, leaving the motorcycle behind.

Emery was sitting on the porch in the yellow light of a bug bulb, eating an apple, when Georgia came up the walk. "Where's the motorcycle?" he asked.

"At Frank's." She walked past him into the hallway, and up the stairs to her old bedroom without pausing, her expression flat and unwavering. Emery watched her go, concern wrinkling his forehead. He walked over to the railing and looked into the dim, pooled light of the streetlights, as if not believing her, as if the motorcycle would be parked down the street or just around the corner. Then he went into the house and stood at the bottom of the stairs, looking up them for a moment before turning to sit on one of the lower steps. With a distracted frown he pulled out his pocketknife and began paring his fingernails, putting the cuttings neatly into his shirt pocket to throw away later. Iris and Bernie were in the living room, waiting for Georgia. They'd made reservations at an Italian restaurant for the final evening of Georgia and Emery's visit.

Emery snapped his knife shut when Iris came out into the hall. "Did I hear Georgia come in? I thought she'd be back by now."

"She's up in her room."

"Well, we should go if we're going. I don't know what time Arturo's closes." She started up the stairs.

Emery sat gloomily on his step and listened to Iris knock on Georgia's door, then the door opening and closing. He could just hear their muffled voices, though the words were inaudible. They continued for a long time. Bernie came out of the living room and looked inquiringly up the stairs, but all Emery could do was shrug his shoulders. Bernie went into the kitchen and Emery heard the sound of the refrigerator door opening, and the rustle of deli paper.

It was another half hour before Iris came back down. "Bernie," she said, "call the restaurant and see how late they stay open. She's coming now." To Emery she said, "She'll be fine, don't worry," and patted him on the shoulder before going to the hall closet for her sweater. She picked up her pocketbook from the hall table and rummaged around in it, glancing up briefly when Georgia, her eyes a little puffy but otherwise looking all right, came down the steps. Emery got up and busied himself, checking for his wallet and combing his hair back with his fingers. Bernie came in from the kitchen saying, "No problem, they're open till eleven."

Georgia took her father's arm as they walked to the car. Emery, trailing behind, saw Bernie lean over to kiss her just above the ear, and heard him ask quietly, "Everything okay?"

"Fine," she answered, her voice nearly steady.

Nobody talked about the motorcycle. Emery wondered if it was gone for good and if so, how they were going to get back to Minnesota. By bus, he decided, and spent the rest of the evening worrying about Georgia. They all talked about the restaurant, the food, about when Georgia and Emery would be back to visit, about Iris and Bernie's plans for Florida.

It wasn't until late that night that Emery tapped on Georgia's bedroom door.

"Can I come in?"

"Sure, come on," she said. She was sitting up in bed, leaning against the loose headboard. She had an old spiral notebook on her lap, and a felt-tipped pen. Emery sat down on a flowered chair.

"Are you all right?" he asked.

She nodded.

"Can you tell me what's going on?"

Again she nodded, but paused to fiddle with her pen, putting the cap on before saying, "You know Frank sent me the bike, right? I already told you how I figured that out at the picnic? ... Well, now I know why he did it." She took a breath and looked up. "But I'm not really sure about anything else. It's kind of confusing," she said, and her voice started to break. "Shit." She took a deep breath, and then another, and went on, "Well, not confusing so much as upsetting. Bad old memories. Anyway, I'm not sure I can keep the motorcycle."

"Oh."

"Not sure I want to."

"That's too bad," Emery said carefully.

"I know. I really love it. It's gotten to be like a part of me. A good part."

"I can see that."

"God," she said with sudden ferocity. "I hate it that something that happened so long ago can keep ruining my life."

Emery just nodded. He could see how troubled she was ... but so much of life with people was a mystery to him.

"You don't know what I'm talking about," she said.

"It's okay."

"I want you to understand, though." She paused. "Something happened to me when I was young. When I was twelve," she said. And then, hesitating for only a second, "Somebody raped me."

Emery had heard the expression "sick at heart." Now he looked at this young woman whom, it turned out, he'd grown to love like a daughter without even realizing it was happening. He wished he could take all her pain on himself, never mind if it lay on his chest like the deadfall that once had pinned him under its weight, almost killing him, back in his lumbering days. If this was what loving was like, he didn't know how so many people could choose to do it of their own accord. He sat still in the chair and listened as Georgia went on.

"It was terrible," she said, "and it really screwed me up in a lot of ways. And now it turns out that the motorcycle is related to it, in a weird way. It's ... it's hard to explain." She stopped and looked at him, as if she wanted to finish but suddenly didn't know if she had the strength. Emery looked back at her, and it came to him that, in a certain way, they were a little bit alike. She didn't completely know how to show her feelings, or maybe even to *feel* them all the way out to the outside, so she mostly kept them inside. And she'd been feeling a hell of a lot tonight. She was pretty well done in, and clearly needed sleep a lot more than she needed an old man prodding her for explanations.

"You don't have to."

She looked at him, and he repeated it. "You don't have to, Georgia, unless you want to. If you'd rather, you can just think things over for a while and then do whatever you figure is right. That's good enough for me."

"It is?"

"Of course it is."

She gave him a weak smile. "Thank you, Uncle Emery."

He stood up. He hesitated for a second, then took a step toward the bed and gave her an awkward pat on her hand. "Just let me know what you decide. We can always take the bus back. If you still want to stay up north, that is. I mean—I want you to, you're welcome. Anyway, good night."

"Emery?"

He stopped on his way to the door and looked back.

"The motorcycle's a good thing, isn't it?"

"I'm not entirely sure what it is you're asking," he began, "but—"
"I don't know either. I'm just—"
"—but I'd have to say it's not one thing or another. It's a tool, you know, to get you around, maybe to have some fun on. But it seems to me that, all in all, it's been a very good thing for you."

Frank sat in the darkened driveway after Georgia had walked away. Libby came to him and he let her guide him into the house. He sat down at the table, then stood back up, pacing while Libby heated leftovers for dinner. Every now and then he'd stop for no particular reason, until some inner prompting set him pacing again. Libby made him sit and eat, which he did obediently, though he didn't know or care what he put in his mouth. Halfway through, he looked up. "I'm sorry, Libby," he said.

"It's okay. Eat."

He looked back down at his food.

He didn't sleep that night but lay still in bed, waiting for Libby to fall asleep, which she didn't. Her breathing grew long and quiet, though, and Frank slipped out of bed and walked barefooted down the stairs and out of the house. He went straight to the workshop. He pulled the door closed behind him but forgot to lock it. Libby came in quietly as he was putting on his coverall. He looked around at her, but she just took the dark goggles from their peg on the wall and sat down on a stool at a side bench. He resumed what he was doing, putting his bare feet into heavy work boots, pulling the helmet over his head.

He worked through the night as Libby watched, her head on her folded arms along the scarred but immaculately clean worktable. He worked with the intense concentration that was characteristic of him—cutting, grinding, welding, all to his own meticulous standards.

But nothing could keep his memories at bay. Images rose up through the bright, hot blue sun at the leading edge of his weld, as searing as if they were burning into his own flesh. He knew this nightmare so thoroughly it didn't matter how fragmented his thoughts were, how incoherent. Each flicker held in its briefest moment the entirety of his memories, like a torturous hologram.

He'd been fifteen when he heard what happened to Georgia, almost sixteen when the case came to trial. He'd cut school to attend, sitting inconspicuously in the back. When it was time for Georgia to testify, the judge had cleared the courtroom of spectators. Frank waited in the corridor. He saw Georgia come out afterwards, her young face pale, empty-eyed. He didn't speak to her, or even stand where she'd see he was there.

He was in awe of the sheer guts it had taken for her to face her assailant, but it seemed to be the last effort she was capable of making. Afterwards, when Donny had been convicted and sent away, and Georgia returned to school, Frank saw her sometimes as he drove past the junior high on his way to his after-school job. He saw how she left the building at the end of the day with a deadened step. How she walked home with a girlfriend or two, smiling sometimes but never laughing, her book bag no longer hung jauntily over a shoulder, but pulled around in front of her like armor.

Frank thought that even if Georgia hadn't come forward, he'd have known that something was wrong by the changes in her. Whether he'd have understood what had happened to her was doubtful, but he realized that although she'd never been in the forefront of his mind all that much, he'd always been aware of her. Through the years they'd lived in this town, crossing paths at school or the movie theater, or thrown together at their parents' affairs, she'd always stood out. She wasn't a super-genius or a beauty queen, she didn't jump around with pom-poms on the cheerleading squad, but she was funny and when she was around, there was energy in the air, as if anything were possible. Bowling balls could leap back out of gutters and make strikes, monkeys could appear on the shoulder of the next man over thirty-seven to come around the corner—because she knew how to imagine they could.

He couldn't believe how unutterably stupid he'd been. Could he possibly have thought that once Donny was done with the little girl in the church basement, somehow that would be the end of it? Could he have thought the girl would go home and forget all about it, and Donny would never do anything bad again? Was that girl even the first? And how many after? How many, he asked himself, had been hurt because of his cowardice? And then ... Georgia.

Soon he'd started doing whatever he could to avoid her, going the long way around to his job so he wouldn't have to pass the junior high, refusing his mother's invitations to accompany her anywhere they might run into Georgia or her mother. He immersed himself in one project after another to stave off the gnawing guilt. As time went on, he learned to live with the grim acceptance of his defective character.

And he never told anyone, until Libby. Not even Jill.

Loving Jill had been a leap of faith, a chance that he might live a normal life in the wondrous sphere of a woman—in love, giving love. He never told her of his terrible shame. In the aftermath of her death, when his mental order crumbled in grief, he was convinced it was this omission, this refusal to reveal his weakness, that had poisoned her life. He'd been certain he was intrinsically incapable of nurturing life and goodness.

Until Libby ... and he realized now what an illusion *that* hope had been.

Frank measured and cut and welded, struggling through the night until, toward morning, exhaustion and the demands of the work had reduced him nearly to the automaton he longed to be. But it didn't diminish the pain.

When light started filtering through the side windows, Libby made him stop and come into the house to get cleaned up for his appointment in Milwaukee. He didn't speak—there was nothing he could say, and his thoughts were too disorganized anyway. She finally stopped trying to get him to do anything but the essentials.

Frank's mind stumbled through its tortured convolutions, but now and then it cleared enough for a coherent thought. When they were out on the highway he finally said, "She deserved to know…. I just hope it doesn't make things worse for her."

"I don't think it will."

"I feel so bad."

A little while later he said, "I should never have told her. It just brought back all of her pain. Now she doesn't even want the motorcycle."

Whatever I do is the wrong thing, he thought. Now what will happen to Georgia? And to Libby? He put his head in his hands. A groan escaped his clenched teeth.

"Frank, what is it?" She glanced over at him and then returned her eyes the road.

"I can't stop it"

"What can't you stop?" But they both knew the answer. He couldn't stop Georgia being raped, or the other girl. He couldn't stop remembering. He couldn't stop the plunging spiral he was descending into.

And, thought Frank, I can't stop loving you, Libby. And because I love you, you'll suffer. I can't stop hurting the people I love—Jill, Georgia, even Julius, when Mom died … and you. Especially you. It'll happen again and I won't be able to stop it. Whatever I do will only make it worse. Whatever I do, or whatever I don't do….

He couldn't stand up and pace, and he couldn't weld. He couldn't reroute his mind, even temporarily. He was breathing now through gritted teeth. Libby reached out and turned on the radio.

I love you, Libby, Frank thought. Soft rock was playing, an old Billy Joel song. Frank pushed scan. It stopped at a classical station, Shostakovitch. He pushed scan again. I love you. And again. He found a song that didn't make him feel like he was going to jump out of his skin, and when it ended he hit scan again.

As nerve-wracking as it may have been for Libby, it at least kept him occupied. For the next hour he jumped from station to station.

The psychiatrist was reassuring. He took Frank's condition in stride. He wanted to try a new medication. "And we've got to get you some sleep, of course, and see if we can pinpoint what initiated this episode."

"We know what initiated it," said Libby.

"That's good. I'm sure we'll make some progress, then. Let's give this new drug a chance. It might take some time. Frank, you've been through this before—you know the ropes."

Libby thought later that what scared her most was how the doctor seemed to treat this as a perfectly normal occurrence. If this was normal, then what was bad? Did someone have to have a complete psychotic break before it was anything other than just another day in the life? She hadn't known whether to be comforted by the doctor's manner or freaked out of her mind.

But for Frank, nothing mattered except that if he could somehow get functional again, then Libby would be able to leave him without guilt, and he'd know she was safe.

18

THERE'S AN ORDER to the world. When things are going well all the separate parts slip into place, fit together with perfect tolerances, and carry a person out into life like a well-tuned machine. In the bad times, though, everything seems to fall apart into impossible disarray. To sort it all out, to repair and rebuild, can seem a crushing task. In a state such as Frank now found himself, hope was the element most sorely required. Without it, life was a meaningless, dimensionless thing with no form or direction. There was no reason to pick up the pieces, because without hope there was no vision, no glimpse of a future that was in any way different or better. The only view Frank could make out was that of a shattered mirror endlessly reflecting the disasters of the past. It was the opposite of hope. His psychiatrist encouraged patience but that had no meaning. Patience without a view was simply despair.

Frank wasn't stupid. He knew Libby had made a bad deal marrying him. She'd ended up with exactly what both of them had feared—a man in pieces. Which wasn't much worse, when he thought about it, than a man so flawed that even put together he'd wreck the lives of anyone he cared about. The only positive aspect of Frank's guilt over Libby—if it could be construed in any way as positive—was that it acted as a counterbalance to his guilt over Georgia. Libby and Georgia—his loves. No, he didn't love Georgia, did he? Of course not. How could he love her? Or maybe he did, and that's what had doomed her.

These were his thoughts until the doctor's drugs plunged him into a blessed sleep.

Once Frank was finally asleep upstairs, Libby sat on the front steps of the house with a cup of coffee. She looked over at the motorcycle. There had been a message on the answering machine from Georgia, but Libby couldn't face returning the call. She went inside and cleaned up the kitchen. She checked on Frank. She brought the dirty clothes down and started the washer, and then she didn't know what to do with herself. It was mid-afternoon, too late to get anything done at work even if she'd wanted to. She was so tired she could hardly stand up straight, but even so, she didn't think she'd be able to nap. Nevertheless, she went back upstairs and lay on the bed next to her husband.

Sleep, that perfectly ordinary thing she'd taken for granted all her life, no longer seemed a sure bet in this house. It was a gift, wrapped in a pill. She reached for the newspaper but the words swam meaninglessly in front of her. She let the paper fall across her chest and closed her eyes. Her head spun like she was drunk, and the images of the past two days swirled past her—the hiss of the cutter and the restrained sputter of the tungsten welding torch, its blue light like caged lightning. Frank's eyes. The doctor's pale waiting room.

The sound of Frank's breathing was the last thing she was aware of until the phone rang around nine that night. It was nobody, a survey. Frank didn't stir, so Libby went downstairs and had something to eat. She watched TV. She cried at odd moments— when two boys in a candy commercial walked down an alley with their arms across each other's shoulders. When a man and a woman laughed over a joke, their voices easy and unafraid. Even though Frank was just upstairs, the house felt empty.

When she finally remembered to call Georgia, she picked up the phone and had already begun to dial before she realized it was after midnight. Tomorrow, then.

Georgia had to leave to get back to her new job. Not only was it the best opportunity she might ever get, but Mel was a good friend and he was taking a chance on her. So whatever she was going to decide about the bike, it had to be soon. She wouldn't risk Emery's life or her own by trying to rush the trip.

She wanted to try calling Frank again. She just thought they should talk, although she honestly didn't know what she wanted to say. Did she want to condemn him? To forgive him? To thank him for the motorcycle, for trying to make amends in such an extraordinary way? She thought she just wanted to see him again and try to sort out her feelings. He owed her that, didn't he, no matter what else? Or perhaps he didn't owe her anything.

Her thoughts had an unreal quality to them, and she didn't trust them. She thought of a friend she'd once had, a girl who'd dropped out of college around the same time she had, then trained to become a merchant seaman. Georgia would occasionally get a letter from her, written aboard ship, full of plans and ideas: I'm going to save up and buy a house in Ireland.... I'm going to go back to school and study for my mate's certificate.... I'm going to quit as soon as I set foot on land, sell all my stuff and join the Peace Corps. But once she was on dry land she'd write again: Forget what I said—my mind at sea and my mind on land are two different things. I don't know what I was thinking. I'm sure it all made sense then, but I can't see it now.

Georgia felt very much at sea herself. She thought if she could only see Frank, sit down and talk with him, she'd know her mind, or would somehow be able to figure it out.

. . .

In the morning Libby woke early and went out to pull weeds. The grass was looking neglected, so she wheeled the mower out of the shed. Frank had been sleeping for nearly twenty hours, and if that still wasn't enough he could sleep through the mowing. She felt like a little kid, wanting to talk to him, to see his eyes open and be reassured he was okay. While she couldn't bring herself to deliberately wake him up, she wouldn't be unhappy if the noise just happened to rouse him. She'd make him breakfast.

If the phone had rung at that point she would still have heard it through the living room window. Then she pulled the starter cord twice and the machine roared to life.

Libby mowed the entire lawn, and when she was done, she still couldn't sit still. Frank hadn't woken up and didn't show signs of doing so any time soon, so she decided to go for a little walk. There was a wind picking up and it looked like it might storm later. Right now, though, the air felt good.

She was four blocks away when Georgia, in her mother's car, pulled up to the house.

There had been no answer when Georgia had called Frank's, but she hadn't left another message. She'd eaten breakfast with her parents and then called the bus station for the schedule—she and Emery would have to leave this evening to get back in time for her job. Then, after stewing about Frank for a while more, she'd finally borrowed her mother's car and driven over to his house.

As she pulled up she saw that her motorcycle—no, *the* motorcycle—was still in the driveway, her pack still over the sissy bar. She went to the door and knocked, but nobody answered, although two cars sat in the carport. She took her pack, and then emptied the saddlebags and the bike's trunk as well. She sat in her mother's car for a while, considering.

Leaving the motorcycle was hard. She loved it ... she loved *her*—Olivia. It had become an extension of herself. It had changed her life. The phrase "blood money" came to mind, though. If it was blood money, she didn't want it. Her blood, though.... It was her blood. Georgia longed for the days at Emery's cabin when the mystery was still unsolved, when the challenge of each moment was so clear and simple—to find the correct part, and using the wonderful manual, which explained everything so truly and precisely, to fit it, connect it, make it a part of the whole, and then go on to the next part.

She rummaged around in the glove compartment for a scrap of paper, finally tearing off the corner of an oil change receipt, and wrote a note. She couldn't think what to say and ended up simply writing, "Please call me, until 6:30," with her parents' number, and below that "after Sunday," with Emery's. She took it to the door—the side door into the kitchen they'd used yesterday evening—and slipped it between the wood and the weather-stripping. Inside the house, Frank turned in his sleep as the storm door slapped closed behind her.

Georgia left feeling uneasy, wishing she could resolve this but not knowing what else to do. Backing out of the driveway onto the street, she tried not to look at the motorcycle, but its soft green and the glint of chrome drew her eye. She couldn't stop herself from glancing over her shoulder as she pulled away. The motorcycle looked so familiar, and in that brief instant, strangely distant, and then she was gone.

When Libby got back home, she went to the shed to lock it up and then circled the house to turn off the hose running to the front bushes. She went inside through the front door. A little while later, as the wind picked up, she heard the side screen door slapping in the wind. She opened the kitchen door and fastened the screen door shut. She didn't notice the little scrap of paper that fell and fluttered away in a swirl of leaves.

———

The Greyhound ride home was a melancholy affair. In the small hours of the morning someone in back threw up, souring the air with the stink of gin and vomit. Georgia and Emery gratefully changed buses in Duluth. They slept off and on throughout the ride, talking quietly when they were both awake. Emery never questioned Georgia's decision to leave the motorcycle behind. He had a shy courtesy that precluded criticism, and she was grateful.

But in some ways she longed to thrash things over. She missed Corrine, who was sure to rant at her and to have all sorts of unrestrained opinions. Georgia thought maybe a little unrestraint was what she needed right now.

She called Corrine from Emery's but caught her at a bad time.

"Mama and I are packing," Corrine told her. "We've got to go to a funeral in Texas. Mama's cousin Deena passed last night."

"I'm sorry. Tell your mother I'm really sorry."

"Thanks, hon. I will."

"When will you be back?"

"I'm not sure. We might stay down for a couple of weeks so we can go to my brother Aaron's baby's christening. I pushed up my vacation at the bank. The home office just has to confirm it. Let me call you from Houston when we get there."

"No, that's okay. You just have a good time."

"It's a *funeral*, darlin'."

"You know what I mean. Have a good trip."

"I know, honey, I'm just messing with you. Are you okay?"

"Yeah, I'll talk to you when you get back."

Frank finally woke up at three in the afternoon. He and Libby sat in the kitchen over sandwiches. Frank gazed out the window.

"She took her backpack," he said.

The sissy bar jutted up behind the seat, reflecting the afternoon sun. Frank finished up and headed outside.

"Frank. Come back in," Libby said. "Wait ... at least get dressed."

"All right," he said, but continued toward the motorcycle. He walked around it, then stopped and touched the handlebars. He looked up at the sky, kicked the bike into neutral, and rolled it into the shop.

He came back into the house. The sedative had mostly worn off but he was still groggy. The antidepressant flowed like slow liquid plastic through his body. The bad feeling was still there, like something stuck hard in his chest, but he was shielded from its pain by the thick buffer that suffused him. He went upstairs and looked at the unmade bed. He thought of climbing back in, but that wasn't really what he wanted. He straightened the covers and pulled on some clothes. Then he headed out to the workshop.

Libby would have none of it. "You can't go out there now. You'll hurt yourself or burn the shop down. Wait until you're not so zonked out from the drugs."

She made him lie down on the couch and turned on the TV. When she looked in on him again he was asleep. She breathed a sigh, and set the timer for the chicken in the oven.

Three days after Georgia and Emery got back to Minnesota,

Georgia opened her eyes to the light filtering into the trailer, and quickly closed them again. There was something wrong but it wasn't the motorcycle this time, it was her head. It hurt like hell. It was time to get ready for work but she could hardly raise herself up from the pillow. In her dream she'd been flying, her wings sparkling green, but when she'd turned to look over her shoulder, bright sunlight reflected like lances into her eyes. The motorcycle was there behind her—a part of her—both heavy and gossamer light, there and not there, and it didn't make any sense ... but was all lost anyway in her waking.

She had to get up. Two days weren't enough collateral to put in for a sick day. She pulled on some clothes and didn't go to the cabin, just took her keys and went straight to her car, the old Citation. She sat there for a minute, digging around in the glove compartment for aspirin. She swallowed a couple with stale water from a plastic jug she kept in case the radiator leaked. Albert had followed her out and now stood next to the car door. He'd taken to following her everywhere since she'd retrieved him from Mel and Barbara's, where they reported that he'd scared Barbara out of her wits by appearing beside her one night in the shower.

"No.... Stay," Georgia moaned. "You can't come with me today."

Emery came out onto the deck with a mug of coffee for her, but she was already turning the car around in the yard, and without looking back, she pulled away down the dirt road. Only the side of her face was visible as she drove off, looking like something floating underwater.

When Georgia pulled up to the garage, Mel was waiting for her. "Emery called. Said he thought you might be sick."

"I'm all right. Just a headache."

"Did you take anything?"

"Yeah, aspirin."

"Why don't you go lie down in back for a while. I'll open."

"You're retired, remember? I'll be fine. Uh, excuse me." She went quickly into the bathroom, and the sound of her throwing up came wafting through the closed door.

"Oh, you'll be fine, all right," Mel called. "Go lie down as soon as you're done puking. I'm calling Barbara."

"No, don't do that. If you really wouldn't mind opening, maybe I will go home for a while."

"Oh, sure. And be barfing out the car door every half mile."

"I feel so bad about this. It's only my third day and I'm already letting you down."

"Hmph," said Mel and went into the men's room for some wet paper towels. When he came out, she was still in the ladies' room swabbing off the sides of the toilet. "Hell's buckets ... go lie down," he said.

"Okay." She grabbed some Glade and squirted it around the room before she left for the couch in the back office.

Mel wrinkled his nose after she left. "That stuff's worse than the puke," he grumbled, and opened the little window high on the back wall.

Georgia still felt bad at noon but at least she wasn't throwing up anymore, so she went to the desk and started on some paperwork. When doing that didn't lay her out flat, she went and opened the door to the front. "How's it been?"

"Pretty slow. Bobby Olson came in and dropped off his Mitsubishi again. Says it's still grinding, but I can't hear it. Mike's gonna take a look at it this afternoon. I called Barbara but she's must be out, and her cell's not answering either, so you're stuck here with me for a while. I could run you over there, but I don't think you ought to be alone, feeling like you do. I left her messages."

"That's all right, I'm fine. You could go home now if you want, Mel. I can take it from here."

"Feeling better?"

"Yeah."

"Like hell."

"All right, have it your way," she muttered, and went back to the desk.

Barbara came in a half hour later with some soup and Ginger Ale. Mel looked at her. "We've got a whole machine full of pop right here," he said. "And bottles in the fridge."

"You don't have Ginger Ale, though. You should stock it." She looked through the door to the back office, where Georgia was slumped over the desk. "Georgia, you should remember to start stocking Ginger Ale." She went to the microwave behind the counter and stuck the soup in.

"And you think chicken soup will cure her? She's just going to throw it up," Mel said.

"It's *turkey* soup and it's only broth. She needs to eat something. I can't believe you didn't send her home."

"She was ... oh, never mind."

Barbara ended up bundling Georgia into a sweater and taking her home with her. She put her to bed in a little converted porch room that had been their son's, and then their grandson's when he came to visit. It had plaid carpet worn down to the backing and ancient baseballs on shelves over a pine dresser.

"I should call Emery and let him know where I am."

"I already did that."

"Albert's gonna be blue."

Barbara smiled. "I'm sure Albert loves you dearly but I don't think he'll disown you if you're not there tonight. He loves Emery too."

Georgia wanted to tell her about how he'd looked so mournful this morning when she'd left him, but she couldn't summon the energy. Barbara stuck a thermometer in her mouth anyway, so that was that.

That evening and throughout the night, Georgia was wracked with spasms of vomiting. Although she tried to protest, Mel and Barbara took turns getting up with her as if she were a sick baby. After a while, with nothing left in her stomach, she was still choking up bile, again and again until she felt as if her whole insides were being torn from her body. Images came to her through the fever and nausea, old images that until a few days ago she was sure she'd put behind her, but it seemed they'd never really been gone after all, just swallowed, lurking inside her. The helpless terror of her rape. Her fears afterward. The horrible sense of being inside out, exposed, not owning her body or her self. And the feeling of falling, like the panicky fear when a plane drops suddenly through space, but never-ending. Then the nightmares that had started up again after Donny was paroled twelve years ago. And all the intermittent years of self-hatred, when she'd secretly felt there must be something wrong with her, and that she was being punished by a just cosmos—that had to be it, didn't it? Because if not, then the world itself had no order, no secure foundation, and that was even less bearable to imagine. All her whole sick past, all the rottenness, seemed to be rising in her nausea.

Toward morning the vomiting finally ended. Purged, weak, and exhausted, Georgia slept. Her dreams, when she had them, were mostly of the motorcycle—as a night bird flying over dark forests, or as an olive tree on a dry hillside swelled almost to bursting with fruit that turned into ripe pimento-stuffed olives that turned into hose connections.

Her waking thoughts turned mostly to Frank. She didn't know whether to feel angry, betrayed, or just to pity him. She'd sorely missed his friendship during her painful teenage years but had only assumed that he was busy with his own life. He was in high school after all, and then off to college. Now she knew better. As her fever rose again and then fell, images of him from their childhood mixed in her mind with his terrible, troubled eyes in the driveway, his hands, their hopeless gesture in the darkness.

She thought of Donny Gerber, too, but it was different now. Her loathing was full of disgust, full of outrage that he could have done what he did, to children no less. To her, and to that little girl in the church basement, and maybe to others. But she no longer felt the impotent rage, the fear, and the furtive shame that had pervaded her life for so long. What hadn't already vaporized in the rushing air of plains and mountains, or burned off in the desert, had been dredged up and vomited out, ending up were it belonged—down the toilet.

Georgia didn't have many long thoughts in the next day or so, her head was too muddled for that, but it did come to her that this illness, this abominable flu or whatever it was, was now the pain of the living, and she was finally, goddamn it, alive. She didn't completely understand how it had happened, and it sure wasn't all fun, but here she was.

She stayed over two more nights at Mel and Barbara's. In that time she found out a few things about them. The first was not a complete surprise. They were sometimes cranky old lovers, but lovers they were. Mel would reach out a hand for Barbara and she would smack it away, saying, "You'd better go wash that dirty old thing." But she'd turn away smiling to herself and Mel would hit the shower whistling. Another was that Mel had false teeth, which gave Georgia a start when she first encountered them solo, but they reminded her of her great aunt Rose, comforting in a bizarre kind of way.

She felt at ease in Mel and Barbara's house. On her third morning, she woke up feeling much better and helped Barbara in the kitchen. Sausages and pancakes filled the house with their sizzle and their smell while Georgia emptied the dishwasher. It was a nice feeling, a privilege, to open cabinets, to hunt for the correct drawer for silverware, for the eggbeater.

Barbara was a tall, shy woman who'd overcome her shyness through long practice in a small community. She thought a great deal of Georgia's uncle, understood his retreat from social situations, and didn't blame him for it or look for underlying causes. But she thought Georgia should move into town, meet more people. "There aren't a lot of unmarried men around here that are worth much, though," she warned. "Not living here full time, anyway. There might be some summer people, but they're mostly couples or families too."

Georgia assured her that looking for men was not her top priority. "I used to think that was my goal in life—to find a man." She shook her head in dismissal. "Romance."

"Oh, you don't necessarily want romance," Barbara said, rolling sausages over in the pan with a fork. "I mean, it's great in its way, but too much of it will put you right into a tailspin. What you want is a helpmeet."

"A helpmeet."

"That's right…. Now don't smile like you know better. You know what I'm talking about. A fellow that'll stick around even if you sometimes don't want him to, so long as you need him. Here, put this on the table for me?" She handed Georgia the plate of pancakes out of the warm oven and added the two from the griddle. "And put yourself in some toast now. This is still too rich for your stomach."

Georgia had toast and juice, and thought that was about right. Afterwards she drove over to the garage and opened up. Mel came in a little later. She told him she was fine, that he could go on home.

"I don't have that much to do at home," he said. "And Barbara'll get sick of me if I hang around too much." So he hung around the garage instead. Georgia wondered if he regretted turning its management over to her.

In a lull after the first spate of phone calls had been answered and the first customers dealt with, she asked him, "Do you miss running this place?" He'd settled himself at the front counter and was comparing parts catalogues online.

He looked up at her. "Hell," he said. "I'm over seventy." And that really did surprise her. "I've had enough of running things."

"I thought you were uncle Emery's age."

"What is he, sixty-five?"

"Sixty-three, I think."

"Guess I'm older, then."

"How long have you been married, Mel?"

"Oh, well let's see. I had a first wife, you know, when I was nineteen, but that didn't last. We had a boy from it. I still hear from him sometimes. I'm sorry to say I didn't have much to do with him after they moved to Missouri—she had family there, my first wife. Then, let's see, I married Barbara when I was twenty-five, after I got out of the service. I have to tell you, though, at first I didn't know if that was going to work out either. I was kind of a shithead back then, if you'll excuse my saying so. It took her a while to reform me." He grinned.

Later, Georgia said, "Mel, I've been thinking about something."

"Uh, oh," he said.

"No, really. You don't have to answer if you don't want. But it seems like everyone I know is avoiding talking to me about the motorcycle. It's like they all know what they think I should do but won't tell me. You've been around awhile, you've made your own mistakes. Would you tell me your honest opinion of what I should do? Or what you would do?"

"I'd get on a bus and go down and get the thing."

"You would?"

"Well, I don't know the whole story, but from what you told me, that guy down there is trying to pay you back for something he did when you were both kids, and it's kind of a slap in the face not to accept it. I mean, a *motorcycle*, that's something. He obviously took a lot time over it, and money. I don't know, but if I was him I might just throw it over a cliff if the girl I made it for didn't want it." He looked at her. "That's just my opinion."

The sliding window from the garage bay opened and Mike Takkunen poked his head in, "I'm gonna need a new fuel pump for Arlene's Saturn," he said. "And I'll be running low on hose soon." He slid the window shut. Georgia went to the computer in back to look them up.

She looked at Mel through the door as she began to type. "Thanks, Mel."

"I'm not telling you what to do, mind you."

Frank wasn't returning her calls. One evening Libby answered and told her Frank was lying down.

"I'd really like to talk to him," Georgia said.

"He's not feeling well. Just give it some time, okay?"

"He's not feeling well because he's sick? Or he's not feeling well because he doesn't want to talk to me?"

"Look, he just can't talk now, but I'll let him know you called. Maybe in a couple of weeks," she added.

"Weeks?"

"Just please don't call for a while. He'll call you when he can. I promise I'll talk to him."

There was nothing Georgia could do about it, so she fretted. She called her cousin Mary Anne, who didn't know much. "He hasn't been in to the restaurant lately, but I'll ask around. Have you talked to your parents? They might know something."

She called her mother but she hadn't heard anything either. "I'll ask Anita Long, she's related to the Morrows somehow, a cousin I think."

"Mom, don't make a big deal out of this, okay? I just want to know if he's all right."

"He was always a nervous boy, if I remember."

"Not nervous, he was just into his own stuff."

"And he had some sort of breakdown once. His mother was very upset about it."

"Mom, just make sure that you don't start any rumors by accident."

"Well, of course not."

Georgia got off the phone feeling less than reassured. But how could she just sit around and do nothing?

That's exactly what she had to do, though. She heard from both Mary Anne and her mother that Frank was taking some time off from work. Her mother said Anita Long thought he was on antidepressants, but nobody seemed to know any more than that. Georgia thought she might know, though. She might know more than just about anybody.

When she thought about it, it seemed it had taken her an awfully long time to come through her troubles. From twelve to thirty eight was a pretty huge chunk of a person's life. During that time she'd grown from a girl to a reasonably mature adult. She'd learned not to look over her shoulder all the time. She no longer stayed at home just because she didn't like going outside at night. And she'd assumed she was all better, back to normal. She saw now, though, how she'd been stagnating—with Jimmy, and the chicken factory, and all the other dead-end jobs she'd had. Corrine had seen it, and had told her in no uncertain terms, but Georgia hadn't listened.

The more she thought about it the more she realized it was Frank's motorcycle that had been the catalyst of her real recovery. How could he have known? What kind of a mind did he have, to have known that a motorcycle, of all things, would save her? A motorcycle! And the truth, of course. His final gift.

And now he was a wreck over it.

A part of Georgia had been bothered by the realization that Frank had been keeping tabs on her. She saw now that it was exactly what she wanted to do for him. She wanted him to be okay. And she wanted to finish the good thing he'd started.

One day after work she sat down on Emery's couch with Albert's head on one knee and a pad of paper on the other. She wrote Frank, saying if he still wanted her to have the motorcycle, she'd be proud to accept it. She wrote to Libby, too, telling her how sorry she was to have upset Frank.

Libby wrote back immediately, a polite letter saying it was not Georgia's fault in any way, but it would probably be better if she and Frank didn't have contact for a while, if she didn't mind. Libby acknowledged that she herself was the one who'd pushed for the two of them to meet in the first place, but now realized it might have been a mistake.

Georgia wrote that maybe one more conversation would resolve things.

Libby wrote that she thought it better to wait.

The irony was that under other circumstances Georgia and Libby might have been friends. Georgia liked Libby's straightforward manner, her underlying fierceness, her determined focus on life's priorities.

For her part, Libby understood what it meant to go through hard times. She'd lost her first husband and knew there was no right way to get through the bad times, and no telling how they'd change you. You grew into your troubles like a tree on rocky ground, holding on however you could. Whatever troubles Georgia had seen, she seemed to Libby a decent person. She even seemed like someone who might be fun, given half a chance. But Libby wouldn't jeopardize Frank any further. After blaming herself for the catastrophic meeting in the driveway, she was going to do whatever she had to, to protect him.

So it was a standoff. And who was to say Libby wasn't right? Maybe Frank needed that time—to hurt, and to think. Maybe he wasn't ready to be forgiven, if indeed that was what Georgia had in mind.

Georgia herself wasn't sure. She just wanted to take the first step, to accept his offering with gratitude. Whether her heart could forgive him for his cowardice—she thought maybe it could, in time.

19

MOST OF THE SUMMER people were gone. The little Boundary Waters town settled into a snug community battening down for the winter—making wood runs, doing last minute roof repairs, getting the last of the hay supplies in. Georgia had plenty to do at the garage. She and Mel worked together on snowmobile and snow blower tune-ups. People checked on their emergency generators, and if they wouldn't start, brought them in for troubleshooting—most had gunk for gas if their owners had been lucky enough not to have needed them for the last few years. Mike and the part time guy, Nathan, were kept busy changing oil and antifreeze, on top of the usual repairs.

At the end of September, the general duck and goose season opened and hunters of every ilk poured into town needing emergency repairs and tows. There was a deep cold snap the second week of October and procrastinators began to rally to the automotive needs of winter. Engines balked, and there was the usual run on engine and oil pan heaters, which the garage kept in stock because Ken down at NAPA never had enough. (Georgia asked him once why he didn't order more in, and he'd just looked puzzled. "I always think people already have them," he told her.) The UPS truck broke down outside of town and Georgia had to tow it in.

Georgia thought of the motorcycle sometimes, and maintained a nagging worry about Frank, but mostly she was too busy learning her job and moving into her new apartment on the top floor of Pat Lundstrom's old three-story, just off the main road. She had her own entrance, a kitchen, a bath, and two bedrooms, one of them small enough for her to wonder if it was once a walk-in closet. She put a bed in there, thinking Emery might want to stay over sometime if bad weather caught him in town. Or if her parents came to visit she could give them her bed and she'd stay in there herself.

In Foxton, as the days got shorter, so did Libby's temper. There were days when Frank was so preoccupied and emotionally absent that Libby felt as if she was still a widow. Frank begged her to leave him, but she wouldn't. If she hadn't known ahead of time what might be in store, she told herself, maybe she could have walked away. But the honorable bastard had told her about his troubles right up front. But it wasn't his weakness that made her stay, or even her vows. It was that every now and then she could see a glimpse of the real Frank through his misery. She'd say some offhand thing, and he'd *get* it, he'd see the point, or the joke, when no one else in the world would have, and she would know she'd found her home. So as lousy as it was right now, she wasn't ready to leave. She'd hang on and see another day through.

When Frank went back to work at the end of September, Libby thought things might get better. But day after day, he came home tired and distracted and farther away than ever.

Frank didn't know himself what he wanted, except some sort of peace, and for Libby to leave him and find her own happiness. He had thoughts of divorcing her but he didn't deceive himself for a minute. He felt too inept to carry out the grocery shopping competently, much less a divorce, and Libby refused to do it herself.

The medication made him feel removed from reality. He often

forgot things, and he slept a lot. He could only do his job because his bosses put him on single-track assignments and didn't divert him once he'd begun.

Talking with his psychiatrist seemed to have no effect whatsoever. The only thing he gained from these sessions was a greater awareness of his guilt. Not only Georgia had been hurt, and the nameless girl in church, but how many others? Frank's mind had been glancing off of the obvious for years. Now he had to face it. There were not enough motorcycles in the world to make up for the hurt he'd allowed.

His doctor was big on overviews. "All right," he'd say. "Let's see where we are. One: You can't go back and undo the past."

"I've got that."

"Two: You can't fix what's done, although I must say that the motorcycle idea was pretty ingenious, and you never know—"

"I understand. I can't fix it."

"All right. So, three: you'll have to find a way to live with it."

"Yes."

"And that's where our work lies. How to put your feelings into perspective."

Frank agreed with this assessment, but other than taking his medication, he felt helpless before the task. What loomed ahead was a future of uncertainty for Libby, as his mental state teetered backwards and forwards. Good and bad, stable and unstable. Decency, and criminal neglect.

"It drives me crazy that you think so little of yourself," Libby said.

But what Frank heard was, "You drive me crazy."

He rallied for Thanksgiving, when Libby's twins came home.

There was some concern before they arrived. Heather and Justin were already in college when Frank and Libby met. They hardly knew him, except perhaps enough to resent the anxiety he was now causing their mother. Frank knew Libby was worried about their visit. "This isn't the home they grew up in," Libby fretted in the weeks before the holiday. "Will they feel like guests? I don't want them to feel like guests. I want them to feel like this is their home, especially Justin. He's always been a homebody, just like his father." But Frank thought her real concern was having a husband who might fall apart while they were here.

Justin arrived with his hair dyed black and a pierced tongue, and Heather was full of opinions and ideas. Frank felt surprisingly easy around them. He liked their energy and their humor. Libby watched them all together and relaxed, throwing herself into the warmth and bustle of the holiday. Frank enjoyed the enthusiasm swirling around him, and was relieved that Libby didn't feel the need to watch him every minute anymore.

Justin left early to spend a couple of days with his new girlfriend's family. Heather stayed for the week but was mostly gone, flying off in a whirl of old friends. Libby and Frank settled down into a comfortable routine. They made breakfast together, read the paper, watched TV, all the things any normal couple did. The conversation that used to come so easily, their thoughts flowing effortlessly around them, began to trickle in again. There was a small sense of optimism.

But after the holiday, as winter deepened, the oppression of the short days and the long, cold nights began to weigh heavily. Frank reduced his medication so he could work more in the shop, and little by little he slipped back into his desolation.

One Saturday afternoon Frank finished grinding a section of beveled steel, part of a dredger design he'd first thought about years ago when he'd known some amateur gold prospectors. He turned around to set it on the workbench and almost jumped out of his skin. Two little apparitions stood side by side before him.

"Jesus," he exclaimed. "You kids can't be in here."

The girl, a tow-headed thing of about eight or nine, encased in a puffy orange parka and snow pants, scowled at him. The boy, in an oversized Packers jacket, kept his eyes on the girl.

The girl spoke. "Jon says you're an inventor."

"No, I'm not."

"He says you are." She pointed to his workbench. "You make things, don't you?"

"Yes. And you shouldn't be in here. It's dangerous."

They conferred for a second. The girl spoke again. "Are you any good?"

Frank blinked, not knowing whether to boot them out or laugh, despite himself. "What's your name?" he asked to gain time.

The boy spoke up. "I'm Jon. I live down the street. She's Muley."

"Muley?"

"My name's Monique. That's just what they call me."

"Oh. Why Muley?"

She stomped her right foot down on the cement floor with a clang. But it was her obdurate expression that made him think the name appropriate. She pulled the leg of her snow pants up to show him her prosthesis. "It's not good enough," she said. "I can't run fast, and it's hard to ride my pony."

"I'm sorry about that, Monique, but—"

"Muley," she corrected.

Frank took a breath. "I'm sorry about that, Muley, but I can't help you."

"I saw a thing on TV," she said. "They make good ones but Dad says they cost a fortune and we haven't got it."

"I'm sorry," Frank said firmly. "But you have to go now."

Muley glared at Jon and stomped out without a backward glance. Jon gave Frank an aggrieved look and followed her out.

Frank closed the door behind them. He locked it securely and went back to work.

Christmas came and went. Libby's kids went on vacations with their friends instead of coming home, and Libby and Frank had a silent, unfulfilling holiday.

Libby's frustration was building. She felt like taking a scalpel from one of her company's medical supplies catalogues and peeling Frank open, saying, "Look—this is you. You're no different than anyone else. Your heart pumps blood, your lungs pump air. You breathe, you bleed, and you screw up. Fix it, or give it up and move on." But short of mayhem she didn't know how to get it across to him.

On New Year's Eve, when Frank didn't feel up to celebrating, Libby threw up her hands and went out on her own.

Alma Petersen, who owned the coffee shop downtown, found her several parties later and thoroughly drunk, teetering down the sidewalk—walking home not because she knew how drunk she was and wisely refrained from getting behind the wheel, but because she'd dropped her keys in the snow and couldn't find them. Fortunately she'd headed off in the wrong direction, toward her old house, which put her directly into Alma's path.

Alma had been detouring past the coffee shop on her way home from a small party with friends, just to make sure all was secure, as she always did on nights of revelry. She found Libby only a block or so away from the shop, so she bundled her hastily into her car and took her straight there, leading her into the kitchen through the back door and flipping on the lights. She guided her over to the work island and sat her down on a stool.

"Shit-fuck-piss," said Libby, with limited but heartfelt eloquence.

"I know, dear," said Alma. "Sam used to make me feel that very same way. They're not fit human company, half the time."

"I hate him," Libby slurred. "He's just a fucking pipass ... a pisa ... oh, fuck."

"That's right, dear, just sit here for a minute and I'll make us some coffee. And here's a nice bucket in case you have to puke."

"You're a good person, Alma."

Alma took off her bangle bracelets and put some coffee on. Then she went to the walk-in refrigerator and came back out with a half-gallon of grapefruit juice, which she poured into a tall glass. "Drink this," she told Libby. "And keep on drinking."

Libby obeyed. Alma pulled a second stool up to the island and sat down with her.

"Now," said Alma. "Do you want to get it off your chest, or do you want to wait till you're sober and decide to bottle it up some more?"

"You're such a good friend."

"I know, dear.... That's right, the bucket's down there on your left—but if you can manage, go ahead and use the bathroom."

"No, I'm not going to heave, I already did that, I think. But I think maybe I broke my toe."

Alma leaned over and looked at Libby's wet shoes. "It's probably just the blood coming back. But you should check for frostbite when you get home. You should never go out without good boots."

"I know," wailed Libby, flinging her hands in the air. "He's making me lose my mind."

"Where is Frank tonight? Didn't he want to celebrate the New Year?"

"He's at home feeling like a failure," Libby said, slumping in her seat. "What's wrong with him? Why won't he get off his butt and *do* something about it?"

"About what, dear?"

"About fucking Georgia!"

"About *what*?"

Libby looked over at Alma. "No, not *fucking* Georgia. Fucking *Georgia*. Oh, you know what I mean."

"Not exactly, but we won't dwell on it.... So who is this Georgia?" Alma rested her chin in her hand, and settled in to listen.

But Libby put her head in her hands. "I can't tell you."

"I see," said Alma. "Well, that's all right ..."

"Oh, Alma. I don't want to go home."

"No, you just sit here awhile. Let's see if the coffee's ready." She gave her a gentle pat on the shoulder as she got up. She poured them each a cup and added a little cold water from the tap to cool it.

Libby pulled the cup toward her and looked blearily from it to her empty grapefruit juice glass. "I'm going to be pissing all night. I'll wet the bed."

"Just drink."

Libby drank her coffee and then she stood up, swaying a little. "Thank you so much Alma. I'd better be going now." She groped around in her purse. "I can't find my keys."

"I'm going to drive you home, but my advice is to wait until tomorrow before you talk to Frank. They're unusual creatures, men, and you never know when they're going to be strong or when they're going to crack like a coconut, so it's always better to have a clear head when you're telling them off. Unless he's got a gun. Does he have a gun, dear? Because in that case it's better to jump in fast, give it all you've got, and get out. I can wait outside for you if you want."

Frank was asleep on the couch when Libby came unsteadily in, carrying the bottle of grapefruit juice. Alma waited until Libby was inside and then, her offer to wait having been declined, drove crunching away through the snow.

Libby banged the bottle down on the coffee table next to Frank's head. His eyes shot open. "Oh…. Hi, Lib."

"This has gone on long enough."

He sat up. It took him a few seconds to focus. "Where have you been?"

"Partying, remember? Happy New Year."

"Oh, yeah. Sorry, Libby. I just—"

"Stow it, Frank. I'm not in the mood."

He blinked. "Are you okay?"

"No, I'm not okay. Get up."

"What?"

"Get up, Frank. Now." He stood up, looking confused and helpless, and hiked up his sweatpants. "Come here," she said. He followed her to the bathroom, where she pointed sloppily toward the mirror. "Look."

He looked into the mirror, past his own reflection to hers behind him.

"Not at me. Look at yourself. Are you a man or a mouse?"

"Libby, are you drunk?"

"Of course I'm drunk. Are you? I mean, are you a man or a mouse?"

"I know what you're getting at. I know I'm a disappointment—"

She slugged him in the shoulder, hard. "GET OVER IT!" she bellowed.

His mouth dropped open in surprise and pain. He turned around to reply, but she leaned in and put her face up to his. "Get over it, Frank," she said. She left the bathroom, closing the door behind her.

It's hard to accept what an absolute jackass you've been without giving in to the idea that it might be a permanent part of your character. Although there had been times that Frank had wished

Libby would leave him, the night Libby came home and finally let him have it, and when he realized she had to get stinking drunk to do it, he suddenly understood how much he needed her, wanted her, couldn't bear the thought of her actually leaving him.

And so he knew he'd have to do whatever it took to live up to her. Whatever he might think of himself was irrelevant. And the antidepressants weren't going to do it for him—they could only help level the battlefield.

Shocked and reeling, and feeling like he was just waking up from a dream he hadn't known he was in, Frank went out to the living room and straightened up the couch, locked the front door, and then went to the bedroom. Libby was already asleep, or passed out. The bottle of grapefruit juice was on the floor next to the bed, upright but uncapped. Frank fished the lid out from under the night table and screwed it on, pulled the covers up over his wife, and got into bed beside her.

He didn't go easily to sleep. There was a knot in his stomach, and a knowledge that he was embarking on something he'd been playing around with all his life but had never truly embraced—being a whole man. If that meant trying his hardest and still coming up short, then so be it. He'd just have to take the chance that his best was not very good. But he owed it to Libby, and to himself, to try. To live out his days trying.

And that meant "getting over it." He wasn't sure he'd ever get over it entirely—all his failures. Certainly he'd never forget, or stop feeling responsible. But he could quit all his piteous self-flagellation. As Libby once said to him, he was not God. It wasn't up to him to mete out his own punishment. And once he stopped worrying about hating himself, maybe he could put his energy toward pulling himself together.

And there was another thing. He couldn't live with only those parts of himself he deemed acceptable. It hadn't worked so far and it never would. He had to put it all together—the bent and the flawed—and hope he could bump along into the world again. And who knows, he thought. He might just be able to hammer himself into shape and have some kind of a decent run.

The motorcycle remained under a tarp in the shop. One evening Frank went out and looked at it, examined the changes that Georgia had made. He couldn't even find where the damage from the accident had been, and that pleased him. He opened the saddlebags to make sure Georgia and Emery had gotten all their things. The only thing left was a book of laminated maps in one pocket. He pulled it out and looked at the pages. He'd never ridden a motorcycle, never wanted to. But for an instant his mind filled with visions of flying across wide yellow plains, across a red desert.

He put the maps back and replaced the tarp, and returned to the house to help Libby with dinner.

That evening he thought of going out to the shop to work on a sculpture he had in mind, a tall woman with feathers at all her joints. He was drawn to the idea of creating something with no other purpose than its own beauty. But he didn't feel like starting anything new yet. Instead he went and found Libby replacing a light bulb in one of the bedroom lamps. He sat down on the edge of the bed.

"Do you think Georgia will ever want the bike?" he said.

"I don't know. Maybe. Probably," Libby said.

"What would you think if I called her?"

Libby hesitated for an instant before she nodded. "She called when you first got sick," she said.

"She did?" When I got sick, thought Frank. "What did she want?"

"I'm not sure. She just wanted to talk to you," Libby said. She turned to face him. "Please don't be mad, Frank. I told her you'd call her when you felt better."

"And then you didn't tell me?"

"No, I didn't."

He looked at her determined face—the caring, and the defiance. "Okay, then."

"Really? You're not mad?"

He smiled a little, "No, I'm not mad."

"Good.... Because, you know, I had to make a lot of decisions in the last few months, and some of them might not be right. And some of them might be right but you still won't like them."

"I know, Libby, and I'm sorry."

"All right," she said. She nodded her head. "I know you are. I forgive you."

And it was as simple as that, he thought. I'm sorry. I forgive you.

The small struggles and contentions of daily life went on. There were tough little fibers of anger left over, and resentment, and worry, but all in all Frank and Libby resumed their married life from that time. The honeymoon was long over, but the bond between them, the understanding and sympathy that had made them fit so well together from the start, was intact.

Frank didn't call Georgia that night, but waited until the next day after work, before Libby got home. He reached Emery, who gave him Georgia's new number. Frank was tempted to ask about her—about how she was and what she was doing, but he thought her uncle probably wouldn't say much. It was good to hear his quiet voice, though. It steadied him, and helped him to see Georgia in his mind as the woman she was, not as the girl she had been, not as the victim.

Georgia answered on the first ring.

"Georgia? This is Frank Morrow."

"Hello, Frank. How are you?"

"I'm fine. I was, uh ... kind of messed up for a while, but I'm fine now."

"Yeah, I heard something about that. I'm glad you're better." She took the phone and sat down by the dormer window at the front of the house.

"I was looking at the bike yesterday. It's in my shop. You did some nice work on it."

"Thanks."

There was a pause. "Would you still like to have it?" he asked her.

"Thank you, Frank. You got my letter?"

"Your letter?"

"It was a couple of months ago."

"I'm sorry, I can't remember. I probably did." He had in fact read it, and wept, and slept, and forgotten it. He'd mixed it up in his mind with his dreams, and thrown it out along with two unopened bills in a confused cleaning binge the next day.

Georgia looked out the window. The winter darkness below was broken in snowy patches of light from the houses along the street. Hard glints of ice reflected here and there. "The motorcycle, Frank—it's a very extravagant gift...." She paused for a second, but before he could respond she added, "A lot of penance for the sins of a scared kid."

He breathed in sharply. She got down to the root of things fast. Not too much penance, though, he thought. Not nearly enough. Not enough to heal you, and not enough to heal me.

And he suddenly realized something. He realized he was wounded as surely, if not as deeply or as blamelessly, as those girls had been. He was collateral damage. Frank was certain his psychiatrist must have talked about this with him. He had some vague memory of it. But he hadn't been capable of hearing it then. That pathway from his ear to his brain had been closed off by his impermeable guilt. But it wasn't holding anymore. Through the breach that Georgia's gentle words had pierced, maybe some sense could finally penetrate.

The pain was there too, catching up to him. He had to speak before it reached him. "Not too much, though" he told her quietly. "Not if it did any good."

"It did a lot of good. I've had a long time to think about this ..." She paused, and Frank could only imagine some of the thoughts she'd had, but all she said was, "You did a good thing giving me that motorcycle. I'm not sure I was worth all the trouble you put into it, but my life's been different since you did. Better," she added quickly. How fragile he must seem, he thought, how likely to misunderstand.

"The crash, though," he said.

"Even with the crash," she assured him. "I don't really even *need* the bike anymore, you know."

"Oh, no," he said. "It's yours, I want you to have it."

"Okay. I didn't mean I don't want it. I meant I don't need it."

"Ah. That's all right then."

So then they talked about the motorcycle and discussed her coming out to get it in the spring. "It'll depend on the weather," she said. "And getting time off from work."

"It'll be here. You can come get it whenever you like."

"Okay. Well, I guess I don't have to worry, then. I was afraid you might throw it in the river."

He laughed. "Not in the river. I'm glad I didn't think of that in September, though. I wasn't thinking very rationally then. Although I probably would have bungled it anyway. No, it'll be here. Don't worry."

"Okay, I won't. And don't you worry either. About anything.

About me."

"All right," Frank said. "It's a deal."

Georgia went to the kitchen to hang up the phone, and stood looking out the window above the sink at the little sliver of the new moon setting over the housetops of the town. What had happened to her at twelve had not been an event that could be dealt with and put aside. It had been a force that had changed the course of her life. How could she have known that then? And suddenly here was this man who, as a boy, had seen that cataclysm begin and had done nothing to stop it. Who, as a man, had given her the tools to put her life back together, or to escape it entirely if she chose. But it had altered him too, buried him choking in guilt. And so she was compassionate, to him as well as to herself. It was not weakness or greed, not magnanimity or pity that had led her finally to accept his gift. And the words she'd offered him in return were not words of bitterness, or of forgiveness either. Just truth. You did a good thing giving me the motorcycle. My life has been better since you did.

20

GEORGIA WENT OUT to Foxton in April. The weather was still too cold for comfortable riding, but she wanted to spend some time visiting her parents, and soon the garage would be too busy to leave. Locals would be wanting oil changes before their 5w-20 started running thin, canoeists and campers would start converging on the town, stocking up on supplies and getting mired in the muddy roads. So she arranged for time off, and after talking it over with Emery, they drove out in his pickup. Albert lolled comfortably on the seat between them, taking his turn at the wheel when they stopped at roadside diners.

Georgia's parents were happy to see them. Georgia looked at their beaming faces, their steady love, and wondered how she could have had so little faith in them for so long.

That night she lay in her old bed and thought about her childhood. The memories flowed around her in an easy tide, lit with a warm light. She'd forgotten so much. Her mind had always balked at looking back, as if to see the good times would mean having to work her way through the intervening years. The factory years, the years with Jimmy, her desperately unhappy high school years.

It seemed to her now that she'd been living all that time in a dull half-light. She wasn't entirely convinced she'd never fall back into such hopelessness, but she had a new faith. She believed in her bones that she'd left that part of her life behind, and if she ever did pass into darkness again she'd at least know the difference. She'd be able to find her way back if she had to.

The next morning she woke expectant and eager, but nervous about seeing Frank. What sort of social conventions were there for retrieving a once-scorned motorcycle-of-atonement? And what about Frank's mental state? Was it so precarious that a misstep would push him over the edge?

She called Corrine for advice.

"I don't know what I'm going to say to him," Georgia fretted. "It seems like he can bring so much pain on himself without any help at all and I don't want to be responsible for bringing on more."

"Honey, if you're going to worry about that, maybe you should just sit home for the rest of your life. He's got some real problems but they're not yours to fix. Remember that time you told me you broke that bathroom stall door at work? You pulled it open and it just came right off the hinges. Do you really think that you broke it all by yourself? You think you just hauled on it and with all that brute strength of yours, you pulled it down? Well, I think Frank's like that door. If he's going to come off his hinges, then maybe he's just ready to. I'm not saying that you need to haul on him, just do what you're going to do. You're not some evil thing who's going to knock him over with pure meanness. Go and talk to him. See what happens."

So Georgia set out in a chilly morning breeze to walk the mile from her mother's house to Frank's.

She knocked on the door with a little shiver. Frank answered and immediately pulled on a jacket and led her to the shop. The tarp was off and the bike had been rolled out into the center of the floor. It sat polished and gleaming in the light from a side window.

Frank watched Georgia's face as she walked in and settled her eyes on it. All her tensions seemed to drain away, and she stood relaxed and balanced. She was completely focused on the motorcycle—no part of her left behind, worried or unsure. If there ever was a doubt in Frank's mind about the value of his offering, it was put to rest.

He stepped back and sat on a stool while Georgia walked around the bike and touched it lightly, the palm of her hand running along the gas tank and seat. Then she swung her leg over and sat down, pulling the bike up to level. She grinned at Frank. "This feels good," she said.

Frank smiled back at her. "I've never seen you ride it," he said.

"I rode it here the last time," she said, regretting it immediately as a shadow passed over them, remembering that day.

But Frank just said, "No, I didn't see you ride then. Maybe you could take it around the block before you go."

"I'll do that," she said. They sat looking at each other for a moment.

Frank nodded.

But Georgia wasn't quite ready to go yet. She let the bike rest back on its kickstand. "I want to know something."

"What?"

"Two things, actually."

He bobbed his head slightly. His eyes were a little wary, not as clear as she'd have liked, but not too bad. She plowed on. "After you built the bike, did you ride it anywhere before you gave it to me?"

"No. I can't ride."

That pulled her up short. "You what?"

"I can't ride a motorcycle."

"You can't...? I don't believe it."

"True, though."

"Why not?"

"They scare me."

"They *scare* you?" She looked at him in amazement. She didn't know what to say. She started to laugh.

He shook his head with a wry smile.

"So of course you build them for other people," she said.

"Just you," he said.

She howled.

"I didn't mean ..." he said, but she was already gone. The tension of the day had left her giddy. Leaning over the handlebars, she laughed helplessly. Frank started to smile, and finally he too was laughing and shaking his head.

At last Georgia pulled herself together and looked at him. Her brows drew together as she considered what he'd said. "I just don't understand how you could have built something like this without even being able to ride it," she said.

"The one thing doesn't really have anything to do with the other." He shrugged, not knowing how to explain the connection in his head between theory and reality—making the components follow the lines he drew on the page. "As far as building it, it's just a matter of getting things to fit together right," he finally said. "Just making it accurate."

"But you designed it yourself, right?"

"Yes."

"How'd you know how to do that, how to make everything run?" She swept her gaze down over the machine she'd become so familiar with, still awed by its complexity and the capacity of all these separate parts to come together into a functioning whole. Though she knew it hadn't been built here, it seemed very much a part of what she saw around her—the metalworking equipment, the neatly organized hand tools, and the half-built project in the corner that was not identifiable at the moment but had an almost sculptural elegance about it that made her imagine it ready to leap into the air.

"Well, I did build a prototype," Frank said, "and then made some modifications—at one point I thought of adjusting the piston stroke a little to increase the compression, but decided not to, in case you ever needed to make any replacements. And I redesigned the frame some, once I knew I was building it for you. I used to work for a motorcycle manufacturer, you know, so that's really where I learned most of this."

"When did you know you were building it for me?" she asked.

"Soon. Right after I started on the first one. Once I realized it would work."

"You thought it might not?" she asked, surprised.

"No, not really."

"So. You just decided to build me a motorcycle."

"That's right." He tapped his fingers absently on the side of his stool.

"I guess I still don't understand," Georgia said.

"Well, my therapist says it was a metaphor. That I wanted to give you freedom. And I wanted you not to be afraid anymore."

"Afraid like you are."

His eyes flickered wide for an instant. He searched her face but saw only straightforward interest. "I suppose," he said. "Yes."

She considered for a moment. "Okay, I get it."

He looked at her.

"I do, Frank. It makes perfect sense. I just wonder what's going to work for you."

"Uh ... for me? You don't need to think about that."

"Well, why not? I'll tell you what I think. I think someone needs to make *you* something. Not a motorcycle, necessarily—but something."

He shook his head. "Drugs work for me. Medication."

"Don't dodge the issue."

They sat in silence for a while. Then both started to speak at once. "I'm going to—" began Georgia. "It's not—" said Frank.

"You first," said Georgia.

"I was going to say that what I've got is not going away. It's chronic, incurable, and manageable, so it's really just a matter of keeping on top of it."

She looked skeptical. "It doesn't seem like you've done such a good job of managing it so far, if you don't mind my saying."

"I'm much better now, though. And the medications are getting better all the time. And I've been able to decrease my dosage lately."

She nodded, but didn't look convinced.

"And maybe I *do* mind you saying so."

She smiled. "Well, I'm going to give *that* some thought."

"Fine, do that," he said. "So what were you going to say?"

"When?"

"Before—what were you going to say?"

"Just that."

"*What?*"

"That I'm going to give it some thought. All of it. You." She gestured towards him, and almost without thought, continued the sweep of her hand to include the shop, his work, all of his projects—that intrinsic part of who Frank was.

"Oh," he scowled.

"Are you mad, Frank?"

"No, of course I'm not mad."

"Uh huh." She grinned.

He shook his head. "You are just as much of a brat at forty as you were at ten."

"I'm not forty."

"Thirty-nine, then."

"Thirty-six."

"All right. No—wait a minute ..." he said.

She laughed, "Okay, thirty-eight."

He narrowed his eyes. "Well, anyway."

They eyeballed each other for a minute, and then Georgia

suddenly started up the motorcycle. It was loud in the enclosed space of the shop and Frank instinctively raised his hands to cover his ears. Georgia looked around and nodded toward her helmet, which sat on the workbench. Frank got up and brought it to her. She settled it on her head and Frank went to the door, opening it wide. A look of sadness brushed his features as Georgia jockeyed the bike out the door, but as she passed him she leaned over. "I'll be back," she laughed. And then she was off down the driveway, turning onto the street in a steady arc. She circled the block once, passing him with a final wave, and then was gone in a purring roar that made Frank proud.

Georgia was more than familiar with the bike by now, but even so, it was a new experience every time she rode. She'd already passed through her first fears, through the first urgent thrill of life rushing toward her and filling all her senses, through the amazement of riding through the world on two fast wheels, then the shock and despair of the accident, then fear and trepidation again. She'd experienced her growing confidence on the road, and the sense that the motorcycle was part of herself, part of her body, moving her naturally from place to place. Now, as she took off from Frank's house, something new filled her. She didn't bother to name it. It flooded through her like water into a quarry. Joy.

When she'd gone to Frank's to pick up the motorcycle, Georgia had planned to ride straight back to her mother's. Now she couldn't imagine doing that. She headed out of town into the countryside, the cool, moist air chilling her as she flew through it. Green shadows fluttered around her, new and thin, the springtime sun filtering through while being passed from cloud to cloud. The earth was waking up. She rode past a newly plowed field, reveling in its rich pungency. Cowshit and wormshit—good. The stink of chemical fertilizer—bad. A skunk—good, until she was almost on top of it, then awful. Some early flowers flickered by. A creek of cold meltwater. By the time she turned back to town, she was chilled to the bone and as alive as she'd ever felt.

On her way back, she stopped at a Yamaha shop out near the highway, and talked them into taking her out-of-state check. With her purchases packed in two cardboard boxes behind her, she rode back into town.

When Libby heard the motorcycle return later that day, she looked out the window. Georgia again. She started to turn toward the door but paused when she saw Georgia dismount, look around, and unstrap some packages from the back of the bike. Frank must be grinding, Libby thought, if he hadn't heard the engine.

Georgia looked back and forth from the house to the workshop, then headed to the shop and set down the boxes outside the door. She tipped her head to one side as if considering something, and then, without knocking, headed back to her bike. She started it up, turned it around with a practiced lean, one booted foot extended to the driveway in a half walk, and disappeared down the street.

Frank sat at the kitchen table looking at the cardboard boxes in front of him. Libby was in the little office off the kitchen, the door open between them. She was leaning over her paperwork, but she was fully attuned to Frank in the kitchen. She listened to him just sitting there. She listened to him staring at the boxes and not opening them. She jumped when she heard his chair scrape the floor, and then she heard him walk to the sink, run water, and fill a glass. He went back to the table and sat down again. Libby thought that in one more minute she'd either have to run in there and tear the boxes open herself, or stay put and tear her hair out. It was all she could do to keep from yelling, *open them already!* But she took some deep breaths and counted. She looked at the phone bill in front of her and tried to concentrate on getting some work done. She heard Frank put the glass down on the table ... and then nothing. She crossed her arms on the desk and laid her head on them. "Lord, give me strength," she whispered.

Frank considered the gifts before him. A large box and a small one. Was this the final forgiveness? Was that even within anyone's power?

He thought back to Georgia as a six year-old, bumping into the pool table in somebody's rec room by accident—so she said—her eyes bright with mischief. And then—accidentally—doing it again, and running off laughing. Georgia at eight pounding up and down the stairs from her backyard to the second story screen porch again and again, to see how long she could do it before she collapsed, panting and clawing her way to a dramatic sprawl across the top step.

And finally, memories he hadn't thought of for years, Georgia at eleven, at twelve—budding, alert, just developing a social conscience. Not her mother's political activism, but a more personal sense of justice. She was an awful tease herself, but just let someone make fun of the new kid with buckteeth or the girl without enough money for the movies, and Georgia would stick out her chin and back the bully down with taunts of her own. "And when was the last time *you* looked in a mirror? Oh, that's right—it's on the wall next to the shower, so it must have been quite a while." Or, "Did your mommy give you your allowance or did you have to earn it by putting a dish in the sink?" Whoever she was standing up for might wind up being more embarrassed by her defense than by the original barb, but nobody told Georgia that. She'd have been mortified if she'd realized it. Then she'd have been mad. "Well, learn to stand up for yourself, then," she might have bristled before stalking off down the street.

Maybe that's one of the reasons why what happened to her was so particularly horrendous, thought Frank. She was ready to take on the world, just figuring out the balance of right and wrong, and determined to tip it to the good. All that spirit, ripped out of her in a single act. She was balanced so precariously on the edge of adulthood. A year, a month either way and the act would have been just as terrible ... but would the results have been as far-reaching, as long lasting? And the red-headed girl, also so young, and then gone forever from his world. What of her? There was no telling, and it would never be his to know. Frank blinked himself back to the table and the boxes.

He felt as if his life was in suspension, but between what two things he didn't know. Whatever awaited him inside that cardboard, it would be the work of seconds to find out, but once they were opened he could never return.

It was probably nothing—nothing of importance—in those boxes with no return address. He could just leave them there, stick them in the corner of the shop maybe. Or he could open them and look, no big deal. He didn't know what was stopping him. He got up and went to the sink for water. When he sat down again, he let his mind wander for a while, not over Georgia's life, but his own. A good life, really, nothing to complain about when you looked at the big picture. He'd lived comfortably, accomplished quite a few things, grown up in a good family. He'd loved his Jill, and he'd lost her. The pain was still there with him, but deep now, not so near the surface where it would rise up and overwhelm him. He sat up straighter. It had been a privilege, really, to have loved Jill, an honor to have been by her during her illness and her death. He would always love her, and that was quite a thing.

And now he had Libby, who'd grown very still there in the office, he realized. She was probably listening, as she did sometimes, worrying about him. Oh, for sure he hadn't been fair to Libby, but he'd do better. He reached out and took the larger of the boxes.

He broke the packing tape and opened the top. The gift inside was wrapped in plain white paper. He felt its smooth roundness under the wrapping as he pulled it out and set it on the table. His hands knew what it was before his eyes saw it. He pushed the paper aside. A helmet. He opened the smaller box. Leather gloves with long cuffs—riding gauntlets.

He glanced up. Libby was standing at the door looking at the gifts on the table. The fingers of one hand rested on her lips and her eyes held a speculative look, as if she didn't know whether he was getting ready to come back to life, or going off to war.

An edge of white paper sticking out of one of the gloves caught Frank's eye. He unfolded it. "You're pretty smart, Frank," it read. "It doesn't have to be a motorcycle."

It was full spring, and Georgia and Emery stood in the sunshine admiring Mel and Barbara's new RV. They'd bought it used, in good shape, and had spruced it up to the point where Georgia wouldn't have minded trading it for her apartment.

She was getting itchy feet herself. Her motorcycle was made to Go, she thought, capital G. Tooling around on the weekends was just not doing it for her. The weather had turned warm, so she invited Emery, Mel, and Barbara over for a barbeque in her landlady's backyard and began to work on her strategy.

"I finally got a photo album put together from my trip," she told them over grilled steak and corn on the cob. "Do you want to take a look?"

By the end of the evening they were figuring out how long it would take to train Mel's nephew Jerome to look after the garage for a few weeks. "He's helped me out before," Mel said optimistically.

"He broke the toilet and completely garbled the register," Barbara objected.

"He was fifteen then. He's helped since then. He was fine."

"He took drugs," she said.

Mel gave her a look. "He was seventeen then. You know he quit that."

"We think he quit. How do we know for sure?"

"Barbara, he's twenty-five now. He's been teaching for two years, not to mention helping in his father's store. I think we should at least ask. Don't you *want* Georgia and Emery to come along with us?"

"Well, of course I do. I just think we should try Lisa instead," she said.

"Your niece Lisa with the twelve dogs and twenty snakes?"

"She does not have twenty snakes. She has two."

Georgia and Emery left them to battle it out, and went for a stroll with Albert in the cool dusk. "I've been taking Albert out in the dog-seat," Georgia said. "I'm thinking about putting on a trailer with a real dog-bed for him. He might like a road trip."

"He could always ride in the RV."

"He could."

"Are you sure you want to do this? Take your vacation with us old fogies?"

"You old fogies are the best thing that ever happened to me," said Georgia. "Shit, Emery. What's the matter with your eyes? Are you tearing up on me?"

"What—you can see in the dark now?"

"It's not that dark, and I think you're sweet."

He cleared his throat and shoved his hands into his pockets.

Georgia turned her attention to Albert, padding along a little ahead of them, poking his nose into this bush and that clump of grass.

"Hey, Albert," she said. "Guess what, you old booger. We're going to see the Rockies."

In the fading light, Emery smiled.

EPILOGUE
Seven Years Later

ON A SATURDAY in early fall, Frank walked out of a low-slung, modern-looking building. He was heading for his car when Julius pulled up in front of him, leaned over, and pushed open the passenger door. "Libby told me you were working today. I thought I'd take you out to lunch," Julius said.

Frank, a tool case hanging from one shoulder and a briefcase in his other hand, came over and leaned down. "I have a house call first."

"No problem, I'll take you there."

Frank climbed in.

"Where to?" asked Julius, as he pulled away.

"The fairgrounds."

"The fairgrounds?"

"That's right."

Julius looked at him curiously, but Frank didn't elaborate. "I thought the VA Hospital or something," Julius pressed.

"Nope."

"You're not going to tell me, are you?"

Frank took out his reading glasses and began flipping through the papers in his briefcase.

As they got close to the fairgrounds, Julius parked at the end of a long line of vehicles without bothering to look for a closer space, a process he scorned.

"I've got a pass," Frank protested. "We can drive right in."

"What's the matter? We can't walk a few steps?"

"What is this, revenge?" asked Frank, but then he sighed and said, "It must be a race day. At least go around to River Street."

Julius relented and pulled down the next street, which ran behind the stables. With no parking space in sight, he drove into the fairgrounds after all, and followed Frank's directions to one of the barns. Frank singled out a folder and grabbed his tool case.

The vet met them outside the stable office. Their young patient was walked back and forth for them while his mother whickered solicitously from the back of the barn.

"A horse?" Julius asked. Then he just stood back and watched, shaking his head in a mixture of amusement and wonder, a familiar sentiment around his brother.

Although it was true that this job was slightly out of Frank's usual line, he'd taken it on and hadn't regretted it for a minute. He was thoroughly enjoying the challenge. He and the veterinarian, Martha Loos, an equine orthopedist, studied the brace on the colt's front leg.

Dr. Loos felt the leg up and down for any suspicious heat or swellings. She nodded her clipped blond head. "It's looking good, I think."

She pulled an x-ray from a large manila envelope and held it up to the sky. Turning a little to put a white cloud behind it, she said, "Here, take a look. It's from this morning." She spent a few minutes pointing out changes to Frank, then said, "I'd like to see the knee take a little more weight."

"Okay. And it looks like he's going to need more length in the frame by next week. I could go ahead and do it now if you like."

"Do it," agreed the vet.

Frank stopped the groom, and stroked the colt's neck before bending down to the brace on the knobby-kneed leg. The colt tried to nibble Frank's neck, but the young groom distracted him by rubbing the inside of his ear, which worked for about five seconds. "I might have to twitch him," the groom said.

"No, I'll be done in a minute," Frank said. He made some adjustments and checked them with calipers and a torque gauge.

They watched the colt walk again. He threw his head a little and stepped gingerly at first, then put his attention to nipping the groom's shirt and began walking with a more natural gait.

"Good," said Dr. Loos. "Nice work." She felt the knee again and turned to talk with the trainer while Frank finished his notes. Frank shut his folder and was turning to leave when another trainer jogged a few lumbering steps to catch up with him.

"Are you the guy that makes prosthetics? For people?"

"That's right," Frank said. "That's what I mostly do. This is a little off my usual track," he added with a smile in the colt's direction. He saw Julius looking his way, and made a small "I'll just be another minute" gesture. Julius nodded and wandered over to the paddock to watch a young bay being trotted around on a longe line.

"I've got a son-in-law who lost a leg a few years ago," the trainer told Frank, "and he's a runner. "He's been looking at some newfangled designs, but he's having problems with his back. I was just wondering if you might know something about that."

"Yes, of course," Frank nodded. "It's actually an interesting problem, getting the weight and the symmetry—"

"Could he call you?" The trainer was a busy man, more interested in horses than humans.

"Have him call me at the Institute, or stop by." Frank gave him a card.

"But you usually do people, right?"

"That's right. This was sort of a favor for a friend."

The trainer nodded, and with distracted thanks, headed off, tucking the card into a pocket.

Dr. Loos was finishing up her notes. She looked up. "And how *is* Muley, by the way?"

"Ornery as usual," said Frank. "She wanted to come today but she's taking her SATs."

"I thought she'd decided not to go to college."

"Oh, she did. But she wanted to show people she *could* have if she wanted, so she's making her mother spring for the tests. She's graduating early, you know, as soon as she finishes up some summer credits." He shook his head in appreciation. "She's got a job already lined up, teaching dressage at a riding school in Toronto."

"She's something, isn't she?"

Frank couldn't agree more. The stubborn little girl in the orange parka had come back to his workshop in an endless campaign until he'd finally broken down and agreed to take a crack at making her a new prosthetic leg. That determination of hers had never flagged in the years since.

Dr. Loos began packing up her notes and X-rays. "Is she taking that goofy cow-dog of hers? I don't think her mom will be too miserable about that."

"No, she's going to be living with an aunt whose son has pretty bad asthma, so she had to give her away. It just about broke her heart, but she knows Winnie went to a good home. A friend of mine in Minnesota took her—she's been dogless for the past few years and I guess she's ripe for some aggravation." Frank smiled as he thought about the latest card he'd gotten from Georgia and the letter inside.

"And that's the mutt to supply it," said Dr. Loos. "Well, you tell Muley I said 'hi' next time you see her."

As they walked back to the car, Frank saw the small smile on Julius's face. "What?" he said.

"You seem happy."

"Well, I am," Frank said, surprised. He paused as they reached the car. His brother walked around to the driver's side.

"I guess I just never thought of you as a people person," Julius said. "But here you are practically in the medical profession, putting people back together, fixing horses."

"It's just mechanics."

"No, it's not *just* mechanics." Julius opened his door and waved his hand toward Frank's briefcase on the seat, stuffed with case histories and diagrams. "I don't think I'd have what it takes. I mean, it seems like you could do some damage if you weren't careful."

"Well, I am pretty careful."

Julius snorted at the understatement.

"I just do the best I can," Frank said with a shrug. He opened his door and slung his tool case off his shoulder onto the seat. He didn't get in, but looked around towards the fairgrounds. "Let's eat here and watch a couple of races," he said.

"Sure, why not?" his brother agreed. In the fresh autumn air filled with the smell of horses, they headed for the stands.

November 30th

Dear Frank,

Thanks a lot for the mutt. Now, if the damn fool will stop hurling herself into my lap every time I sit down to write, I might get this letter off before Christmas. She's a wonderful dog most of the time, though, when she's not tunneling her way out of the yard to rummage through my neighbors' garbage cans or hauling turkey carcasses through the living room. A couple of weeks ago I walked her down to the drug store, teaching her to heel off the leash, and I stopped to talk to a friend for a second. The next thing I knew, that little weasel had snuck off. A lady in the Laundromat heard me yelling for her and told me to try the bar. The bar! Sure enough there she was, scrounging cheese doodles from drunks. I swear!

Anyway, things are going fine here. We put up a new sign on the garage and it looks great. Guess what it says— Johnson and *Dunn*! Mel made me a partner. He says he wants me to feel like I have a stake in staying here. As if I didn't already. Uncle Emery's doing fine, except he's starting to get a little arthritis in his knees and I'm kind of worried about him living so far out in the woods all alone. He's happy, though, and I can't blame him for wanting to be independent.

I'm glad to hear things are going well for you. I won't be out to Foxton this Christmas (my folks are coming here this year, and also my friend Corrine and her mother—a first for them, since they usually go to Texas, but they went at Thanksgiving instead.) Anyway, the next time I come out your way, maybe I can see some of the work you're doing. That spring-loaded ankle thing you're working on sounds interesting. Maybe I'll ride Olivia out next summer. You'll be proud to know how well she's been running. The headlight shorted out this fall but that was just me being lazy—I nicked a couple of wires when I was messing around one day and I didn't get around to replacing them. It's all fixed now though.

I've been doing quite a bit of motorcycle work lately, when I'm not busy with running the business. The other day Mike Takkunen, our mechanic, actually asked me to help him solve a problem on an old Harley. Now, that's progress!

Winnie's finally asleep and she looks so innocent you'd hardly imagine that just this morning I caught her chewing gum. Now where on earth did she get gum and how did she know not to just scarf it down like she does everything else she gets her teeth around? And where would it have ended up if I hadn't made her give it up and she'd decided to spit it out somewhere? I shudder to think. Oh, while I'm thinking of it, could you send me Muley's new address? I thought she might like a photo I took of Winnie being chased by a goose.

Okay, she's finally fallen asleep, and now that she's not listening, I have to admit that I think she's really great.

I do sometimes miss my old Albert, though.

Happy holidays to you and Libby.

                        Love,
                            Georgia

ACKNOWLEDGMENTS

More thanks than I can express go to Judy Logan, who took on the monstrous task of editing my first drafts. You made all the difference, Judy. Warm thanks to my earliest readers for their help and encouragement—Lisa Erickson, Diane Madigan, Sharon Reynolds, Judy Katz, and especially to Jan Demorest, who was also my final reader in the text editing stages. Many thanks also to my (very special) later readers for their enthusiasm and helpful comments—Dr. Michael Small, Monika Zschaebitz, and Shaun Lawrence. My gratitude also to Kelli Gannon and Gary Gannon for their ongoing encouragement and for the title of the book, and to Kathy Hopwood, for her help in the homestretch.

Many others gave me information, insights, and corrections on matters large and small, most notably Lance Dean, Jon Licht at Great Basin College, and a number of wonderful folks at the Elko Motorcycle Jamboree who gave generously of their time and expertise, including Bill Skinner, Bill Pennell, Victor, Tony Lau, and Mad Brad. Thanks also to Dan Richardson, Jason Hansen, Cindy Ryder, Donna Garcia, Michelle Gonzalez, the Great Basin English Department staff and computer techs of 2001-2002, and Drs. Ron Schouten, Jim Hoffman, and Bob Deckelbaum.

To all of you, and to those whom I've most lamentably forgotten to include, or whose names I've mislaid due to my flawed (read: virtually nonexistent) organizational system, I am extremely grateful for your help.

ABOUT THE AUTHOR

Beth Carpel is a writer and photographer. She grew up in Washington, DC and has lived in various parts of the country, including several years in Minnesota. She now lives in northeastern Nevada, where she raised her two children. Her website is www.bethcarpel.com.

3164433

Made in the USA